I0675638

Robyn I

Michael Peron

Copyright © 2020 Michael Peron
All rights reserved.
ISBN-13: 978-0-9863143-3-9
Cover art copyright © 2020 Anita Tung.

Dedicated to Alex, who helped shape each of my novels.
Thank you for your time and patience!

1

I was born in an off-white shell with a bed in the middle. I felt the comfort of the mattress underneath me and the warmth of the covers on my chest. My eyes opened to a blinding light, but with each blink, the surroundings came into focus. I picked up on a soft hum and noticed the curve of the walls forming a dome over my prone body.

Glancing around the periphery, I saw a door etched into the wall beyond my feet. Small tubes slithered out from under the covers, hanging off the side of the bed. There, right at the edge, I saw my hand for the first time. Three fingers poked out from under the sheets, and instinct beckoned me to curl them. So I did.

What was meant to be a tiny impulse became a bolt of lightning, activating my entire nervous system. Crisp detail spread across every centimeter of my body, mapping the contours of the blanket draped over me. Unfortunately, this newfound clarity highlighted the tubes sliding underneath my skin, and I cringed with discomfort.

What was happening? Despite my location and surroundings, I felt no pain. Why was I here?

Before my thoughts went any further, the door in front of me slid open with a hiss. A woman walked in, smiling at me. She held a tablet of some kind against her chest, pressed into her white uniform. I did not recognize her.

"How are you feeling?" she asked.

"Fine," I answered.

My voice. I had never heard it before, but I knew it was mine. The woman came to the right side of the bed, peering at something just underneath me.

"Don't be alarmed, you aren't in any danger."

I noted her soothing tone but ignored it. Alarm was not what I felt, just curiosity.

"What am I doing here?"

She looked up at me, as if it were an odd question.

"Before we talk about that, can you tell me your name?"

We stared at one another, the silence answering before I did.

"I don't know."

The woman showed the subtlest of hesitation, then brought back her smile. But this smile was different, it used different muscles.

"What's the last thing you remember?"

I reached into my mind to answer the question, but there was nothing to be found. No memories, no past... nothing.

"I— I don't know."

She frowned, and I felt a hint of dread.

"What's my name?" I asked.

Her expression gave away the answer before she said it.

"I'm afraid I don't know either, but we're doing everything we can to figure it out."

I shared the next half hour with this woman, who turned out to be a doctor assigned to me. Unlike me, she had a name: it was Chellet. Chellet told me everything she knew about me, but it did little to clarify my situation. I had been found, unconscious but breathing, inside a busy spaceport. This was the port hospital, where I had arrived immediately after my discovery about sixteen hours earlier. And then, without warning, I was born.

The way I see it, birth is the process of being brought into existence. As far as I knew, my existence began in that hospital. And while most births do take place in a hospital, they are typically not of twenty-something year olds.

What made the least sense to me was my amnesia. I had knowledge of many things, but memory of none. When I asked Chellet why I didn't have an ID chip, she had no idea. But how did I know what an ID chip was? I even knew it was supposed to be embedded somewhere in my upper thigh or upper arm, and had a vague idea of what it looked like.

"What planet are we on?"

The question occurred to me as important.

"Kurotar."

Again, I knew exactly what she was talking about.

"What year is it?"

"477 by the Terian calendar."

Terian—we were in the Terian empire. It consisted of twenty-three worlds, one of which was Kurotar. But the Terian empire was just a small piece of a much larger whole, a whole that held millions and millions of colonized worlds: the Milky Way.

"What galactic year?"

The woman was surprised by the question.

"I can't remember."

I wasn't surprised by her answer. The Terian empire was isolationist. I didn't know why I knew that, but I did. And isolationism meant a disregard for the greater galaxy, along with its time standards.

"Could I have some water?"

Her smile returned—finally a question she could handle.

"Of course."

She stepped behind me, beyond my original field of view, to a sink protruding from the wall. Using a small cup sitting on the left, she poured me some water. I watched all of this unfold with my mind on the empire.

All twenty-three worlds came to me immediately, but one stood out: Raviir, the capital world. Something about the place drew me. I wanted to go there, but I wasn't sure why. At that point, it was the only lead I had.

"I'm going to lift you up, okay?"

I nodded in response. Chellet, holding the cup of water in one hand, pressed a pedal with her foot, folding the bed so I could sit upright. As I moved upward, the blanket slid down my chest, and I noticed a white, skintight outfit on my body. Whatever it was, I didn't feel it.

"What happens if I don't have a chip?"

She handed me the cup before answering.

"Well, this is an unusual situation. Since we cannot get a positive identification, we have contacted a Fleet officer for assistance; they'll take the appropriate measures."

The Fleet—the Terian empire's governing authority and military force. The muscle behind the system's expansion. An officer could be good news, but it could also be very bad. I sipped at my water apprehensively.

"Why wouldn't I have a chip?"

Chellet shrugged.

"Usually, if someone doesn't have a chip, they're a foreigner. But we've never had someone without a chip have total retrograde amnesia."

She paused, giving me yet another smile. This one was genuine, but it was also sad.

"In any case, if you remember anything, you can signal me using the blue button next to your hip."

I looked down and saw an assortment of colors to press.

"For now, I've put you into our system as Robyn. It sounded better than Unknown Female."

I smiled. I liked Chellet, and I was a little worried to see her heading towards the door.

"Thanks, Chellet."

She looked at me and flashed a happier smile.

"Of course. See you soon."

With that, she stepped out of the room and pressed a button, sliding the door shut behind her. I stared at that part of the wall for a few seconds before trying to process what was going on.

Chellet had presented me with the most likely explanation for my missing chip, but it wasn't the only one. Perhaps I had taken it out myself? I knew it was difficult to remove ID chips without leaving a trace, but depending on how desperate you were to hide your identity...

I paused, surprised by my train of thought. How did I know so much about ID chips, yet couldn't seem to conjure even one memory? And why this fixation on removal? When the officer came, would he inform me I was actually a wanted criminal?

I shuddered at the thought. The Fleet wasn't known for their mercy or kindness. Depending on my crimes, my punishment could range from a simple beating to laborious servitude to summary execution. None of those sounded like good options to me. My head began to hurt, a dull pounding that cleared my thought process. I decided to focus on Raviir.

Raviir was one of the first of the twenty-three worlds to be colonized, eventually becoming an offshoot of the neighboring Moffan empire. It was on Raviir that Terius, the empire's namesake, spent most of his young life—the same Terius who rebelled against the Moffans with the help of six other worlds, forming the new empire and what would later become the Fleet.

All of this information ran through my brain at breakneck speed, and once again I struggled to understand how I could know so much and remember so little. I tried to come up with something related to Raviir that was personal to me—an image, a sound, even a smell—any memory to prove my existence before this day. It was useless. All I had was knowledge, general information that could be found in an encyclopedia.

With my mind drawing a blank, I started to panic. Frankly, even if I was labeled a foreigner rather than a fugitive, my outlook was poor. The empire wasn't just lightly isolationist—most citizens held a great deal of disdain for the rest of the galaxy, and foreigners were treated with little respect. Chellet had shown me a surprising level of empathy for a potential outsider, though that was to be expected in a spaceport hospital. But the Fleet? They wouldn't be as accepting as she was.

This thought process continued in futile circles for the next half hour until it was interrupted by the hiss of the door opening. A man in uniform stood in the doorway, with the insignia of the Fleet on his lapel. The officer was here.

2

His uniform was black outlined in crimson—simple but sharp colors that demanded attention and respect. He wore black gloves over his hands, and a black cap with a crimson outline on his head. On the front of the cap and on each of his shoulders was a red star with one thick line underneath, a symbol I recognized. A pin in the shape of the Fleet emblem on his right chest broke the red and black pattern, its gold glinting under the light of the room.

He stepped inside without a word, the door hissing shut behind him. There was a vague air of irritation in his short walk to my bed—he didn't want to be dealing with this. He came to my left side and gave me a once over. In that moment, I thought I saw a hint of the irritation slip away.

"Good morning, I'm Lieutenant Folent. I've been assigned to your case. Your doctor informed me that you have complete retrograde amnesia and no ID chip, is this true?"

His eye contact was intimidating and unbroken.

"Yes, sir."

"At this point in time, do you remember your name?"

"No, sir."

He gave a small sigh at my response, looking away.

"But you can call me Robyn."

He looked back at me.

"Robyn? Is this the nickname given to you by Dr. Rolt?"

I nodded.

"Very well. Robyn, I'm here to assess your claim of amnesia and determine the proper action to be taken."

Assess my claim? That seemed like a job for a doctor, not a military officer, but I kept my mouth shut.

"Is there anything you remember before waking up?"

"No. But I know things."

The lieutenant gave me a confused look.

"What do you mean?"

"I know the twenty-three planets of the empire. And I knew that star with one line under it made you a lieutenant."

His expression darkened.

"You say you know all twenty-three planets of our empire?"

I hesitated, wondering what I had done wrong.

"Yes. Alder, Borrin, Dathleran…"

He raised his hand to stop me and pointed at the star on his cap.

"And this? What about no star with one line?"

"Private."

"And a full star with no lines?"

"Ensign."

He looked me up and down, frowning.

"Do you think a foreigner would know so much about our empire?"

At these words, my heart rate jumped.

"We've spent the last twelve hours cross-referencing our database of current foreigners in our empire on a visitation, and foreigners on special permits. Your face hasn't matched anyone yet, and we're running out of candidates. If you're not found on that list, you're either a Terian fugitive or a foreigner in our empire without a permit, and therefore still a fugitive."

I was only half-listening, desperately searching for absolution in the dark recesses of my mind. Why was there nothing? Shouldn't there be something?

"However, given your knowledge of the empire and until you can prove otherwise, you'll be considered a Terian fugitive who willfully removed their ID chip. You'll be taken to a detainment hospital and placed under Fleet supervision for a month's time. If there has been no progress with your memory or other forms of evidence for or against your case, you will then be prosecuted to the full extent of Terian law. Do you understand?"

I gave a weak nod, still searching my uncooperative memory.

"Of course, any additional information you give me could lighten your punishment. Is there anything you would like to say?"

Yes there was, but I didn't know what. I wanted him to know I wasn't lying, and if I was a Terian, I had no idea why my ID chip was missing or why I ended up in the port. The fact that I still had a month to recall things didn't ease my fears—to me, it seemed if there were no memories coming now, there wouldn't be any coming ever.

I looked up at the lieutenant and saw the suspicion in his eyes. He thought I was lying—he thought I was faking the amnesia.

"No, nothing."

He gave a short nod of acknowledgment, disappointed by the lack of confession.

"Very well. You will be transported to the detainment hospital in approximately four hours. I will come back at that time and escort you. Be advised there are Fleet soldiers throughout the spaceport and hospital, and you have been placed on a watchlist."

With one more cursory nod, the lieutenant turned away and walked out the door. I watched it close behind him, then pressed the blue button at my hip.

3

When Chellet walked in three minutes later, I felt a wave of relief. For the brief time I had been alive, she was the only comfort I had.

"They told me you've been assigned to a detainment center," she began, standing a little farther than before.

A hint of pain spread in my chest, and I had my first taste of betrayal.

"You think I'm dangerous?"

She looked away in embarrassment.

"I..."

I interrupted her.

"I understand, but I need someone to talk to. How can I get my memory back?"

Chellet turned back toward me and, with a look of determination, came to my side.

"I'm sorry. With all that's going on right now..."

She gave me a concerned look.

"I shouldn't treat you like one of them."

I stared at her, confused.

"One of them?"

She looked away, ashamed.

"The MR. I thought you might be a terrorist..."

She looked back at me, frowning.

"I'm sorry."

I frowned in turn. The Moffan Resurgence was an insurgent group bent on disrupting Terian control over what were once Moffan worlds. If the Fleet thought I was one of them, I'd be dead before the end of the day.

"No, Chellet, I understand..."

Worst of all, how did I know I wasn't? I decided not to share that thought with her.

"Please, do you know any way for me to get my memory back?"

I saw the pity in her eyes and, for the second time, knew the answer before she said it.

"I'm sorry, Robyn, but no. If I did, we would've already tried. Almost all cases of retrograde amnesia are cured by a spontaneous recovery."

I frowned again.

"Is there a timeline? How long will it take?"

Chellet shook her head.

"I can't say."

It was difficult to hold back my frustration, the emotional catharsis pushing and pounding the walls of my brain. Every answer was another wave against a weakened dam. I needed to find a productive outlet, a useful goal.

"What can you tell me about Raviir?"

She looked at me curiously.

"Raviir? What do you want to know about Raviir?"

I realized how abrupt my change of subject had been.

"I'm not sure…"

I saw the confusion in her eyes, but before she had time to respond, the door hissed open and a Fleet ensign marched into the room.

"There's been a change of plans. We need to prep her for departure immediately."

My heart sank. My four hour window had been cut down to ten minutes.

"What? Why?" Chellet asked.

The ensign seemed annoyed by her tone, but ignored it.

"That is none of your concern, doctor."

Chellet was ready to respond but I interjected.

"Where is the lieutenant?"

"Lieutenant Folent is no longer assigned to you."

"I was told I would be escorted by the lieutenant."

The ensign shot me a dirty look. I knew I was pushing it, but I wanted to take his attention off Chellet.

"Would you like me to call him to confirm?"

I hesitated, then shook my head. I had pushed far enough.

"In that case doctor, detach her."

Chellet worked her way around the bed, gently removing the various tubes. I felt no pain, just a small pinch with each pull. On the last one, she leaned closer to my ear, reaching under the bed, and whispered, "Good luck."

She gave me a small smile as she stood, but the ensign broke the silence before I could respond.

"What's your name?"

I glanced at Chellet.

"Robyn."

"Okay Robyn, it's time to leave."

I looked down at my legs, still hidden under the covers, and realized I had not used them yet. They swung out from under the blanket, over the right side. As far as I could tell, my body was working without issue. Why couldn't my brain get on board?

As I processed my status, the ensign turned around and walked to the door. I hopped to the ground and saw the outfit covered my entire body, except my hands and head. I knew it was some sort of medical clothing, but even my encyclopedic knowledge didn't have an entry for this.

The ensign stopped at the door and I looked at Chellet.

"Do I have any clothes?"

The ensign responded, "Your belongings have been taken care of. The medsuit is sufficient for the transition."

I glanced down at my body. It might be sufficient for them, but even if it wasn't transparent, it hugged my skin a little too close for comfort.

The door hissed open and I scurried behind the ensign, shelving my complaints for the time being. I had to accept my freedoms were limited until further notice, and I had to follow this young soldier or my month of supervision would be bypassed in favor of immediate punishment. Unless it already had?

I stepped out the door and turned my head, barely catching a glimpse of Chellet as it hissed closed. I felt a new pain in my chest, but this was not the pain of betrayal. It was one of loss.

4

I followed the ensign through the wide, off-white hall, my eyes darting up to look out the glass ceiling. Dozens of spaceships dotted the sky, flying in every direction. Soon, I would be among them.

"How long is the flight?"

I was close enough to know he could hear my question, but I got no reply. We took a right into the next hallway and continued our march, doctors and other medical workers standing clear of our path. I wondered what would happen if I just turned around and ran. I was relatively certain I had seen another ensign in the previous hallway, but I had yet to see a weapon. How could he stop me if he didn't have a weapon?

I glanced at the ensign's gloves. They were the same black as the lieutenant's, and something about them triggered some buried knowledge...

"Ow."

A sharp pain shot through my forehead and I brought my hand up instinctively, but the feeling was already gone. What was going on in my brain? Part of me hoped this might bring back some of my memory, but as far as I could tell there was no change.

I spent the next few minutes following the ensign in silence. He guided me down another hallway into a large, hexagonal lobby—what looked like the hospital hub. In the center was a circular desk with medical staff, and each of the six walls opened into a grand hallway—all except one.

We made our way towards the exception, an ominous steel door with two Fleet privates on either side. As the ensign approached, the guards nodded in unison, and the door opened. I realized I was walking into the military section of the spaceport and took a glance back at the people in the lobby. Was this the last of my freedom? Did I even have any now?

I turned back around and rushed after the ensign, into a room about ten meters by ten meters, with another large steel door in front of us. The door behind us closed, muting the outside world and locking us inside. I didn't know how I knew, but we were being watched.

After a short silence, the second door opened, and a massive hangar stretched out before us. I looked up and saw three fighters fly through one of many great arches that supported the huge dome, the columns forming a structure at least three kilometers in diameter. On the floor in front of us were rows of craft as far as the eye could see: fighters, bombers, even some frigates off in the distance. The larger ships dominated the midsection, and everything tapered down to the smallest scouts. It was both impressive and overwhelming.

"Let's go."

I had let myself stop and stare long enough to annoy the ensign, who led me leftwards along the edge of the hangar. I continued to admire the row of ships on my right, noting that I knew the difference between an interplanetary and interstellar bomber. Now why couldn't I replace that knowledge with my real name? Or how I got here?

About thirty meters ahead, next to a shuttle entrance ramp, stood another Fleet lieutenant. He watched our approach with contempt, and I wondered if any of the Fleet had a sense of humor, or even knew how to smile.

The ensign stopped just short of the ramp and gave the lieutenant a nod. The lieutenant returned the nod, then the ensign turned back toward me.

"Go up and take a seat."

He gestured toward the ramp. I looked at the lieutenant but he continued to stare down at me with disapproval. What was his problem?

I went up the metal ramp in front of me, into the belly of the shuttle. Inside were twelve seats arranged in two columns of six, each one wide and cushioned, with ample room between them. Thick windows formed the midsection of both walls for the entire length of the shuttle, and an open door up ahead led into the cockpit.

Standing at the back eyeing the decor, I couldn't help but wonder why everything seemed so… luxurious. It was not what I had expected from a prison transport.

Of the twelve seats, three were occupied—the front right, second left, and back right. I couldn't quite see the people in the front, but the man in the back right seat turned around to face me, smiling. What I had originally thought to be another prisoner was actually a Fleet commander.

So much for them not smiling.

5

"Please, have a seat."

He gestured to the seat next to his, and I followed his polite order.

"I'm Commander Hurren, what's your name?"

Now that I was next to him, I noticed he was rather short.

"Robyn."

Concern flashed across his face.

"Robyn? You remember your name?"

"No, this was the name given to me by my doctor."

The concern vanished, and I grew uneasy. What was this about?

"Robyn, I'm here to inform you that you're no longer being transferred to our detainment hospital—at least, not yet. We've decided to give you a different option."

My unease grew.

"Though I'm sure it caused you discomfort, your amnesia and lack of ID chip could be a valuable asset to the Fleet. You have a choice: either continue your detainment process and face a severe punishment..."

He glanced toward the front of the shuttle.

"...or, effective immediately, begin training as a Fleet cadet at the Academy."

Commander Hurren looked back at me and resumed his smile. I could see he was excited to give me this opportunity, this apparent way out. After a few seconds of tense silence, his smile began to fade.

"Well?"

"Sorry, I don't understand. What's the Academy?"

A hint of the enthusiasm came back as he responded.

"The Academy is the Fleet's premier training institution, meant only for the best minds and bodies in the empire. A cadet is one of our most valuable assets. Assuming you are able to succeed in the training, you will become a full-fledged officer of the Fleet. You'll learn more about the program once you have joined. Until then, most information pertaining to the Academy is strictly classified, particularly to a potential criminal."

I stared at the commander, waiting for the punchline. The Fleet's premier training institution, for the best minds and bodies? And they deemed me—a potential criminal with amnesia—qualified?

The commander held my gaze with a hint of apprehension and it dawned on me that I had leverage. Something about my situation was enticing to them, and even though they had presented me with a choice, I could tell they were keen I make it in their favor. Of course, this only made me more suspicious.

"What will I do at the Academy?"

I saw a flash of disdain in Hurren's expression before he responded.

"As I said, you'll learn about the program when you join. Until then, what you might do is classified."

These answers did nothing to assuage my concerns. Even if this was not some convoluted ploy, even if I was actually being offered a spot in this program, I still knew nothing about the Academy. The name was vaguely familiar, and when the commander explained its purpose as an officer training school, that too seemed familiar. But I knew nothing about the training; what if it was worse than the punishment they had in store?

"If I join the Academy and manage to become a Fleet officer, will my restrictions be removed?"

Now it was Hurren who eyed me with suspicion.

"Your current restrictions as a fugitive will be removed. However, you will have more numerous and far greater restrictions as an officer of the Fleet."

I nodded.

"I understand."

I looked up the aisle toward the other passengers, but I couldn't see their faces. As far as I could tell, there wasn't much to think about. I had been given two choices: one suspicious and likely dangerous, the other straightforward but certainly dangerous.

"I accept this offer."

I looked back at the commander, his smile wider than ever.

"Excellent."

He stood from his seat and looked toward the front.

"Seal the ramp and set a course for Alder."

I heard the ramp moving behind us and felt a small vibration as the shuttle came to life. The commander looked down at me, still smiling.

"Enjoy the flight."

He walked up the aisle to the front, taking an empty seat, and I noted that he was even shorter out of the seat.

We were headed to Alder, the oldest inhabited planet in the Terian empire, colonized over four thousand years prior—older even than Raviir. Was the Academy on Alder? I knew Alder was the site of an important Fleet base, but I couldn't quite remember what it was...

A slight jolt let me know the repulsion systems were engaged, and we began to cruise forward. I watched out the window as we approached one of the dome's archways. The experience of flight seemed normal enough to me, which made sense for someone who woke up in a spaceport. I even knew a trip from Kurotar to Alder would take somewhere between 3-8 hours, depending on the power of the shuttle and my incomplete knowledge of the empire's flightpaths. The real questions were how did I know all of this and what would happen once I got there?

We reached the archway and passed out of the hangar, the shuttle pitching upward to start us on our journey. I could see at least a dozen other ships, military and civilian, crisscrossing the slice of sky visible through the side window. Most of them were busy going about their daily routines, unperturbed by significant life events or severe neurological issues. I realized with a bit of sadness I might never remember that feeling, if I was ever able to experience it.

I closed my eyes and sat back in the chair, fighting the flood of questions on the edge of my conscience. I didn't want to spend the flight in light depression, contemplating my unknown future or searching for my unknown past. I wanted to sleep.

6

When I opened my eyes again, I saw the blackness of space out the window, punctuated by two other vessels and hundreds of stars. There was something both calming and magnificent about the view, and I stared out in wonder. How many of those glimmering lights were inhabited systems? How many had yet to be explored?

As I watched, three more ships came into view, and I realized we must be approaching the Kurotar gate. I sat up straighter, excited at the prospect of what I was about to behold.

Interstellar travel was the key to galactic colonization, but most habitable planets were separated by many light-years, making conventional spaceflight impractical. The only way such flights were possible were via jump gates: massive, astonishingly complicated devices that created temporary wormholes between specific nodes of a grander system.

Jump technology made interstellar travel possible, yet no one in the galaxy knew how it worked. The gates themselves were ancient—a vestige from galactic colonization thousands of years ago—and despite centuries of research and scientific investigation, the secrets of the technology remained beyond reach. As a result, no new gates could be constructed; in order to travel between planets, an already-extant gate had to be utilized. There were still plenty of gates to go around—many of the older planets had three or four—but their number was, of course, limited.

What would happen when they ran out, I wondered.

I couldn't see Kurotar's gate yet, but I knew what it looked like: seven hexagons stacked in a large circle, one in the middle and six around it. Each of the hexagons created a separate wormhole measuring nearly two kilometers wide, meaning the entire honeycomb of seven wormholes was over five kilometers in diameter.

While the details of jump technology were lost, the gates were still very much programmable. In essence, the Fleet—or any galactic entity—could control which two sub-gates were currently connected and remove or create new connections as necessary based on the flight plans of all the ships in their jurisdiction. Between certain nodes, there could be thousands of jumps an hour, so these connections needed to be very well synced.

I took my mind off the gates for a moment, pondering all of the information that just came from somewhere in my brain. Clearly I was familiar with spaceflight and jump technology, but why? Was all of this common knowledge, or had I spent significant time on ships? I tried once more to dig a little deeper, to find something to latch on to, but all I could find were general facts, impersonal information. Nothing that could answer the only question that mattered: who am I?

The other ships were closer now, close enough that I could make out three shuttles and a squadron of six interceptors escorting a small frigate. On my right, past the empty chair where Commander Hurren once sat, I saw two more shuttles and two larger frigates. It was fascinating to me, this density of travel. So many people, all with their own missions and stories.

A moment later I caught sight of the jump gate out of the edge of the window, and I stopped paying attention to our caravan. We were going through one of the outer sub-gates, and our orientation made it so I would see almost the entire gate system as we approached. The farthest sub-gates came into view first, large metal hexagons of black and gray. If you looked through the sub-gates themselves, you might not know they were activated—there was just more space on the other side. But by paying attention to the stars and the way they moved with respect to your position, you could tell you were looking at a different part of space.

More sub-gates came into view, and an entire fleet of ships was visible, separated into distinct clusters heading to and from each sub-gate. I watched one of the sub-gates closely, hoping to catch a switch between clusters. The last of the caravan went through, and the next group of ships was a fair distance behind, so I knew it was coming.

In the blink of an eye, the star pattern on the other side of the sub-gate changed as a new connection was made. Fascinating.

I looked up the aisle toward Commander Hurren and the other passengers. All of them were gesturing in the air, interacting with some virtual interface I couldn't see, oblivious to the large number of craft around us. To them, the jump gates must seem routine, mundane. But as much as I knew about these massive space structures, this would still be my first time actually seeing one—at least as far as I could remember. Perhaps my past self was just like them, bored and uninterested... I hoped not.

Finally, our sub-gate came into view. At this point, the front end of our convoy was most likely in the Alder system. What did a jump feel like? As with most things, I couldn't remember. Would it feel like anything at all?

I stared at the edge of the sub-gate, the black and grey hexagon surrounding us on all sides. The hardest thing for me to imagine was I was actually looking at two halves of two separate sub-gates, each one hundreds of lightyears apart—it all looked seamless to me. The transition itself was just as seamless, and as the ship passed through the portal, I felt nothing different, no change. It was almost a let down.

I watched the new gate emerge from the other side and realized we were oriented differently than we had been before. My mind tried to understand how I was not seeing what it expected to see, and a faint dizziness made me close my eyes.

Fascinating. I didn't understand how the other passengers could ignore it.

7

Less than an hour later, we were entering the atmosphere of Alder. There was a hint of vibration and a distant rumble, but otherwise the ship's interior was still and silent. No doubt it had an advanced entry-suspension system and extensive soundproofing.

I turned my gaze to the dancing flames of plasma in the window. I couldn't see any of the terrain yet, but I knew Alder was almost exclusively artificial, a product of its development over thousands of years. This was a dense planet with a rich history, some of which I knew. Why?

Before my mind could even attempt to answer, the plasma cleared and I saw the surface. Alder was mostly black and grey, with patches of blue water and one pocket of dark green. Pocket was a word reserved for this altitude—the area looked to be thousands of square kilometers in size, a forest and mountain landscape cutting a neat rectangle into the never-ending city.

It was clear our shuttle was headed for this natural area, and I peered through the window as we approached. A segment of what was once a vast mountain range created a natural boundary along the southern and eastern borders of the expanse; the imposing, snow-capped peaks ending abruptly at the edge of the grounds in massive, sheer walls of rock. The northwest segment was mostly trees, a vast and dense forest, tapering and thinning toward the middle. If this was our destination—if this was the Academy—it was beautiful.

The descent lasted another ten minutes, but it wasn't until I could feel the braking thrust that it hit me how real this was. I was just as confused by the situation I found myself in as I was by my elusive past—letting a potential terrorist join the ranks of the Fleet elite, a woman with a broken brain becoming a cadet... it didn't make any sense. Unless, the thought suddenly occurred to me, they were connected.

What if my past wasn't a secret? What if one of these people knew something I didn't? I shot a glance up the rows and saw the commander working the same virtual interface. Did he know more than he was letting on?

The pilot brought the shuttle over a landing pad, pausing for a moment just above the ground. A subtle nudge let me know we had landed, then I heard the ramp open behind me. There was a rush of cool air from below, and a pit formed in my stomach.

The commander stood and came down the aisle, stopping next to my seat.

"Welcome to Alder. Come with me and we'll get you processed."

He continued down the ramp, but I hesitated. What was I getting myself into? Before I let my mind wander too far, I remembered I was on a short leash and jumped out of my seat to try and catch up.

The first thing I noticed when I stepped off the ramp was the climate. The air was thin, but the light breeze and gentle sun were pleasant. I wondered how they kept the planet this temperate with so little vegetation on its surface—there had to be some heavy climate control going on. I also didn't feel any change in gravity—the shuttle must have employed a gradual shift during our flight to acclimate us.

The second thing I noticed were my surroundings: groups of tall, green trees some hundred meters away and tremendous mountains in the distance. These views managed to distract me from my worries, if only for a moment.

"Welcome to the Academy, Robyn," Commander Hurren announced.

I turned to see him waiting a few steps ahead, a small smile on his lips. Behind him was a singular building: a wide, one story structure that immediately caught the eye with its polished black exterior and red trim. I forgot all about the trees and the mountains as I stared at those pitch black walls, my wonder and awe replaced by dread.

"We need to get you inside for processing. Follow me."

I took a glance back toward the shuttle, expecting some of the other passengers to join us, but no one else was coming down the ramp. I turned back and hurried after the commander.

"Will I ever receive my personal items?" I asked.

He responded without looking back.

"The items found on you in the spaceport?"

"Yes."

He shook his head dismissively.

"No, but you aren't going to lose anything. Just a set of clothes, not even a communicator."

He stopped, turning toward me with a stern look.

"Also, you need to refer to me and all other officers as 'sir.'"

"Yes, sir."

He gave me a small nod then continued toward the building.

"What is processing, sir?" I continued, the pit in my stomach growing.

"We need to evaluate your physical health and put you in a uniform. That's processing."

They were planning to evaluate my physical health, but what about my mental health? Wouldn't a premier military institute need recruits of sound mind? Besides, hadn't they already decided my mind and body were among the best?

We reached the front of the building and a door slid open, revealing a red and black interior, just as imposing as the exterior. The commander led me down the main hallway, into a room on the right. Inside was a Fleet doctor, a senior lieutenant whose uniform was white instead of black, though lines of red still highlighted her frame.

The doctor had me enter a medical pod in the corner. Since I was wearing a medsuit, she let me stay dressed while scanning my body. The process took all of ten seconds.

"We received your file from Kurotar and everything looks normal. Our pod scan was all clear. Is there anything you know that may affect your ability to train?"

I shot a glance at the commander, who eyed me curiously. Should I tell her I don't know who I am? Should I tell her I don't know why I'm here?

My eyes went back to the doctor.

"No, sir."

She nodded and looked at the commander.

"She's all yours, sir."

"Thank you, doctor."

The commander led me to another room and asked me to wait by the entrance. I watched him walk over to the wall and press a button, revealing a shelf of black uniforms. He grabbed one, closed the panel, and brought it toward me.

"Take this."

He held the outfit in front of me, and I took it from his hand.

"Now, according to Lieutenant Folent, you have a certain level of knowledge of the Terian empire and the Fleet, is that correct?"

"Yes, sir."

"Do you know what it takes to put on that uniform you've got in your hand?"

I shot another glance at the garment before responding.

"No, sir."

A sort of amused pity came over his expression.

"Fleet recruits have to undergo basic training, and then only the best of the best are chosen to become cadets. Do you happen to know what percent of Fleet recruits end up going to the Academy?"

"No, sir."

"Less than three percent."

Once again, everything the commander told me sounded familiar, as if I was being reminded of things I had forgotten but once knew. How much knowledge was hidden in my broken mind? And why was it hidden at all?

"Now here's the interesting part. My superiors have decided that you will be skipping basic training and jumping right into the Academy. Do you know what that means?"

"No, sir."

"That means you're about to join the ranks of the best recruits in the Fleet with zero training. You'll be expected to adapt and fit in among the top three percent when you yourself can't even stand at attention."

I straightened my posture, and the commander laughed.

"I pity you, Robyn. I think my superiors saw an opportunity and they're jumping on it without thinking it through. Of course, I'm sure they have their reasons, but in this line of work, you get used to having more questions than answers."

Then his demeanor changed, and he eyed me sternly.

"There are, however, two things I can tell you with utmost certainty. First, if you fail to adapt and assimilate, you will be removed and taken to your originally scheduled detainment. And second, if at any time your memory returns and you do not immediately report this to your primary liaison, you will be summarily and unceremoniously executed. Is that clear?"

I felt the pit in my stomach again, deeper than ever. What had I gotten myself into?

"Yes, sir."

Commander Hurren smiled and patted my shoulder.

"Now put on that uniform, cadet. And welcome to the Fleet."

8

After Commander Hurren's abrupt announcement, all I could do was stare at the outfit in my hand. The cadet uniform was the same black as an officer's, with the same hint of crimson, though I saw no shoulder patches, gloves, or hat. This was odd, as I knew cadets should have all three, but my mind was still focused on one of the man's threats: if I failed to adapt to the program, I would face my original punishment.

Why even bother? They wanted me to jump into the Academy, among the best recruits of the Fleet, with exactly zero training? I eyed the object of clothing with a hint of fear. There was also the second threat he had made, the one about my memory returning…

"Stop staring at it, Robyn. We don't have time to waste."

I glanced up at the commander then down at my medsuit.

"Sir, are you…"

I left my question unfinished and he eyed me sternly.

"Robyn, modesty has no place in the Fleet."

I looked at my medsuit again, then back at the commander. Slowly, and with a look that made me wince, he turned around.

"If my superiors weren't so invested in this gimmick I'd expel you right here and now."

I tried to ignore his words and the fact that he was still two meters away, focusing instead on how to take the medsuit off. After a few seconds of deliberation and one or two false starts, I was able to strip down. Naked in this strange room, I suddenly lost all hesitation and hurried to put on the uniform. It slipped on easily, tightening automatically to fit itself to my body's proportions. Although it was more comfortable and less revealing than the medsuit, something about it hugging my shape felt almost constrictive—a literal and metaphorical pressure.

"Done, sir."

The commander turned around and looked me up and down, smiling.

"Like a typical transie!"

I didn't understand the term, but he moved on.

"Okay Robyn, you have one more day until the session starts. Do you understand?"

"The session, sir?"

I could see a hint of irritation in his expression, but he answered all the same.

"A cadet's time at the Academy is normally divided into three sessions, each lasting 400 days with 100 days of specs in between—1500 days total. The next session starts in one day, which I would assume is the entire reason you're here."

He gave me a knowing look.

"Again, I think my superiors haven't thought this through, but it's not my place to question their orders. Your appearance was perfect timing, in their eyes."

Though I kept the thought to myself, I disagreed with this assessment; if anything, I woke up at exactly the wrong time. With 500 days to a session, this was a cruel coincidence. Why couldn't I have woken up in the middle of one, or even ten days in? Maybe then I wouldn't be standing here, wearing a uniform I didn't earn, about to join the ranks of the military elite without so much as a shred of experience.

"What that means is we have only one day to get you as caught up as possible. Your primary liaison will guide you through that."

Now I understood why there was a hint of urgency in my transfer to Alder. Maybe if I had woken up ten or twenty days before the session, I'd have enough time to prepare, to train. But with just one day left? How could I fit all of basic training into one day?

"Obviously we'll focus on the most important facets, and you'll have some gaps to fill later on. Again, your primary liaison will handle the details."

He gestured toward the door.

"Follow me."

I followed him back into the hallway and wondered what time it was. I had seen no windows inside this building, but more surprisingly, I had seen no more than five other people. It was an awfully large structure to be so empty.

The commander led me to a wide room with several desks along the walls. Standing in the middle of this room was another commander.

"Robyn, this is Commander Kelt."

While her height matched my own—both of us about ten centimeters taller than Commander Hurren—Commander Kelt still managed to look down at me. There was something intimidating in her stance and stare, something that gave me pause.

Commander Hurren cleared his throat, breaking the spell and unlocking my gaze.

"Robyn, this is a superior officer, you are expected to give a customary nod."

It was something I already knew—lower ranks were supposed to give a small nod to higher ranks, which the higher rank would acknowledge with a nod of their own—but there was still a disconnect between the uniform I was wearing and the person underneath it.

"Sorry, sir."

"Don't apologize to me. Just do it."

I looked back at Commander Kelt and gave her a small nod. She returned the gesture without breaking eye contact.

"Details like that will get you kicked out of the Academy," Hurren added.

I heard the disappointment in his tone but didn't care—his statement gave me an excuse to break away from Commander Kelt's gaze.

"Commander Kelt will be your primary liaison here at the Academy. She will be in charge of bringing you up to speed during your first session. You'll be seeing a lot of her over the next few months, but your relationship with her will remain strictly confidential, as will any interactions you two have. You may not disclose anything about your relationship or any of your interactions to anyone unless directly authorized by Commander Kelt to do so. Is that clear?"

I hesitated. This imposing figure was my primary liaison? And our relationship was a secret? I saw a hint of impatience in Commander Hurren's expression, and rushed to respond.

"Yes, sir."

"Good. This is where I leave you, Robyn."

He gave me another once over, then flashed a false smile.

"Good luck. You're going to need it."

I watched him walk out the door and felt a surprising desire to follow. While the man hadn't been particularly kind, he was not malicious—just indifferent. Despite not having heard her say a word, I wasn't sure if I could say the same for Commander Kelt.

9

"Good afternoon."

Her voice was curt, cold. Exactly what I would have expected, exactly what I had feared.

"Did Commander Hurren brief you on the details of your situation?"

After a moment's hesitation, I brought my eyes to hers.

"Yes, sir."

Though her expression hid it well, I could hear the subtle disdain in Commander Kelt's tone. What had I done to warrant such treatment? Perhaps she knew I was a criminal, perhaps she knew I didn't belong…

"Does this mean you know and understand your cover as a member of the integrated commission program?"

The what?

"No, sir."

She gave a slow nod, a nod of unsurprised disappointment.

"You will have a better understanding of your cover after you have completed the basic knowledge assessment. But before we can do that, we need to install your lenses and chip."

An ID chip? Wasn't part of my original appeal my lack of chip?

Commander Kelt held out her hand, a small black box with one red line through the middle in her palm.

"Take your lenses and install them."

I hesitated, eyeing the tiny box, then took it from her. A moment after it hit my palm, it opened upward along the seam, revealing two small, transparent, concave circles.

Lenses—these went on my eyes. How did I know that?

With care, I used my free hand to grab the lenses and place one on each eye. As they attached to my cornea, I expected some display or perhaps sharper vision, but I noticed no change. When both were in place, the box closed itself, and the commander took it from my hand.

"Are you familiar with the lenses?"

Her expression was neutral, but I could tell what answer she expected.

"No, sir."

She paused, holding my gaze for a moment before continuing.

"Your lenses enable false holographic display of information, usually controlled by a combination of gestures and audio cues. You will learn how to use them with your squadron. At this time, they are display only, and will show you only what needs to be shown. Do you understand?"

Again, that tone in her voice: she was treating me like a child, someone who needed their hand held through the process. To be fair, this wasn't far from the truth.

"Yes, sir."

"Now your ID chip."

She gestured toward my right arm.

"Expose your upper arm."

The commander turned around to grab something from a nearby desk, and I pushed my sleeve up. She turned around with what looked like a fat pistol in her hand: an insertion gun.

I stared at the device as she lifted it toward my skin. How deep was an ID chip implanted? Was this going to hurt? A shiver coursed through my body when the cold metal tip met my tricep. I had a half-second to ponder the level of pain I was about to feel before a light jab startled me. All that worrying for nothing.

She gestured toward one of the desks along the wall.

"Replace your sleeve then take a seat."

The commander turned away and I did as told, covering my arm then walking over to the desk. As soon as I sat down, the surface lit up: a large, interactive interface, with instructions on how to begin. I looked at the commander.

"Follow the instructions to complete your basic knowledge assessment," she said.

Thus began a lengthy session of reviewing and testing on rudimentary Fleet knowledge, from nomenclature to protocol. Questions and diagrams flashed before me, and each time I learned something ostensibly new, it felt as if I had already known it all along. Some of the information came slowly, but all of it came, and I was surprised by just how much I could remember. I waited for some part of this knowledge to unlock my mind, to bring back my memories and tell me who I was... but even the few questions about Raviir did nothing more than remind me of an itch I couldn't seem to scratch.

For her part, the commander didn't seem impressed by my rapid progress, though I did my best to ignore her presence. During the testing, she stood over me and said nothing, a situation I found both awkward and intimidating.

The testing lasted a full three hours, during which I was given water but no food. I began to feel the objections of my stomach about halfway through, reminding me that I hadn't eaten in my recallable lifetime, but I waited until it was over to voice my discomfort.

"Sir, may I eat?"

I saw a flash of disgust in her eyes, followed by strained neutrality. Why did she hate me so?

"Yes, dinner is waiting for you in your chamber. Come with me."

I stood and followed her back into the hall.

"Sir, is there no more training?"

"Not today. You will begin the session tomorrow as planned."

She guided me toward the back of the building, and my mind raced to understand her answer. I had passed a basic assessment, and that was enough to blend in with the top three percent of Fleet recruits? This was a terrible idea. Commander Hurren was right to doubt his superiors—how could they possibly think this would work?

"The only thing left to do is understand your cover. As I said before, you will be put in the integrated commission program. I trust you understand what that means now?"

"Yes, sir."

The basic knowledge assessment had filled me in. There were two main ways to become an officer of the Fleet. The first was to go through basic training, show extraordinary promise, and proceed directly to the Academy. This was the most common method, for more than 90% of cadets. But there was a subset of already-enlisted members of the Fleet who would apply and/or be pushed toward becoming an officer at some point in their careers. If approved for admission, a committee would decide how many sessions and which courses would be required to become an officer. In most cases, their enlisted experience would shorten their time at the Academy to two or even one session instead of the standard three. This was known as the integrated commission program. In other words, I was pretending to be an already-enlisted member of the Fleet working on becoming an officer.

"Good. Understand that your instructors and the cadet-officers in your chain of command will know you were already enlisted, but your activities and placement are classified. Therefore, they will not ask about your past. On the other hand, they will expect you to be more proficient than a typical cadet in standard drills, weapons training, and fitness. In these regards, you're expected to do your best to blend in. If you fail to do so, you'll be removed from the Academy and taken to your originally scheduled detainment."

She stopped in front of a door and pressed a button to open it.

"This is your chamber. Dinner is inside. There's a cot for you to sleep on and a small basin for waste. This door will lock behind you. Tomorrow morning an alarm will sound at 200 and I will meet you at 205 to take you to the matriculation ceremony."

She gestured inside and I stepped into the small room. I turned around, ready to ask her another question, but the door was already closed behind me.

Part of me was upset at having my question unanswered, but a bigger part of me was relieved to be away from her. What a charming primary liaison. I hoped our future interactions would be rare and brief, though I doubted I would last longer than a day here.

After scarfing down my dinner, using the waste basin, and getting into the provided sleepsuit, I lay in the cot awake for hours, unable to close my eyes, my mind reliving the past day over and over, searching for reason, searching for understanding. But there were no answers, there was no understanding.

What was I getting myself into?

10

I woke to the sound of an alarm at 200 and wondered what time I had finally fallen asleep. Somehow, I wasn't the least bit tired. I stood and removed the sleepsuit, putting on the black cadet's uniform a second time. Was this really about to happen? Did I even have a choice?

The door opened at 205 with Commander Kelt standing just outside. I gave her a small nod and she replied in kind.

"Good morning, Robyn. Follow me."

"Yes, sir."

She led me down the main hallway, just as empty as the evening before.

"Today you may be asked about your basic training or your transitional time. In either case you are to answer that you are on the integrated commission program, and that your previous operations are classified. If they persist, you will resist."

During my lengthy testing, I had learned a lot more about the typical path to the Academy, which was surprisingly intertwined with planetary time standards. For starters, Fleet recruits entered basic training at one of over a thousand bases spread throughout the empire. Basic training was an intensive program combining all sorts of mental and physical preparation, but it was hard to standardize: one planet's days—and minutes and hours —could be twice or half as long as another's.

To combat these differences, the empire used Raviir's rotation as an interplanetary standard known as Terian time, and the Fleet set basic training at a certain number of Terian days. Therefore, although no planet's rotation was the same as Raviir's, each base did their best to squeeze or stretch the program into an equivalent duration.

But there was only one Academy, on one planet, and each session lasted a full Alder year—over a thousand Terian days. During that time, tens of thousands of up-and-coming cadets would graduate basic training throughout the empire, and many were left with hundreds of days to kill before they could matriculate.

This problem was rectified with what the Fleet called transitional time. Recruits selected for the Academy would leave their original bases and come to Alder as a transitional cadet. Transitional cadets handled all of the low level work at the Academy: cleaning, cooking, etc. This allowed the Fleet to save on support staff, though it also led to many unfair situations: some people spent hundreds of days in transitional time, while others had less than twenty. It all depended on when the recruit completed their basic training with respect to the Academy's running sessions.

Of course, none of this applied to me, as I was supposed to be on the integrated commission program. But the more knowledge I had of the process, the better I could blend in and understand.

"Most importantly of all, you are never permitted to speak about your time on Kurotar or the conditions that brought you here. Is that clear?"

"Yes, sir."

It was clear, but that didn't mean it wasn't lunacy. The classified bit would help, but what about when I had to prove my experience?

Commander Kelt stopped short of the main door.

"There's a junior lieutenant with a hovcar waiting outside to take you to matriculation. I'll be in contact with you as necessary."

The door opened, letting the crisp Alder morning rush in. As the cold air hit my body, I felt the uniform react: a noticeable warmth emanating from beneath the fibers. I glanced down at my sleeves, wondering what other secrets this outfit held.

"You're dismissed."

I looked up and gave Commander Kelt a parting nod, but she didn't return the gesture. Was that considered rude? I had no idea.

I stepped through the open doorway and felt the familiar relief of leaving her presence. Something about the commander did not sit well with me. If anything was going to motivate me to do well today, it was the hope that I wouldn't have to see her any time soon.

Somehow I wasn't all that confident.

11

Ahead, floating above the pad we had landed on the day before, was a vehicle about 3 meters long and 2 wide. In the front, behind what looked like a control module, sat a junior lieutenant. Behind him was another cadet-to-be, sitting in one of the passenger seats. I was happy to see someone else without their cap, gloves, and shoulder patch.

I approached the side of the hovcar and gave the junior lieutenant a small nod which he returned.

"Hop in, transie. Time to get that cap."

I stepped up and into the hovcar, unsure if his statement warranted a response. What did transie mean? I had thought it meant transitional cadet, but I was on the integrated commission program...

The hovcar took off, maintaining a steady half-meter of clearance off the ground as we made our way across campus. At least I knew what a hovcar was—the testing didn't need to explain that to me. The question, as always, was why.

"Hi, I'm Loreen."

The other cadet gave me a half smile and a curious look, but I glanced at the lieutenant to be sure speaking was permitted. When he didn't say anything, I turned back to Loreen.

"Hi Loreen, I'm Robyn."

"You ready to get your cap back, Robyn?"

Thanks to yesterday's testing, I knew what she was talking about: recruits selected for the Academy were given their caps when they left basic training as a symbol of their acceptance into the ranks of the cadets.

Once they reached Alder, however, these caps were taken away, to be returned after transitional time.

"I never had a cap."

She gave me a curious look.

"What do you mean?"

"I'm on the integrated commission program."

An eagerness came over her expression.

"You too? So that's why we're together."

I hesitated. Now I was in the presence of an actual, formerly-enlisted member of the Fleet. Would I be found out in the first two minutes away from Commander Kelt?

"Where were you stationed?" she asked.

I did my best to give her a knowing look.

"I'm not allowed to say."

At my words, her curiosity only seemed to grow.

"Classified? Well, forget I asked."

We accelerated through the open plains, flying just above the green and yellow grasses. There were groups of trees in every direction, and what looked like a dense forest a few hundred meters to our right. Most of the area had light changes in elevation, and the hills gave way to mountains toward the horizon.

With the morning light shining down, I realized just how beautiful the Academy was. This was a near-pristine natural landscape, interrupted only by the occasional building, each one the same stark red and black. It was these intermittent structures that reminded me of the conditions of my visit and prevented me from truly appreciating my surroundings.

"What command are you, Robyn?"

Again, I hesitated. Had she not heard me before?

"I can't tell you," I replied, somewhat confused.

She shook her head.

"I'm not asking where you were, I'm asking where you're going."

Now I was even more confused. I knew what a command was, even before the testing: the highest organizational unit of the Fleet, it represented an entire star system. There were 21 commands in the Fleet, each led by an admiral who reported directly to the Emperor. I figured she was asking me where I had been stationed, but asking where I was going didn't make much sense: we were a few sessions away from that still.

"I don't know."

I didn't know what other answer to give, but this wasn't the right one: her confusion grew, and I wondered if I had already let too much slip.

"They haven't told you yet?"

I held her gaze, trying to keep my composure.

"No…"

She eyed me curiously for a few more seconds, then the junior lieutenant broke the silence.

"You're both in Puric."

Loreen raised her eyebrows at me, seemingly satisfied by his reply, but the feeling wasn't mutual. Puric? Puric was a planet of the empire, but we were nowhere close to it. Puric Command would be the command associated with that star system, but that still made no sense. We were on Alder, in the Alder Command. Had they already selected our eventual placement, before we even started? That seemed irrational.

I waited for clarification, but when the lieutenant spoke again, he changed the subject.

"A word of advice to the both of you: keep the integrated commission program to yourselves."

Loreen looked at him curiously.

"What do you mean, sir?"

He replied without looking back.

"I mean once the other cadets find out you were enlisted, they might treat you different. Maybe they won't, but I was in your shoes a few years ago, and I saw it happen."

I saw the value of his advice, but it was hard to take him seriously. The other cadets will treat me different well before they learn about the integrated commission program, I thought. Probably as soon as I try to perform a drill.

"Remember our strength," he added.

The lieutenant was referring to the Fleet's motto: our strength is unity. Something useful for Loreen to remember, but for me?

"We're approaching the main campus. I'll lead you to the rest of Puric Command, and you'll file in from there to be seated."

"Yes, sir."

"Yes, sir."

I answered a beat after Loreen, and she gave me an amused look. It was clear we were approaching our destination, as hundreds of people in near-identical outfits walked about in groups, all weaving between the red and black buildings. I noted with relief that none of them were in formation—at least I wouldn't have to pretend to know how to do that yet.

When the lieutenant brought the hovcar to a stop, a piece of text appeared in my vision, with a line pointing to the mass of cadets ahead. It read *Puric*.

"This is Puric Command. Follow the instructions in your lenses to find your spot."

"Yes, sir."

This time, we answered in unison.

I stepped out of the hovcar with Loreen right behind me, watching her to make sure I didn't have to nod at the lieutenant again—I didn't.

I turned to face the mobile mass of cadets and saw a new line in my lenses, this one ending with a pulsating red dot.

"Well, see you later, Robyn."

I looked at Loreen.

"Bye."

She gave me another curious look, then walked away. Our interaction had been short, but already my dry and awkward tone had caught her attention. I turned to the hundreds of cadets filing toward matriculation and wondered how I could possibly fit in.

Before my hesitation caught too much attention, I started walking toward the spot indicated by my lenses. A small reading in my peripheral vision gave me distance to destination, the number decreasing as I got closer. Once I was within visual range of the dot, I saw it was pulsing in a gap between two other cadets.

Even with the word *Puric* hovering in the air, I couldn't understand what was going on. We were hundreds of lightyears from Puric, what did this group of individuals have to do with that planet?

A few meters away, other cadets turned to watch my arrival, conversations pausing at my approach. Besides Loreen and I, I hadn't seen any other cadets out of line—already I was attracting unwanted attention, breaking the so-called unity. I avoided their stares and took my spot, the dot and the reading disappearing from view as soon as I was in place.

Silence held for a few seconds before a few of my neighbors started talking again. As they returned to their conversations, I felt some of the tension leave my body, but not all—even though we weren't marching in formation, I did everything I could to match the movements and posture of these neighbors, to not seem out of place. It might be overkill, but it served to distract me from the reality of where I was, of what I was getting into.

Our march lasted about ten minutes, during which the doubts in my mind demanded more and more attention, and I did everything I could to ignore them. Who I was, where I came from, how I could possibly expect to survive so much as a day here... none of these questions would get me out of this line, out of this spot between the cadet in front of me and the one behind. Unless some memories decided to show themselves, I was out of luck.

Finally I caught sight of our destination: a massive building, its importance clear by its central position. Snippets of conversations around me let me know that this was the Academy's hall of ceremonies, one of the largest buildings on the grounds.

I stared at the black walls towering upward, sparse lines of burning red cutting across horizontally. Inside I would matriculate—I would officially join the Academy. With each step of this journey, I regretted my decision more and more. I had no idea what the rest of the day held, or the week, or the year. Would I even make it that far?

12

If the hall of ceremonies was formidable from the outside, it was even more impressive from the inside. As we filed into the main chamber, I could not believe my eyes: there were thousands upon thousands of cadets, arranging themselves via lens instruction into 21 seemingly even groups.

21—that was not a coincidence. There were 21 star systems in the Terian empire. Is this what Loreen and the lieutenant had meant by Puric? Were we divided symbolically, like the empire itself?

It took about thirty minutes to get everyone settled. We stood in our groups facing a raised balcony where several officers watched from above. A general stepped forward and the lenses called for quiet. Almost immediately, thousands of voices were silenced and I glanced around in awe—it was almost disconcerting how effortlessly and simultaneously the entire hall had hushed.

The general began a rousing speech about the Terian empire and the Fleet, but his empty phrases did little to hold my attention, and my mind wandered to the same questions I now struggled to ignore.

Back in the shuttle with Commander Hurren, I had leverage. Back in the shuttle, I had made the choice to go to the Academy because I thought the whatever punishment they had waiting for me would be worse. But how did I know that? What if what the commander had called severe wasn't as severe as this?

After this ceremony, I would be among the cadets, interacting in a manner hopefully more natural than my interaction with Loreen. But what about when I had to walk in formation? Or perform some kind of drill? Even the customary nod was something I had to actively think about; once the session officially started there would be hundreds of minor social cues I needed to understand and perform with little to no hesitation.

After the general finished, a handful of commanders walked among us, handing back caps to mark the beginning of our first session. I grabbed a cap I had never worn before, the same black as my uniform with an empty star on the front. Everyone else had earned this cap, this symbol of excellence. I just happened to wake up without a past.

A pit formed in my stomach, a product of the doubt plaguing my mind. Here I was, worried about the future: about what was in store for me, about trying to fit in, about not going to detainment... but at least these questions had a timeline, at least these questions would be answered.

The other question, the bigger question, the one about my past... it didn't have a timeline, it might never be answered. And that terrified me more than any of this ever could.

13

Matriculation ended with little fanfare, after which the lenses directed us out of the hall of ceremonies, back onto the grounds. As we approached a nearby forest, a specific path through the trees was laid out before me, weaving between plants and cadets alike. It looked as if certain groups of cadets were being led down certain paths, the system working to keep thousands of us moving as seamlessly as possible.

The forest ended about ten minutes later, revealing three rows of identical buildings. I could see seven in the first row. Three rows of seven made 21: one building per symbolic command?

Hundreds of upper-session cadets meandered among the structures, their gloves giving away their senior status. I glanced at my bare hands and wondered when we would receive ours. More curiously, why weren't they part of the uniform? I could feel the answer in the back of my mind, but it eluded me. That seemed like a piece of information that should have been on the basic knowledge assessment.

My lenses directed me to the first building of the third row, and I filed inside with the rest of what had been labelled Puric. As I crossed the threshold of the main door, my directions updated, pointing me to the 7th floor via a set of large stairs. I made my way up, watching others peel off at each floor as their senior counterparts tried to squeeze by.

On the 7th floor, my directions updated a final time, and two minutes later I was at my destination: a large room with eight other cadets inside. One of them—an upperclassman—stood at the front, while the other seven formed a semicircle around him. I glanced at the scene and filed in as symmetrically as possible.

"Good morning, cadets," the upperclassman announced. "I'm Pell, your new cadet-captain, and this," he gestured toward the lot of us, "is your division."

He smiled, and in his smile I saw a friendliness I never would have expected.

"In your time at the Academy, your division will be your closest companions, but it is your squadron that will act as the fundamental unit during your three sessions."

With Pell's introduction, I finally understood the Academy system. I had learned in my assessment that some cadets took leadership roles, and with Pell calling himself a cadet-captain and calling the eight of us a division, it all clicked into place: the Academy was modeled as a microcosm of the Fleet. The 21 dorms were called commands, which were then subdivided down and down, presumably all the way to squadrons, divisions, and elements, the final three groupings in the Fleet structure. A captain in the Fleet would preside over a squadron, so a cadet-captain at the Academy would lead a model squadron.

I wondered how far up the ladder this model went: were there cadet-admirals for each command? Was there a cadet-emperor of the Academy?

"Your element is you and your bunkmate. These assignments will rotate monthly, so every 5 weeks you'll have a new bunkmate from your division. I'll give you your current element assignments now. Once you have your assignment, go to your room and arrange your things. Inside, you'll find your gloves. Put those on and keep them on—gloves should be worn at all times. If you have any questions, I will be here, in the squad room, until 480. Otherwise, I will see you in the wing cafeteria at 500 for lunch and to introduce you to the squadron."

Wing cafeteria—a wing was another, larger subdivision of the Fleet. If the Academy was a direct copy of the Fleet, the commands would be divided into forces and then wings.

Pell began listing off pairs of names, each pair leaving the room after being called.

"Drel and Robyn, room 7-1711."

I followed the lead of those before me and made my way toward the exit with my future roommate. As soon as we were in the hall, she smiled at me.

"Hi Robyn, I'm Drel."

Another friendly face? I liked her already.

"Hi Drel. Any idea where 7-1711 is?"

She pointed to our right.

"Probably this way."

I followed her lead and glanced at a few of the doors. She was right.

"Where are you from, Robyn?"

My smile disappeared, and I nearly stopped in my tracks. Drel noticed my sudden change in demeanor and eyed me with concern.

"Are you okay?"

I gave her a half-hearted smile.

"Yes, sorry. I just— I don't like to talk about it."

This was the truth, and thankfully Drel seemed more apologetic than frustrated.

"Oh, sorry. I didn't know."

"It's fine."

Before an awkward silence could take hold, I shot the same question back at her.

"Where are you from?"

"Puric." She gave me a look. "Ironic, isn't it?"

I smiled again. Even with my odd reaction, Drel had not given me the same curious looks as Loreen, which I appreciated.

We came upon 7-1711 and the door opened, likely sensing our ID chips. I took one step inside and was pleasantly surprised by the accommodations. The room wasn't large, but it certainly wasn't small. It stretched about five meters from the door to a large window, and there were matching beds on either wall. The foot of each bed led to a nice desk with a chair, finishing with a locker in each of the corners closest to the door. Better than prison, I thought to myself.

Each bed had folded sheets and a small pile of personal items; Drel's pile was clearly larger. On top of both our piles lay our gloves.

"We have to be in the cafeteria at noon, right?" Drel asked.

"Right."

I lifted my arm and turned my wrist toward me. Three white digits appeared along the cuff: 479. This was not a buried memory—the basic knowledge assessment had taught me how to read time on the uniform. And while it hadn't taught me how long each each of Alder's 1000 minutes lasted, the events of the morning had acclimated me to the planet's standards—we had plenty of time.

"Let's try to get out of here by 485 since we don't know where it is," she suggested.

"Good idea."

She walked to her pile of personal items and began arranging her things, so I followed suit. Besides the gloves, my pile included shoulder patches, a sleepsuit, hairbrush, and mouthcleaner. I put the patches on, placed the brush and cleaner in my locker, made my bed, then grabbed my gloves.

I stared at these extensions of my uniform, wondering why I still knew nothing about them. Pell had told us to wear them at all times—why? Did we wear them while we slept?

"You ready?"

I glanced up and saw she had already put them on.

"Yes."

She waited while I slid mine onto my hands then gave me a smile.

"Let's go."

14

Just outside our door, we ran into another element of our division, Crim and Deena, and we introduced ourselves.

"Do you know where the wing cafeteria is?" Crim asked.

"No idea," Drel replied.

There was a brief silence as each of us waited for someone else to say something.

"Let's go back to the squad room, maybe Pell is still there," Crim suggested.

We nodded in agreement and made our way back. Right before we reached the door, three cadets emerged from inside—no one we recognized.

"Excuse me, could you tell us where the wing cafeteria is?" Drel asked.

They paused, and one of them smiled.

"That depends, what squadron are you in?"

The four of us exchanged glances, expecting one of us to know. Finally, I spoke up.

"Our captain is Pell."

All three laughed.

"Then we can help you. I'm Rolin, and these are Bett and Wilor. We're in your squadron."

They looked at us expectantly, and we introduced ourselves.

"Nice to meet you all," Rolin said, then turned to me. "One thing, Robyn: Pell isn't a captain. He's a cadet-captain. A great one, but you have to be careful with nomenclature here."

I nodded, and he looked at the others.

"Come with us—we're headed to the cafeteria now."

We started walking with the upperclassmen, and I tried to wrap my head around their friendly behavior. This was not the welcome I had expected. In fact, this was not the Academy I had expected—the Fleet had a reputation, and these individuals seemed to negate that reputation. These people were friendly, helpful—even kind. Maybe this wouldn't be so bad after all?

"So what squadron are we in?" Drel asked, clearly wanting to know what we should have said.

Bett laughed, smiling at her.

"17th. You're in Puric Command, 7th Wing, 17th Squadron, and, at least for now, 3rd Division," he replied.

"Third division? But we're first-session cadets."

Bett nodded.

"True, but we count divisions backwards."

Rolin added, "In fact, we call the third session the first class, and the first session the third class, so you're going to have to do some mental gymnastics. Us second-session cadets have it easiest."

We reached our destination quickly, and it was soon clear why: the wing cafeteria was much larger than I had anticipated, occupying almost half of the floor. Rolin, Bett, and Wilor led us to one of many large round tables —I counted twenty in all. If I had to guess, that meant twenty squadrons were in a wing.

Others, including Pell, were already seated at the table. Everyone was capless, and I watched as the three second-class cadets took their caps off and hung them on a prong attached to the back of each seat.

"Welcome, new cadets."

I gave a slight nod to Pell's greeting, as this was the only official form of salutation I knew.

"Crim, right here. Deena, over here. Robyn, here. And Drel, there."

The cadet-captain gestured to each empty chair as it was assigned, and we took our seats following the example of our new friends—taking our caps off and hanging them on the back before we sat.

"Before we start our lunch, I want to give a few more introductory comments. The people seated around you are your squadron. These are your new team. Most operations in the Academy are squadron-based, so you'd better get used to all of us."

He smiled. My mind had been distracted with so many things today, but now I was focused—focused on him.

"Today, each of you must choose your courses for the coming month. For help, I direct you to the squadmate on your right."

I turned to Rolin, who smiled at me.

"This is your second-division partner. They will act as a mentor for your first session, starting with course selection."

He paused, and I brought my attention back to him.

"During our lunch, your second-division partner will explain the academic system here at the Academy and walk you through what you need to do for this first month. We're all in this together, so don't be afraid to ask as many questions as possible. You're not transies anymore."

Pell gave me another friendly look, and I realized something inside of me was changing. After a morning full of doubts, I was starting to feel comfortable. How was that possible?

"Any questions?"

A thought occurred to me, and I raised my hand. Several of the senior cadets chuckled.

"Robyn, you don't need to raise your hand to address me."

"Sorry, sir."

"You also don't need to call me sir while we're capless."

"Right."

I hesitated. The momentary embarrassment had derailed my train of thought.

"Who is our cadet-commander?" I asked.

Since each grouping had a leader, who was leading our newly-formed division?

"Good question. You will elect one at the end of the month, until then I will act as your direct cadet-officer."

I nodded.

"Now, if you have any other questions, your squadmates will be able to help you. It's time for lunch. We line up by division, upperclassmen first."

With that, he stood, and the squadron followed suit. I saw many of my divisionmates being introduced to their second-class counterparts. I tried to remember all these names: Crim and Deena, Rolin, Bett, Wilor...

"Don't worry about that, it happens every year."

Rolin interrupted my train of thought.

"What happens every year?"

"Not knowing how to interact with the cadet-captain. It's your first time with the squadron, of course you don't know."

I knew he was trying to be nice, but it irked me. Had I really seemed that embarrassed? I let him go ahead to the line and focused on my surroundings.

Our squadron was heading toward one of many food dispensaries lining the walls of the cafeteria. There looked to be one for each squadron, which made sense. If there were 3 divisions plus a cadet-captain in each squadron, that made 25 cadets per squadron. With 20 squadrons in a wing, the cafeteria had to service 500 cadets at once. Spreading that out by squadron made it much more manageable.

"What kind of food do you think we'll get? More goop?"

Drel came up next to me while we waited. I didn't understand what she meant, but one of the first-class cadets responded.

"More goop, but it's better than what you had as a transie, don't worry."

When we got to the dispensers, I saw what Drel meant by goop: the food was some kind of nutritional paste. Even though it didn't look appetizing, when I got back to the table, I found it surprisingly palatable.

"So Robyn, I'm going to give you a breakdown of everything you need to know but if you have any questions or don't understand something just stop me."

I nodded, surprised again by his warmth.

"Courses are based on monthly units," Rolin began. "You have 8 months in a session, so this gives you some flexibility. However, many courses have several parts, and every cadet has to eventually choose one or more specialties that will decide which course paths are right for you."

"And the special assignment?"

Commander Hurren and the basic knowledge assessment had taught me that each Academy session lasted one year: 400 days of classes, plus 100 days of a special assignment. But they had not taught me what these special assignments were.

"We won't worry about specs for now. For all intents and purposes, you won't be doing any coursework during specs."

He paused and I nodded. Maybe they were in-field assignments? I would ask about them again later.

"Now, the weeks within each month are typically the same, but there is some day-to-day variation. The first 8 days alternate between an odd schedule on odd days, and an even schedule on even days. The weekend is for special activities. Courses on each day are divided into hour slots, and each cadet is expected to have 8 slots every day. So in total, you have to fill in 16 hours of courses: 8 hours on odd days and 8 hours on even days."

"Is each course one hour?"

"No. Some are more than an hour, and all of them cut off 5 minutes at the start and finish to give you time to get between places. So a one hour course isn't actually 50 minutes, it's only 40."

I nodded. I hoped everything was close to the dorms, 5 minutes didn't seem like an awful lot for this massive complex. It had taken more than 10 minutes just to get to the ceremonial hall.

"Also, some courses are on both odd and even days, so your odd days and even days won't be completely different. It just depends on your courses."

He paused, smiling.

"I know it's a lot to process, but don't worry, a good chunk of your first session is preplanned—all third-class cadet have certain required courses. As time goes on, you'll get more and more specialized, which give you more freedom to choose."

Freedom to choose, I thought to myself. Would Commander Hurren allow me that?

"You'll have three main performance metrics throughout your time here: PPA, APA, and MPA. Your PPA is your physical performance average, an assessment of your fitness and health. The APA is your academic performance average. As you can guess, this is where most of your coursework will be lumped in. The MPA is your military performance average. This one is all about your behavior as a member of the Fleet. Simple stuff like drills and protocol, but also leadership, and some coursework might make its way in here too. Sometimes you will see these three combined for a cumulative performance average, or CPA. These four numbers will allow or deny you access to certain courses, tracks, and careers. Depending on what track you take, one might be more important than another. An analyst won't be as worried about PPA, for example."

"What kind of tracks are there?"

He smiled again.

"Many. And I wouldn't try to pin that down until at least four months in. You have to explore a bit and see what works for you."

What works for me? The optimist within me took hold, and I felt a hint of excitement. Rolin had managed to put me at ease, and as he explained the upcoming session, I tried to see the situation through the eyes of a typical cadet: this was the start of an exciting journey at the Academy, the path to becoming an officer.

It was all happening so quickly, a wave of new experiences pulling me under, drowning out the complaints in the back of my mind. But those complaints would not go down without a fight. I had been on this planet for barely a day.

Why had the higher-ups in the Fleet decided to throw me in here? There had to be more to it than timing. Timing made no sense. They could have sent me to basic and waited another Alder year, when I'd be really prepared.

Of course, I knew that was a question I might never answer. So as I listened to Rolin explain the ins and outs of the upcoming session, I pushed those doubts into the back of my mind and focused on that growing excitement.

After all, I was a cadet now. I had to start acting like one.

15

Two hours later, I left the cafeteria. Pell and the first division had long since departed, along with some of my divisionmates. Rolin had told me everything I needed to know and more, and that I had until about 715 to access my desk and input my desired courses. At 720, third division had a meeting in the squad room before dinner, and when we returned to our dorms at 800 we would have our courses finalized.

Drel was still in the cafeteria, so I was alone in 7-1711. I sat in my chair and tapped the surface in front of me, bringing it to life. After a few gestures I reached the course input screen, and considered my options.

The program had already included my predetermined courses: for example, my first month had Officer Training listed as an 'all-day' course, meaning it met on both odd and even days. This particular class gave me hope—perhaps it would fill the blanks left by the knowledge assessment—but there were other required courses that worried me, threatening to extinguish all of my earlier excitement.

Military Training was listed as a one hour, all-day course, and thanks to Rolin, I knew it would extend well beyond the first month: every cadet in the Academy was required to take it throughout their three sessions. According to him, it was a mix of old and new drills and protocols, something he brushed off as easy. But how easy would it be for someone who didn't know any of these drills yet, adapting to them on the fly?

Then there was Weapons Training—another one hour, all-day course meant to last throughout a cadet's tenure. How would I fare against the rest of the cadets, who had undergone at least a hundred days of such training before their arrival?

Finally, every cadet was required to take one physical fitness course. Here, at least, I had some options—there was a range from easy to extreme—but I also knew the introductory versions presumed a certain level of skill carrying over from basic training. And if my instructor knew I was on the integrated commission program...

I could feel the fear and doubt returning, threatening to erase my new perspective, so I skipped over this choice, opting to read about the academic courses. Physics, biology, chemistry; all of the sciences were well-represented, and I was equally curious about advanced tactics and Fleet history. I had 4 hours to spare on both even and odd days, but that wasn't enough to fit everything I wanted. Even with these safer subjects, I had some difficult decisions to make.

Of course, I couldn't stall forever. I went through the interface and put together a course list. As I was wrapping up, Drel walked in.

"So many choices," she announced. "This is way better than basic."

I smiled in reply and submitted my selection.

"Any idea what track you want?" she asked, sitting down at her desk.

"No, you?"

She turned to face me before responding.

"Not sure—I think space engineering. I want to work on capital craft."

She paused, giving me a curious look.

"You're not thinking of going over 8 hours, are you?"

I raised my eyebrows.

"You can do that?"

She nodded.

"Swir told me you could, she even warned me not to. Apparently a lot of new cadets overestimate what they can handle and try it out."

She paused, looking away as if searching for her next words.

"In a way I don't blame them. You make it to the Academy so of course you're gifted, but now all the outliers are together in one place. It's easy to think you're still better, or special."

Her comments only fueled my doubts. What would happen tomorrow, when classes began? How could I keep up with these cadets, physically or mentally? I wanted to confront Commander Kelt or Commander Hurren and ask them what in the world they were thinking. How could a basic knowledge assessment put me up with these outliers?

But they were not the reason I was here, I thought to myself. Hurren had mentioned his superiors more than once. Would I ever know who was really responsible for my fate?

16

At 715 we headed to the squad room for our pre-dinner meeting, where Pell introduced us to some basic commands for our lenses, including how to check the time, the weather, our course list, and how to message other members of our squadron with either text or audio. We spent a few minutes practicing these commands, and the cadet-captain told us we were to keep our lenses on at all times.

"Even when we sleep, sir?" someone asked.

"Yes, same with the gloves."

Lenses and gloves on at all times, even when asleep. I wondered why.

We returned to our table in the wing cafeteria for dinner at 750, and the upper classes helped ignite conversations about what courses we had chosen. Snippets of their experiences helped me paint a picture of what was coming, and some of my earlier excitement returned.

According to the upper-session cadets, most Academy courses were engaging and informative, and the material covered caught my attention. I paid particular attention to one of the upperclass cadet's discussions of Interplanetary Tactics, one of my own selections. Apparently it was a popular course—required for many tracks—and a good one.

As our meal came to an end, Pell addressed the third division once more.

"When you return to your rooms, you'll be able to see your final schedule. Most of you won't see any difference, but some of you may have one or two changes. If you have any questions, send me a message."

Most of the first and second division had already left the table, and while Pell spoke to us, the rest of the upperclassmen took their leave.

"Lights out is at 900, so make sure you're in your dorm before then. You're expected to stay in there until at least 180, except for toilet breaks."

Pell stood, looking at us with a smile.

"Welcome to the squadron. See you tomorrow."

He grabbed his cap and headed out the door, and after a few excited glances, most of our division followed suit.

"Ready to see what we've got in store?" Drel asked.

I smiled.

"As ready as I'll ever be."

Back in our room, Drel and I activated our desks. I opened the finalized course list, looking at each time slot and the associated class. A few of the selections were no surprise: the requirements I knew I would be taking, and one of my own choices. But everything else? Everything else had been changed.

In truth, I was not surprised. Somewhere, someone else was pulling the strings. Commander Hurren? Commander Kelt? Their mysterious superiors? It didn't matter. The alterations were a clear reminder of the reality of my situation, and served to quell my illusions of freedom.

"So, how's it look?"

I glanced up to see Drel eyeing me expectantly.

"A few changes."

My answer was brusque, almost rude, and I winced internally.

"Oh, nothing bad I hope?"

Thankfully, she seemed to take it in stride.

"No, I don't think so."

I smiled at her. I could tell she was being patient with me, and I appreciated it. Thank goodness this was my roommate for the first month.

We spent the rest of the evening chatting about our courses then made for bed around 870, opting to get a little extra sleep. But as I lay in my bunk with my eyes closed, my mind drifted, contemplating the events of the day just as I had the night before.

Waves of dread had mixed with moments of excitement… how many more crests and troughs did I have waiting for me at the Academy? I thought back to my earlier surprise: Drel, Rolin, and even Pell had made me feel at home, and so far everyone else seemed nice. Yet my first encounter with the Fleet—the lieutenant on Kurotar, the one that came to my hospital bed—was so imposing, so cold. Surely one day, years ago, he must have been here, sitting among his own squadron of cadets, smiling and excited. What had changed? What had happened?

War, I thought to myself. The Fleet was dealing with an increasing number of terrorist attacks, the work of the Moffan Resurgence sprouting up throughout the empire. These incidents were always condemned by the Moffans and the Confederation, but one had to wonder who was funding them, who was directing them.

I paused my train of thought, fear gripping me. Why did I know so much about this subject? This wasn't on my basic knowledge assessment.

Was I actually a terrorist, an agent of the Resurgence? I took a moment and tried to reach back, beyond the day on Kurotar, to the past unknown, searching desperately for something to prove me wrong...

It was almost a shadow of a thought, but it was unmistakable: red all around me, a familiar place, somewhere I knew...

And then I was back in my bunk, eyes staring into the darkened room. I glanced around nervously and heard Drel snoring lightly on the other bed. What had I just seen? I tried to bring it back but it was gone, beyond reach. Commander Hurren's threat came to mind and a cold dread came over me. Was that a memory? It felt so distant, I couldn't even be sure it was really me...

But I knew exactly where it was—that background was unmistakable. Raviir, the red planet, capital of the empire. Clearly, that world held the key to something about who I was, something about my past. The question was when I'd be able to unlock it—and if I even wanted to.

17

At 230 the next morning, my lenses lit up, waking me from my troubled slumber. That night, like the one before, I had barely slept. After my bizarre flash of Raviir, all I wanted was to understand what I had seen, but I was nowhere closer to the answer now than I had been in the hospital on Kurotar. Besides, I'd have to shelve these thoughts soon: I had Fitness Review in 20 minutes.

Fitness Review was meant for cadets who had spent a significant amount of transitional time on Alder and had fallen behind on their training. As far as I could tell, it was the most basic fitness course offered, and I considered it my best option. Luckily, whoever had rearranged my schedule had not changed this particular selection.

Of course, that didn't mean Fitness Review would be a walk in the park. I would still be among cadets who had undergone all of basic training and finished in the top three percent of their class. And if my instructors knew I was on the integrated commission program, they might ask why an already-enlisted member of the Fleet would take a course so low on the podium. Thankfully, my sleepless night had provided me with a solution to this dilemma: since my activities were classified, I could always say I'd been physically inactive for a long period of time and chose Fitness Review to get back up to speed.

"Good morning."

Drel was sitting up, stretching and yawning all at once. Pell had told us all new cadets would have their lenses programmed to wake us 20 minutes before their first scheduled course, so both of us woke up at the same time.

"Good morning, Drel."

I sat up, wondering how I looked after a night with little to no sleep.

"Ready for the review?" she asked with a smile.

"I don't know," I answered.

Last night, we had shared our schedules with one another. When I mentioned Fitness Review, I was worried Drel might ask about my transitional time but thankfully, the subject never came up. Yes, I had my cover story, but I wanted to follow the advice of the lieutenant in the hovcar and avoid that conversation for as long as possible. If Drel or the rest of my division found out I was enrolled as a previously-enlisted member of the Fleet, who knows how that might alter our relationship, particularly at such an early stage. As he had said, our strength is unity.

I hopped out of bed, made quick use of my mouthcleaner, and changed into my uniform. We left our room and walked across the hall, my lenses guiding me down the most optimal path to my course location. It looked as if most cadets on our floor were up and about, hundreds of them heading to their morning classes.

Before we reached the stairwell, four of our divisionmates joined us: Crim, Deena, Epore, and Kulee.

"Morning," Crim gave us a nod as we continued down the hall.

"Hiya," Drel replied.

"Either of you heading to one?" Crim asked.

Drel nodded in reply.

"You?" he asked me.

"Fitness Review."

"Long-term transie?" Epore asked.

I hesitated.

"It's the best fit."

He nodded.

"All three of you headed to one?" Drel asked.

"Yep," Crim replied.

We reached one of the main stairwells and, as the crowd thickened, I noticed the lenses giving me subtle directional cues, trying to minimize traffic and maximize efficiency. Of course, it was up to the humans behind the corneas to actually follow these directions, and that wasn't always the case. Thankfully, the buildings had been designed with high occupancy in mind, and the thousands of cadets in Puric had eight stairwells to choose from, each wide enough to handle the load.

As we descended so did the temperature, and my uniform reacted with a subtle warming of the innermost layer. By the time we reached the bottom floor and saw the culprit—all of the doors were open, likely to improve traffic flow—only the uncovered part of my head was cold— even the cap felt warm.

Were these door always open? I hoped not—the cold would only get worse in the coming months. The Academy was located in the southern hemisphere of Alder, a planet with an above-average axial tilt and hence very pronounced seasons. We were entering the first stages of winter, a winter that would last almost the entire session. As we stepped onto the grass outside, I wondered how long it would be before it was covered in snow.

A few meters past the door, my path deviated from the rest of my division.

"Bye," I announced abruptly.

"Have fun," Drel replied with a wink.

I watched the five of them walk away, all headed to the same course, then continued to my own. Fitness Review met in a small clearing between dorm buildings only a few hundred meters from Puric. A quick glance at my cuff told me I had over fifteen minutes until the start of class, but I wasn't the only early one: twelve other cadets were conversing among themselves in the flattened grass. I opted to hover on the sidelines, a knot forming in my stomach as the minutes passed.

Would this be the end of the charade? My first course, ousted as an outsider? Yes, these other cadets had spent a long time as transies, but they were still part of the top three percent, and their hiatus was at most ten months long. When was the last time I had done something active? Had I ever done something as active as what I was about to do?

18

At 255 sharp, a junior commander called everyone to form two lines. I watched the other cadets and scrambled to follow their lead. We did as ordered, standing in formation just in front of him. I was at the far right of the back line.

"Good morning, cadets. Welcome to Fitness Review. Since you are the most behind, we'll skip the introductions and let the class calibrate as we go. Over the next four months, my job is to try to get you ready for Fitness II. So let's get to it."

He clapped his hands together, then pointed down the wide expanse to our right.

"Right rotation."

Everyone made a ninety-degree turn, and a half-second later, I followed suit.

"Jog forward."

There was a split second of hesitation where it dawned on me I was now leading one of the two lines, and that split second was too long for the instructor's liking.

"Cadet! Pay attention!"

I jumped into a run, doing my best to mirror the person on my left and ignore the instructor's comment. A few seconds later, my arms and legs matched my companion, and I wondered if that was good enough. Would I need to change our speed? Was this a good speed?

I let the other cadet set the tone and focused on my breathing. We ran along an expanse of mostly flattened grass, heading toward the edge of the dorms opposite where we had entered the day before. There was a sliver of trees ahead, behind which more buildings stood—the academic halls. Between us and the trees, I saw two more groups running in similar formations. Other fitness classes, maybe other sections of Fitness Review?

"Rotate!"

The instructor's command caught me off guard. Rotate? Were we supposed to turn?

I noticed my partner leaving my peripheral vision, opening up room for the person behind them, and it clicked. I made an awkward shift to the right and slowed enough for the other pairs to pass, then filed back in at the end.

"Looks like someone skipped basic!"

I felt the knot in my stomach tighten but did my best to ignore it. This was only the beginning; I had to be quicker on my feet.

Over the next ten minutes, the only other commands the instructor called out where "Left!" and "Right!", both of which I managed to understand without issue. We continued running between the dorms, never quite reaching the surrounding trees, until the instructor stopped us for a water break. Only during that rest did I realize how well I'd managed. Yes, I was struggling with the instructions, but the exercise was reasonable, and I didn't feel too tired. Perhaps I'd survive this course after all.

After taking a few sips of water, I saw two small gauges appear to the right of my field of view.

"Okay cadets, time to get serious. The readouts you see in your lenses are speed and formation targeting. The top metric indicates how far below or above the desired speed you are holding, while the bottom metric indicates how well the entire group is holding formation. Green means good, yellow means bad. I'm not even going to mention red, just don't let it get there."

He paused, giving us a small smile.

"We're going into the forest, so the formation metric will be more forgiving than usual, but that doesn't mean it'll be easy. Ready? Right rotation."

I was happy to be in the middle of the pack this time—at least for now. He wanted us to hold formation while we ran through the trees? This would be interesting…

"Go!"

A small timer counted down from 5, and the speed gauge turned red while the formation gauge turned green. As soon as we took off, red turned to yellow, and before the timer reached zero, we hit the desired speed.

The timer switched to 15 minutes, and I realized the first jog was just a warm-up. The speed target had us holding quite a pace, which only made formation more difficult. Different gaits made matching movements practically impossible, so I focused on staying in line with the cadet on my left. For now, both gauges were green.

As we approached the edge of the forest, the ground beneath us began to change; gone was the flat grass, replaced by small mounds and rocks of various sizes, ready to trip us into one another.

"Keep formation, cadets!"

Running into the forest, we knew the instructor's command was impossible. All we could do was keep the best formation possible given the circumstances, and hope the gauges were set with enough tolerance to stay off the red. Moving at a considerable pace, eyes scanning for rocks and trees, I tried to keep in line with my partner. Everyone in our group was fighting the same battle, but for the time being, both gauges stayed green.

The crisp morning was losing its effect, and I felt the uniform cooling me down, dissipating the heat and drying my sweat. Despite its valiant effort, it could not remove all discomfort—this was a task of increasing difficulty.

About four minutes into the forest, the formation gauge started to show flashes of yellow, brief blips at first, then steady dips for two to three seconds.

"Stay in line, cadets!"

The instructor's voice came from behind us, and I wondered if he was running with us. I knew I was in line with my partner—five times so far a tree had come between us or forced us closer together, but never enough to hit yellow. I also didn't see any issues ahead of me, though it was hard to glance at the rest of the class when I had so much sensory input to process.

"Ten minutes left!"

He didn't need to tell us, the timer was clear in our lenses.

"Right!"

The gauges dulled and a small timer counted down from ten as we reacted to the command. I saw both faded metrics in the red and was thankful changes in direction were accompanied by a grace period. But the formation gauge stayed red through five, into four, into three...

Just as a hint of panic entered my system, it turned yellow, and the countdown ended two seconds later.

"You're gonna need to do better than that. Left!"

Thankfully, we didn't make any more errors for the remaining ten minutes. The junior commander had us running in circles through the same patch of forest until I started to recognize some of the trees. Our performance declined as time went on, but even though we were often in the yellow, we never once saw red. Only in the last minute did he let us pass through to the other side, and we managed to get our formation back to green just before the timer ran out.

"Nice work, cadets! Let's take it to the gym."

The instructor led us to a large gymnasium space inside the nearest building, filled with all sorts of soft surfaces and climbable walls. We stood in formation on a large mat, and he explained how the lenses would guide us through a series of isometric holds and dynamic movements, focused on strength, flexibility, and balance. With each exercise, the system would measure our performance and adjust accordingly.

"Okay, you're all on your own now."

With his announcement, we split off to our first assignments, following the instructions on our lenses. Where the run had stressed me out, I found myself enjoying the exercises, working up the ladder of each progression with relative ease. I noticed I was advancing much quicker than my peers, and by the time I was halfway through the third set of exercises, some of the other cadets were staring at me.

"Cadet, come here."

I stopped mid-movement and went to the instructor, thirty-odd pairs of eyes watching me travel across the gym floor.

"Yes, sir?"

He looked me up and down with suspicion and my mind raced, trying to understand what I had done wrong, where I had messed up...

"Where did you do basic?"

I felt the knot in my stomach again. This was a superior officer, not just a fellow cadet. How could I avoid answering his question?

"Sir, I—"

He put up his hand and looked behind me, to the rest of the class.

"What do you think you're doing? Get moving, cadets!"

There was a flurry of movement from the group, and his eyes came back to mine.

"Well?"

I realized it was silly to dodge the question—I'd been given the cover story for a reason, and this man wasn't part of my squadron.

"Sir, I'm on the integrated commission track."

He raised his eyebrows.

"Ah."

Then the suspicion returned.

"Then why are you in this course?"

This, at least, I had anticipated.

"Sir, I apologize. I thought this would be the best fit for me."

I wanted to elaborate, to say that I had been physically inactive for a long period of time, yet something inside of me protested, cutting my statement short.

"The best fit for you? Cadet, you thought wrong."

He gave me a skeptical look, but when he continued, his tone was softer.

"You kept within a tenth of a percent of your target speed the entire duration. I've never seen such a precise and consistent run. That's either incredibly lucky or just plain incredible."

I stared at him, not sure of what to say. Had I really done that well?

"Sure, you had a few hiccups at the beginning, but you're too advanced for this course. I will send an immediate advancement notice and put you in Fitness II starting tomorrow. Is that clear?"

Fitness II? I wanted to object, but I caught myself before the words could leave my mouth.

"Yes, sir."

He gave me one more curious look.

"You're dismissed. Tomorrow, you'll be in Fitness II. Good luck."

I gave him a nod and left the gym, some of the other cadets watching me exit. As I made my way back to Puric for breakfast, I tried to understand what had just happened, to understand how I had done so well… but all I had to work off of was a cryptic flash of red.

19

I had decided to keep the events of the morning a secret to avoid any unnecessary attention, but our cadet-captain foiled this plan as soon as he joined the table for breakfast.

"Robyn, I heard you're being upgraded to Fitness II starting tomorrow?"

My spoonful of goop stopped halfway to its destination, and I felt the stares of my squadmates from all sides.

"Yes."

"Underestimated the shape you were in, huh?" Bett asked.

"I guess so."

I brought the spoon to my mouth and took the bite. I knew my responses were curt, but I was still set on keeping the integrated commission program a secret from my division.

"Robyn, we're in the same OT class, right?"

Drel's question broke the momentary silence, and I appreciated her attempt to plot a new conversational course.

"I think so…"

"Do you know how to check your course list on your lenses?" Rolin asked.

I shook my head.

"Wait, I know this," Drel interrupted.

She spent the next two minutes teaching me how to access my course list. Apparently, the second-division cadet she was paired with—Swir—had taught her a great deal on the lenses.

"Do you know how to pull up a map with your course location?" Wilor asked.

"No, how?"

While Wilor explained to Drel, I scanned the false holograph of my course list currently occupying a small section of my vision.

Today was 1day, an odd day, and I had already gone to Fitness Review from 255 to 295. All of us had an hour for breakfast—300 to 350—and my next course was Officer Training from 355 to 395. There was a note beside each class letting me know any squadmates that shared the course with me. Drel was right—her name was listed next to Officer Training, as were Tyla's and Grie's, another element pair from our division.

"And now, focus on the map with your eye, put your finger on it, and say 'Share with Robyn'."

"Share with Robyn."

A small map flew into my field of view.

"There you go."

We had barely scratched the surface of these lenses and already I was impressed.

"Are you two in the same courses most of the day?" Crim asked as he joined us at the squad table. "Deena and I have four hours together."

Drel looked at me then shook her head slowly.

"No, only two I think."

I glanced over the schedule again and nodded.

"Officer Training then Weapons Training later in the afternoon."

"How was Fitness Review?" Crim asked.

Before I could get a word in, Drel responded for me.

"She's being upgraded to Fitness II starting tomorrow."

She gave me a sly look, but I didn't share her enthusiasm. Before Crim could react, Rolin interrupted our conversation from the other side of the table.

"What about tactics?" he asked.

I didn't know he had been listening.

"What do you mean?" I replied.

He gestured to Drel and I.

"You're not together for tactics?"

I shook my head.

"We're both taking interplanetary, but Drel has it today and I have it tomorrow."

"What do you have today?"

He seemed to be fishing for something.

"Terrestrial."

He raised his eyebrows, impressed.

"Double dosing?" he asked.

Wilor gave out a whoop, and I stared at both of them, confused.

"Double dosing?"

Rolin smiled before answering.

"You're doing space and terra at the same time. That's quite a workload, and it can get very confusing conceptually."

I didn't know what to say. I had chosen Interplanetary Tactics as he had suggested. Terrestrial Tactics was added to my schedule by whoever was pulling the strings.

"Some people manage," Bett responded, glancing at Pell.

The cadet-captain noticed the glance and smiled before replying.

"All of you will be together most of the afternoon anyways."

He was referring to the hour we had set aside every afternoon for multi-level military work. I still wasn't certain what that was, but I guessed it would be where a lot of our MPA would come from. Now that I had survived my fitness course, this was next on the list of courses I was worried about. The drills this morning had been simple, but an entire hour of them? I wasn't out of the woods yet.

20

After some more chatter, Drel and I made our way to Officer Training with Tyla and Grie. The sun was higher in the sky now; a bright, yellow orb whose pleasant warmth fought with bouts of cool wind. For the time being, the star was losing the battle, but I had a feeling by the middle of the day the weather would be almost perfect.

"At least it's close by," Grie commented.

He was right: Officer Training looked to be just beyond the ring of trees that surrounded the dorms.

"That's by design," Drel replied.

"What do you mean?" I asked her.

"Swir was telling me the halls are assigned by popularity, so the most popular courses are closest to the dorms. OT is one of the most popular courses, if not the most."

We walked along the large paths between the dorm buildings, toward the sliver of forest separating us from the main academic halls. With the amount of traffic this area encountered, it was a miracle the grass wasn't dead. How did it manage to survive thousands of footsteps day after day?

When we reached the front edge of the band of trees, Tyla broke the silence.

"So what happened this morning, Robyn?"

"This morning?"

"In Fitness Review."

I almost winced. I knew they meant well, but couldn't they just let it go?

"I got upgraded."

My reply was more curt than intended, and Tyla gave me a confused look.

"Right, but how?"

I tried to answer with a friendlier tone.

"We did a forest run in formation then worked on some exercise progressions. About halfway through, the instructor pulled me aside and told me I was moving up."

"So you beat everyone else by a mile?"

She gave me a knowing look, but I shook my head.

"No, not really."

The intrigue in her expression faded, my blunt answer extinguishing her excitement. I felt a little guilty, but how else was I supposed to change the subject? After an awkward silence, I tried to salvage the situation.

"And you guys? How was Fitness I?"

When Tyla didn't answer, Drel shrugged.

"They had us running tests to measure our strength, endurance, so on. Today was about calibration, making sure everyone was in the right spot," she nodded at me, "and figuring out their fitness plan for the next few weeks."

She paused in thought.

"Honestly, I don't know why they don't just use the records from basic."

"For some of us it's been a long time since basic," Grie responded.

"Ah," she replied. "Right."

We reached the building for Officer Training—not as tall as the dorms, but just as black and just as red—and walked inside. In place of many floors with hundreds of small rooms were just two floors with several large chambers. Our lenses directed us to one of these grand classrooms and, once inside, I saw rows of podiums forming soft arcs toward a lone podium at the front. My lenses showed me which of the hundreds of podiums was mine, and I stood behind the interactive interface with Drel and Tyla on either side. At 355, a commander took the front podium and addressed us.

"Good morning, cadets. I'm Commander Fost. Welcome to Officer Training. While this course will be somewhat of a review at first, I suggest you don't underestimate its importance. You'll use the protocol we go over in this class on a daily basis, and lack of knowledge on these topics can negatively affect your MPA. To be clear, cadets have been expelled for not knowing some of the basic things they need to know."

He eyed us intently, emphasizing his last words.

"So consider this your two-month reminder period, and pay close attention."

He didn't have to tell me twice. After the introduction, the commander dove right into customs and rules at the Academy the others might have forgotten, while one cadet in particular had never actually learned. In other words, Officer Training was exactly what I needed: a more in-depth version of the knowledge assessment.

Between this pleasant discovery and my surprising success that morning, some of the earlier enthusiasm came back, a small dose of hope in my anxious mind. I was far from making it through the first day, but so far so good.

21

After class, I parted ways with Drel, Tyla, and Grie, the lenses guiding us in different directions. For the next two hours—from 405 to 495—they had Interplanetary Tactics I while I had Terrestrial Tactics I. My course was a little farther away, and as soon as I reached the classroom, I understood why.

The room itself was less than a quarter of the size of Officer Training, though it had the same layout. Inside were just under 30 cadets, and a captain stood behind the front podium. I glanced at some of my classmates, wondering if any of them were double dosing, then stood behind my podium until the official start time.

"Good morning, cadets. I'm Captain Ennin. Welcome to Terrestrial Tactics I."

This was the highest ranking officer I'd seen in such close quarters, and I wondered if there were any higher ranked professors. Colonels? Surely not generals?

"As most of you know, the terminology and concepts in terra tactics can cause some issues with learning or retaining terminology and concepts in any of the space tactics. This is because the information we go over is both different enough and similar enough to be confusing. I say this not as a threat, but as a warning. It would be in your interest to heed this warning."

He scanned the class before him, then dove into an explanation of the various situations involving terrestrial tactics in the Fleet, a mostly space-based entity, and his explanations shed light on some of the Fleet's organizational details.

"The Fleet has two major, terra-based sections: the Guard and the Infantry. The Guard is the Fleet's police branch, tasked with day-to-day peacekeeping on each of the twenty-three planets. Most of their activity is terrestrial, but they do not engage in high priority operations—these are reserved for the Fleet Infantry."

Some of this was review from the knowledge assessment, but some of it was new to me.

"While the Infantry was typically the least active section of the Fleet, today's climate has changed that somewhat. In any case, they will represent the majority of our terrestrial tactic discussions and simulations."

As he spoke, a hologram appeared above our podium, and the captain explained how we would study tactical formations and movements via interactive diagrams created by a combination of the podiums and the lenses. Even before he started discussing the details, I was hooked. There was seemingly endless customization available here: changing viewpoints, running time lapses, zooming in and out of levels of command... it was no wonder the Terrestrial Tactics courses lasted the entire eight months of the session.

Would I have to go through all of them? A part of me hoped that was the case, but another part of me realized just how absurd that was. I took a step back, still seeing the projection in front of me without letting it absorb me. I saw all the other cadets around me, each one with their own interactive display, and last night's questions came to me once more.

Who was I? What was I doing here? Part of me was beginning to accept this identity, but was that merely a coping mechanism? I worried about falling into complacency, about letting this become my reality, but I wasn't sure I had much of a choice. Besides, there was a chance this identity was preferable to my actual one. Did I even want to know for sure?

22

I left terra tactics at 495 and was in our cafeteria by 500 for lunch.

"How was terra?"

Drel sat down next to me with her portion of goop, and I was surprised by how happy I was to see her.

"Good… interesting. We went over a lot of introductory material."

She smiled and, after a beat, I realized I needed to be socially proactive.

"And you guys?"

Drel nodded.

"Same."

Bett joined the table and Drel turned to him.

"Bett, what's military training like?"

After lunch was our hour of military work, the second course that threatened to expose my truth. I focused on Bett's reply, hoping for some insight into what awaited us.

"MT? Today is just an introduction for you, but it could be anything. Drill work with your division, your squadron, the wing," he gestured around the cafeteria, "even the entire command. Protocol testing, tactic implementation, historical review, the list goes on."

Drills and protocols—exactly what I was afraid of. Like my run in the morning but more involved, and with more opportunities to bring attention to myself. Everyone else in my division had already practiced formations and drills for some 100 days, perhaps many more: I wasn't sure if transitional cadets did any drill work, but I didn't consider that a safe question to ask.

For the rest of lunch, I tried to determine if there even was a safe question to ask, but by the time we were in the squad room, I was clueless as ever.

"Hello, Puric 7-17. I trust we've all had a productive first day so far."

Even Pell's smile couldn't put me at ease.

"For those in our third division, welcome to your first day of military training, the only course you'll have to take the entire time you're here."

I remembered Rolin saying this would be one of the easiest courses we had. A cadet failing to keep up in one of the easier courses would certainly stand out, and if Pell knew I was on the integrated commission program...

"For your division, today will be a simple introduction: your second-division partner will provide examples of past courses to give you an idea of what to expect. Tomorrow, we do the real thing."

With one sentence, the cadet-captain erased all my fears.

"First division, out with me."

The first-class cadets filed out after Pell, leaving us with our second-division partners.

"You look relieved," Rolin said.

He gave me a smile but I didn't return it. Had I been that transparent with my thoughts?

"Let's take two desks and get started," he continued.

All of the upperclass cadets were leading their underclass partners to paired desks and initiating the interfaces. We chose a set off to the side and did the same.

"So the first thing I'm supposed to tell you is MT will alternate timing by session. Did I mention that yet?"

I shook my head.

"No. What do you mean?"

He seemed surprised.

"Hm. Well basically, right now, 11 commands have military work after lunch, including us. The other 10 have it before lunch, and we switch every session—so next session we'll be before lunch and the others'll be after."

From an organizational standpoint, this was unsurprising. The Academy held around 90000 cadets at one time. Trying to have all of them out doing drills simultaneously would be chaotic, not to mention a waste of potential class time. In fact, I wondered why they didn't spread it out even further.

"Another thing you should know is MT isn't always at the squadron level. Sometimes you'll be in your division, sometimes all of Puric will work together, and sometimes we will mix and match in various ways to test you. You saw how the first division went out on their own today— that'll happen a lot."

He gave me a sly smile, but I didn't catch any underlying meaning.

"Okay."

"How good were you with drills in basic?"

There it was. I'd wondered who in my chain of command already knew about my integrated commission. I was almost certain Pell did, but it looked like he hadn't shared that with my second-division partner.

After a moment's hesitation, I decided this was not the time for obfuscation.

"I didn't come from basic. I'm on the integrated commission program."

I watched his expression shift from confusion to intrigue, and he glanced around the room before responding in a whisper.

"Integrated commission? That makes so much sense."

I gave him a confused look, which he noticed.

"The double dosing."

"Oh."

Then he gave me a curious look.

"But why Fitness Review?"

"It was the best fit for me."

I answered as if on auto-pilot, and he peered at me suspiciously.

"Where were you stationed?"

There was so much eagerness in his tone, I almost felt bad shooting him down.

"I can't tell you—classified."

He raised his eyebrows and leaned back in his chair. My answer seemed to impress him, fueling his curiosity.

"Really? Wow."

He paused, staring off into the distance for a moment, then returned his attention to me.

"Well then, you probably want to keep that information as private as you can for as long as you can, right?"

I nodded, relieved at his suggestion.

"Yes, I do."

Rolin gave me a wink.

"Don't worry, Robyn. I've got you covered. I'll try not to treat you differently, but I can't make any promises."

I nodded. Clearly the lieutenant's advice was right.

"Thanks, Rolin."

He smiled.

"Of course. Now, where were we?"

"You asked about my drills in basic."

He nodded.

"Right, so even if you haven't done basic in a few years, you'll have a chance to catch up. The first week or so of military work will be review for the long-term transies."

He paused, looked around the room again, then lowered his voice.

"And I just realized you didn't have to do that either. Consider yourself lucky. Transition is a real pain in the ass."

I replied with a nervous smile. This falsified revelation regarding my origin seemed quite enticing to Rolin. Would he share the news with the rest of his division, despite his promise? I had barely known him half a day, I had no idea if I could trust him...

As these thoughts went through my mind, I saw the intrigue fade from his expression, replaced by a frown.

"I'm sorry, Robyn. I'm going on and on about something you want to keep secret."

Before I could react, he pointed to the desks in front of us and brought his voice back to a normal volume.

"Let's take a look at some of the military work we've done in the past year to give you an idea of what you have coming up."

The rest of the hour Rolin kept a professional demeanor with me, explaining the many facets of the course. I was glad for the change in tone, but it was almost too professional—as if he was forcing it. He would need to do better than that to keep my secret, though if my hand had already been forced with him one day in, I wasn't sure how much longer I could keep it from the rest of the squadron. Sooner or later, everyone would find out. Hopefully later.

23

I left the squad room and made my way back to the academic halls for my 605 to 645 course, Galactic Biology I. This was an odd-day course—on even days, the same time slot was taken by Communication Analysis I.

Like terra, biology was smaller, with some 30 cadets. Our instructor was a senior commander and, as I would quickly decide, my favorite so far —her presentation was engaging, as was the material: there was something fascinating about the greater biological trends of the galaxy, a topic I looked forward to exploring in more detail. Even though I had originally chosen an engineering course for this time slot, I found myself thanking whoever up my chain of command had made the change.

After biology I had Galactic Politics I, another odd-day course paired with Galactic Militaries I on even days. This class was almost as small as bio, with about 40 cadets. After a brief introduction, the instructor explained that the two courses were designed to be taken together, and those of us in both would meet him tomorrow in the same room. Worked for me.

The first day consisted of a brief history of galactic colonization, which truly had to be brief: like jump technology, most facts regarding pre-galactic history had been lost or forgotten, although not for lack of record. In fact, it was the exponential expansion of data that led to such loss: the human race was oversaturated with information and had trouble keeping track of the necessities of the present, let alone the past. In short, the sheer volume of information available was expanding so rapidly that our methods of navigating it couldn't keep up. It was a fascinating and— from a certain standpoint—terrifying situation, but for now I tried to absorb what few pieces of this vast knowledge I could.

With regards to galactic colonization, all that was known for sure was humanity and their robots emerged from one planet and spread dramatically with the help of jump technology. How long this lasted, nobody knew for certain. Likely thousands if not tens of thousands of years. Eventually, the Galactic Confederation was formed, joining some three million worlds divided into tens of thousands of kingdoms, empires, republics, dominions, etc.

Presently, the Galactic Confederation was over 6000 galactic years old, comprising approximately three quarters of all habitable planets and over 70% of chartered space. Each member of the GC was known as a Galactic Region. The Terian empire was surrounded by five such regions and the H'lee Collective, another independent sector.

As he discussed the history of these six neighbors, there was one detail our instructor omitted: the Moffan Galactic Region, formerly the Moffan empire, had integrated with the GC almost two hundred years ago. This coincided almost perfectly with the end of the Terian War, the war that led to the formation of the empire. This was no coincidence, of course. While the Fleet would never admit it, once the Moffans joined the GC, Terius was forced to end his conquest. There was something to be said about power in numbers.

Again I had to ask myself why I knew these things. Or, more to the point, why did I know the history of the empire better than my own history?

24

After Galactic Politics, I ran into Drel, Tyla, and Grie. All four of us shared the same course to close out the day: Weapons Training I, the third and final course that threatened to expose me.

"Hey Robyn! How was—"

Drel paused mid-question, searching her memory for the answer.

"Bio and politics," I said, filling in the blank.

She smiled and nodded.

"Right. How was bio?"

I gave an enthusiastic nod.

"Very good."

Tyla gave me a curious look.

"Really? I might have to try it next month. Chem was a bust."

I smiled at her, happy to see our earlier conversation hadn't soured her opinion of me.

"Give it time, Tyla," Grie replied. "Remember what Olla said: it's supposed to get better after the first week."

"And politics?" Drel asked me.

I nodded.

"Also good. And you?"

"Great. Material Studies covered a lot of information today—more than I expected—and Ship Design was pretty dry but I'm excited to learn that stuff."

I envied her a little: I had originally signed up for Ship Design. Something about the way spacecraft were built fascinated me.

"All three of you were together?" I asked.

"For Ship Design, yea," she replied.

"I think this is it," Grie announced.

We reached the classroom and cut our conversation short. Like Officer Training, Weapons Training had about 100 cadets in it, but this room was different. There were no chairs or tables, just an assortment of large, black spheres along the walls, each about as tall as my waist. A junior commander stood at what seemed to be the front.

"Good afternoon, cadets. Welcome to Weapons Training I."

He glanced around the room, as if to make sure we were all here.

"Today we're going to introduce you to the most important weapon in your arsenal, one unique to officers, one you have not yet used."

He reached his arm toward one of the spheres, palm out. An arc of white light erupted from his hand and connected with the sphere, which turned a crimson red. It was over in the blink of an eye, and the red sphere faded to black almost as quickly. Only a subtle hint of smoke betrayed what had just occurred.

"Your gloves are your most versatile and powerful short-range weapon, but they require a certain level of skill to operate."

The gloves? That energy came from his gloves?

"Cadets, please form one large circle around me."

The commander moved to the middle of the room and we shuffled into place. Drel was on my right while an unknown cadet stood to my left.

"I want everyone to bring their wrists together like so."

I watched the commander place the insides of his wrists together in a perpendicular manner and copied him. As soon as they touched, I felt a minor vibration, then a subtle but persistent tingling in my hands. What in the world?

"This is the ceremonial activation method. To deactivate, repeat this process but hold for five seconds."

He gestured for us to do so, and we did. After five seconds, the vibration repeated, and the tingling disappeared.

"Now, in a hostile situation, ceremonial activation could be cumbersome or dangerous. Thankfully, the gloves are fully integrated with your lenses. I want everyone to cross their eyes."

As soon as I began the movement, I felt the tingling return.

"Easy, right? Now use your right hand to grab your left arm."

I hesitated, then did as I was told. Nothing.

"Also easy, right? Go ahead and let go."

He paused and a self-satisfied smile spread across his face.

"Now take your right hand and grab the arm of the person on your right."

I looked at Drel, who looked at me. I was supposed to grab her arm? I felt a strange pain in my forehead, like a headache but deeper—

"Oh!"

The person to my left had grabbed my arm, and I jumped in surprise. But there was no electricity, no pain. In fact, her touch seemed to clear my head as well. What was that headache? Was it related to—

"Cadet?"

The instructor's voice brought me back to reality and I grabbed Drel's arm. He gave me a curious look then continued.

"As you can see, the weapon does not discharge at all times. Now let go and deactivate them."

We did as we were told.

"Your gloves aren't just connected to your lenses, they're also connected to your uniform. You may not know it, but your uniform has several, highly sophisticated sensory systems in place to monitor everything from your heart rate to minute muscle contractions. Because of this, we have a rough measurement of intent to fire, and this is translated to your gloves. But you have to train this skill, so you fire exactly when you intend to—no more, no less."

These gloves seemed like an integral part of the officer persona. Why hadn't they been included on the basic knowledge assessment? More curiously, this piece of knowledge didn't seem as familiar to me—I wasn't remembering something I already knew, I was learning this for the first time. Or so it seemed.

"Cadets, pair yourself up with one of the targets along the wall and stand close enough to touch it."

Again, we arranged ourselves as commanded. I looked at the large black object next to me and wondered why it wasn't rolling. Was it that heavy?

"Cadets, please activate your gloves ceremonially then lift your target up."

Well, I was about to find out. I touched my wrists together then placed both hands underneath the sphere and lifted. It wasn't too heavy, but I could feel why it wasn't rolling: it was hollow with a small weight inside.

"As you can see, moderate physical exertion is not enough to activate your gloves. Please lower the target back to the ground."

I put my sphere back down.

"Now, finally, we're going to try to use our gloves offensively. Please place one hand on your target and, with intent, attempt to fire upon it. If you are successful, your target should turn a shade of red."

I put my hand on the sphere. With intent? Okay...

A sudden, searing heat forced me to jerk my hand back. Before I could comprehend what had happened, the feeling was gone, my glove and hand comfortably cool. The same burnt smell permeated the air, and my sphere was bright red.

No one else was performing the exercise—all eyes were on me. Even the junior commander hesitated before noticing his surroundings.

"Staring at her won't make you any better, get back to work!"

The instructor regained his composure and gestured for me to come to him. I did as I was told, an uncomfortable feeling of deja vu accompanying my walk.

"What is your name, cadet?"

"Robyn, sir."

"Robyn, is this the first time you have used your gloves?"

The tone of the question indicated he thought the answer to be no.

"Yes, sir."

His skepticism remained.

"Are you lying to me, cadet?"

"No, sir. This is the first time, sir. I don't know what happened, sir."

My plea seemed to work, and his expression softened.

"Very well. In any case, you don't belong in this class. You'll need to be tested for your next placement."

He made a small gesture.

"Puric, 7th Wing, 17th Squadron?"

"Yes, sir."

"Okay Robyn, you'll receive a message after dinner for an assessment to determine your next Weapons Training placement. You're dismissed."

25

I made the walk back to the dorm alone, lost in thought. When I had been upgraded out of Fitness Review, I was surprised to find I was physically fit. But this? This was different. The instructor clearly thought I had previous experience with the gloves—a weapon unique to the Terian empire.

I reached the forest ring and made my way through the paths between the trees. The sun was low in the sky, and a chill was coming over the grounds. There were maybe a dozen other cadets in the vicinity, an odd sight compared to the thousands I had seen between my other classes. I wondered why each of them was out here right now: how many had a gap hour, how many were running some kind of errand, how many had been dismissed because it turns out they already knew how to use the gloves.

As I walked, I pondered the only explanation I could come up with, a theory that had the potential to explain everything. What if I had been a Fleet operative? What if I had had an accident or—and here I let my paranoia shine through—what if my amnesia had been induced? Perhaps they had brought me to the Academy knowing I would catch on with no issue because I had already been an officer in a past life. After all, that made more sense than throwing a potential criminal into the top educational institute of the Fleet...

But that begged the question: why? Why would the Fleet induce amnesia in an operative and then throw them back into the Academy? It made no sense, and part of me considered the absurdity of the idea enough to dismiss it. At least, until I thought about my performance with the gloves.

I stepped through the open doors of the dorm and made my way up the stairs. There had to be a way to find the truth, but how? The only person who might know was Commander Kelt, but I had no idea how to contact her and I was meant to keep our relationship a secret.

The door to my room opened and another thought occurred to me: I didn't have an ID chip when I was found. This seemed to poke a hole in my hypothesis: while ID chips could be removed, the process was purposefully difficult. And again, why bother?

If I really was a Fleet operative and my ID chip had been removed, they would have had to go to great lengths to falsify my medical data in the Kurotar hospital. Unless everyone I had seen and met were part of an act, part of the deception... perhaps even Chellet was in on it?

No, that was too preposterous. I sat at my desk and tried to clear my head, to take a step back and see the bigger picture. Why go through all of that trouble? Why not have me wake up in the Academy hospital? Just to make me believe it was real?

There was another hole in my theory. While it was true I had a surprising amount of knowledge about the Fleet and certain things seemed familiar to me, the majority of my experiences were totally new to me. Matriculation, the Academy grounds, the Academy system, much of Officer Training, most of tactics and biology... even the gloves, the same gloves I seemed to know how to use. All of this was new to me, none of it held the vague familiarity I had felt with the flash of Raviir.

A cold fear came over me as I considered that apparent memory. It wasn't frightening in itself—I couldn't even evoke an image of it now, as much as I tried—but the implication I might be remembering my past meant I was already in direct violation of Commander Hurren's order.

No, I told myself, that wasn't a true memory. A true memory would stick with me, I'd be able to relive what I had seen, what I had felt… but it was beyond reach, beyond remembering. And yet, somewhere in the back of my mind, I knew it was there. I couldn't see it, I couldn't even feel it, but I knew it was there.

Should I tell Commander Kelt? Again, I didn't know how to reach her, and frankly, I didn't want to. Besides, a part of me was beginning to see the cadets as my way out, my path to a normal life. What if reporting my memory meant I'd be expelled, sent to prison… or worse?

No, for the time being, I would keep this information to myself. If I started to remember more, then I'd speak up… depending on what I remembered.

26

Before my thoughts could wander too far, I received a message in my lenses: I was to report downstairs immediately, where a hovcar was waiting. No sender was listed.

My heart raced as I left my room and made my way down. What could this be? Would Commander Kelt be waiting for me? Or maybe Pell? But when I reached the ground floor and stepped outside, I saw an unfamiliar lieutenant in the driver's seat.

"Robyn?"

I gave him a nod.

"Yes, sir."

He returned the gesture.

"Step in."

I got in the hovcar, eyeing him curiously. Before I could sit down, we were pulling away, rushing through a gap in the tree ring. The wind bit at my face, my uniform fighting against the cold of the approaching night. Already the sky was turning orange, the sun almost at the end of its journey. I wondered what the stars at the Academy looked like—my first two nights I had been indoors.

The lieutenant took me well away from the academic buildings, closer to the mountains. It took about 10 minutes to reach our destination, but I recognized some of the surroundings along the way. By the time he stopped outside the red and black outpost, a familiar dread—the pit in my stomach—had returned.

"Go inside," he said, gesturing to the door.

I stared at the building for a moment then looked back at the lieutenant.

"Yes, sir."

I stepped out of the hovcar and made my way toward the entrance, my mind still racing to find an explanation. Had I already failed in integrating? Would I be taken off Alder, stripped of this uniform, and thrown into prison?

The door opened at my approach, and I stopped just inside. I was in the same small hallway with several doors on either side, and part of me couldn't believe it had only been a day. An officer stood before me—someone as familiar and off-putting as the building itself.

"Good afternoon."

Commander Kelt feigned a smile, but there was no effort to make it seem real. I gave her the customary nod.

"Good afternoon, sir."

Even now, standing a meter away from her, I knew I could not ask her any of the questions I wanted to ask. If my theory was right—if I had been a Fleet operative before my amnesia—then either they didn't know or they weren't telling me for a reason. Asking her about it would get me nowhere… or might make my situation worse.

"Your first day has gone well, I imagine?"

Again, there was no sincerity in the question.

"Yes, sir."

She nodded.

"Do you know why you are here?"

Because I failed? Or because you plan to tell me the truth?

"No, sir."

She gestured toward one of the doors.

"Come inside."

I followed her into the room, a small space about eight meters by eight meters with some kind of padding on the floor. In the middle of the room was a black target sphere. The commander turned to face me, and I stopped about a meter away from her.

"We're going to figure out where we need to put you for weapons training."

Some of my tension faded. This wasn't what I was expecting, but at least it was safe.

"Yes, sir."

She gave me a curious look, then gestured to the target.

"First, demonstrate what you did in Weapons Training I."

"Yes, sir."

I approached the sphere, crossed my eyes, placed my glove on it, and fired. This time I was able to hold back a bit of the heat. The target turned a dark red, then faded to black.

Commander Kelt stared at the sphere for a few seconds, a frown spreading across her face.

"Now fire on the target with your glove a few centimeters from the surface."

I obliged.

"Now with the other hand."

This continued for several minutes. The commander had me firing with either hand or both from several different distances. The progression helped me learn how to control the intensity and direction of the arc, but there was something off about her instruction. Each time I progressed, she seemed more disappointed than happy. It was almost as if she didn't want me to succeed.

At some point we reached what seemed like the end, but Commander Kelt hesitated, staring at me for an uncomfortable amount of time.

"Let's try a different target."

There was something in her eyes that worried me—a subtle excitement that contradicted all of her earlier disappointment.

"Yes, sir. What target?"

I saw a smile spread across her face, but this time it was real.

"Me."

I hesitated.

"You, sir?"

She took a small step toward me. I could reach her now, if I tried.

"Yes, Robyn. Me. Fire on me with your gloves."

There was something very wrong about this situation, but I couldn't put my finger on it. The eagerness in her voice, the discomfort I was feeling... I tried to raise my arm but it felt heavy, useless. A sharp pain came through my forehead, a sudden, surging migraine that rose up from within.

"Cadet, that's an order."

Her voice was stern, but I barely heard it. The pain in my head was so potent, so sudden, so...

"Enough."

I took a step forward, nearly stumbling. The pain vanished as quickly as it had appeared, and I caught my breath, dumbfounded. When I regained my composure, Commander Kelt had taken a step back, her enthusiasm replaced by a shade of fear.

Fear?

"You are dismissed. The lieutenant is waiting in the hovcar outside. You will receive your new course assignment this evening."

I gave a small nod then exited the room, eager to leave her presence. But as I made my way outside and got back in the hovcar, relief turned to concern.

What was that pain? And more to the point, what was that fear?

27

My divisionmates from Weapons Training were already at the table when I made it to the cafeteria.

"Robyn! How did you do that?"

The encounter with Commander Kelt had taken over my thoughts, and for a moment I had no idea what Drel was talking about.

"By the end of the class we could barely get the things to work, but you... that was amazing!"

Her excited tone helped distract me.

"What happened?" Wilor asked.

"Robyn showed us all up in Weapons Training," Tyla responded.

"With the gloves?"

"Yea. The instructor let her leave immediately."

Wilor raised his eyebrows.

"Nice job, Robyn."

Drel looked from the conversation to me.

"What did he tell you?" she asked.

"I'm being reassigned," I replied.

She smiled.

"Look at you."

I glanced around the table. Everyone seemed excited for me; even the senior cadets were paying attention to our exchange.

"You're not going to leave me alone in OT, are you?" Drel asked.

She gave me a pat on the back, and I managed a smile. I had been so worked up by the bizarre encounter with Kelt; all of this was a welcome reprieve, a temporary but important distraction. I got lost in the conversation, letting it carry me through the end of dinner.

After the meal, Pell had our division and second division meet in the squad room for a quick review of the day. We sat at the same pairs of desks we had used for the explanation of military training.

"Most days, you will have two hours of personal time after dinner. The squad room is open so long as there isn't a meeting—like this one—and so is the wing cafeteria, if you want a little more space. You're also welcome to reserve one of the open rooms or halls on the ground floor, just ask me ahead of time and I'll take care of it."

He looked at each of us as he spoke, and when his eyes locked on mine, I felt a warmth much like the uniform's—it made me feel like I belonged.

"Does anyone have any questions?"

No one did.

"Alright, you and your second-division partner will have a quick review of the day, then you're dismissed. We'll have another meeting like this tomorrow then it's up to you two to arrange any others. You're also welcome to come to me if you need anything."

With that, he left the room, and conversations broke out among each pair.

"So, upgraded out of two classes, not a bad start."

Rolin gave me a knowing smile, and this time I actually smiled back. Sure, I might not know why I was upgraded—and there was a chance this whole thing was a setup—but I had to admit part of me was proud.

"You plan on doing the same thing tomorrow?" he asked.

I shook my head, still smiling. After a moment, Rolin's expression grew more serious, and when he spoke again, he did so softly.

"Listen, I know you don't know me very well, but I want you to know you can trust me. I won't tell anyone about your situation."

I nodded. There was a sincerity in his tone that put me at ease.

"Thank you."

He smiled, then cleared his throat.

"Okay, so anything you want to talk about? Something I can help with?"

After a pause, I shook my head. Unless he could explain the gloves, Commander Kelt's fear, or the vision of Raviir, there really wasn't anything I needed to discuss.

"Oh. Okay."

There was a hint of defeat in his expression and, for a few seconds, we sat in silence.

"Well then, I'm going to run some simulations. If you need anything, let me know."

He gave me a nod then activated the hologram on his desk.

"Thanks, Rolin."

I stood and walked into the hall, starting toward my room then stopping abruptly. It turned out I did have something I needed to discuss, but not with Rolin. I turned around and headed the other direction, until I reached room 7-1700.

I hesitated, staring at the door, then knocked. A moment later, it opened.

"Robyn. How can I help you?"

A flash of adrenaline threatened to take away my composure, but I pushed through it.

"Sir, I wanted to talk to you about the integrated commission program."

Pell stared at me for a moment, then leaned into the hall. After looking to both sides, he brought his eyes back to mine.

"I'm guessing you want me to keep your status a secret, right?"

I nodded, and he gave me a reassuring smile.

"That was the plan all along."

He glanced in both directions again then continued.

"I've seen your file. I know your assignments are classified, and the last thing we need is curiosity creating a divide in our squadron or in your division. If that's what you're here to talk about, you don't need to worry."

He paused, giving me an inquisitive look.

"Is that what you wanted to talk about?"

I hesitated. There was still a shadow of a smile on his face, and I couldn't help but stare.

"Yes, sir. That's what I wanted to ask."

He smiled again.

"Of course. But remember: this is a temporary solution. This morning, at breakfast, when I told everyone about your upgraded fitness assignment —I know I might've upset you, but I did it on purpose."

He gave me a knowing look.

"You don't want to keep any secrets you don't have to, Robyn, especially not from your team. If you keep your past hidden too long, it will cause more damage than sharing it too soon."

I stared into his eyes, fixated on their sharp blue hue. What was it that made his presence so therapeutic?

"Do you understand?"

His question snapped me out of my trance.

"Yes, sir."

He nodded.

"Well then, enjoy the rest of your evening, and welcome again to the Academy. I hope we can find something to challenge you with."

I hesitated for a second time, then nodded hastily.

"Thank you, sir."

Before I made a fool of myself, I turned and walked down the hall back to my room.

28

As soon as Drel walked in, she shot me a smile.

"One day down, less than four hundred to go!"

I laughed.

"What did you think?" she asked.

I shrugged.

"Not bad for a first day."

Truth was, it was far better than I had expected, though that wasn't necessarily positive. My level of fitness was a welcome surprise, but what happened in Weapons Training was more concerning than exciting. Besides, I had yet to tackle what I considered the final obstacle, military work. What would happen tomorrow, when I had to perform those drills? Still, the fact that I was in the dorm laughing with Drel and not on a ship leaving Alder was an unexpected turn of events. Most surprising of all, I actually liked it.

"You ready for tomorrow?" she asked.

I shrugged again.

"Ready as I'll ever be."

She smiled, opening her locker and pulling out her sleepsuit.

"I have a feeling it's going to be a good session," she said.

I tried to imagine another 399 days, blending in, becoming a cadet of the Fleet... the optimist in me could see it happening, but the realist knew better than to judge the session on its first day.

"I hope so," I replied.

She closed her locker and looked at me, suddenly serious.

"Robyn, I'm glad you're my roommate for the first month."

I smiled, surprised by her sincerity.

"Thanks, Drel. I'm glad to have you too."

She smiled back.

"Now it's only been one day, so don't prove me wrong."

I laughed.

"No promises."

She smirked, then started changing into her sleepsuit. I let the warmth of the moment take over, an escape from my dormant worries, but it didn't take long for a new question to appear: what about what Pell had just told me, about keeping a secret too long? When would be the right time to tell Drel?

But when I got into bed, these were replaced by the realization of what had happened last night: this was about the time I had had my flashback. Would I have another one tonight? Or had my experience with Commander Kelt rewired my brain?

The pain I had felt in the room, the surging headache... I didn't understand it, but it had to be linked to my issues, linked to my amnesia. Maybe these sudden migraines were a byproduct of my memories trying to resurface? Maybe my spontaneous recovery was just around the corner?

Of course, the opposite could be true—maybe they were erasing my past, pushing me ever further from the truth... but I didn't want to consider the possibility.

29

My first even day started with my new fitness assignment, Fitness II. After a brief walk in the cold, my lenses directed me to a gymnasium similar to the one where I had finished Fitness Review. Even though we had seven minutes until the start of class, I saw the other cadets already in formation and made my way over to join the line.

"Cadet, come here."

I veered off course to meet the junior commander at the front.

"Sir?"

He eyed me curiously.

"You missed our first day of aerobic calibration. Your run data from Fitness Review gave a general idea, but you still need to complete at least one practice run today in addition to the already-scheduled progressions. I'll send the routine to your lenses and have you perform it now. When you're done, you can join us in the gym."

"Yes, sir."

The instructor made a few gestures, spoke a few commands, and the routine was uploaded to my lenses.

"There it is, cadet. Start immediately."

"Yes, sir."

I took my leave, following the instructions to make my way outside. When I reached the designated starting location, a small description appeared, outlining the parameters of the run. According to what I read, my speed and distance targets would adjust according to my performance. Just as I finished reading the text, a small timer appeared, counting down from 5. Here we go again.

The run began much like the day before, sending me into the tree ring at a decent pace. I had the same speed gauge, colored green, but this time it displayed a target speed. In place of a formation gauge was a distance progress bar, with corresponding data. After two minutes, I saw the target speed and target distance variables increase, and I was given five seconds to accelerate.

This pattern repeated itself every two minutes. The lenses had me weaving among the trees, avoiding any cadets walking through the area. By the tenth minute, I could no longer feel the cold around me, and by the sixteenth minute, I was at a near-sprint. Even though the distance and speed increases were smaller with each update, I started to wonder if it would ever end. Finally, at the twenty minute mark, the distance bar was filled, and I was instructed to jog back to the gym.

If that was any indication of what to expect in Fitness II, I was in over my head. Coming down to a jog made me realize just how tired I was, and each step was harder than the last. I was so relieved to reach the gym and see the routine disappear from my lenses that I bent over, ignoring my surroundings while I caught my breath.

"Cadet!"

The instructor's sharp tone brought me to my senses, and I scrambled over to him, standing at attention.

"Sorry, sir."

He looked at me with a disdain that was all too familiar.

"Cadet, why are you wasting my time?"

I hesitated.

"Sir, I finished the routine as fast as I could without exceeding the target speed."

This answer only angered him further, and when he spoke again, his voice was raised for all to hear.

"Cadet, are you playing games with me?"

My mind raced, trying to understand what was going on. In my peripheral vision, I saw some of the other cadets pause mid-exercise, turning to stare.

"No, sir."

He continued to stare down at me, clearly frustrated.

"Your behavior will be reported. You are dismissed."

I hesitated, waiting for some kind of explanation or clarification.

"Cadet, if you don't leave this instant, I'll have you running transie duty all week."

I turned around and hurried out of the gym, confused as ever. What had I done wrong? The speed gauge had stayed green the entire time, and it wasn't my fault the routine took a full twenty minutes. What did he expect?

I stopped just outside the gym and wondered what to do next. He said my behavior would be reported, what did that mean?

I brought my arm up and checked the time: 277. I had over twenty minutes until I needed to be in Officer Training. Enough time to return to the dorm, but I had no reason to go back.

After a quick look around, I started walking along a wide path between the academic halls. A spatter of clouds blocked the rising sun, and with the heat of the run wearing off, my uniform began to warm. The morning air was crisp as ever, and I breathed in deeply, trying to clear my mind.

When would we get our first snow, I wondered. Even now I could see the white tops of the mountains in the distance, and I knew the soft powder would eventually make its way down to the lowest parts of the Academy. How a planet with so little natural land managed to have such clear weather patterns was a mystery to me, though I knew it had something to do with terraforming performed many thousands of years ago.

Was the Academy landscape an accurate image of ancient Alder? Probably not. The trees and grass I saw were likely hybrids, mixes of species from all over the galaxy. Rare was the planet with indigenous life, especially after thousands of years of human presence. But I didn't mind. The Academy was absolutely beautiful.

After wandering around for fifteen minutes letting the landscape occupy my thoughts, I headed to Officer Training, my mind cleared and my mood improved.

"How was Fitness II?"

I ran into Drel as she entered the academic hall with Tyla and Grie.

"I—"

I hesitated, and she gave me a curious look.

"I made the instructor angry."

This seemed to make her even more curious, but I didn't know how to elaborate.

"Angry?"

I nodded.

"He dismissed me without an explanation."

"Really?" Tyla asked.

I nodded. I wondered if I would get any answers before the next class. Maybe it was worth bringing up with Pell at lunch?

"Well, don't get yourself kicked out of OT."

Drel gave me a nudge, and I smiled. If she was thankful to have me as a roommate, she couldn't imagine how glad I was to have her too.

30

Today's Officer Training was about our lenses. The instructor explained a number of advanced features and had us attempt several workflows. I learned we could send text, audio, or video messages to any number of individuals or groups. We could even send a message to the entire Academy, if we had the correct permissions. I also learned how certain courses or situations stopped these sorts of notifications, so someone in Weapons Training wouldn't suddenly have a message jump into their field of view.

After Officer Training was Interplanetary Tactics. My divisionmates had discussed it in detail the day before, so I had a rough idea of what we were going to go over. What I didn't expect was another small class, about the size of my terra course. Drel and the others had had about 100 in theirs.

"Welcome cadets, I am Captain Berge."

I recognized a few faces from the day before. Perhaps those were the other double-dosers? It would be useful to have some peers to work with.

"This is Interplanetary Tactics I, your first space tactics course. As most of you know, over eighty percent of all Fleet operations are in interplanetary space. For this reason, it serves as the basis for your space tactics knowledge. However, do not assume any of these subjects will transfer to planetary or interstellar tactics. Those subjects are very different and, for the time being, more advanced."

Those were the four main domains of action for the Fleet: terrestrial, planetary—also known as atmospheric—interplanetary, and interstellar.

"For those of you taking Terrestrial Tactics simultaneously, I will repeat the warning I have no doubt one of my colleagues gave you yesterday: there is some overlap between these courses but it is often convoluted."

While I was sure Captain Berge knew what she was talking about, I had to assume the similarities between planetary and interplanetary, or interstellar and interplanetary, were more convoluted than those between interplanetary and terrestrial. In reality, all these fields blended into one another: terrestrial operations would likely have atmospheric components, while planetary battles would have interplanetary support, and so on.

"Rolin, both instructors warned us about double dosing."

I was back with the squadron at lunch.

"Ha, told you. And?"

"And what?"

"Are you going to take both?"

I gave him an incredulous look.

"Of course."

He shrugged.

"As you wish. I won't underestimate you, Robyn. Not after yesterday."

"Robyn's a machine, she can handle it," Drel chimed in, winking at me.

A message popped into my field of view. Pell wanted to speak with me in the squad room before military training. I had been waiting for him to join us at the table, but it looked like he was skipping lunch. I finished my meal quickly and headed to the squad room.

"You wanted to see me, sir?"

He was seated at a desk, a meal in front of him. When his eyes met mine, I felt another flash of adrenaline, and his smile only made it worse.

"Robyn, I'm capless. You don't need to call me sir."

I nodded, trying to hide my embarrassment.

"Please, have a seat."

He gestured to the desk across from his and I sat down.

"Do you know why I wanted to see you?"

"Fitness II?"

He nodded.

"Tell me what happened."

His tone was friendly, and his smile hadn't faded. I relaxed a little in my chair.

"I was asked to perform a calibration run. I did exactly as instructed, but when I was done, the instructor got angry and dismissed me."

Pell nodded slowly.

"He got angry and didn't tell you why?"

I shook my head.

"No, sir."

I caught myself just as the word came out, but Pell was gracious enough to ignore it.

"I'm not surprised. I received quite a note from this instructor…"

He paused, shaking his head with a smile.

"Long story short, I wouldn't worry about it."

"Sir?"

Pell raised his eyebrows, amused. I could feel the blood rushing toward my cheeks.

"Sorry… what do you mean I shouldn't worry about it?"

There was something in the cadet-captain's look that only deepened my embarrassment, but I listened intently as he answered my question.

"I mean it's not worth worrying about. He thought you were wasting his time, joining the course when it was clearly too easy. He may have taken it personally, or had a bad day, or any number of things."

I tried to hide my surprise—too easy?

"But that's not the only reason I wanted to talk to you, Robyn. I know your activities are classified, so I'm not sure how much you can tell me, but I'm curious: why did you sign up for Fitness Review?"

I stared at Pell, a new feeling creeping in: fear. I didn't want to get trapped in a corner with the cadet-captain.

"I thought it was the best fit for me."

I repeated the words I knew so well, but they were more of a defense mechanism than a real answer. Pell peered at me curiously and I braced myself for a follow-up question, but it never came.

"Okay. Well, you've been reassigned once more. You'll be in Advanced Fitness starting tomorrow morning. You can take a look at your schedule to see the details."

He gave me another smile, but there was something different about this one, as if some of the warmth had escaped.

"I'll see you for MT in 16 minutes. We're meeting in front of Puric."

I took that as my cue to leave, and gave Pell one last nod before exiting the squad room. In the hallway, I stopped to take a look at my schedule. Advanced Fitness started at 205 and went until 295. It was two hours instead of one, meaning I was now in nine hours per day instead of eight.

I was an outlier among outliers.

31

My new course load was concerning, but it was beyond my control. Besides, I had a more urgent issue: my first real military training course was in 16 minutes.

I made my way from the squad room back to the cafeteria in the hopes of asking Rolin a few questions, but he was already gone.

"What's wrong?"

Crim was leaving the cafeteria and noticed my concern.

"Have you seen Rolin?" I asked.

"He left a few minutes ago."

A notification came into my lenses: Pell letting the squadron know to meet outside.

"Well, he'll be downstairs in 15 minutes," Crim added, seeing the same message. "You heading down? I'll come with."

I nodded absentmindedly, my mind trying to remember everything I had seen and heard the day before. Today we would be doing real drills, real formations—a live exercise in front of my division and maybe even the entire command. For the most part I was nervous, anxious of what might happen, but there was a part of me that worried it might go well— too well. What if this was a repeat of Weapons Training?

The crowd heading down the stairs was thicker than usual, and when we reached the doors I saw why: all of Puric was assembling for military work outside, some four-thousand cadets separated into their respective squadrons.

A small notification grabbed my attention: my lenses asking if I wanted to be directed to our squadron's designated starting point. I accepted and a small area about twenty meters away was highlighted.

Just outside, we ran into Kulee and Epore.

"What do you think it's going to be today?" Kulee asked.

Crim shrugged.

"Introductory, I guess."

He turned to me and pointed toward the highlighted area ahead.

"There he is."

Rolin was talking to Wilor and Bett.

"Thanks."

In truth I didn't know what I might have asked him if I seen him in the cafeteria, but down here with the rest of the squadron, I opted not to ask anything at all.

"Hey, where were you?"

Drel joined us just as we reached the designated area.

"I was waiting for you in our room," she added.

Before I could answer, Crim interjected.

"She came with me, she's my friend now."

He stepped between the two of us.

"She doesn't want to room with you anymore."

Drel laughed and pushed him out of the way.

"I don't believe you."

While my squadmates joked around, my mind replayed all of the scenarios Rolin had introduced to me the day before. There were many ways an hour of MT might pan out, though the most common was drill work.

Drill work was less about actual operational movements and more about obedience: the ability to receive, understand, and execute commands efficiently and effectively. I knew we might be asked to hold certain formations, walk, jog, or run in specific ways or groups, or even mix and match with other groups. Some of the commands might come from Pell, some might come from other cadet-officers. Some would come verbally, others through the lenses. At times, we might be given conflicting commands, or even fake ones, and we were meant to identify these in real time and react accordingly.

For most of my peers, all of this was building off of what they had done in basic training. And as we began to get into formation, I realized something else: Pell would assume I had some number of enlisted years behind me, making me more a veteran than even the upperclassmen. Could I play off any issues as being rusty, like I had planned to do with Fitness Review?

Before these thoughts could wander too far, instructions appeared in my lenses, and I scrambled to follow them. Pell had us rearrange ourselves in thirty different formations in rapid succession, and it was immediately clear who the weak link was. I was always a half-second behind everyone else, nearly causing a few collisions. I was sure the cadet-captain and my peers had noticed, but I was too busy trying to keep up to see their reactions.

After the thirtieth formation, we started a command-wide march. This began much slower, and I had less trouble matching their movements, but the reprieve was short-lived—soon, different parts of the whole began to deviate, breaking off and regrouping into new combinations. This complicated dance lasted another 25 minutes, and while I managed to improve, I was still the clear outlier. We finished with a few more formation rearrangements, then the hour was up.

As soon as we were dismissed, I felt the stares of my squadmates. Several members of the first division gave me odd looks, though no one ventured to say anything. I thought Pell might make a comment, but he was already on his way back inside.

"Little rusty, aren't you?" Drel asked.

Her tone and expression were lighthearted, and I appreciated her effort to assuage me.

"I'm doing my best," I answered.

"It'll come back quick," Rolin suggested.

"I'm just glad I can beat you at something," Tyla added, with a smile.

"Yea, drill work. Congratulations," Grie responded, rolling his eyes.

Both of them laughed, and I couldn't help but smile. Though my performance was subpar, my squadron's reaction put me at ease. And Rolin was right: I could learn to keep up, I just needed some more practice.

Yet as we parted ways for our next courses, I found myself trying to reconcile my performance with my latest theory. How could I be a former Fleet operative if I struggled so much with the basics? Was drill work less prevalent after graduation? Probably, but after basic training and three full sessions, I imagined all the drills would be second nature—even with some time off. After all, the gloves seemed to be second nature…

Clearly, there were many questions to answer, and as always, no answers to match.

32

After military work, I headed to Communication Analysis I. Unfortunately, the course didn't live up to the wonderful teaching style of its odd-day counterpart, biology. In fact, it was the most boring lesson I had been to thus far: a physics-based discussion of electromagnetism, as well as a review of uses and regulations related to the electromagnetic spectrum. It might have caught my interest were it not so encyclopedic— these were the kinds of things I already seemed to know.

Next came Galactic Militaries I, the course paired with Galactic Politics I. Here, I had an equally boring lesson: a review of Terian military hierarchy and Fleet structure, something the original basic knowledge assessment had already reminded me of. There were a few interesting tidbits such as the number of generals and colonels in the Fleet and how those numbers corresponded to specific Terian necessities, but overall I learned nothing new for two courses in a row. After the second one wrapped up, I headed to my new Weapons Training course.

"Once activated, your drones will begin mild, random maneuvers. It's your job to keep them targeted, but don't fire upon them while in their current, neutral color."

Commander Kelt had upgraded me all the way to Weapons Training V. There were 12 of us out here—a very small class—in a clearing among the academic halls. With the sun already on its way to the horizon, the air was much cooler, and a sharp wind numbed my ears and nose.

"When the drone activates its green color pattern, that's an opening to fire. The drone will turn red briefly to indicate a hit, and then modify its program to adapt to your ability level. Random movements will give way to evasive maneuvers of growing complexity."

The instructor had paired each of us with a small drone about the size of a human head, sitting inert on the ground next to us.

"Okay cadets, any questions?"

None.

"The exercise begins now."

All 12 drones activated at once, lifting gently into the air. My right arm was already outstretched, palm open, targeting the flying machine and waiting for any hint of green. It drifted lazily in one direction, then dropped a bit, to chest level. I was focused on its movements but could see similar things happening around me—I needed to make sure I didn't run into another cadet or drone.

I barely registered the change of color when I realized I had fired, a flash of green turning into a dark red. The drone stopped abruptly, gave out an angry tone, returned to its original black, and started its flight once more.

This time I had to walk quickly to keep pace, and it changed directions frequently. I passed by several other cadets but never lost sight of the target.

Green. I fired. Red. It stopped again, complained, then darted off with purpose. Now I'd done it!

It lifted up to about 5 meters, much higher than before, and began a very sporadic flight pattern above the class. I kept my eyes and palm on it, watching it zig zag and drop behind some of my classmates. I ran through them, weaving between their bodies and ducking to avoid someone else's drone.

There! It was green, but it was right next to another cadet, and I hesitated long enough for it to turn black again. It lifted up, just above our heads, and continued its bizarre dance.

I kept my hand steady—I wasn't going to let it slip by again. It dropped and turned green, but this time it wasn't close to anyone. I fired—another hit.

After what sounded like an even angrier tone, it flew off at a speed I couldn't keep up with. I ran through my classmates, trying not to knock into anyone. I could barely keep my palm on it, it was moving so erratically. I reached an open area and did my best to stay underneath it, watching it move with my hand ready to fire. It stopped and I stopped with it, arm poised, waiting for the green light. But it didn't change colors. Instead, it dropped rapidly to chest level, hovered about a meter away, then knocked into me at full force.

I hadn't expected it to actually hit me, and I fell to the ground in shock. I saw it flash green for an instant, as if in mockery, before flying off. This machine was pissing me off.

I got back up and followed it. The other cadets were out of my periphery, and though I wasn't sure where they were, I kept my focus on the task at hand. Another green, I fired—just missed it. My chest was sore from where it had hit me. I didn't know where the rest of the class was, I was no longer running into them.

Finally it stopped again, dropping to chest level. I knew this dance. It charged forward, but this time I braced myself and grabbed it. As soon as it was in my hands it fought my grasp, pushing and pulling against my hands. It was strong, but not strong enough. After a few seconds of struggle it flashed green and I fired with all my might.

I felt the heat from my hands and let go. The drone dropped to the ground, charred and smoking. Victory.

As soon as my job was done, I felt the stares of the others on me and turned to see 12 stunned cadets, their drones buzzing around unattended.

"Show's over, cadets! Get to work!"

The instructor beckoned me over and pointed to two fresh drones. "Both."

And so began my next dance.

33

I woke the next morning at 180, an hour earlier than most of my peers. Today would be my first day in Advanced Fitness, and unlike my other fitness courses, this one met quite a ways away—I would need most of my 20 minutes just to reach class.

With that in mind I jumped out of bed, used my mouthcleaner, and changed into my uniform as quickly and quietly as possible. I shot a glance at Drel before stepping out the door, jealous of her extra sleep. Why did I have to be different?

The cold hit me in the hall, noticeably worse than the last two days, and I wondered if it was a particularly chilly morning or just the earlier start time. While the corridor was almost empty, I spotted three other cadets heading to the stairs. Classmates in Advanced Fitness? I would know soon enough.

I hustled past the toilets, hoping nature wouldn't call midway through class, and made my way to the ground floor. My uniform rushed to warm me, but it wasn't fast enough—by the time I got outside, I was rubbing my arms with my hands, trying to create some friction.

I activated my lens directions and power-walked toward my destination. Advanced Fitness was the first course I was taking without a numeral designation, and I had spent a few minutes the night before finding out why. Apparently, the course was meant for the top tier of Academy cadets and had no specific progression. Instead, each student would have a program calibrated to their strengths and weaknesses, even more individualized than the typical fitness courses.

Surprisingly, this put me at ease. I didn't have to keep up with the best of the best, and I also wouldn't have another instructor yelling at me for passing a test with flying colors. At the same time, this meant whatever I had in store would be truly difficult—exactly as difficult as I could manage.

Our meeting point was indoors, another gym a little farther from the dorms. This one was more spacious, with a larger variety of equipment inside. Twenty other cadets were standing at perfect attention near the front of the space, facing a lone commander. I filed in line with four minutes to spare and waited for class to start.

"Good morning, cadets."

The commander addressed us at exactly 200.

"Your lenses have your prescribed routine for the day. Robyn, come speak with me. Everyone else, you may begin."

While the other cadets hustled to get started, I approached the commander.

"I must say I've never seen a cadet jump from Fitness Review to Advanced Fitness in two days, but having reviewed your file and the performances in the previous courses, I can only guess you underestimated what you retained from your enlistment. In any case, this entire week is calibration. Follow the instructions on your lenses and if you have any questions or issues, let me know. Understood?"

Her tone was serious, but there was no disdain in her voice.

"Yes, sir."

"Very well. You may begin."

She made a gesture and the routine activated in my lenses, prompting me to begin yet another run. I gave the commander a nod and went on my way.

The subsequent two hours proved to be the most difficult I had ever endured. What started as a simple run soon evolved into an obstacle course through the gym, incorporating various climbs, crawls, and jumps. I was given a brief water break then guided through several strength and balance exercises on bars and rings, moving through progressively harder variations in order to find my ability level. After a longer water break, the lenses led me to a pool and directed me to swim.

I hesitated, unsure of what would happen to the suit or gloves, and glanced across the gym at the instructor. She was watching me at that moment, and our eyes locked. There was something in that look—curiosity, maybe even encouragement—that made my hesitation disappear. I turned my attention back to the water and jumped in.

As soon as I hit the surface, I felt a subtle pressure at my wrists and neckline, and I realized the suit had sealed. My cap also morphed, spreading and flattening to fit my head. It was an odd sensation, as if a creature were crawling in my hair, but it was over in less than a second. The lenses reminded me I was supposed to be swimming, and I put my face in the water to start.

The swim proved to be the final piece of the routine, and I hopped out at 290, 5 minutes before the end of class. I was given another water break —how generous—then told to report to the instructor. I saw my fellow cadets doing the same, arranging themselves in the same pattern as before.

"Good work, cadets. That's it for today. We have five more days of calibration, mostly fine-tuning. You're dismissed."

I half-expected her to hold me back, to berate me for some reason or another, but she turned and walked away. I followed my peers out of the gym and, despite all the pain, I couldn't help but smile—things were improving.

34

The walk back to Puric was slower than usual, and I grabbed a second serving of goop at breakfast.

"Where were you this morning?"

Drel gave me a suspicious look when I sat next to her, and I realized Pell was the only one in the squadron who knew about my most recent schedule change.

"Advanced Fitness."

I answered quietly but a few heads turned at my words.

"Advanced Fitness?" Rolin asked, a hint of shock in his voice.

I nodded, hoping I wouldn't hold the spotlight for long.

"It's two hours?" Drel asked.

"Yep," I answered.

She nodded, and I could almost see her thought process: yes, I was in nine hours now.

"Well, if we do any inter-squad competitions, Robyn's on my team," Crim added with a grin.

"Hey, roommates stick together," Drel replied, laughing.

Crim glanced around the cafeteria then leaned in before answering.

"Look, Deena is nice and all but I can barely get two words out of her."

His tone was more serious than joking, and I realized just how right he was: I hadn't heard her say a word since our first gathering in the squad room. Yes, I knew Drel and Crim the best out of my division, but I had had several conversations with Tyla, Grie, Epore, and Kulee. Everyone except Deena.

Regardless, each of us would get to know one another well at some point; Pell had mentioned we rotated roommates every month. What would the month with Deena be like? Did her and Crim really not speak?

Just as these thoughts ran through my mind, she sat at the table.

"Deena, what did you think of today?" Crim asked.

She looked up from her goop and shrugged.

"Pretty easy."

Crim gave us a knowing glance.

"I agree," Epore added. "I might try to jump into two next month."

The standard fitness progression was every four months: Fitness I and II for the first and second half of the first session, then Fitness III the first half of the second session. After that, cadets could stay in Fitness III, move on to specialized fitness courses or, if qualified, upgrade to Advanced Fitness.

"Me too. I've got to catch up to Robyn somehow," Crim replied, giving me another grin.

After breakfast I went to Officer Training and reviewed all of the differences, overt and subtle, between enlisted members of the Fleet and officers of the Fleet. Each group had its own ranking system, and the empty star on a cadet's cap indicated our future: anyone with a filled star was an officer, while anyone without a star was enlisted.

Our instructor made sure to emphasize the most important difference between theory and practice: while full-star officers technically outranked all enlisted, we needed to respect and follow the advice of senior-level enlisted according to what was colloquially known as the "line rule." In essence, the number of thick horizontal lines on a cap gave a degree of experience equivalency between each ranking system: a captain, with three lines under their star, was about as experienced as a sergeant, whose cap had three lines without the star. If an enlisted member had more lines than you, yes they would still call you sir and yes you would still make the decisions, but you had better do what they suggest.

It was only during that course I realized I had yet to see any enlisted at the Academy. Everywhere I looked I saw either officers, cadets, or—rarely—transies. I knew the Academy had a Guard detachment and many of their members were enlisted, but I hadn't run into any of them yet.

Speaking of the Guard, my two hours of Terrestrial Tactics delved into a more in-depth discussion of this police force and their various duties. While the Fleet had major bases dotting every planet in the Terian empire, these strongholds were isolated from most civilian activity. In regular cities, towns, and settlements, the Guard was the major Fleet presence. Only when things got truly out of hand would the Infantry get involved.

"How's the double treating you?"

I had barely started my lunch when Rolin came and sat next to me. I finished another bite before responding.

"Fine, but it's only been three days."

He nodded, giving me a curious look.

"How was Advanced Fitness?" Grie asked from across the table. "I heard you got moved up."

I nodded.

"It was hard."

Grie stared at me for a moment.

"Well, okay, but what did you do?"

I gave him a summary of the class.

"Hm, sounds like a harder version of one," he said.

"Imagine that!" Drel exclaimed.

I laughed. My morning class had put me in a surprisingly good mood, and even with military work around the corner, I was feeling optimistic. Yes, I still had no idea why I was so physically adept—or anything about my past—but what good did it do to question it? If my spontaneous recovery came, I'd deal with the fallout. For now, why not enjoy my success?

35

After lunch we had more drill work, this time with our sister squadron —7th Wing, 17th—of Printo. Pell and their cadet-captain traded us off, mixed us and matched us by element, division, you name it. It was overwhelming, especially trying to remember 24 new names, and I found myself struggling even more than the day before. While I made it all the way through, I couldn't help wondering how this might affect my military performance average.

Meanwhile, I felt almost as confident in my academic average as I did in my physical one. Biology and Galactic Militaries expanded their introductory remarks, delving into animal and plant classification systems and military hierarchies throughout the galaxy.

It wasn't until I left Galactic Militaries that I noticed a change in my schedule: I was no longer in Weapons Training V. In its place was a course named Special Elective, located just in front of Puric dorm. No teacher was listed.

I hesitated, staring at the information projected before my eyes. Every other upgrade had involved a direct conversation with the instructor and a clear notification. I didn't recall seeing this change when I glanced at my schedule earlier in the day. Had I just missed it?

The location didn't make sense either. Right in front of Puric? I had had classes in the spaces between the dorms, but this mystery course happened to be in front of my own? A faint dread began to take hold, and I closed the display in a hurry. Maybe it was a coincidence, I told myself.

As I made my way back through the forest ring, a light rain began to fall. The drops rolled down my cap and uniform, sticking to my face. Would this class be outside? There was something about the rain and the gloves that reminded me of my swim that morning, but I hoped we were indoors—the rain only exacerbated the encroaching cold.

I rounded the corner to Puric and stopped in my tracks. Just in front of my building I saw a familiar hovcar with a familiar lieutenant.

My good mood disappeared, and the knot in my stomach returned. Why this? Why now? What had I done to warrant another meeting with that monster? I remembered the commander barking at me to fire at her, the pain in my mind, the fear in her eyes when she told me to stop…

The lieutenant caught sight of me and I put my thoughts on hold, hustling to the vehicle.

"Sir."

I gave him a nod and he replied in kind, gesturing for me to get in. I did as I was told.

The hovcar took off, sheets of light rain hitting our bodies as we made our way to the secluded outpost. When we reached our destination, the lieutenant gestured for me to go inside.

What, he couldn't speak now?

I stepped out of the hovcar and walked inside.

"Good afternoon."

Commander Kelt stood just inside the doorway, her eyes filled with the same disdain.

"Good afternoon, sir."

It was hard to get the words out, but I did what I could to hold my composure. I didn't want her to know the effect she had on me.

"This way."

She turned around and led me to the exact same room as before, though this time I saw no target sphere. Was this another assessment?

"According to your current Weapons Training instructor, he will run out of material for you by the end of the week. Therefore, you will no longer be in Weapons Training V. Starting today, you will have a private weapons training course during the same time slot, in this location, with me as your instructor."

It took a moment to process what she was telling me. Starting today I would spend an hour every day in this tiny room with Commander Kelt, eight days a week. That was 40 hours a month, or 320 hours per session.

"Do you understand?"

I snapped out of it.

"Yes, sir."

"A hovcar will wait for you at the base of Puric every afternoon at 700. You are to arrive at the hovcar no later than that time. Is that clear?"

"Yes, sir."

I glanced at my surroundings, wondering how this room could be used for weapons training. There was no space for theatrics, no fields to chase down drones.

"Good. Let's begin."

I barely had time to register her arm rising, palm open, before I felt a dull and total pain cover my body. It was over in an instant, but I stumbled to keep from falling.

"This is what an unexpected hit feels like. Your enemies, of course, will not stop immediately. Hopefully this won't matter, as it is your job to make the unexpected expected."

She raised her arm again and I raised my own, mirroring her.

This seemed to catch her off guard, as she stared at my arm in surprise.

"Where did you learn that?"

There was a hint of suspicion in her voice and I glanced at my outstretched hand.

"Sir?"

Suspicion gave way to irritation.

"You know how to catch?"

How to what?

"Catch, sir?"

I saw another flash of irritation in her expression, then a flash of light from her glove. But instead of falling over in pain, I watched the energy go into my palm and disappear. Besides a minor pushing sensation, I felt nothing.

"Your gloves emit electrical energy, but they can also absorb it."

She spoke in a forced manner, as if she thought I was lying and already knew what she was talking about.

"This is called catching, and it's your most effective form of defense."

She moved her arm again and I mirrored her. I didn't want to get hit again.

Her other arm came up quickly, and she fired both at once, but I managed to copy her in time, catching both shots.

"Well done."

Her expression did not match her words: I could tell she had hoped to hit me.

She strafed and contorted suddenly, and with my mind on her tone I was a half-second too slow. Every muscle in my body tensed simultaneously then let go, and I collapsed to the floor in convulsions. While certain muscles continued convulsing at random, a dull pain swept over me, and I realized just how much she had held back on the first attack.

Once the convulsing subsided, I got to my feet and collected myself. Commander Kelt gave me a self-satisfied smile, and an anger erupted inside of me. How was this professional? How was this okay?

"Remember cadet, make the unexpected expected."

And then she made another twisted move and I was on the floor again.

36

I struggled up the stairs of Puric, frustrated and tired. Commander Kelt had put me through such a beating I wondered how I would survive Advanced Fitness in the morning. Still, this wasn't the same as our last encounter—I was sore and miserable, but it was all in my muscles, in my body. Two days ago, it was all in my head.

The difference was clear enough: today, she had hit me multiple times with the gloves, while the day before yesterday, she hadn't fired on me once. That time, Commander Kelt wasn't the source of my pain—I was. But why?

"Robyn!"

I paused, turning to the familiar voice.

"Hey Crim."

He rushed up the stairs to reach me.

"Ready for dinner?" he asked.

We continued our way up to 7th, and I tried to hide the pain in each step.

"Yes. And ready for bed."

He laughed.

"Weapons training that bad?"

I gave him a look.

"You have no idea."

"Guys!"

We paused, and even before I turned around, I smiled.

"Drel."

She was with Tyla and Grie, no doubt coming from my original Weapons Training class. As they made their way up to us, Tyla shivered.

"It's so cold in the rain."

Grie nodded in agreement.

"Imagine having to do MT in that."

When she was at our level, Drel gave me a once over.

"You okay?"

I sighed, still smiling.

"Ask me after dinner."

She smiled back, and we walked as a group toward the cafeteria. I could feel my time with Commander Kelt in each step, but the presence of my friends helped distract from the pain.

Friends—were we already at that point? Yes, I realized, we were. And even my special elective couldn't erase that.

37

"I think they're reaching a calibration point now," Crim opined.

"I think they've passed the calibration point," Tyla replied.

Crim laughed, then turned his attention to me.

"How about you, Robyn? Advanced Fitness found your level yet?"

We were at breakfast the next morning—4day—and my divisionmates were complaining about their fitness courses, already anticipating the next workout.

"If they haven't, they're close," I replied.

In truth, that morning's class had been extremely difficult, but it was more the fault of my special elective than the routine itself.

"They usually calibrate for the first week then work from there," Swir informed us.

"You realize it's only been four days?" Bett responded, verbalizing what I was thinking.

Tyla groaned.

"Don't remind me."

We laughed.

"Say Pell, what're we doing this weekend?" Crim asked.

Our cadet-captain finished his bite before answering.

"Team-building exercise. Division based."

Crim raised his eyebrows.

"So, it's a secret?"

Pell shook his head.

"No, the other divisions should remember it."

The senior cadets laughed.

"Yea, no secret, I know what you're doing," Bett added, winking at Crim.

Crim leaned in, giving Bett an inquisitive look.

"Am I going to like it?"

Bett brought his index finger and thumb to his chin and stroked it dramatically before responding.

"Hmmm… maybe."

Having sat at the squad table almost a dozen times now, I began to notice certain behavioral patterns. The third division—my division—socialized with one another and with the second division. The second division socialized with everyone, but the first division kept mostly to themselves, occasionally conversing with the second division.

In a way it made sense: they were on their last session, the people that had mentored them had graduated, and since they mentored the second division they kept those relationships open. But it was still a shame the first and third divisions didn't really interact. Or maybe I was overthinking things? It was only four days in, after all.

Regardless, it reminded me of my cover story and the lieutenant's warning. Would I be treated differently when the other members of my division found out I was on the integrated commission program? Would the social norms shift, and I'd be an outcast?

Now I was definitely overthinking things.

"Your peers are complaining about the fitness course, but I think you have a much more legitimate cause. How's space and terra?"

Rolin's question snapped me out of it.

"Still no problems," I responded. Then, after a pause, "It's only day four."

He smiled at my dry tone.

"I know, I know: I asked you the same thing yesterday… but I'm not sure you understand how hard it's going to be."

I gave him a curious look. Two days ago he had said he wouldn't underestimate me, yet here he was asking the same question day after day. As much as I liked Rolin, it was almost patronizing.

"If you ever need any help with the space side, let me know," he added.

I smiled. Maybe I should give him the benefit of the doubt. After all, wasn't I just musing on the importance of maintaining relationships between divisions?

"Thanks, Rolin. I'll let you know."

"And if I ever need any help with my gloves, I'll just come to you," Crim added, smiling.

"Careful, if you annoy her she can really mess your day up," Drel replied from across the table.

I caught her eye and she gave me another wink.

One person who I hadn't noticed for a few meals was Pell. He was either in late, out early, or sometimes not there at all—which I assumed had to do with his cadet-captain duties. But I found myself keeping an eye out for him: hurrying to grab my food if he was already at the table or staying a bit longer than necessary if he came in late. Why was I doing it? I had barely talked to him. Besides our two short meetings, the most interaction we had had was during military training, and that was usually as a squadron.

Actually, I knew why I was doing it, I was just in denial.

38

Even though we were only four days in, I found myself settling into my schedule. Officer Training and Interplanetary Tactics continued to explore basic concepts, and while I struggled to keep up in military training, I was pleasantly surprised by Communication Analysis—it was anything but the boring lesson I had expected.

The topic was jump waves, and right away, the instructor's discussion had me hooked. Using the same technology as the jump gates but on a much smaller scale, it was possible to send information from one location to another instantaneously. Effectively, the speed limit placed on electromagnetic radiation—the speed of light—was a non-issue.

Like the jump gates, jump wave technology was ancient and enigmatic, a relic of colonization. But unlike jump gates, jump wave devices were relatively common. No more of the devices could be created, but there were thousands upon thousands in the Terian empire alone. This was a major tactical asset, particularly in space, which explained why we were covering this subject so early in the course—they were the main method of communication between distant ships.

What made jump waves particularly useful also made them particularly aggravating: since they weren't actually waves, they existed only at the origin and the destination—nowhere in between. Therefore, there was no known way to intercept them. This was great for the user, but a nightmare for intelligence operations.

Both the jump gates and the jump waves led to a very interesting and, in some ways, worrisome question: where did the knowledge to create these technologies originate, and why had it disappeared? It was a fascinating question, but not one we would dwell on in Communication Analysis. Instead, we focused on the current supply of jump wave devices, how they were assigned to different parts of the Fleet, and how they could, would, and should be used.

After such a captivating lesson in Communication Analysis, Galactic Militaries left me relatively unsatisfied. But in some ways, I was glad we weren't covering anything fascinating: my mind was focused on the class I had next, the only thing in my schedule I hadn't adjusted to.

Groups of cadets walked to and fro, making their way around the hovcar. As I made my way over and stepped in, I wondered what would happen when someone recognized me. What would I say if they asked about my daily hovcar trips? Had Pell seen the change in my schedule, and if so, did he have any idea what I was doing?

The lieutenant took us through the tree ring, and I began to ponder the extent of this secret arrangement. How many people knew, and how much did they know? Did this man in front of me have any idea why he was picking me up? Did he have to wait while I was with Commander Kelt, or did he run other errands?

These thoughts helped distract me until I could no longer avoid where I was, until I had to step out of the hovcar and into the building.

"Good afternoon."

"Good afternoon, sir."

She turned around and led me to the same room.

"Today we will continue to develop your defens—"

Her arm shot up and I saw a flash of white before collapsing to the floor.

"Have you been paying attention, Robyn?"

I struggled to my feet, wincing in pain at the occasional after-spasm.

"Yes, sir."

"Clearly not enough."

This time I barely registered her movement but my body was already matching it, opening my palm to catch the attack.

"Better."

The commander stared at my open hand, the anger in her eyes betraying her true feelings. Then she moved even more dramatically, attacking with both gloves in opposing positions, but I was able to mirror her movements and catch the hits once more.

"Good."

She almost barked the word at me, but I barely noticed: she was moving toward me now, firing shot after shot with intense hostility. I caught each one while backing up, aware I didn't have much room left, aware I was running out of space. My back hit the wall but Commander Kelt didn't stop, marching forward with frightening intention. Three meters away, two meters away, one meter away...

Her palms hit my own and she pushed forward. I felt as if I had no strength, as if I couldn't resist. My arms went limp, her gloves hit my shoulders, and a burning heat shot through my back, up my neck, and into my head.

Everything went black, and then it went red. I saw red grass all around me, as high as my waist, and someone in front of me. More of a presence than a person, more of a feeling than a memory...

And then the darkness returned as I collapsed to the floor.

39

I woke in an unfamiliar bed, the black walls with red lining reminding me of my location, of my situation. This was the Academy, this was Alder, this was day four.

While I didn't recognize the small room I was in, when I noticed my uniform had been replaced by a medsuit, I assumed it must be some kind of medical area or infirmary. How had I...

My mind flashed back to the classroom—to Commander Kelt's aggressive attack—and an anger came over me. Why was I training with a psychopath? She had every intention of harming me, and she had clearly succeeded. I was supposed to spend an hour with her in that room every day?

Then I remembered the image, the memory. I was on Raviir—this time I was sure of it. The capital planet, the red planet. It was the same memory as before but with more detail, enough to erase any doubt I had had. Of course, if that was a real memory, that meant...

The door opened, cutting my thought process short. I looked up and saw a woman walk in, distinct red lines accenting her white uniform—the same doctor who had assessed me a few days prior.

"Good evening, cadet. How are you feeling?"

I stared at her for a moment, knowing if I didn't report what I had remembered, I would be in direct violation of Commander Hurren's orders.

"Fine, sir."

She eyed me curiously, and suddenly I felt trapped, cornered on this strange bed in this strange room. Did she know about the memory? How could she?

"Do you know your name?"

"Yes," I answered. Then, after a beat, "Robyn."

She nodded slowly, still eyeing me curiously.

"Robyn, can you tell me where you are?"

I gave her a confused look, then it clicked: she was concerned about my earlier condition.

"I remember everything, sir. I'm at the Academy, it's 4day, I was—"

I stopped mid-sentence. My class with Commander Kelt and all of our activities were strictly classified.

"You were…?"

The doctor leaned forward, watching me intently.

"Sorry, sir. I was in class."

"In class? And you just collapsed?"

I eyed her cautiously, wanting to tell her everything, wanting to scream at her that a commander had viciously attacked me and that she should be suspended immediately… but I couldn't.

"I can't say, sir."

"You can't say? Or you can't remember? What class were you in?"

She leaned in even closer, eager to hear what I had to say, but there was something suspicious about her persistence.

"I… who brought me in, sir?"

She gave me a lingering look, then leaned back and smiled.

"Commander Kelt."

Just as I heard the name, she came through the door. For whatever reason, her casual entrance didn't surprise me.

"Well done, Robyn. You kept our interaction classified."

She gave me another of her self-satisfied smiles, and I felt a fury ignite within me.

"Yes, sir."

I answered through clenched teeth and instantly regretted it: Commander Kelt's smile disappeared.

"Doctor, leave us."

The doctor stood and walked out of the room, closing the door behind her. I eyed the commander warily, wondering how I would defend myself with my gloves off.

"Robyn, in case you've forgotten, you're nobody. You have no past, and if you're not careful, you won't have a future. You've been awarded a very special privilege, and you should be eternally grateful for the series of circumstances that brought you here. I suggest you channel your frustration elsewhere—for example on your defensive maneuvers."

She paused, eyeing me with the same frightening intention as when she had backed me into the wall. I hoped she had a level of self-control beyond my own.

"Yes, sir."

She gave a slow nod.

"Good. The doctor has been informed of everything that happened during our class and you're free to tell her anything you deem necessary. I will see you tomorrow."

With that, she left the room, and the doctor came back inside.

"Your vitals are good. You may return to your dorm."

I stared at her for a moment, unsure if I had heard right.

"That's it?"

She gave me a stern look.

"Cadet, you need to check your tone."

I felt the frustration welling up a second time, but I did as Commander Kelt had suggested and channeled it elsewhere.

"Sorry, sir. What happened to me?"

Her stern look lingered.

"You suffered a direct hit."

Again, I stared at her.

"The commander's attack knocked me unconscious?"

She held my gaze for a moment, hesitating.

"We aren't sure. Normally gloves don't cause blackouts—not to this extent and not at nonlethal doses. This is almost certainly related to whatever induced your retrograde amnesia."

That's what I was afraid of.

"Is there any damage?"

Again, she hesitated, a hint of pity breaking through her expression.

"What do you want me to tell you, cadet? This is what you signed up for."

No, it wasn't. It was this or severe punishment, what choice did I have?

"Thank you, sir."

She stared at me a little longer, then gestured toward the wall.

"Your uniform is in the cabinet." Then, after a glance at the door, she added, "Be careful. It would be best if you didn't end up here again."

40

The doctor left me to my devices and I changed back into my uniform. A quick glance at my cuff let me know it was 744—I must have been out for just under 30 minutes. But why was I out in the first place? If it wasn't the gloves, what was it?

I thought of the memory: the red grass, the presence in front of me. So familiar yet so alien... I was certain this memory belonged to me, but it only led to more questions. If I was Terian, I should have had an ID chip. So why did I have this memory of Raviir?

Maybe my worst fear was true: maybe I was a foreign agent, a military operative working for the Resurgence. That would explain my level of fitness and my knowledge of all things Terian, but there was a hole in that plot: how well I had used the gloves. As a foreign agent, I could have learned to use this weapon to blend in, but any double agent in a sensitive enough position to use gloves would certainly need an ID chip.

Unfortunately, all I had to work with was a blurry recollection that appeared to me in a time of great stress. While I was desperate to learn more, I wasn't desperate enough to go through another attack by Commander Kelt.

Just the thought of her made me angry, and for a moment I stood in the room, frustrated and terrified. Everything else was falling into place, but this? Just as I was beginning to get the hang of things, just as I was starting to fit in, she had to go and ruin it all.

Stress was threatening to consume me, so I made a concentrated effort to move on, to distract myself. I stepped out of the small room and almost ran into my chauffeur: the lieutenant who ferried me to and from class.

"This way, cadet."

"Yes, sir."

I followed him through the hallway, noting I was still in the outpost. While I fought the anger festering inside of me, he led us to the hovcar then drove me back to Puric. It was dinner time when I arrived, but I wasn't sure I was hungry: the situation had me on the verge of nausea. Still, I made my way to the wing cafeteria and forced myself to line up for food.

"Robyn, how was the rest of your 4day?"

Crim gave me a smile as he lined up behind me. It took a moment to clear my head and give him an answer.

"Painful," I replied.

He gave me a concerned look, and I jumped on a follow-up question.

"How was yours?"

He stared at me for several seconds, clearly worried by my deflection, then shrugged.

"More and more information. Ship design has really piled it on, even in four days. I mean, I like what we're learning, I just don't know how they think we can keep up."

I reached the front of the line and pressed a button on the dispenser, a small sensor reading my ID chip and dispensing my evening goop into a bowl. I waited as Crim did the same, then walked with him to the squad table.

"And you, why was it painful?" he asked.

I hesitated. I knew he meant well, but this was only adding to my frustration.

"Weapons training," I replied.

"Ah," he said. "Wait, what level are you now? Did you advance again?"

We took our seats at the table, and I had a minor panic. How could I answer his question? What was I allowed to say?

"I— I did, but I don't know what level I'm at now."

It was true, the special elective was an advancement, but it wasn't labeled like the normal Weapons Training courses—I had no idea what level it corresponded to.

Crim gave me a look.

"You can't even keep track of the level? Teach me your ways."

I nodded politely, then ate my food in silence. My mind was consumed by the commander and the red memory—I hadn't mentioned it to Commander Kelt, but really, what good would it do? Would she believe me, or even care?

No, now I was making excuses. I didn't want to admit I had made a conscious decision to withhold that information, and I was now doing something Commander Hurren had explicitly described as punishable by death.

As soon as my plate was clear, I went back to my room and laid down. Had I made the right choice? For some reason, I thought it best to keep my returning memory a secret, despite the commander's threats. After all, the whole reason I was at the Academy was my amnesia. If that went away, what would they do with me?

"Robyn, what's wrong?"

I was so absorbed in my thoughts, I hadn't noticed Drel come into the room.

"Are you okay?" she continued.

Her soft tone put me at ease, and I gave her a thankful smile.

"It's been a rough day," I responded.

She nodded, taking a seat on her bed.

"I think we'll have a lot of those here, unfortunately."

I nodded absentmindedly.

"Drel, have you ever been to Raviir?"

She peered at me curiously.

"Raviir? Yes—twice, why?"

Why indeed. When you were there, did you happen to see me in a field of grass?

"I've always wanted to visit, but I haven't had the chance."

Obfuscating the truth was easier than lying. I would have to get used to that, even with Drel.

"Oh, well, it's beautiful. At least the parts of it I saw. Very red."

She paused in thought.

"Honestly, I prefer Alder. Or at least the Academy. Some of the grounds here are more beautiful than anything on Raviir, at least that I saw."

I nodded, half-listening to her assessment, half-trying to conjure the memory in my mind. The second iteration was clearly more detailed than the first—did this mean I was on the path of spontaneous recovery? Would I woke up tomorrow with all of my history, all of my past? If I did, would I tell my superiors?

I knew it depended on what these memories revealed, but I also knew what would happen if they ever found out I was hiding them. Per Commander Hurren: summarily and unceremoniously executed.

41

Thanks to the incident with Commander Kelt and my decision to withhold information about my vision of Raviir, I was on edge all 5day. Advanced Fitness was tougher than usual, but I barely noticed. Military training took a detour from drill work, but I hardly felt relieved. Tactics, biology, politics: it was all a blur. The only thing I could think about was my last class: the hovcar that would be waiting for me, the drive over, stepping onto the padded floor…

This was exactly the sort of thing I was afraid of when Commander Hurren gave me a choice. Yes, I wasn't in a detainment center awaiting punishment, but what kind of freedom was this? After only four days, I'd been sent to the infirmary. How was this any better?

These thoughts swam through my head all day but did nothing to slow the passage of time. Before I knew it, the nightmare was a reality, and I stood before Commander Kelt once more.

I studied the woman in front of me, arms ready to jump into action at the first hint of an attack. There was a change in her demeanor, a subtle dominance derived from the day before. Deep down, I felt resentment and rage, but I needed to be careful. I was nothing more than a puppet of the Fleet, and this psychotic woman was holding the strings.

"Good afternoon."

"Good afternoon, sir."

I tensed in anticipation, eyeing her gloves, but they stayed deactivated.

"We'll start with catching practice. Follow my movements and absorb my attacks. Ready?"

She paused, but my eyes didn't leave her gloves as I responded.

"Yes, sir."

Her arm came up slowly, deliberately, and she fired a shot I caught with ease. Her other arm came up faster, but when the white arc escaped her glove, I was ready. I watched her drop her arms to her side, resetting her position before starting another move.

For the full hour, I anticipated a surprise that never came. The commander led me through a series of progressively more difficult maneuvers, and I practiced catching her attacks. As we reached the more advanced stages, she managed to outdo my defenses, but even when her hits connected, the pain was manageable—I didn't fall over once.

I left the course thoroughly confused. Was she trying to lull me into a false sense of security? After all, she had told me more than once to make the unexpected expected. Her behavior was certainly unexpected. In some ways, it made me angrier. Was this a game to her? Was she toying with me? I tried to ignore these toxic thoughts, but they plagued my mind through dinner and into the night.

I truly hated Commander Kelt.

42

6day proved to be more of the same, as did 7day. Thankfully, by 8day I had so many other things on my mind—coursework, budding friendships, all the usual demands of a cadet's first week at the Academy—that my incident with Commander Kelt began to fade into the background, as did my obsessive thoughts.

"Where are all the transies?"

I looked up from my lunch at Kulee's question.

"What do you mean?" Wilor asked. "You know it's only the first week."

"Right, but… don't transies do all the work? Who's cleaning the buildings? Cooking the food?"

There was a sincerity in her voice that made some of the senior cadets chuckle.

"The ones here are doing all the work they need to do. How long were you a transie, Kulee?"

"57 days."

The same upperclassmen gave each other knowing looks.

"Lucky you," one of them said.

"You had a pretty short transitional time, so they put you to work," Wilor explained. "But while you were cooking and cleaning, the transies that had already been here for hundreds of days got to take a break. It's more fair that way."

His explanation was friendly and matter-of-fact, but I could tell Kulee was a little embarrassed. In her defense, I had wondered the same thing. I was told these transitional cadets would be coming in droves, waiting for the start of the next session while performing all of the menial work on the Academy grounds. But eight days in, I had only seen a handful of the capless newbies.

"How long were you a transie?"

Drel's question was quiet enough that most of the table didn't hear, more of a curious inquiry from a roommate than a topic of discussion for the squadron, but it still managed to catch me off guard.

"I…"

She eyed me curiously, a few of my divisionmates also waiting to hear an answer. Was this it? Was this the moment I had to reveal the integrated commission program? It was much sooner than I would have liked, but what choice did I have?

"I'm more curious to hear what you were doing as a transie," Rolin interjected. "Did you run laps between every hovcar you cleaned?"

He gave me a smile, and I smiled back. Thank goodness he had been listening to our conversation.

"There's no other explanation," Crim added. "That and sneaking into the officer's quarters to practice with the gloves."

Unfortunately, if I had been sneaking in extra glove practice, my final session with Commander Kelt proved it wasn't enough. While her attacks still weren't knocking me over—or knocking me out—they were connecting more frequently than I would like. With each hit I tensed, waiting for the commander to change her mind, to decide to increase the power and send me back to the infirmary. But today was not that day.

I rode the hovcar back, relieved to have the next two days off. Whatever this weekend held, it was better than dealing with that psychopath. My mood improved even more when Pell joined us at the squad table for dinner.

"Ready for tomorrow?"

He directed the question at our division, but I could swear I saw his eyes linger on mine.

"Well," Crim replied, leaning back in his chair, "Bett said I will maybe like it, so I'll say I'm maybe ready."

Pell smiled.

"Fair enough. We'll head out directly after breakfast."

"We? I thought this was division based?" Drel asked.

"It is," Pell replied, "but I'm coming as an observer."

I fought the urge to smile, turning my attention back to my plate.

43

After breakfast the next morning, Pell led us out the dorms and through the tree ring. It was clear a good portion of the class was participating in this exercise: more and more cadets joined the march, until there were several thousand of us crossing a sparse section of forest. After about ten minutes of walking in this crowd of people, we reached a clearing full of shuttles. I had never seen so many ships in one place—not even the hangar on Kurotar. There had to be at least three hundred of them, enough to carry the thousands of cadets converging on the clearing.

Pell took us through the maze of ships to one shuttle in particular, and we boarded through the open side door. Inside was a cadet-colonel, who gestured toward a row of seats along the wall. As we took our spots and strapped in, another division boarded. Just behind them came another, and then one more. Soon, almost all of the open seats were filled, and I noted their familiar faces—they were from different squadrons in our wing, people I had seen in our cafeteria.

"Welcome, cadets. I'm cadet-colonel Porr."

Cadet-colonels led groups: at the Academy, that meant four squadrons worth of cadets. In the shuttle there were four cadet-captains, but only the third division from each squadron.

"This weekend we're doing a team building exercise at the division level. You and every third division in five commands are being spread across the grounds at randomized wilderness locations between 30 and 50 kilometers from the dorms. Once you've been dropped off, you will attempt to return to the dorms as efficiently as possible. The cadet-captains will be with you for any necessary aide or in case of major error."

She pressed a button on the wall and the side door slid shut.

"Part of this exercise is location awareness, which is why the maps in your lenses have been deactivated and we've chosen these armored shuttles."

I looked around and saw what she meant: no windows and a sealed cockpit. Only the growing rumble from the engines and a slight pressure let me know the shuttle was lifting.

"Each division will be dropped off separately, in numerical order of their squadron. Until then, you can relax and enjoy the flight."

The cadet-colonel strapped in next to the cadet-captains and broke into quiet conversation. I tried to pick up on what they were saying, but the ship's rumble had grown to a roar. Between the noise and the way my seat was vibrating, I realized just how luxurious the shuttle from Kurotar must have been.

"First class service," Crim announced with a grin, nearly shouting.

Before anyone could reply, the craft accelerated dramatically. I felt the straps press tightly against my uniform, keeping me planted firmly in my seat. Epore and I shared a nervous glance, then the shuttle dipped to the side and punched into a sharp turn, holding for almost 200 degrees before evening out.

I shot a worried glance at the cadet-officers, but they continued their conversation unfazed. That's when it hit me: location awareness. The pilot was trying to disorient us. What followed was a flurry of violent loops and rolls, and I could only imagine how complex the flight pattern would be for hundreds of shuttles performing similar maneuvers in close quarters. Whoever was piloting us clearly knew what they were doing.

After a few minutes, the chaos subsided. Our shuttle held a heading without any major deviations, and I relaxed in the still-vibrating seat. Despite the tumultuous start to our journey, I was smiling; I had been a little nervous about this exercise at first, but now I was excited. For all intents and purposes, this would be a hike through the beautiful Academy grounds with my division and the cadet-captain. What more could I ask for?

Fifteen minutes later, the craft began to descend. I glanced at Pell, who had broken away from the conversation among the cadet-officers and was doing some work on his lenses. If we were going by squadron number and there were four squadrons in a group, 17th would be first.

The shuttle slowed to a near-stop, and Porr and Pell both removed their straps, standing from their seats.

"17th Squadron, you're up."

We unbuckled ourselves to stand while the cadet-colonel opened the door.

"Go ahead."

She gestured outside and Epore, standing closest to the exit, hopped out of the hovering craft to the ground below. The rest of us followed one by one, with Pell holding the rear.

"Good luck."

With those words, she closed the door, and the shuttle lifted off. I watched it fly away then took a look around.

We had landed in a small outcropping inside the typical Academy forest. As far as I could see the area was flat, but the surrounding trees blocked most of the view. There were a few mountains poking up behind them, but not enough to tell where we were.

"Okay third division, the goal here is minimal interference. I won't give guidance or aide unless required. I'll follow you wherever you go, but don't ask me to participate in the exercise any more than necessary. The sooner you get back, the higher chance you make it in time for dinner. Otherwise, breakfast was your only meal for the day. It's 408 right now."

Pell nodded at us, and we formed a circle on our own.

"Okay, let's get someone up one of these trees and see if we can figure out where we are," Epore announced.

I was surprised to hear his voice—I had expected Crim to take the lead.

"I'll go," Tyla replied.

She headed toward one of the trees at the edge of the clearing, but I wasn't sure this plan would work. I had no doubt she could get to the top

—the trees of Alder had thick, well-spaced branches that made them ideal for climbing—but this tree was about fifteen meters tall, and there were almost certainly older and taller trees around us. Would she be able to see past them? At best, she could use the mountainous edge along the south and east borders of the Academy as a bearing, but it wouldn't be very accurate.

It took her about three minutes to get up to the highest point she could stand, then another five minutes to clamber down.

"The mountains are all along here and here, and rather close."

She gestured toward the mountaintops peeking over the trees on the other side of the clearing.

"We are south-southwest of the dorms, looks to be about 35, maybe 40 kilometers. We need to go this way."

She pointed her finger straight into the forest.

"Ok, lead the way," Epore replied.

She started off in the indicated direction, and we followed her into the trees. The forest was quieter than I would've expected, with only the soft crunch of our footsteps reaching my ears. Were there no animals here? There had to be, I had heard about them.

As if to answer my question, a series of chirps came from one of the trees nearby. I glanced up to get a look just as one of my divisionmates stepped on a fallen branch.

The loud crack brought the forest to life, and a dozen birds came darting out of the branches a few meters overhead. They were small creatures, about the size of a human fist, covered in dark blue feathers that contrasted sharply with the browns and greens around them. I watched them weave among the trees as they made their escape, fleeing the perceived threat below.

"Beautiful," Drel commented.

I had to agree.

We moved at a good pace, aided by a slight descent, but as time went on, I felt like we were deviating from our path. I glanced at my divisionmates, wondering if anyone else had noticed, but no one said a word. Was I imagining things?

An hour in, I couldn't hold back any longer.

"Should we reassess our direction?"

The rest of the division stopped in their tracks, surprised by the break in silence.

"Do you think we need to?" Tyla asked, somewhat confused.

"I think we've deviated," I answered.

"It's worth checking," Drel added.

Tyla shrugged.

"Okay. You going to check?"

I glanced at the trees next to us, much taller than the ones by the clearing.

"Sure," I answered.

I approached the nearest trunk, eyeing the arrangement of branches at the bottom. The truth was, I didn't think I needed to climb. I felt like I already knew where we needed to go. But if they wanted me to climb, I would climb.

I made my way up the tree carefully, checking each foot and hand placement before putting my weight on each branch. I had no idea if I would actually see anything near the top, but my division didn't need to know that. No matter what I saw, I could decide where we should go. Of course, that would happen to be the right direction.

The right direction. Why was I so sure of myself? Where did this feeling come from?

I got about two-thirds of the way up—as far as I could with the thinning of the branches—and took a look around. The trees around me blocked most of my view, but I could see the mountains exactly where I expected them to be.

I clambered down just as carefully, jumping off the last branch to the ground below.

"We need to go that way."

I pointed to the dorms.

Tyla stared at my finger.

"So the same way we were going?"

I nodded.

"Almost."

She gave me a small smile.

"Right. Take the lead, Robyn."

Gladly, I thought.

"Hold on," Pell announced.

We all turned to our cadet-captain, who had remained silent until that moment.

"You've done a good job with location awareness, but it's time to raise the stakes."

He gave us a knowing smile.

"The rest of the exercise will incorporate active evasion tactics. You are to assume we're in hostile territory until you reach the front edge of the tree ring, and every other division is the enemy. As we converge on the dorms, if any division spots you and marks you, you will lose your meal privileges for tomorrow. You won't be notified of this until you arrive at the dorms."

He paused, then tapped his temple with two fingers.

"But you're not just hiding. If you see another cadet, you can mark their division with your lenses. Each division you successfully mark gives you protection from one marking. Therefore, you have to spot at least the same number of divisions that spot you in order to eat a meal tomorrow."

His smile widened, then he took a seat on the ground.

"Also, I'm your injured companion. Please return me to safety unharmed."

And with that, he laid back on the soft ground, still smiling.

44

After a moment's hesitation, messages began firing off from one set of lenses to another, and we set about deciding who would carry Pell and for how long. Drel got the first shift and, as she lifted our cadet-captain onto her back, I gestured for everyone to follow single file.

These new conditions certainly complicated the situation. We would be cutting it close before Pell's announcement, but now? Even if we weren't spotted, it was unlikely we'd make it in time for dinner. Of course, better to skip one meal today than three tomorrow.

I watched my steps carefully, searching for more broken branches or anything else that might give us away. Grie and Deena were right behind me, acting as eyes and ears, looking for threats among the trees ahead. Crim and Epore scanned any direction they weren't covering, and Tyla stayed with Drel, ready to help at a moment's notice.

Despite the increased stress level, it was encouraging to see us work so seamlessly as a unit. Every 20 minutes, we took a 3 minute break, rotating our positions through the line. Unfortunately, this brought back the feeling of deviation—we were creeping ever-so-slightly off course.

This presented an issue for me. I could let it slide—after all, we probably wouldn't make dinner anyways—but that wasn't what this training was about. I needed to help my division. I could attempt to redirect us, but on what grounds?

I got my chance about two hours later, when we crossed a creek and took a short break. I sipped at the cold water, surprised by how thirsty I had become, then took a seat on the ground against a tree. While the rest of the division took their turns at the stream, I composed a message on the lenses.

"*Verify heading?*" I asked.

They gave me uncertain looks. Some shook their heads, others shrugged.

"*Climb, noise,*" Epore answered.

I had to concede he was right, climbing could be noisy enough to bring attention to our position, and besides, it would be easier to spot a cadet in a tree than on the ground.

"*Increase pace?*" I asked.

They acquiesced, but I could see some reluctance in their expressions.

I glanced at my cuff to check the time. 592. We had been going for almost four hours and were still short of halfway. In just over four hours, dinner would be over. It was a pain, but we needed to—

Short of halfway? I glanced at the distance gauge in my lenses. We had covered 20.23 kilometers. According to Tyla's original estimate, we were 35 to 40 kilometers from the dorms at the landing site. So why was I so certain we were short of halfway? Did I think we had deviated that much?

"*Let's go.*"

The message from Drel signaled it was time to move out, and it was my turn to carry Pell.

The cadet-captain had played the part of the injured companion faithfully, his body going limp as soon as someone went to pick him up. It was only during our breaks that he would revert to normal, watching us carefully as we planned our next move. I wondered how we would be graded on this exercise. Surely this fell under the umbrella of the military performance average? Or perhaps some of it was in the physical one?

I knew I shouldn't hesitate, but I couldn't help myself; as I approached Pell, I felt the familiar rush of adrenaline and fought to focus on the task at hand. I squatted down, placing my arm under his upper legs and my shoulder into his stomach, then lifted him in one motion. I needed to ignore those distractions; we had a drill to complete.

Thankfully, carrying a human being for several kilometers proved difficult enough to take my mind off exactly who I was carrying. The task was more strenuous than I had imagined, and Deena helped me shift him from shoulder to shoulder to help even the load.

"*Down!*"

Crim's command came through our lenses and we hit the ground as quickly and quietly as possible. With Deena's help, I did my best to bring Pell down softly and swiftly—in a way one would treat an actual injured companion—but I wasn't sure if it was fast enough. Had we been spotted?

After several tense seconds of silence, Crim sent a follow-up.

"Slow scan here."

His message included a position shared to our lenses, and I lifted my head to help take a look, my body still prone on the ground. When no one reported anything, he asked if anyone was close to directional cover—a tree or some other object between themselves and the indicated area. Tyla responded in the affirmative, then moved to a seated position behind a tree trunk, peeking around the side while gradually standing, trying to see if anyone was out there.

"All clear, but verify," came her message on our lenses.

The rest of us stood just as carefully, eyes locked on a specific piece of forest, peering for the smallest hint of movement. Nothing. We sent our all clears one by one, until the entire division was satisfied.

There was no way to tell if we'd been spotted, but we had followed protocol almost perfectly—more than likely we were safe, and Crim had marked the other division, granting us one layer of protection. Unfortunately, the ordeal had taken almost 10 minutes, and as we reformed our line and prepared to depart, we did so more cautiously, more slowly. If all of the divisions were converging on the dorms, these delays would only compound.

Marked or not, we would go hungry tonight.

45

The back half of the exercise was, as expected, more populated. Trees gave way to buildings, and after six more drop-and-hide encounters, it was clear we wouldn't be eating that evening. We finally managed to reach Puric at 824, 24 minutes past the end of dinner and well into the dark.

Pell had us meet in the squad room, where we awaited our results with growing impatience. Having already skipped lunch and dinner, we could scarcely imagine another day without food. I knew we had marked seven other divisions, but how many had marked us? Was it enough?

"First off, I want to congratulate everyone on a well-executed exercise. Your division worked cohesively and effectively as a team, even when conditions were suddenly changed. There were certainly mistakes made, and tomorrow I will meet with each of you to discuss specific things I witnessed over the course of the day, but overall you exceeded my expectations."

The cadet-captain paused, eyeing us with a hint of pride.

"I won't keep you guessing any longer. You marked seven other divisions, but only five divisions marked you."

He smiled, and Crim gave out a whoop.

"You're all dismissed. Get some sleep, your body needs it."

He was right—I fell asleep without issue. Eight hours of wilderness hiking with evasive tactics would do that to someone.

Thankfully, 10day was a reprieve. After breakfast, all third divisions stayed in the cafeteria for a wing meeting. We met the cadet-general of 7th Wing—the top cadet-officer of the wing—and she talked about various things of varying importance, after which we had only one thing on our agenda: our individual meetings with Pell.

"This is great. We basically get the day off. I wonder how rare that is?"

Drel and I were back in our room after breakfast.

"Definitely rare," I answered.

None of the other members of our squadron had been at breakfast. In fact, throughout the cafeteria, only the third divisions were present. Perhaps the senior cadets had some long-term exercise carried over from the day before?

"You have any work to catch up on?" I asked.

I knew Drel had several sets of simulations for Interplanetary Tactics —I had the same ones. But I didn't know what her other courses had assigned.

"Quite a few. Mostly sims. You?"

I nodded.

"Same. Sims for space and terra, and reviews for the others."

Both tactics courses assigned simulation work, while my other classes assigned reviews: summaries of the lectures for each day and the week, combined with testing to check knowledge retention.

Drel gave me a knowing look then smiled.

"So different from basic, right?"

I tried to smile back, but it didn't feel right.

"Drel…"

She noted my tone and gave me a concerned look.

"What?"

I hesitated, part of me still unwilling to share my secret, but I knew it was time. At least for her.

"I'm on the integrated commission program."

My words hung in the air for a few tense moments, and I watched Drel's expression, expecting confusion, or perhaps even anger. To my surprise, she just leaned back and smiled.

"Thank goodness."

I gave her a confused look, and she elaborated.

"I've been wondering why you were so much better—this makes much more sense."

She leaned forward again.

"Plus, this explains why you're struggling with the drills. It's been a long time, hasn't it?"

I wanted to agree with her, to latch on to her convenient explanation, but technically, I couldn't. There was one more detail left to share, one that prevented me from telling her whether or not it had been a long time.

"Drel, my activities are classified."

Her eyes widened, much as Rolin's had.

"No wonder you've kept it secret. Does anyone else know?"

I shook my head.

"Just Pell and Rolin. None of the division. I'd prefer if—"

"I didn't tell them, got it."

She gave me a wink.

"Don't you worry Robyn, your secret is safe with me. Besides, it makes me feel special."

I laughed. Despite my initial worries, Drel's reaction put me at ease, and I felt like a small burden was off my shoulders. I knew at some point, I'd have to share this secret with the rest of my division, but not yet. Not until I felt as comfortable with them as I did with Drel.

46

We spent the next hour working together on simulations until I had to leave for my one-on-one with Pell. At 398, I entered the squad room and found the cadet-captain sitting at the same desk as last time, the only difference being the cap on his head.

"Good morning, Robyn. Please, have a seat."

I took the chair in front of him.

"Before I tell you anything, why don't you tell me how you think you did?"

I noticed something different about his tone, the way he was interacting with me. Was it because we were in an official meeting now?

"Sir, I think we did well. We followed protocol near perfectly. If I had to mention any weakness, it would be speed. We were unable to perform the tasks quickly enough to make dinner."

Pell stared at me, a curious look in his eye.

"Robyn, I asked how you think you did, not how you think the division did."

His response caught me off guard.

"I... I think I did well, sir."

He nodded slowly, still peering at me. Something about the look made me uncomfortable, and I fought the urge to look away. Finally, he broke eye contact, looking down at the illuminated desk.

"In any case, I agree with your assessment."

"Sir?"

"Of the division. Your main weakness was speed. There were several communication inefficiencies that caused this. I have compiled a list of them and will share it with you now."

He looked up at me again.

"Interestingly enough, you didn't cause any of these inefficiencies. In fact, within the division, your tactics and communication were the best."

In those last few words, a hint of the unofficial Pell came through, catching me by surprise.

"Good work, cadet. Study the communication breakdown and enjoy the rest of the weekend. You're dismissed."

I left the squad room with a sort of tepid satisfaction. Yes, Pell was proud of me, but to him, my performance was no surprise: a formerly-enlisted cadet would excel at tactics and communication. I was also proud of myself, but I knew my performance wasn't a product of my first week at the Academy—it was a product of my unknown past.

47

While the first week was designed to give new cadets some breathing room, the second week gave far fewer concessions. Individual courses only ramped up a minor amount, but the cumulative effect was immediately noticeable: more coursework, tougher exercises, and harder drills. The complaints I heard from my division increased in frequency and severity, but I was quietly thankful for the heightened load: it served to distract me from my demons—even the one I had to see every day.

Commander Kelt remained strictly professional, but that did little to ease the anxiety I felt each time I hopped in the hovcar. Day after day I expected her to snap, to press me into a corner and send me to the infirmary, but so far she had done nothing of the sort. Having said that, just because she wasn't rendering me unconscious didn't mean it was easy. And with Advanced Fitness nine hours later, my body never had quite enough time to recover.

After a particularly brutal 4day morning, my movements at breakfast were stunted enough for Rolin to notice.

"Advanced Fitness finally calibrated, huh?"

"Yes."

It was true, the course had calibrated to my level, even if it wasn't the cause of all my discomfort.

"Well at least you've hit the ceiling," he replied.

I forced a smile, but my train of thought continued: were these rough sessions with Commander Kelt affecting my performance in Advanced Fitness? Would it be enough to reduce my PPA?

"Rolin, how can I check my performance averages?" I asked.

"You'll get an update at the end of the month, but you should have a general idea of where you stand based on how classes are going."

He gave me a curious look.

"Why, you worried about something?"

I shrugged.

"Maybe."

The PPA, APA, and MPA were all measured on 100-point scales with 100 being perfect—and therefore impossible—and 0 being so terrible you would have long since been kicked out. I knew the importance of each number depended on a cadet's selected track, but I still had no idea what track I wanted to do—or if I even had a choice. Did Commander Kelt or Commander Hurren expect me to pass a certain threshold on all three? I assumed if I was faltering she would call me into a meeting… and that was the last thing I wanted.

"Well, I doubt you need to worry about anything—not even your drill work—but if you're really dropping, the instructor should let you know."

I nodded.

"Thanks."

Despite the physical load, I managed to stay alert and absorbed in my classes—particularly when something interesting came up, as it did in that morning's Officer Training.

The instructor discussed the hierarchy of the Fleet, which followed the same pattern as the Academy's microcosm: 21 commands, each with forces, then wings, groups, squadrons, divisions, and elements. In the Fleet proper, an element was typically a specific number of ships rather than a specific number of people—it was a fleet after all.

Within each command, there were 4 special groups that did not belong to wings or forces, but instead reported directly to that command. These were the Fleet Guard, Fleet Infantry, Fleet Intelligence, and SOD. It was this last one—SOD—that caught my attention. The instructor made no elaborations about this special group, despite in-depth explanations of the other three, and for whatever reason, this series of letters were foreign to me—something missing from my encyclopedic knowledge. When I tried to look into it on my own, all I could find was the full name: Special Operations Division. That, along with the lack of supplemental data, was enough to clue me in on its purpose, but not enough to quell my curiosity. Maybe my second-division partner knew something I didn't?

"What's SOD?"

Rolin smiled, amused by my question.

"Don't bother," he replied, then continued eating his lunch.

I stared at him for a moment, confused.

"What do you mean?" I pressed on.

He shook his head, still smiling.

"OT mentioned it today didn't they?"

I nodded.

"So?"

"So that's about as much as you'll learn for the next three years."

I gave him a look and he shrugged.

"Trust me, we're all just as curious, and there're plenty of rumors, but no one really knows."

Then he put his spoon down and looked around the table before leaning in closer, close enough to whisper.

"You should know more about that than us, shouldn't you?"

His suspicious look lingered, and it took me a moment to realize what he was talking about: my classified past. I wanted to shake my head, but I knew I couldn't confirm or deny anything, so I just turned back to my meal, slightly embarrassed by my slip-up. He was right, of course: if anyone at this table knew anything about SOD, it would be the formerly-enlisted cadet with a secret past.

And for a moment, lost in my own thoughts, contemplating all the inconsistencies and coincidences of my first week and a half at the Academy, I realized maybe it wasn't so far from the truth.

48

I spent most of the afternoon unable to shake this hypothesis, though I knew even if my past was somehow related to SOD, it didn't explain all the discrepancies in my experiences. It wasn't until I found myself face-to-face with Commander Kelt, prepping myself for another day that could go horribly wrong, that I was able to escape these thoughts.

At the beginning of the second week, the commander had introduced some new techniques, and I found myself spending more time on the ground than off it. But I was adapting. Here, three days later, I managed to hit the ground only twenty-one times. The next day, it was down to twelve, and on 6day, seven. On 7day I only went down twice.

By 8day, I felt the week's worth of accumulated pain, but I was in a good mood. Maybe I could wrap up the week with no hits from the commander? As we sat at lunch, I was sad I couldn't share my excitement with anyone.

"Two weeks in, how's it feel?"

Swir, Drel's second-division partner, directed the question to both of us. We shared a glance before Drel answered.

"Pretty good. Finally feel like I'm finding my stride—at least in some courses."

She nodded.

"That's good to hear. And you, Robyn?"

Swir's question provoked quite a reaction within me. We were nearly two weeks in—twenty days—and I was still here. And not just still here, but actively integrating into the Academy: taking classes, forming relationships, and being a cadet.

That was the crux of it—I was starting to feel like a cadet, like this was where I belonged, what I was supposed to do. With no more blurry red episodes, only the special elective with Commander Kelt reminded me of my unique circumstances.

"Robyn?"

She gave me a concerned look and I shelved my wandering thoughts.

"Yes, same. I feel challenged, and sometimes I'm still surprised, but I've learned to expect the unexpected."

I smiled at my little inside joke.

"You're definitely not talking about OT," Crim said, joining our conversation. "There are no surprises there."

We laughed, though I couldn't help but think 4day's class had proved him wrong.

"What about the MT?" Swir prodded.

He hesitated, then nodded.

"Okay I'll give you that. It's like what Robyn said, I'm surprised but not surprised, if that makes sense? It's always something new but also always useful."

I agreed with his assessment—military work had been the most variable course of all. Sometimes we were reviewing protocol as a division in a classroom, and sometimes we were running drills as an entire wing. Most importantly for me, I was starting to bridge the gap between myself and my peers; in the end, drill work was more or less predictable, it just took practice. A few more weeks, and I would be right in line with the rest of my division.

"Robyn, you're taking biology right?" Wilor asked from a few seats away.

I nodded.

"Yes."

"How is that? I took it my first session and it was one of my favorite courses."

I nodded again.

"Very interesting. We've been talking about lifeforms in the Terian empire, but next month we're supposed to expand to the galaxy."

"Ah, yes. That's the best part, just you wait."

I had expected another, specific question to come at the dinner table, but it waited until we were heading out for MT.

"What about tactics?"

"I was waiting for you to ask."

I smiled at Rolin and he smiled back.

"I'll admit it's starting to overlap a bit, but so far so good."

He shrugged.

"You know where I am if you need me."

As we got into formation for our first set of drills, Rolin's words reminded me of the surprisingly familial aspect of the Academy. After all, the kindness of my peers was the main reason I was starting to fit in, but I couldn't get over the contrast between their friendliness and the psychopathy of Commander Kelt. Was her behavior a product of her past? Had combat shaped her into a vile monster?

Then it hit me: what happened after I graduated? Now that I was starting to succeed, I realized I might actually make it through the Academy and become an officer of the Fleet. If that happened, was I destined to a fate like Commander Kelt's? Had I foregone an unknown punishment to become a broken woman?

I ignored these questions, focusing on Pell's orders. I had a long way to go before I needed to worry about any of that.

49

After military work, Communication Analysis, and Galactic Militaries, I hopped in the hovcar with a sense of purpose. Today was going to be the day I wouldn't let Commander Kelt hit me, not even once. The lieutenant dropped me off outside the complex and the commander led me to our staging room. As soon as I crossed the threshold, she turned on me with an immediate and decisive attack. I fell to the ground just inside the doorway, shocked in more ways than one.

"What did I tell you, Robyn?"

There was a derisiveness in her tone that ignited my old anger, but I bit my tongue: she had hit me harder than usual, and something about her demeanor made it clear she was hoping for a reaction. The last thing I needed was to give her an excuse to send me back to the infirmary.

"Except the unexpected, sir."

I got to my feet and into a defensive position, palms out and ready to absorb anything she threw my way. Yet despite the surprising start to our lesson, the rest of the course played out the same as the day before. She was angrier, yes, but the attacks went back to normal, and in the end, I didn't fall a second time.

On the ride back to Puric, I couldn't help but wonder if the commander had done that on purpose to deny me a clean day. But did it even matter? The week was over, and I didn't have to worry about her for another two days.

"Do you know what we're doing this weekend?"

I directed the question at Crim, who paused his dinner and shrugged.

"I assume it's another surprise."

"It is indeed!" Bett interjected with a grin.

Crim rolled his eyes and continued his meal, but my curiosity wasn't satisfied.

"Are all the weekends a secret?"

"No," Rolin answered. Then, after a pause, he added, "I told you about the pattern, right?"

I shook my head.

"No."

He raised his eyebrows.

"Wow… I'm sorry Robyn, I thought I told you."

"You didn't tell her!?" Bett interjected, shaking his head mockingly. Then, turning to me, he added, "You kind of got the short end of the stick with Rolin here, sorry Robyn."

Rolin laughed.

"Bett, do you even know what classes Deena is in?"

Bett lifted a finger as if to speak, took a dramatic breath, then dropped his finger and shook his head in defeat. Rolin laughed a second time, then turned his attention back to me.

"So the actual exercises are a secret, but the weekends follow a monthly pattern, at least for you newbies. First weekend is division-based and second is squadron-based. The third is a bit random, but it is usually a little easier. The fourth is group-based for your class, and is always the hardest. The fifth weekend is for room changes, schedule changes, and other administrative stuff. That one's not secret."

I nodded, excited by the prospect of a squadron-based weekend—it meant one person in particular might be joining us, one person who once again was missing from dinner. I looked around the cafeteria and saw we were not the only table with an empty chair.

"Olla, do the cadet-officers have meetings during meals?"

Olla was the second division's cadet-commander, so I figured she might know.

"Yes, usually just the captains but sometimes we do too."

"Why, you eyeing the commander position?" Crim asked, grinning at me.

No, Crim, I thought. I'm eyeing our captain.

50

The first day of the second weekend introduced me to a new weapon: the rifle. While the gloves remained the officer's weapon of choice in close combat, they were unstable at moderate distances and useless at long range. Normally, this is where the rifle would come in, but today we put a twist on that paradigm: we used the rifle for close combat.

Out in a designated segment of wilderness, we ran an assortment of competitions under Pell's command. Our lenses created false walls to keep us in the zone of play and update us on various metrics, depending on the exercise. The patch of wilderness had been sprinkled with pipes, boxes, and the like to increase complexity.

"Okay, first and second divisions off the field, we're going to let the third division compete. Last individual standing. Third division, in position."

The senior cadets joined Pell just outside the artificial boundary and the eight third-division cadets met at the designated starting point.

"Third division, you have 20 seconds to spread out. Ready, mark!"

A small timer appeared in our lenses and Drel gave me a wink before we went our separate ways. That bush? No. This ditch? Too close. I bumped into Tyla at the 10 second mark but we shot off in opposite directions. I found a thick tree and crouched down behind it, scanning the perimeter for any other cadets. Seemed clear.

The timer hit zero and I heard a beep from my rifle. I put the weapon on my shoulder and leaned out one side of the tree.

At first, I wasn't sure whether to expect another drill situation, where my proficiency was noticeably lower than that of my peers, or another glove situation, where it was suspiciously higher. I knew from snippets of conversation that everyone else had used the rifle during basic training, but I lucked out with the close quarter combat: while it was clear I wasn't as proficient in its use, none of them had used it like this before, which evened the playing field.

I caught sight of movement to my right, but it disappeared before I could pan the barrel. I hopped in a trench on my left and crouched for cover, poking my head up for another quick scan.

There—movement, in a large pipe about 3 meters from me. Several holes along its side clearly showed someone crawling through it. I lined up my rifle at the next hole and fired.

"Damn!"

Got Grie. I did another quick scan and saw someone jump behind my tree just a meter away. I turned around and lay back in the trench. Had they seen me? I kept my rifle pointed up, trying to make sure the front end didn't come out of the trench.

A rifle came around, then a head, and I fired. A grunt, then Tyla emerged, shaking her head at me.

I smiled, then got back up in a crouch. I wondered if Drel was still in.

I lifted my head over the lip and was greeted with an angry tone from the rifle along with a message in my lenses—I had been hit.

I stood and made my way out of the play zone. I saw Drel already outside, along with 4 others. Only Kulee and Crim were still in. By the time I reached the boundary, just Crim.

"Congratulations, Crim. Full squadron now, with teams of elements. Play continues down to the last element or individual. In position."

All 24 of us met at the starting point.

"20 seconds. Ready, mark!"

With three times as many cadets, finding a good hiding place was a challenge. I ran faster this time, bumping into one of the first-division cadets hard enough to bring us both to the ground. She took off right away, but my muscles still ached from a week's worth of pain and it took me a moment to compose myself.

The large zero in my lenses and the beep from my rifle let me know I needed to find cover. A few bushes and a small wall nearby were my best bet, so I jumped behind them. Just ahead, I noticed two of my squadmates. My rifle came up and I fired two quick shots—both hits.

My lenses had a small counter telling me how many of us were still active. Right now it read 19/24.

I peeked around the side of the wall, using the bush as cover. I saw someone dash between two trees but they were too quick. I pivoted back behind cover, did another scan in front of me, and saw a large pipe about 2 meters away. I poked my head over the wall, didn't see anything, and took four quick strides to get myself behind the pipe. The side of the pipe and an adjacent tree made a nice wedge I could hide in, so I tucked myself between them and did another scan. There was a wall next to a trench nearby, and I saw a rifle sticking out just above it. I waited a few moments until the rifle moved. Wilor was trying to hop from behind the wall into the trench, but I didn't let him.

15/24. I had to stand almost all the way up to get a view over the pipe, but I didn't make the mistake of leading with my rifle. I popped my eyes over the edge, scanned from left to right, then dropped right back down. I had seen two people, one moving, the other facing away crouched near another tree. I brought the rifle up and fired where the person had been, but they were gone. I dropped back behind the pipe and did a scan behind me. Was that someone behind that bush off to the left?

A rustle to my right caught my attention. There was someone on the other side of my tree, less than a meter away. I tensed, the sound of my heartbeat coming through my ears. My adrenaline was so high I thought I saw my display flicker. Now or never.

I strafed around the tree and fired, hitting Kulee.

"Ah!"

A large red 'ABORT' appeared over my lenses but I barely noticed it. Pain flooded my head and I fell to my knees, the rifle dropping beside me.

"Robyn, are you okay?"

It was Kulee. Somehow her words reinforced me, clearing my mind. The pain left as quickly as it had come, but a small ache lingered, a tingle behind my eyes.

"What happened?" I asked as she helped me to my feet.

"I don't know, I guess the shock is on?"

A first-division cadet came out from behind the bush, where I thought I had seen someone moments earlier.

"You two okay?"

"Squadron, to me," Pell called out.

We hustled over to him and saw the concern in his eyes.

"The rifle shock was reactivated mid-exercise," he announced.

The rifle shock—I had heard about this too: the rifle could emit an electric shock, alerting its owner of a hit in a more painful manner. It was sometimes used in exercises, but it wasn't supposed to be on for this one…

"Based on the messages I am seeing, this was a simultaneous, Academy-wide malfunction. Was anyone hurt?"

"We got hit, sir, but we're good," Kulee answered, gesturing to the both of us.

My display flickered again, and this time I knew I wasn't seeing things. Pell immediately confirmed my observation.

"There. That flicker was the system resetting. The shock is deactivated."

He paused, reading a message on his lenses.

"We have the all clear. We'll restart that exercise. Squadron, in position."

By the time I reached the designated starting point, my headache was gone, but the memory of it lingered. Something about the pain reminded me of my time with Commander Kelt, and then it hit me: an Academy-wide malfunction? Whatever Pell had read must have been reassuring enough to have us continue, but I myself was no longer a believer of coincidences. The random reactivation of our rifle shock was certainly a good way to expect the unexpected.

51

I woke up on 10day expecting more rifle exercises, but Pell told us over breakfast we had something else on the agenda: a tour of the Academy.

"We're going to show you five key areas on the grounds, areas that most of you will get to know very well by the end of your time here."

Despite reaching a surprising level of competence with the rifle, I was happy for today's change: yesterday's games, along with the rifle shock incident, had left me physically and mentally drained. It wasn't the same soreness I got from Advanced Fitness or Commander Kelt, but my body was clearly in need of rest.

After breakfast, we boarded shuttles in a manner similar to the first weekend—again, the sheer number of ships amazed me—and were ferried to our first destination: the trainee spaceport. The Academy had three spaceports: the action spaceport, the supply spaceport, and the trainee spaceport. This one, as the name implied, was meant to train new pilots, and was about two kilometers south of the dorms. The other ports were much farther, on the far west side of the grounds.

Pell led us through slowly, in front of 18th Squadron and behind 16th Squadron, explaining what we were seeing as we walked. The trainee spaceport was enormous, and with good reason: every senior cadet had courses here, meaning a good 60000 people ran through it almost daily.

"Most of you will begin introductory pilot training in your second session and specialize in your third. These courses are typically two hours per day on odd and even days. Depending on your track, you could have anywhere from four to sixteen months of pilot training before you leave the Academy."

Rolin had glossed over this on my first day, saying I would learn more about pilot training later on, and we had touched on the subject in Interplanetary Tactics, but not in detail. All I knew for sure was every cadet had to be able to perform basic interstellar maneuvers, mostly simulated. More advanced students moved on to atmospheric flight, which involved many more variables: different planets had different atmospheres and gravities, and pilots had to be ready to adapt. The top students finished with interplanetary flight, including the most impressive feat: the transition from atmospheric to interplanetary flight in one trip, a transition between two very different sets of physics. I hoped to be able to get to that point one day.

After the trainee spaceport, we did a flyover near some of the northernmost mountains, and Pell described the activities that took place in some of the buildings below. I stared at the red and black structures, standing out in stark contrast to the snow around them. Our lives were so sheltered in the dorms and academic halls, I had almost forgotten the Academy was a fully-functional Fleet base. This helped explain why only about a quarter of the grounds was dedicated to cadet activities. In fact, most of us would rarely venture to the western half barring special circumstances, like today's tour.

We ended the day deep in the southwest quadrant. A large dome hangar, much larger than Kurotar's, dominated the skyline. As we approached, I saw more and more ships coming in and out, but we made a landing on a large field of pads about a kilometer away.

"Welcome to the Academy's active spaceport."

Pell gave us a knowing grin, and we began our walk toward the impressive structure. This was clearly the highlight of the tour.

"This hangar can hold an entire Fleet force, except of course the cruisers. It's the second largest hangar in the empire, second only to Raviir Prime."

The closer we got, the more daunting it looked. I judged Kurotar's hangar to be about three kilometers in diameter. The Academy's had to be at least five. The arches forming the dome were tall and wide, made to fit the largest frigates. Even from this distance, I could tell the ships tapered outward like on Kurotar, with frigates in the middle and scouts at the edges. If the clearing full of shuttles was amazing, this was awe-inspiring.

My basic knowledge assessment and my time in Interplanetary Tactics had reminded me of the four types of ships present in the Fleet: light, medium, heavy, and capital. Light ships included fighters, bombers, scouts, and the like. Medium ships were almost exclusively shuttles, although some were designed for other uses. Heavy ships were known as frigates and acted as squadron flagships, commanded by a captain. The largest ships in the fleet were the capital ships, known as cruisers. Cruisers were so large they were constructed and operated strictly in space, with only one cruiser per wing, each helmed by a general.

While there would never be any cruisers here, I counted three frigates. They were the real jewels of the day, and we got to walk alongside one while Pell described a few of its features. At dinner, the hangar was the main topic of conversation.

"It's one thing to sit in IP and learn about the tactics but to actually see some of the craft up close... the frigates were huge!"

Several of the senior cadets smiled at Crim's enthusiasm.

"You've never seen a frigate before, Crim?" Tyla asked, surprised.

"Well, yes, but never in a hangar."

"Which one did you look at?" Wilor asked Pell.

"The scout," he replied.

Wilor raised his eyebrows.

"There's a scout frigate docked at the milport?"

Pell nodded with a smile.

"Why's that a big deal?" Grie chimed in, confused.

"Scout frigates are usually off on long-range missions. You lot just saw the rarest ship that lands in that hangar," Wilor explained.

After dinner, Drel and I continued the discussion in our room.

"Those scout missions must be lonely. Can you imagine being in space for decades at a time?"

I nodded. Scout frigates had to be outfitted with several unique capabilities in order to keep the entire crew alive for that long. But every once in a while, their efforts would be rewarded tremendously. It was up to scout frigates to determine a planet's habitability, check for resources in uncharted areas, and patrol contested borders in deep space—such as the one between the Terian empire and the Moffan Galactic Region, a border the Fleet considered the main entry point for MR agents.

A knock at the door interrupted my thoughts. Drel and I glanced at each other, neither of us expecting a visitor. She went to the door and opened it.

"Good evening, ladies."

Grie and Tyla stood just outside our room, grinning. What was this about?

"May we come in?"

Tyla shot a few glances around her. Whatever was going on, they were acting awfully suspicious.

"Sure."

Drel stepped aside, let our two divisionmates come in, and closed the door behind them.

"Okay, sorry for acting weird, but they told us to be careful."

They gave us a knowing look and Drel glanced at me, confused.

"What are you talking about?"

"There's going to be a party in the squad room tonight," Grie replied. "Second division invited all of third division."

"A party? Are you insane?" Drel asked.

Grie threw his hands up defensively.

"Hey, it's the second division's idea!"

"Who told you?" I asked.

"Wilor and Bett came by our room and Epore and Kulee's room," he answered. "They told us to tell everyone else. They're meeting in the squad room at 900."

I looked at my roommate and couldn't tell if she was more intrigued or terrified.

"Are you going?" she asked them.

Grie looked at Tyla before responding.

"Yes."

Several questions popped into my mind. I hadn't heard about any parties at the Academy, but it made sense that they happened. I wondered if they were common, or if this was, in the words of Drel, insane? How much of second division was involved? Was this some complicated joke?

"And if we get caught?"

I asked the question I thought most important, but Grie didn't have an answer.

"They said we won't."

Drel rolled her eyes.

"Oh, okay, then we're all good."

Sensing a bit of hostility, our divisionmates took their leave.

"Well, the invitation stands."

"No promises," Drel replied.

After the door closed, she looked at me.

"They're crazy, right?"

I nodded in agreement, trying to understand the logistics. A party in the squad room? Wouldn't the halls be patrolled? Weren't ID chip entries and exits logged and reviewed?

These thoughts followed me to bed, though I fell asleep without issue. At 950, however, there was another knock at the door.

I sat up and looked at my roommate, who gave me a look.

"Are they out of their mind?" she asked.

A second knock made me jump out of bed.

"I got it," I said.

"If it's those two again…"

But it wasn't.

"Robyn."

There was something off about Rolin's appearance, but I couldn't put my finger on it.

"Why aren't you at the party?" he asked.

"We didn't want to come," Drel answered for me, a hint of anger in her voice.

Rolin put his hands up.

"Ah, sorry, just wanted to know. You sure?"

He was answering Drel but looking at me. What was different about him?

"Yes, we're sure."

Drel had gotten out of bed and joined me at the door. Before I could say anything, she pressed the button to close it shut.

"Can you believe him? Coming here like that? He's going to get us expelled."

She went back to bed but I didn't move. I was trying to understand what I had just seen.

"What was wrong with him?"

"He's high, Robyn. They must have relaxants at the party."

Drugs? And these were cadets in the Fleet?

52

Breakfast was awkward the next morning. Drel kept quiet, clearly upset, and Rolin sat on the opposite side of the table, avoiding my gaze. It occurred to me this was a problem I couldn't ignore—such background conflicts could divide our squadron—and I spent most of my morning classes distracted, trying to come up with a clean fix. Unfortunately, while I had an idea of how to handle it, I wasn't sure I would call it clean. At lunch, I made a point to speak with Drel alone—I wanted a second opinion.

"Drel, I think I'm going to tell Pell."

She hesitated before responding.

"I don't know if that's a good idea."

I stared at her, surprised.

"Why not?"

She shrugged.

"If you tell Pell, they could get expelled."

I felt the frustration growing within me. Of course they could get expelled. Relaxants were extremely dangerous. She would rather have one of them develop an addiction and potentially endanger others? I could imagine the excuses: these were our friends, it wasn't necessarily our business... but I didn't agree. Our friends had made a mistake, and as members of the same squadron, it was our business. That kind of behavior was unacceptable for a cadet.

I sent Pell a message saying I needed to meet with him privately as soon as possible. He suggested after dinner, and I agreed. Until then, I had one more obstacle to overcome.

"Good afternoon."

"Good afternoon, sir."

I stood at attention in the familiar room, wondering just how many months I would have to come here. The entire first session? The entire time I was a student?

"Your defensive techniques are up to standard, but you can't survive on defense alone. It's time to implement offensive techniques."

As I processed her words she made a swift move unlike any other I had seen. I tried in vain to absorb the attack, but her hand was too quick, and I felt the familiar texture of the floor crash upwards into my body.

"As you may have noticed, my glove was too fast to match, but my body was not. A direct hit to the chest would've put me on the floor."

Slowly, I got to my feet, all of the weekend's recovery seemingly erased by one hit. Worst of all, something about her attack brought back the headache, emerging from the recesses of my mind as if it had never truly left.

She made another move and I tried to follow her instruction, to attack her directly, but the pain surged through my head, clouding my focus. Muscle memory took over, a muscle memory devoted to defensive response, and I hit the ground in convulsions.

The headache subsided, replaced by the pain of the hit itself, and I felt an anger come over me. What was going on? The commander had attacked me countless times since the episode in the infirmary, so why was the headache happening now? Was it because of the rifle exercise?

I got back up and tried again, but the pattern repeated itself: she made a move and the pain distracted me, forcing my trained response to take over. As frustrating as it was, I understood my weakness: everything up to then had taught me absorbing attacks was the only way to avoid them, so my reflexes acted against me. I had to unlearn what I had learned.

Time and again, the commander knocked me to the ground, but while I couldn't seem to switch tactics, I did notice the headache fading—with each attempt, my focus was sharper, and the pain was weaker. Still, I left class as battered as I had been the week before, without so much as one hit to the commander.

Sitting in the hovcar on the way back to Puric, it wasn't my failure that bothered me, but the familiarity of it all. I was here to avoid severe punishment, yet I was dealing with constant torture by a psychopathic commander. On top of that, I had to endure intense pain stemming from unexplained neurological issues, issues related to an unknown past.

I took a deep breath and tried to clear my head. While all of this was true, there were positive aspects to the choice I had made. In fact, I had an appointment with one of these positive aspects that very evening.

53

I ate my dinner quickly, wondering if the cadet-captain would join us or if I had to go find him.

"Meet me in the squad room when you're ready."

Pell's message arrived just as I took my last bite of goop, and I left right away, ignoring the curious look from Drel.

I found him at a desk, pouring over some information on the interface. He stopped when I entered, turning off the surface and looking up at me.

"What do you need, Robyn?"

"Sir, I need to talk to you about some of my squadmates."

He smiled.

"Again, Robyn?"

I gave him a confused look and he laughed, pointing at his bare head.

"We're in the squad room off hours, you can treat this as a capless zone."

I nodded and removed my cap, but stayed standing.

"It has to do with potential illegal behavior."

He sat up straighter, his smile disappearing.

"I'm listening."

"Last night there was a party here in the squad room. At least one cadet in our squadron seemed to be under the influence of relaxants."

It wasn't hard to say the words, but it wasn't necessarily easy either. Pell raised his eyebrows.

"Can you be more specific? You heard about the party, or you were there?"

"I wasn't there, sir. Drel and I were invited but elected to remain in our room."

He nodded.

"And it was when you were invited that another cadet exhibited these symptoms?"

"No, sir. We were invited and then about two hours later someone else came to our room. I noticed they were acting peculiar, and Drel told me it was drugs."

Pell gave a gentle smile before responding.

"Robyn, not only are you refraining from naming anyone other than Drel, you're giving me very circumstantial evidence. You did not attend the party and you did not actually see this mystery cadet taking relaxants, correct?"

I nodded.

"Yes, sir."

He sighed and relaxed in his chair. I waited for a few moments before he continued.

"Well, I should say you coming to me was the correct course of action, and I'm glad you did. I'm also lucky your account has so many gaps in it…"

He raised his hand as if to reassure me.

"Not that I don't believe you. But if you had irrefutable evidence one of our squadron was taking relaxants, that would very likely get them expelled and…"

He straightened once more, eyeing me intently.

"It would also ostracize you from the group completely."

He gestured to the chair next to him.

"Robyn, do you mind taking a seat? I may begin to ramble here."

He smiled and I felt a familiar rush as I sat down.

"Are you uncomfortable?"

His question was sincere, but it only made things worse.

"No, sir. Just confused."

He chuckled.

"Well first off, I already told you once, we're capless. You can quit calling me sir."

I nodded, ignoring my growing embarrassment.

"I just want to talk to you about something they won't teach you in Officer Training, or Weapons Training, or anywhere for that matter. You know the Fleet's one-word motto, of course?"

"Unity."

I had to fight not to say sir.

"Unity. Exactly. It seems so simple, so clean. But as with anything in this galaxy, it's not. In fact, it's neither."

His voice was soothing, calming. Was it always like this, or more so now?

"Robyn, between your secret past and the things you've done these first three weeks, I have no doubt you have a very decorated career ahead of you. But you have to be careful."

He locked eyes with me and I felt another rush.

"You are more experienced than the other cadets. You are faster, stronger, and, in some ways, smarter. You know it, I know it, and they know it. I can tell you're keeping a low profile, not getting in anyone's face, but that might not be enough. And therein lies the dilemma. How can there be unity when you are by and far the best? Of course they should support you, and hopefully, when they learn about your integrated commission, things will simmer down. But it'll never go away, not completely. Jealousy is ugly, and there's not much you can do about it. If it comes up, it comes up. If you feel the need to, you can always come to me. But as long as you aren't arrogant, don't let anyone's jealousy hold you back."

He looked to me for a response, but all I could do was nod. His words gave me mixed feelings. On the one hand, I was being reminded that I was different, but on the other hand, there was a hint of pride in his voice—I found it intoxicating.

"I'm sorry, Robyn. I know this is an uncomfortable topic for you, and I'm not saying you need to reveal your history to everyone just yet. In fact, I've digressed from what I was going to talk about, but it's related and I felt like I needed to mention it."

His expression was sincere, and I could tell he was a bit embarrassed. Somehow, that only made it worse for me.

"What I really wanted to mention was the dark side of our motto. A senior cadet takes relaxants and puts himself and possibly others in danger. A junior cadet comes to the ranking cadet-officer and explains the situation, while the others rally to shield him from repercussions. Which side is united?"

He took a deep breath and let it out slowly.

"It's a shame, really. These things happen more often than anyone would like to admit."

What things, I asked myself. Parties? Drug use?

"Who was the senior cadet you thought might be drugged?"

"Rolin."

Where I expected to see anger, I saw a moment's hesitation, and then relief.

"This might not be so bad after all."

Pell leaned in toward me, suddenly more animated.

"Listen, Robyn, I have an assignment for you. This is not one of my typical orders. I am honestly a bit ashamed to ask, but it's the best path to take."

I hesitated, surprised by this turn.

"Sir?"

He smiled, then continued.

"I need you to speak to Rolin yourself, privately, and voice your concern. Be honest with him, but make sure it's just you and him. Now—and this is the part you won't like—I also need you to keep our conversation a secret from him. Can you do that for me?"

I didn't understand. I was supposed to guilt Rolin? To what end? And what if he asked me directly if I had told anyone...

"Robyn, I need you to do this. For you, for me, and for Rolin. Okay?"

I felt cornered, trapped. His eyes pleaded with me. How could I say no?

"Yes, sir."

His smile unleashed another wave of endorphins and, for the moment, I ignored the repercussions of what I had agreed to.

54

"You talked to Pell, didn't you?"

Drel barely waited for the door to close behind me before starting her interrogation. I tried to read her expression, to see if she was upset or happy, but her face betrayed no emotion.

"I did, in private."

"And?"

I took a few steps forward and sat at my desk.

"And he wants me to speak to Rolin. Also in private."

Drel raised her eyebrows.

"He wants you to do his job?"

I shook my head.

"No, not like that. Rolin and I are close—the dynamic is different."

Drel pondered my words.

"So he's not going to be expelled?"

"Pell says since I didn't see anything directly, I don't have proof."

She nodded slowly, her expression still as guarded as ever.

"Fair enough."

I expected her to elaborate, but she turned to her desk and continued her work.

"Drel?"

She looked up at me.

"Are you upset with me?"

She held my gaze for a moment then shook her head.

"No. I do have one question though."

She leaned toward me, a coy smile spreading across her lips.

"Did anything happen?"

I stared at her.

"What?"

She leaned back, rolling her eyes.

"Oh come on, Robyn. I've seen the way you look for Pell when he's not at the table."

I felt the heat in my cheeks and did my best to keep my composure.

"What're you talking about?"

Her smile faded.

"Careful, Robyn, or I will be upset with you."

I sighed in defeat.

"Fine, yes, I like him."

She smiled in victory.

"Of course you do. You mention him in practically every conversation we have."

I sighed again, embarrassed. Was this really a necessary conversation?

"Okay, moving on," I said.

She wagged her finger at me.

"Nuh-uh, you still haven't answered my question."

I gave her an incredulous look.

"No, of course nothing happened! He's a senior cadet and I'm one of his squadron."

She shrugged.

"True, but you're also formerly-enlisted and he knows that, right?"

I nodded.

"See? You're not exactly a normal cadet."

Truer words had never been spoken.

55

It wasn't until 5day that I found a way to speak to Rolin. It wasn't that he was hard to find—I saw him at every meal—but I needed to speak to him in private, not with the entire squadron. Besides, ever since the weekend, there was a subtle change in behavior between myself, Drel, and

Rolin. Pell had noticed as well: he glanced at the three of us a little more often than usual.

At first I considered sending him a message like I had with Pell, but I didn't know how he would take it. Would he even answer? Would he just say no? I also considered catching him between classes or after a meal, but I didn't know what to say without putting him on the defensive. Not until 5day at lunch, when the idea finally came to me.

He was getting in line for food just as I arrived, and I managed to get right behind him.

"Rolin."

He tensed at the sound of my voice then turned to face me.

"You said you could help me with IP, right?"

His stance relaxed, but there was a hint of suspicion in his expression.

"You need help?"

No, but I wasn't going to lie. Just twist the truth.

"I want to sit down with you. Can we meet up today after dinner?"

He hesitated, and for a moment I wondered if I should have just lied.

"Sure."

He relaxed even more and I mirrored him, my own nervousness fading.

"Thanks. I just have a few questions."

He nodded and smiled.

"Of course. I'm happy to help."

And like that, the wall started to come down. During lunch we spoke more frequently, and during dinner things were almost back to normal. I caught Pell's eye and almost expected a wink, but he just smiled.

"You ready?"

Rolin pushed back his chair and grabbed his cap.

"Yes," I replied.

As we walked out of the cafeteria, I still wasn't sure what I was going to say. What exactly did Pell want me to convey? Disappointment? He had said to be honest, and that was how I honestly felt.

"Squad room okay?" Rolin asked.

I figured he might suggest that, but there was no way it was going to be private on a weekday evening.

"Is there anywhere we can go with less distractions?"

"Uh, no… not unless you want to go to one of our rooms…"

He seemed uncomfortable with the suggestion, but I didn't have a choice. I knew Drel was studying in our room.

"Let's go to yours. I haven't seen a second-division room yet."

"They're the same as yours…" he began.

"Drel's studying in mine," I replied, with a knowing look.

He nodded. That was enough to convince him. Now the question was whether or not his own roommate was there. Thankfully, when the door opened, an empty room greeted us. He gestured to the desk on the left.

"You can use Swir's desk, she's going to be in the squad room for a bit."

I nodded and sat. The room itself was almost a replica of ours. Rolin activated his desk then turned his chair to face me.

"So, what do you need help with?"

The eagerness in his tone brought a pang of guilt. But this wasn't for me, it was for him.

"Rolin, I haven't been completely honest with you."

He tensed again, concern marring his expression, but I pushed ahead before he could react.

"I wanted to talk to you about what happened this weekend. About you coming to our room."

His eyes no longer held mine, and anger started to replace confusion. I had to act fast.

"Please, hear me out. I respect you, Rolin. You've helped me so much these past three weeks. You've made me feel like a part of this team, and you've kept my secret, like I asked. I don't think you understand how much I appreciate that."

Some of the anger faded, and he looked me in the eye.

"Right now I need your guidance," I added. "I'm new here, I don't know what's normal, what's expected. I'm not planning to tell the entire squadron what you did or what anyone else did. Of course not. But I need to know, from you, the truth."

He sat back in his chair, less tense, but still guarded.

"What truth?"

"The truth about 10day. Was that normal?"

"You want to know if parties are normal?"

"I want to know if drugs are normal. Are they common at the Academy?"

The rest of the tension disappeared, and a sad smile preceded his words.

"They're not, Robyn."

He turned off his desk.

"You're right, you have a right to know. In a way I'm glad you came to ask me, and I understand why you weren't straightforward. If you had gone to Pell instead, this might have ended differently."

I betrayed no outward response, but I felt another pang of guilt, deeper than the last.

"Parties are not normal, no. It's rare that we have an opportunity like that, and we've been planning it for a while. We being myself, Bett, and Wilor. The three of us wanted to celebrate our second session together, especially after not seeing each other all specs. When the opportunity finally presented itself, we took it. Since we were already two weeks in and we liked your division, we decided to invite you as well. In some ways, I regret that now, and not just because of you and Drel."

He took a deep breath and let it out, then nodded to himself. Wherever he was about to go was clearly making him uncomfortable.

"We managed to get a hold of a bottle of relaxants. These were medical grade pills, and strictly prohibited. Getting caught having a party would have gotten us in trouble, yes. But with those relaxants there, everyone was in danger of getting expelled."

He looked up at me sheepishly.

"And then I decided it would be a great idea to come to your room under the influence. I'm sorry about that, Robyn. You're completely right. I'm supposed to be a role model, and I failed."

I knew at that moment he was asking for my forgiveness, and I took a deep breath before I replied.

"Rolin, I want to be a part of this squadron. If my fellow cadets have a party, it makes me uncomfortable, but it's not a big deal. Relaxants are. I can't force you to do anything, but if drugs are a part of your lifestyle, I have to keep my distance."

He shook his head as I was finishing my sentence.

"No no no, they're not a part of my lifestyle. Robyn, that was the only time I've ever used a relaxant. But it doesn't matter. You're right."

He chuckled, which caught me off guard.

"I can't believe this. I'm sitting here being lectured by my third-division partner. And she's right. You're right. I can't risk my career like this. You don't need to keep your distance. I tried it, it was a mistake, and I'm done."

He smiled.

"Thank you for talking to me, Robyn. I owe you one."

I smiled back, and stood.

"Don't mention it. I'll see you tomorrow at breakfast."

That wasn't so bad after all.

56

My entire third week, besides dealing with inter-squadron drama, I was being absolutely crushed by Commander Kelt in our special elective. All eight days passed with zero hits. I had fired a few times, but always too slow, always missing. And they were half-hearted efforts, because as soon as the beam started I knew I was going to miss.

At this point, the headache was gone, and it was hard to blame everything on muscle memory. Day after day, I saw zero progress. I wasn't hitting the ground less often—if anything, Commander Kelt's attacks were connecting more frequently. I kept waiting for some kind of instruction, some kind of direction, but the commander did little more than bark at me to get up. It was frustrating and painful, but a part of me was happy not to be knocked out.

As the weekend approached, I hoped for a break, for some respite from the pain. Rolin had said the third weekends were usually lighter, and I held onto hope all the way through 8day evening, when Pell pulled me aside before dinner.

"Robyn, I wanted to let you know: this weekend, you have a special exercise, separate from the rest of your division."

I gave him a curious look.

"A special exercise, sir?"

He nodded.

"I just got the news. All Puric students in Advanced Fitness are partaking in a special exercise this weekend. A few other members of our squadron will be doing the same thing, but it's an individual exercise, so you won't be with them or anyone else."

With these words, my hopes of a lighter weekend were dashed. Pell noted my disappointment and frowned.

"I'm afraid that's as much as I can tell you, sorry."

I nodded. This wasn't his fault.

"Thank you, sir."

He gave me a quick nod and left the cafeteria. Drel approached me, looking from the departing cadet-captain to me.

"Bad news?"

I shrugged.

"I'll find out tomorrow."

She nodded, then looked around and leaned closer.

"By the way, how was your talk with Rolin? Seems like it worked."

I shrugged.

"It wasn't as bad as I expected. I told him I was disappointed in him, and he agreed he made a mistake."

Her eyes widened.

"Wow, way to go. I don't know if I could tell a senior cadet to get their act together, even Swir."

I shrugged again.

"I just did what Pell asked me to."

She leaned back and gave me a coy smile.

"Of course you did."

I rolled my eyes and started walking to our table.

"I'm leaving now."

57

The next morning, I woke at my usual time with an unusual message.

"Reach the target location by 250."

Next to the words was a map, indicating a position just under 80 kilometers west of Puric dorm.

I leapt out of bed, threw on my uniform, and ran out the door. I was supposed to travel 80 kilometers in less than two hours—on foot, that would be impossible. A hovcar might get me there in time, but the Academy grounds were covered in pockets of dense forest. Depending on how the expanse between me and this location looked, even a hovcar might not be fast enough...

But I didn't have time to consider that. As I jumped down each flight of stairs, weaving around a few bewildered cadets, I sent a quick message to Pell, asking how to get permission to use a hovcar. The vehicles were typically reserved for officers, although I knew they sometimes made exceptions for cadets who asked in advance.

How long would it take to get permission? What if Pell was busy, or still asleep? Maybe I could flag down an officer on an errand? But why would they help me...

As soon as I was out the door, my eyes locked on the three hovcars parked in a neat row to my right. There wasn't an officer in sight, and Pell had yet to respond. If I waited, I would be late. But if I got in now, I might make it on time. So I hopped in the hovcar and started it up.

Apparently—and luckily—it didn't need ID clearance. I had watched the lieutenant drive me every evening to and from my sessions with Commander Kelt, and I was confident I knew the controls. I pointed myself west and took off, some of the nearby cadets watching me with mouths agape.

In my three weeks at the Academy I had explored enough of the surrounding area to know some of the hovcar routes. When I arrived on Alder I assumed these vehicles were only used in the open, grassy areas of the Academy, but I had since learned that was not the case. While they weren't useful in the heavily forested areas—which accounted for more than half of the grounds—they were used much more than I had realized. The problem was I didn't know if a hovcar would get me all the way to the target location. Even if it could, I certainly didn't know the hovcar routes all the way there.

So what did I know? I knew up ahead the trees would thin out a bit and I would hit a group of buildings, past which I had never ventured, except for the Academy tour. At that point, I was traveling blind. How would I know which routes went which direction? There were a few holes in this plan…

My thoughts were interrupted by a loud, low-pitch horn, followed by the hovcar's immediate deactivation. I gripped the seat as it came to a halt, not quite enough to launch me out but enough to knock the wind out of me. What just happened?

I composed myself and stood, turning to face the sound, which came from above. A small vessel hovered over the tree line, shining its lights on me as two members of the Fleet Guard leaned out either side.

"Stop right there!" one of them barked.

They were on a planetary patrol vehicle, a bigger and more powerful cousin of the hovcar, capable of long flights at high altitude—standard Guard issue. It came to a hover just above the ground and the two guardians hopped out, rifles aimed in my direction. Helmet visors hid their faces and amplified their voices.

"Do you have authorization for the operation of this vehicle?"

I shook my head.

"No, sir."

They stopped about a meter from the back of the hovcar, rifles still armed and ready.

"What are you doing with this vehicle?"

He pressed a button on the side of his helmet, lifting his visor. His partner remained covered.

"I'm trying to complete my assignment, sir."

"Assignment? Is part of this assignment to use a hovcar without authorization?"

"No, sir."

"Verified. Puric 7-17. Robyn, first-session cadet on integrated commission."

The other one spoke for the first time, then pressed the button to lift her visor. Both guardians lowered their rifles, and I saw their demeanor relax considerably. The first one looked amused.

"Did you forget where you were?" he asked.

I shook my head.

"No, sir."

He gave me a confused look.

"Cadet, I'm not an officer. Aren't you integrated commission?"

I realized my mistake—this man wasn't an officer, I shouldn't call him sir. Someone who was formerly enlisted would know that.

"Sorry, habit."

He nodded slowly, still confused.

"Right... now why did you steal this hovcar?"

"To complete my assignment."

He raised his eyebrows.

"As long as that star on your cap is empty, you don't have any of the privileges you had before you came here. You need to ask permission before you use a hovcar."

I nodded, trying to ignore my growing impatience.

"Sorry, it's been a stressful morning."

I glanced at the other guardian then back to the first one.

"I was given an assignment to reach a target location by 250. No other information was given. When I realized I wouldn't make it in time without a hovcar, I decided to take the appropriate actions to complete the mission."

They shared a glance and the man shrugged. The woman picked up the conversation.

"Cadet, you are not permitted to use hovcars without prior authorization except in case of emergency. Would this qualify as an emergency?"

"No, sir."

She gave me an incredulous look, and I looked away, embarrassed.

"Sorry, habit."

"What's the target location?" the man asked.

I shared the location with the guardians, just like Drel had taught me. They shared another glance, then the man turned to me.

"Hop in, we'll get you there," he said.

I hesitated. Did I hear what I thought I heard?

"What?"

"Don't make us change our minds," he added.

And with that, they turned around and walked back to the patroller. I jumped out of the idle hovcar and caught up to them.

The patroller had two doors on each side, a front half for the guardians and a backseat for passengers, willing or unwilling. There was also a significant amount of storage space below us, above the engines—all told it was about twice the size of the hovcar.

I hopped in the backseat and the door closed behind me.

"Why are you helping me?" I asked, strapping in.

The patroller started its ascent and the woman answered.

"You think we want all star-heads to be fresh out of basic? At least a former enlisted will actually understand who they're commanding."

"Plus," the man added, "when your superiors hear about the hovcar, you'll get in plenty of trouble, don't worry."

I sat back in the patroller, oddly satisfied with their explanation. This marked my first interaction with enlisted members of the Fleet—at least since my awakening—and it was much more positive than my first interaction with officers.

A quick glance at their shoulder patches told me one was a vice sergeant and the other a corporal. I wondered how often they had to take orders from star-heads, as they called them. The Guard was like any other segment of the Fleet, composed of enlisted and officers, with the former acting as enforcers and the latter as administrators. No doubt the dynamic could get strained at times, especially if they didn't follow the line rule.

As soon as we cleared the trees, the sergeant pitched the nose down and we shot forward at twice the speed I had managed in the hovcar. The good news was I would make it on time. But what would happen when I got there?

58

We spent most of the ride in silence, and I stared out the side window at the grounds below. The trees thinned out for a while, then returned with a vengeance, a thick forest of green covering the ground below. To the south, the mountains rose to snowy peaks, and I wondered what the edge looked like. The senior cadets had mentioned those sheer walls where the mountains were cut, and I got something of a glimpse in the shuttle from

Kurotar, but I wanted to see them up close. I wondered if I'd ever get the chance.

"We're ten minutes out," the woman announced.

I glanced at the read-out on my cuff. 212. I hadn't seen a building in several minutes, and only the occasional hovcar path broke the blanket of forest below. The sergeant brought the patroller to a stop over one of these openings, then dropped down to a hover about a half-meter above the ground.

"Here we are," he announced.

The side door opened, and the sergeant turned to look at me over his shoulder.

"Your target location is about 800 meters from here. Good luck."

I was already verifying his claim on my map and checking the time: 222, 28 minutes to spare.

"Thank you," I said.

He gave me a small nod, then a stern look.

"Don't let the filled star fill your head."

I nodded then got out of my chair, hopping out of the side door onto the ground below. The patroller started its ascent, its door closing as it cleared the tree line, then took off the way we had come.

The hovcar path was a cut sliver of forest, about fifteen meters of grass between two walls of trees. I glanced at my map one last time then entered the forest in front of me. Even with time to spare, I didn't want to take any chances.

A few minutes later, I saw the target location: a small, red circle on the forest floor—a false image projected onto my lenses. As I approached, I noticed not everything was a holograph: inside, lying on the pile of leaves on the ground, was a metal box about the size of my head.

I reached the circle and stepped inside, bending down to inspect the object. As I did so, a new message appeared in my lenses.

"Deliver the box to updated target location."

I glanced at the map attached and saw a position about 30 kilometers south of me, just two kilometers shy of the Academy border. I was taking this box up into the mountains.

In an attempt to temporarily forget the daunting task ahead, I closed the map and inspected the box, picking it up and feeling its weight. It was surprisingly heavy: at least fifteen kilos. Fifteen kilos up into the mountains? Great. At least there wasn't a time limit for this one.

Rather than let my thoughts wander, I pointed myself in the direction of the target location and started my trek. With the change in terrain ahead of me and the weight of the box, I should be able to reach the location before 850.

850! That was twelve hours away... twelve hours without food. I had skipped breakfast in my haste to reach the target and already I was starting to feel hungry. Still, thinking about it wouldn't get me there any faster. Right now I needed to walk—so I walked.

59

The first two hours passed much like my division's wilderness trek, and I found myself admiring the surroundings. I cut through several hovcar paths, but not once did I see another person or vehicle.

Around the third hour, the trees began to thin, and a soft incline let me know I was getting closer to the mountains. While the path had yet to bother me, the package in my hands seemed more awkward than when I had started. Its sharp metal edges dug into my gloves and slipped on the fabric, complicating an already difficult endeavor.

Soon I had to complete my first set of switchbacks, and the sharp elevation change slowed me down considerably. Still, the surroundings kept me distracted. The air was cool under the trees, and with the sun shining down above, the scenery was beautiful. Beneath my feet, rocks interrupted the soft ground, and I realized just how well the uniform's foot coverings protected me.

At some point around the fifth hour, I hit my first patch of snow and my first climb. Normally a climb wouldn't be a problem, but I had an inconvenient package I was dragging along, and I found it difficult to maneuver up a sometimes-slippery rock face with a fifteen kilogram metal box. Thankfully, I hadn't been told to care for the object, so I simply threw it above the wall then pulled myself up.

After the climb, I reached a small creek and bent over to drink some water. It was just past midday now, but the air grew cooler, even as the sun rose in the sky. This was a point I had forgotten, but the occasional strip of snow was now reminding me: as the day wore on and my altitude increased, the temperature would drop dramatically. If I was still walking when the sun went down, it would be colder still.

I took generous sips of the clean, crisp water, letting the sensation push my worries away. Were the other cadets in Advanced Fitness out in other parts of the Academy, each one facing an equally daunting task? Would we all meet at the target location, or did we all have our own separate treks?

Somewhere deep in the back of my mind, I doubted it. Somewhere deep in the back of my mind, I knew there was something off about this assignment, something weird. But I ignored this premonition and grabbed the box, heading up the mountain towards my destination.

I broke the tree-line about an hour later, pausing to admire the view. Snow-covered rocks dominated the mountainside ahead, with patches of green and blue plant-life fighting against the white powder. Turning around, I noted just how striking the tree-line was. There were a few smaller trees trying to take hold up ahead, but their efforts were in vain.

Over the next two hours, I faced several elevation changes, and I struggled with the box both uphill and downhill. I was truly in the mountains now, the same area I had flown over last weekend, but there were no buildings in sight. I knew if there was an emergency I would be able to find civilization—I had a map in my eyes, after all—but what about later on, when I was even higher up? Were there any buildings there? At least one, I thought to myself—the destination was marked as a small outpost deep in the mountains.

Two hours later, the sun slipped behind the peaks and the already cold temperatures started giving my uniform trouble. I had to stop every few minutes to put down the box and stick my hands in my armpits, fighting for extra warmth. Even through the gloves I could feel the cold metal on my fingers, and each passing minute only made things worse. The trees were long gone, and as if to spite me, the wind picked up as soon as the sun set.

I found a small shelter among some boulders and put the box down to give myself a quick rest. I wasn't having much trouble seeing where I was going, but Alder had no moons or close celestial bodies, so the sky was truly black. Only the sporadic glitter of the thousands of stars in the Terian empire lit her night.

Again, it was beautiful. It was cold and I was miserable, but it was beautiful. Beautiful and dangerous. I knew I couldn't stay out here much longer: the temperature was still dropping and my uniform was not keeping pace. I was about 5000 meters higher than the main grounds now; the difference at this height was hard to believe.

A rustle off to my left caught my attention. What kind of wildlife was on the Academy grounds? I hadn't really thought of Alder as harboring many animals, but if there were any they would likely prefer the green down below to the gray and white up here.

I stood and looked over the boulder, scanning the surroundings. The wind was even faster now, whipping at my hair and making it hard to keep my eyes open. Nothing. Nothing but the barren mountainside covered in a thin layer of snow, interrupted by boulders large and small.

I had been sitting for about five minutes—that was enough. I grabbed the box and continued, exiting my shelter and facing the cold wind.

Another rustle, closer this time. I paused. It came from behind me—I was being followed.

I put the box down on the ground and turned around. This time, I saw it: a large silhouette, about one meter tall and wide, on top of three limbs.

Whatever it was it wasn't moving, and it occurred to me it probably hoped I couldn't see it. It was definitely a creature of some sort, and I could make out what looked like a set of openings along one side of its body. Mouths, eyes, something else... I had no idea. The surface looked to be some kind of flat skin of a dark color, although I really couldn't tell from this distance. The variety of animals in the galaxy was staggering, and trying to make any educated guesses from over forty meters away in the dark of night was silly.

So why did it feel like I knew this animal? Why did I feel like I was in grave danger?

I took a step forward and it tensed. I took a few more steps, and it moved. Slowly, carefully, it dropped a bit lower on its limbs. I froze. It was in a position of attack.

I surged forward. There was no escaping now, I had to face the threat. The creature responded with an astounding leap, clearing over thirty meters, and was now aiming to land on me. I jumped to meet it in the air, reaching for two of its limbs, managing to lock on and send us both to the ground in a tumble. As soon as it had leverage, it kicked my arms with enormous force and I let go immediately. Those legs were strong.

I pushed away from it, another kick driving into the ground centimeters from my head. Scrambling to my feet, I tried to get a clear shot with my gloves, but the animal was very strong and very fast, and the cold was slowing my reflexes: I fired two arcs that missed completely. It braced for another jump and I dropped onto the ground just in time, sending it overhead, landing a few meters behind me. If it hit me with one of those jumps I would be dead.

For some reason, I was reminded of my sessions with Commander Kelt. But this thing wasn't the commander—if it knocked me out, it might just eat me.

The creature set up another leap, leaning into position, and I scrambled behind a boulder. That turned out to be a mistake—it jumped anyway, hitting the other side of the boulder and bringing it down on top of me. I heard a few loud cracks inside my torso and screamed in pain, the giant rock pinning me to the ground.

Just as the pain threatened to take me under, I noticed one of the creature's holes within reaching distance. Without thinking, I gave it a hard punch. When my hand made contact, I felt the same rush of heat as the first time I used the target sphere, and the creature gave out a screech, collapsing to the ground beside me. It kicked around in the snow, still smoking from my attack, then stopped, going limp. It was over. It was dead.

A surging pain came over my body as the adrenaline faded, replaced by the realization that I was pinned down by a boulder with several broken ribs. I tried to breath but this only made things worse, my shattered innards exacerbating the blinding pain. A faint light came into view, but I wasn't even sure if it was real. It seemed so far away, so distant, so… red.

And then the darkness took me away.

60

This time was different. When Commander Kelt knocked me unconscious, I was completely out until the moment I woke up. There was no grogginess, no hazy recollections. But now I was hearing things that didn't make sense, snippets of conversations that could have been real or imaginary.

"…why would they…"

"…was reckless…"

"…her suit…"

I would open my eyes to blurry surroundings then close them for indeterminate amounts of time. I knew I was being healed, knew I was somewhere safe, but I had no idea how I had gotten there, how I had been found.

Then I opened my eyes, the surroundings weren't blurry, and I had a brief flashback to my birth. Tubes were coming out of me, and I was in a medsuit. The room wasn't white or round, but black with a hint of red. It wasn't Kurotar but it also wasn't the room I had woken up in before.

I found I didn't have much trouble breathing. Was I already healed? How long had I been out? I was left to my own thoughts for about five minutes before a door opened and a familiar Fleet doctor came in.

"Hello, cadet."

"What happened?"

I almost barked the question at her, and she stopped in her tracks, eyeing me sternly.

"…sir."

She held her glare for a few more seconds before reprising her walk to my bedside.

"You broke seven ribs: a few clean fractures but mostly shattered. You're all fixed up now, and should be clear to return in two to three days."

As she spoke, she tapped on her tablet, her eyes jumping from me to the device.

"How did I get here?" Then, after a pause, "Sir?"

She eyed me with disdain and I thought back to what she had told me last time: it was best if she didn't see me again.

"You were brought in by two guardians."

She continued her diagnostics and I tried to digest that information. Two guardians? Out there, in the middle of the night?

"And the creature, sir?"

The doctor looked at me curiously.

"Have you forgotten your orders, cadet?"

It took me a moment to understand.

"Sir, Commander Kelt told me I could tell you anything I deem necessary. I deem this a necessary question."

She held my gaze for a moment then chuckled.

"Fair enough. The creature was a trone."

A trone. I had never heard of it. Or had I?

"How long have I been here, sir?"

"Four days."

She looked me up and down, the disdain reappearing.

"Any more questions, cadet?"

Four days? And I was already healed?

"No, sir. Thank you sir."

I nodded and she nodded in response.

"If you need anything, there's a small blue button by your hip that will call me."

Her tone indicated she would be less than pleased if I decided to do so.

61

I spent two more days in the hospital bed recovering my strength. The doctor checked on me intermittently, but I made no attempts to engage in conversation—I knew it wouldn't lead anywhere. With the rest of my time, I used the interface attached to my bed to complete assignments from my courses. While all of my outgoing communication abilities were suspended, I got enough messages from my squadron and my instructors to figure out they knew I had been injured and they knew I was on the mend. Why I wasn't allowed to respond I didn't know, but apparently that must have been addressed as well, as none of the incoming messages asked questions or expected a reply.

Despite this, Drel really outdid herself, sending me innocuous updates on a regular basis. I smiled each time I saw her name pop up, and I wished I could thank her—the coursework kept me busy, but her messages—

along with those from Rolin and other members of my squadron—
reminded me I had friends out there that cared.

But even with the coursework and the messages, I had plenty of time
to let my mind wander. This wild encounter was both terrifying and
intriguing. Once again, I was not a believer of coincidences, and finding
that animal out there then somehow being saved just in time?

No, it didn't sit right with me, but there was something that bothered
me even more: the subconscious familiarity. Something about that creature
was connected to my memory of Raviir, I was sure of it. Unfortunately,
this certainty did nothing to answer any of my questions, and I was too
afraid of outside monitoring to research trones myself.

I continued to worry about these things until the evening of the second
day, when Commander Kelt came into the room.

"Good evening."

I tensed unintentionally and winced—my abdomen still hurt.

"How are you feeling?"

She approached the bed, looking down on me with her familiar disdain.
I couldn't imagine her actually caring about how I felt—if anything, she
was asking in the hopes I was still in pain.

"Better, sir."

She nodded absentmindedly, eyeing the tubes around me.

"Good. You will be dismissed shortly for dinner."

The news made me smile, though I regretted it immediately:
Commander Kelt scowled, and her next words were harsher in tone.

"Your encounter with the trone will remain a secret. Your injury was
reported as an accident on the mountainside during the exercise.
Specifically, while climbing, a boulder pinned you down and broke your
ribs."

She eyed me intensely, leaning closer.

"Do you understand?"

I couldn't help but cower from her intimidating glare. Why did she hate
me so?

"Yes, sir."

Even after I answered, she stood over me, the fury clear in her eyes. There was a visceral anger behind the expression, something I had only seen one other time—moments before she had knocked me out. My heart pounded in my chest, pushing against my sore bones, but I barely felt the pain—I was watching her hands out of the corner of my eye, moving ever-so-slightly as if to attack...

And then her eyes glazed over, and the fury and anger disappeared. In that one brief moment, I saw it again: fear.

"The doctor will dismiss you momentarily."

She turned around and walked out the door before I had a chance to understand.

62

As soon as I reached the cafeteria, my questions washed away, overwhelmed by the welcome I got not just from my division but from the entire squadron.

"Robyn! Welcome back," Crim pat me on the back with a grin.

He pointed to my stomach and asked, "All better?"

I hesitated.

"Almost."

I wasn't all better, not yet. Even getting off the hospital bed was uncomfortable, not to mention walking up the stairs to the seventh floor. While it didn't seem too serious now, I had more than stairwells to tackle tomorrow morning, and I wasn't sure how Advanced Fitness would react to my injured state.

Thankfully, it reacted with a plan for gradual readjustment. My medical records had been shared with the instructor, and she and the system came up with a challenging but safe series of exercises to start getting me back in shape. It wasn't until my special elective that I felt the full extent of my injured state.

"Do you think your injury makes you special? Do you think your enemies will care if you're in pain?"

Commander Kelt changed nothing about her class, attacking me with clear indifference to my suffering. While her words made sense, I failed to see how injuring me further helped my lackluster offensive training. If anything, I was falling more behind.

The good news was that it was already 6day, meaning I had only two more days before the weekend. The bad news was this would be the fourth weekend—what Rolin had said were the hardest ones for my class. I made a point to find Pell in the squad room after dinner.

"I know you're not allowed to tell me details, but am I fit to complete the exercise this weekend?"

Pell gave me a concerned look.

"Do you feel you aren't fully recovered?"

I hesitated, then shook my head.

"Not if this is the hardest weekend yet."

He nodded, frowning.

"I checked the manifest. Medical has you toning down Advanced Fitness, but there were no changes to this weekend's plan."

He scratched his head for a moment, staring off into the distance, then met my eyes once more.

"Let me see if there's anything I can do."

I smiled.

"Thanks, Pell."

He gave me a curious look, one he had never given me before, and I realized this was the first time I had called him by name. My smile vanished, and he raised his eyebrows with a smile. He knew I was uncomfortable, and it made him smile…

I turned and walked out of the room, stopping abruptly in the hall—my quick exit had made my abdomen sore, and I gripped my side, trying to relax. Clearly, I needed to take it easy. I hoped Pell would find a way to get me out of the exercise, but when I saw him the next morning, his smile was gone.

"Sorry, Robyn. No change to this weekend."

I sighed. The hardest weekend yet and I was recovering from seven broken ribs.

"Still, I have some good news," he continued.

I looked at him curiously.

"I talked to Porr. She will be in charge of your exercise, and she agreed to take your condition into consideration. Hopefully that'll be enough."

I nodded. Porr was the cadet-colonel of our group—the one we had met on our very first wilderness excursion, during the shuttle ride. Rolin had said the fourth weekend was group-based for our class, so it made sense she'd be the one leading the exercise.

"Thank you, sir."

He smiled, then turned and walked away. At this point, the injury wasn't the only thing on my mind. While I was sure Porr was a capable leader and I was glad to have her aware of my condition, there was only one cadet-officer I wanted to see this weekend. Hopefully he'd be joining us.

63

Unfortunately, Pell was nowhere to be seen 9day morning, and it was Porr who led us and the three other third divisions of our group to another shuttle. Besides our cadet-captain's absence, the fourth weekend began much like the wilderness excursion and Academy tour: the same massive crowd of cadets marched to the same army of shuttles, and we even entered the exact same one—or at least one parked in the exact same spot.

Once we were in the air, Porr unveiled what we had in store.

"Cadets, your fourth weekends during your first session will be spent doing climate excursions: tours of various parts of the Academy—some natural, some artificial—meant to imitate some of the most challenging environments in our empire. For this first weekend, we're going into the mountains of the Academy for high altitude conditions. It's up to you to survive through tomorrow 600. After we are dropped off, no one is permitted to go below 4000 meters of elevation excepting an emergency. Are we clear?"

"Yes, sir!"

My voice almost cracked in response. We were heading back into the mountains, the same place I had just been attacked and wounded. Was this some kind of cruel joke?

Immediately, I faced a dilemma. While the cadets around me chatted about what we had in store, I could only think of the trone and the danger such an animal posed. Did Porr know about these creatures? Would we be warned about the possibility of dangerous wildlife?

I wanted to pose these questions, to alert my divisionmates to the danger ahead, but I was strictly forbidden from discussing my encounter. Did that mean hiding my knowledge of the existence of the animal as well? I wasn't sure...

It didn't take long to realize the cadet-colonel was tougher than Pell: while she let us chat amongst ourselves in the shuttle, her commands were more direct, her tone more curt. And when we landed in a light snow storm, she looked pleased.

"Ah, even better," she announced.

I worried this attitude might negate any reprieve Pell had negotiated for me, but as soon as we were out of the shuttle, she pulled me aside.

"Your cadet-captain showed me your records. While it is ultimately Medical's responsibility to clear you or not clear you for an exercise, I will keep it in mind when grading your performance. I suggest you communicate your situation to the other divisions."

Her words eased my fears, but they did nothing to ease the pain. Each breath of thin air pinched my chest, and as our group searched for shelter among the boulders, I struggled to keep up. The blizzard picked up after the first hour, and I could see the frowns pointed my direction—I was slowing everyone down.

"Nice and crisp, isn't it?" Drel asked with a smile.

I felt a pat on the back and saw Crim come up alongside me.

"Got a few complainers out there, want me to get rid of them?"

He shot me a grin and I couldn't help but smile. At least my division had my back.

It took another hour before we found a suitable refuge—an outcropping of boulders forming a small shelter. While the space wasn't big enough for everyone at once, it was well-protected from the blizzard, so we started discussing a rotation system. Before I could get a word in, Crim and Drel were pushing me inside.

"You rest, we'll take care of this."

I tried to protest, but they wouldn't hear it. Besides, as soon as I let myself sit down, I knew they were right—I was in far more pain than I cared to admit.

A few minutes later, more cadets came inside, including Drel.

"Good news, you're staying in here the whole time."

"But—"

She shook her head emphatically.

"No buts! You need to rest. We're going to try to find some food, and you get first dibs on that too."

"What do you mean she gets first dibs?"

Drel whipped around to face the other cadet, but someone had already put their hand on his shoulder.

"She's hurt Teer, just drop it."

He shook his head in anger, then stepped away. Drel turned back to me with a frown.

"The blizzard is getting worse. But some of the mosses might be edible. I'll be back soon."

I watched her leave with a hint of guilt—what was I doing to contribute to this exercise? Worse yet, what if there was another trone somewhere out there?

"How are you feeling?"

Deena sat down next to me as the shelter started to fill. I saw Crim trying to reach us, but there wasn't anymore room.

"So so," I replied, smiling.

I peered at her curiously. Not much had changed in the past three weeks; she was still the least outspoken of our squadron, though sometimes I wondered if being roommates with Crim exacerbated her perceived quietness.

"It was up here, wasn't it?"

She gestured to my abdomen and I had a moment's panic. Did my squadron know I was injured in the mountains? How much information had been shared? Then it hit me: they knew I was pinned down by a boulder, and there weren't many boulders down in the forest. I raised my eyebrows, impressed by her deductive reasoning.

"Yes it was."

She nodded absentmindedly, then glanced at the boulders surrounding us.

"I hope these don't move."

I followed her glance, eyeing the rocks that sheltered us from the dying storm.

"Me too."

We sat together in silence, but it wasn't long before I felt someone's stare. I looked up and saw the same cadet glaring at me, watching me from across the refuge.

I looked away, uncomfortable. Why had Drel been so vocal about my situation? Like Porr had said, I was cleared for this exercise, so why was I getting special treatment?

When the group came back with some of the edible mosses, I made a point to wait until they had been fully distributed. Deena bid me farewell —it was her turn to be outside the shelter—and Crim took her spot.

"How did you do that?" he asked, sitting down.

I gave him a curious look.

"Do what?"

"Deena. She opened up to you. I can't get her to say more than two words."

I shook my head.

"She barely said more than two words to me."

He looked up, watching her leave the shelter.

"Still, she seemed comfortable with you. I've never seen her like that."

I frowned, following his eyes to Deena. He was right, that was the most relaxed I had ever seen her, but the rest of the exercise, we didn't speak. Whatever had caused her temporary comfort, I didn't know how to replicate it.

64

We came back for dinner on 10day exhausted but proud of ourselves, and closer to the other cadets in our group—or at least some of them. While the one cadet had given me dirty looks the entire time, I couldn't really blame him—I hadn't taken the cadet-colonel's advice and mentioned the extent of my injury, so how was he supposed to know?

At first I thought pride had kept my quiet, but in truth it was caution— I was afraid of even talking about the situation, lest I say something classified. If one of my peers saw me in a negative light, so be it—that was better than the alternative.

Of course, none of this strategic silence granted me any sort of reprieve in Advanced Fitness the next morning, and I wasn't the only one in pain. Our entire division walked slower and talked less at breakfast on 1day.

"Feeling the weekend, are we?" Swir asked a clearly exhausted Drel.

She managed a nod in response as she hunched over her food.

"Don't worry, next weekend's easier."

Drel nodded, but she hardly needed the reminder. The fifth weekend was administrative, meaning we dealt with course changes, room changes, and command changes. While I was looking forward to the break, I couldn't help but worry about the room change: who would be my new roommate? While I was relatively comfortable with everyone in my division, I wondered what our absence at the party meant. I hadn't noticed any outward tension, especially after speaking with Rolin, but there were subtler signs: Tyla and Grie, the ones that had invited us, seemed to speak to us less. Maybe I was just overthinking it?

"Who do you think is going to be your commander?" Bett asked.

This weekend we would elect the first cadet-commander of our division. Unlike the higher cadet-officers, a cadet-commander remained a part of the division. It was a sort of stepping stone to the higher positions, a way to see if you wanted to continue down that path. A new cadet-commander was elected every month, although reelection of incumbents was common. Changes were even less frequent higher up the ladder: cadet-captains were chosen every 4 months, while cadet-colonels, cadet-generals, and cadet-admirals were chosen every session.

"Either Epore, Drel, or Robyn," Crim answered.

Drel laughed.

"Me? What about you? Don't give us that false modesty."

Before Crim could respond, Kulee interjected.

"Yea, no offense to my roommate, but the list is you, you, and you," she said as she pointed to Crim, Drel, and myself. "The three of you are the most active among the division, at least so far."

"None taken," Epore chimed in sarcastically.

"Some taken," Grie corrected with a laugh.

"It's division-voted, right?" Tyla asked Bett.

He nodded.

"Yep. Choose wisely! Look what we got ourselves into," he gestured toward Olla, who rolled her eyes.

These conversations continued through the fifth week, lifting my spirits while I tried to recover my strength. Commander Kelt's complete disregard for my injury made me fall behind on my Advanced Fitness trajectory, but by 5day I was seeing some progress: my movements were less stiff, my breaths less shallow. Everything continued on a positive trajectory until one particular, seemingly innocuous lecture.

In biology, we were spending one lesson on each of the seven animal kingdoms in the Terian empire. Today's lesson focused on the kingdom thought to originate mostly from Raviir, and my attention peaked at the mention of the planet. As if that wasn't enough, our instructor spent a good deal of time on one animal in particular.

"Trones are one of the most dangerous animals in the empire. Most biologists agree that trones evolved from ancestors originally on Raviir, before human colonization."

This was a big deal. Raviir outdated the Terian empire by thousands of years. Jump technology was not the only thing lost in all that time. As humans expanded across worlds, they encountered many new types of life. But they also brought many types with them, and depending on the planet, they made minor or major changes to terraform it. In the end, each planet was a complex mix of original species, introduced species, and human modifications.

"Their musculoskeletal system evolved with spring-like joints, allowing them to leap with great force over large distances. Their three legs are a prime example of interplanetary evolutionary convergence. Like many prime species, trones have two major leg segments with a joint in the middle."

Prime species were species thought to have originated or directly evolved from those of humanity's native planet. While our instructor continued to describe the trones, our lenses showed a holographic representation of one at the front of the classroom.

"These holes along the side are equivalent to mouths. Once a trone has neutralized its prey, it will lay on its side and absorb nutrients for several hours."

So I had shot it in the mouth? I had to admit just seeing the hologram was enough to make me uneasy, but my intrigue outweighed my anxiety. All this time I had been longing for Raviir, and a little piece of it had come to me.

I tried in vain to focus on the rest of the lesson, but that was out of the question. I wasn't surprised, of course—I had already known, at least subconsciously, that the trone was related to the capital planet. But having that information paraded in front of me and my classmates only seemed to make things worse.

I thought back to my second vision, my second memory: all that red, and the presence. Was that why I had recognized the danger, out there on the mountain? No, I realized. The presence wasn't that of a trone, it was of a person. But who?

65

9day morning was spent with Pell and the second division as they explained to us what it meant to be a cadet-commander. Every person in the division was given one vote. We would vote in rounds, eliminating the lowest-scoring candidate or candidates until there were only two choices left. At that point, a majority was needed to win. In the event of three ties in a row, Porr would come and choose for us. Pell emphasized that we didn't want to get the cadet-colonel involved if we didn't have to, especially since it amounted to chance—she didn't know us all that well.

We were given lunch to think about it but—in the words of Pell—not too hard.

"Make it clear to your divisionmates if you aren't interested. They may still elect you, but at least you told them not to. Remember, we have a new election every month, and this position is just dipping your toe in the pool."

Deena made it clear she wasn't interested, but she was the only one. The rest of us shared nervous glances during the meal, wanting to talk about it but feeling the eyes and ears of the senior cadets on us. When lunch was over, our division went back to the squad room with Pell.

"Okay, I'll share the vote to your lenses and you can make your selections immediately. It will refresh every round until we are down to two candidates."

Eight names popped up on the screen, including my own. I picked Drel. After a few moments the names disappeared, then reappeared. Deena, Grie, and Kulee were out. I picked Drel again. Another refresh, now Tyla was out. I picked Drel a third time. The list refreshed without her name.

Robyn, Crim, Epore. Now I was less sure. Of the three listed, I felt like I was the most qualified, but something about voting for myself seemed wrong. Pell hadn't said anything about that, but still… I chose Crim.

"Okay, we are down to the final two. Please choose wisely, as this may be your last vote."

The list refreshed. Crim and Robyn.

Robyn? I was on the short list? I hadn't expected that. I started to contemplate winning. Did I actually want this? Apparently not too much. I chose Crim again.

"Okay, that's it. Congratulations, Crim. You're now cadet-commander."

"Thank you, sir."

Pell shook his hand and it was done—we had a new cadet-commander. It had taken all of five minutes.

"Now I'm going to send you all of our performance averages. Please take a moment to look over them. If you have any questions, you can speak to me, send a message to an instructor, or do whatever you feel is necessary. Sharing your averages amongst yourselves is entirely up to you.

Some cadets are willing to talk about it and others aren't. Don't feel pressured either way."

The grades came in and I opened the message. APA: 98, MPA: 88, PPA: 92, CPA: 93.

I took a moment to process these numbers. The near-perfect APA was a pleasant surprise, but so was my military average. I had expected a lower number given my performances in military training; maybe I was catching up faster than I thought. Only the physical average was disappointing; I thought it would be at least 95, but I knew where the drop came from: my special elective effecting my Advanced Fitness performance.

Still, for someone who didn't think they'd make it through a day, a cumulative average of 93 was excellent. I had done it, I thought to myself. I had proved myself worthy of the cap, worthy of the Academy. Part of me couldn't believe it—Commander Hurren's superiors weren't so crazy after all—but right then, surrounded by my divisionmates, I didn't bother wondering how it was possible. I was here, I was succeeding, and for once, I was happy.

66

The rest of the afternoon was dedicated to course changes, if necessary. Since none of our division had any changes to make, Pell told us we could go off-cap in the squad room—in other words, we could relax. Crim asked if he needed to do anything, but Pell said they would discuss it after dinner. He left the room to us.

"So, how's it feel to be the cadet-commander?"

Tyla exaggerated her words as if she were in awe, and the rest of us laughed.

"Well, first off, you get to do the high altitude exercise again for that sass," he responded.

After some more laughter, he looked at me.

"Honestly I'm surprised you people chose me over her. What were you thinking?"

The laughter was a bit more reserved this time, with most eyes on me.

"I voted for you, Crim. There's more to leadership than taking high level courses."

My words were met with nods of approval.

"Okay but you do it next time, I'm already tired of it, deal?"

The laughter continued through the afternoon, and even Deena participated in the banter. This was the most fun I had had at the Academy—which, by extension, was the most fun I had had in my life. If I had had any doubts about my relationship with Tyla and Grie, that afternoon erased them completely. In fact, when we got our new rooming assignments and I saw I would be with Grie, we grinned at each other.

"This'll be interesting," he said.

"You know he's trying to catch up to you in fitness?" Tyla interjected.

I gave Grie a look.

"Really?"

He nodded with a smile.

"I've been upgraded to Fitness II starting 1day."

I raised my eyebrows, impressed. He was a month ahead of the average.

"Only two classes to go," Tyla added sarcastically.

He shrugged, but I was quick to defend him.

"Hey, I don't see anyone else moving up with him."

The teasing continued at dinner, where our good humor spread through the whole squadron. Everyone was enjoying the fifth weekend—some well-earned rest and reprieve. I rode the high all the way to its abrupt end: a notification, a message to report downstairs.

"What's wrong?"

Drel's hand was on my shoulder, and I saw the concern in her eyes. The rest of the squadron was starting to leave the table, some going back to their rooms while others headed to the squad room.

"Something came up," I replied.

I saw the confusion in her expression, but there was nothing else I could say.

"I'll see you in the room," I said, standing.

"Don't take too long," she quipped, smiling.

I turned around and headed out of the cafeteria, trying to control the emotions inside me. Why did it always have to be at the worst possible moment?

Still, I thought to myself, maybe I was exaggerating. I would get this over with and be back in time to spend my last night with Drel. I wasn't going to let Commander Kelt get in my head, was I?

67

"Good evening."

She stood in the middle of the room, eyeing me with a contemptuous smile.

"Good evening, sir."

The words came out, but the delivery was flat. Why was she ruining this perfect day?

"Congratulations on your first month. You have exceeded most of our expectations."

"Thank you, sir."

I watched her carefully. This was unfamiliar territory: would she attack me without notice?

"However, there is one area in which you continue to fail. You know what I'm referring to, don't you?"

I did.

"Offensive weapons training, sir."

She smiled again, and I felt the pit in my stomach, a premonition I tried to ignore.

"Offensive weapons training. Exactly. Tell me, how useful is a cadet who cannot effectively fire their gloves?"

I wasn't sure if it was a rhetorical question, but after a moment, she continued.

"Before you leave this room, you will show me you can use your gloves offensively. Activate them now."

I did as I was told.

"Now aim at me."

I felt a chill down my spine and the pit in my stomach grew. This again? I tried to lift my arm but something about the situation terrified me; I couldn't get my body to comply.

"Still having problems I see?"

I ignored her words, concentrating even harder on the task at hand. I couldn't let my previous experience affect me like this—I couldn't let her affect me like this. Finally, and with considerable effort, I was able to lift my arm, palm open and ready to fire.

This seemed to surprise her, and for a moment I saw hesitation in her eyes.

"Now fire on me."

Here it was, the opportunity I had always wanted. This woman, who had tortured and berated me day in and day out, stood undefended, ordering me to strike. So why, despite the bubbling rage I felt within me, did I struggle to fire?

My mind jumped to the last time this had happened, to the indescribable pain that had accompanied that moment. I didn't want to experience that again. No matter how much I wanted to fire on the commander, this memory refused to cooperate.

I dropped my arm, defeated.

"So be it," she announced.

The door behind me opened, and I turned to see the lieutenant drag a limp body into the room. When I recognized her face, my heart stopped, the pit in my stomach tearing up my insides. I watched, paralyzed by shock, as the lieutenant dropped Drel's unconscious body next to the commander.

"Leave us."

The lieutenant did as he was told, but my eyes were locked in horror on my roommate.

"Don't worry, she's alive. For now."

Commander Kelt lifted her arm and opened her palm, aiming directly at Drel...

Two white hot flashes of light erupted, one after the other, and a burnt odor filled the room. Both of the commander's arms were up, one facing Drel and one facing me. One facing me... mirroring me. My arm was up, palm open, pointing straight at Commander Kelt.

"Good."

The pain—searing pain. I stumbled to catch myself as it hit, but no one was attacking me. This pain was from within. And with it, clarity. The commander had fired on Drel with more power than I had ever seen and I had reacted immediately. I had fired on her, as commanded.

"Again," she announced.

I stared at her in shock, but she nodded toward Drel.

"Do it now."

I raised my arm and aimed at her open palm. There was a hint of resistance, but most of the weight was gone. I didn't want Drel to be hurt again.

"Too long."

Another two flashes in rapid succession, but this time the commander staggered backward—she had dropped her hand on purpose. I braced for the pain but it was a shadow of its former self, nothing compared to what I had just felt.

"Better."

Once again, her expression didn't match her words. I saw an anger in her eyes and wondered why in the world she had dropped her arm.

"Next month our lessons continue, but I expect you to fight back. If not, we will have to do this again. Is that understood?"

I wasn't able to answer. This afternoon, I was laughing with my squadron. Now, because of me, my best friend was lying unconscious, having suffered two direct hits at the hands of this psychopath.

"Cadet, I asked you a question. Is that understood?"

I nodded.

"Yes, sir."

"Good. You're dismissed."

I hesitated, glancing at Drel's body.

"She will join you tonight, unharmed and none the wiser. I don't need to tell you this entire event is to remain strictly secret?"

I felt the rage within me threatening to lash out, ready to make up for all the hits I hadn't given her... but I held my tongue.

"No, sir."

Next time she asked me to attack her, I would be more than happy to oblige.

68

I was returned to my dorm without a word, my anger turning into nausea. The lieutenant avoided eye contact; he didn't bother to see if I gave him a cursory nod, and I didn't bother to try.

I sat in the room feeling sick and restless, waiting for Drel's return. Finally, about 30 minutes after my arrival, she walked through the door.

"Are you okay?" I asked, shooting up out of my seat.

My concern took her by surprise.

"Wow Robyn, what did they tell you? I'm fine."

Words stumbled through my brain, trying to form a cohesive statement —first the truth, then a lie... the nausea and pain hit me, and I fell back into my chair, overwhelmed by a whirlwind of emotions.

"Are you okay?" she asked, concern in her eyes.

Now Drel was worried about me. This was too much.

"I'm fine. Tell me what happened."

She shrugged.

"Doctor says my glove malfunctioned. Apparently I shocked myself so hard I passed out in the hall! Someone saw me and took me in, they checked me out, woke me up, and here I am."

A glove malfunction? Passed out in the hall? I wanted to scream the truth at her, to tell her to run away from here. But where would she go? Would she even believe me? I was having trouble believing it myself.

"Robyn, are you okay?"

I was gripping my forehead again.

"Yes, just…"

She gave me a concerned look, and I pressed on.

"…your glove misfired? Did they tell you why?"

She shrugged.

"They didn't know, but I'm not too worried. They gave me a new pair and did a brain scan—nothing abnormal. I have another checkup tomorrow morning just in case."

I nodded absentmindedly. Was this the life I had chosen? Was this what it meant to be a cadet at the Academy? That night, for the first time in my life, I didn't sleep.

69

At breakfast the next morning, everyone else in my division was carrying the excitement from the day before and looking forward to their new rooming assignments. It was the same table, with the same people, yet for me, everything was different. Every time I laughed, it was without conviction—a half-truth. Commander Kelt would be pleased. I could almost see her smug smile now—the thought made me sick.

After breakfast, I gathered my things, ready to move into my new room with Grie.

"Hey, you sure you're okay?"

Drel's concern was almost too much to bear.

"I—I don't want to leave."

It was true—I felt like I was abandoning her.

"If this is about last night, Robyn, I promise I'm okay."

I frowned. If only she knew the truth…

"Listen, before you go, I wanted to thank you again. You've made the first month here so much better, and I'm going to miss rooming with you."

There was a sincerity in her words that managed to break through my suffering, and a flicker of warmth took hold inside of me.

"You know, you didn't end up proving me wrong," she added, smiling.

This callback to our first day together helped reinforce the feeling, but before I could reply, Epore walked in.

"Hey Robyn. Do you need more time?"

I glanced at Drel.

"No, Epore, you're good."

With my handful of personal items in hand, I left my old room and walked into my new one.

"Hey Robyn!"

Grie, for one, seemed excited to have me.

"I start tomorrow," he added.

I put my stuff on the bed and looked at him.

"Pardon?"

"Fitness II. I start tomorrow."

"That's great," I replied, starting to arrange my things.

"Do you have any advice?"

I paused, surprised by his enthusiasm, but when I looked in his eyes, I saw a mix of respect and friendship that helped fuel the warmth Drel had ignited. To Grie, I was still the same Robyn—between yesterday and today, nothing had changed.

"Of course."

I spent the rest of the morning preparing Grie for his new course, embracing my role as mentor, and by the time we left for lunch, I was feeling much better. At the table, Drel sat next to me and whispered in my ear.

"I miss you already. Epore is kind of a pain in the ass."

I held back my laughter as she cleared her throat. Her new roommate took a seat on the other side of me.

"Is she talking trash already? Damn it woman I told you I didn't mean to knock into you."

We laughed some more, and this time I meant it. Pell took his seat at the table.

"Everyone settled in?" he asked.

We nodded.

"Yes, it took me hours," Grie quipped.

He hadn't actually changed rooms, Tyla had moved out and I had moved in.

"Careful, you're with Robyn now, she'll whip you into shape," Tyla replied.

"Fitness II will whip him into shape," I responded.

"What do we have the rest of the afternoon?" Epore asked, looking at Pell.

"For you? More down time."

"Really?"

Pell laughed.

"Really. Enjoy it, this only happens once a month."

We did. I did. It was true, the weekend had changed me, but it was nothing compared to how the month had changed me. I had many questions left to answer: some about my past, others about my future… but at least one of them, I had already answered.

Did I belong here, as a cadet, in the Academy? Yes, yes I did.

70

Unfortunately, feeling like I belonged didn't excuse me from my special elective, and I spent all of 1day dreading the inevitable. It was a sad type of deja vu, even worse than after I had been knocked out: as the day went on, a growing nausea overcame me, and by the time I reached the hovcar, I felt like I was going to puke.

The lieutenant avoided my eyes as I got in, but the sight of him brought back images I didn't want to remember: the commander, Drel, the white-hot flashes of light…

I leaned out the side of the moving hovcar and emptied my stomach on the grounds below. Some of the vomit splattered against the side of the vehicle, and I expected some kind of reprimand, a reaction from the lieutenant, but none came. He remained silent as ever, still avoiding my eyes when we reached our destination.

"Good afternoon."

I found myself struggling to look her in the eye, but the fury within me persevered. If I looked away, she'd win. She'd smile that smug smile and after everything she had done… I wouldn't let that happen.

Commander Kelt didn't even wait for me to respond, making an elaborate move to set up an attack. But something was different this time. This time I was ready.

I fired at her center of mass decisively, and she failed to catch it, falling to the ground in convulsions. A sharp pain rushed through my head but I was ready for that too—I fought against the feeling, focusing on the satisfaction of my hit. It was the first time I had knocked her down in class, ever.

"Good job."

The words came through clenched teeth, and I knew I had surprised her. In the only way I knew how, I was exacting my revenge, retribution for what she had done to Drel. It didn't make up for what had happened, but it was the best I could do.

She got to her feet and our dance continued. It was a relatively even match that first day, with each of us hitting the other many times, but I knew I could do better. Part of the problem was I was fighting two battles simultaneously: one against Commander Kelt and the other against my trauma. With every hit, images of an unconscious Drel passed through my mind, clouding my focus and slowing my movements.

Still, over the course of the week, things improved. The continued distractions of my friends and classes helped ease my inner suffering, and each time I entered my special elective, I managed a few more hits, a few more blocks. Of course, I had to ignore the root of my improvement—that the trauma I had endured was the only reason I was getting better.

This was a weight I had to bear, and one I had to keep secret. I only hoped the rest of the cadet experience could make up for it.

71

On the opening weekend of the new month, Crim had his first major test as leader of our division. We were competing against the other three third-class divisions in our group in what was essentially a larger version of the rifle exercises we had done as a squadron. All four cadet-captains were there to make sure we knew the instructions of each exercise, but it was the cadet-commanders who made the tactical decisions.

There were two key differences between this exercise and the last: one, our play zone was quadrupled in size, and two, the gloves were included, forcing us to use both weapons as necessary. Oh, and since the gloves were in there anyways, they activated the rifle shock.

All told it made for a very painful experience. During the first round of exercises, the four divisions started at each of the four edges and played until only one division was left. We were repeating this process until one division won three games total. After the fifth round, the winners were 18th, 17th, 20th, 17th, and 20th.

Crim gathered us in a huddle before the start of the sixth round.

"Okay guys, either we win or 20th loses, but I prefer the former. Tyla and Epore, I want you up ahead again, but take the left pipe instead of the wall and try to get as many as you can from there. Cover for Grie and Deena, who will come up and around the left. Stay hidden as long as you can. Kulee and Drel, take the right as best as you see fit. Robyn, you're with me. We'll hold back, then Tyla and Epore will cover us into the other quadrants."

He was starting to get better at this. The timer on our lenses read 34 seconds until the start of the next round.

"How long do you want to hold back, sir?" I asked.

He didn't seem to hear.

"Sir?"

"Ah sorry Robyn I'm still getting used to the sirs. 30 seconds, give or take. On my mark."

I nodded.

The timer reached zero, and the rest of the squadron darted off. I held back in a crouch next to Crim with my rifle up and scanning, waiting for his mark. Our displays showed the current standings of each division. So far, 3 people had been hit, none from 17th.

"Mark."

He called it right at 30 seconds, rushing forward to the first wall, and I noticed someone in our division was out. My lenses just had the numbers, but Crim's told him everything.

"Deena. Our cover is secure."

We sprinted to the next major stopping point, almost halfway into the zone. I saw Tyla and Epore scanning behind us from a nearby pipe. Someone popped up a few meters away—I aimed and hit.

"Thanks, Robyn," Tyla announced, her voice sounding off in my head.

"Don't mention it."

My reply wasn't very loud, but I knew she had heard it: all of us were wearing our earwigs, small devices that extended from the edge of our caps into one of our ear canals. With them on, we were able to communicate verbally instead of typing messages on the lenses. The earwig was designed to pick up sounds from inside the ear canal rather than the environment, meaning ambient noise was excluded. Of course, we were still getting used to them, and with an open channel, every once in a while…

"Got you, son of a—"

"Grie, cut it out we can all hear you."

"Sorry sir!"

Nine people out so far. I was waiting for Crim to give the signal to go into enemy territory.

"Robyn, now!"

We jumped out from behind our cover and I prayed Tyla and Epore were paying attention. Crim shot off to my left while I went straight to a large wall, bracing against it and scanning my immediate surroundings.

Nothing, nothing, someone jumping out right next to me, them lifting their arm, my rifle dropping, my hand coming up, absorbing their hit, responding with my own, and they were down.

"Holy shit, Robyn."

Epore's response let me know he was watching but I ignored his comment, lifting my rifle and turning around to finish my scan.

"Hey… Hey!"

The tone in Epore's voice tipped me off and I twisted back around, dropping my rifle and raising my hand instinctively to catch another hit from the downed cadet.

"Game over, report in!"

Pell's voice came over the earwigs and our lenses went blank, the numbers and data replaced by a large, red 'ABORT.' I saw the cadet gear up for a third shot and prepared to absorb it.

"STOP RIGHT THERE!"

A cadet-captain jumped between us and someone grabbed my arm.

"Come on."

Pell pulled me away while the other cadet-captain started yelling at my attacker. I saw Epore and Tyla staring at them, mouths open wide.

"Epore, Tyla, back to the start point, now."

Pell's voice was harsher than I had ever heard it. I looked back over my shoulder at the cadet, remembering the last time I had seen him, the glares he had given me during the first climate excursion...

Pell took us to the start point, and Crim was there half a second later.

"Sir, I'm sorry, I should have—"

"That's enough, Crim."

Crim shut his mouth and Pell sighed, putting a hand on the cadet-commander's shoulder.

"This had nothing to do with you. You did everything you were supposed to do."

He took his hand off Crim and looked back the way we had come.

"I want everyone to wait here while I talk with the other cadet-captains. Understood?"

"Yes, sir."

He took his leave and everyone stared at me.

"Are you okay?" Drel asked.

"Okay? She destroyed him!" Epore answered.

"Let her answer," Crim replied.

There was concern in their eyes, but nothing had happened to me. I guess I could thank Commander Kelt for that.

"I'm fine. I didn't—"

I hesitated, and their curiosity intensified.

"You didn't what?" Drel asked.

"I didn't even realize what was happening."

Epore shook his head in disbelief.

"See? What'd I say? Destroyed!"

"Wasn't that the guy that gave you attitude on the climate excursion?" Drel asked.

I nodded.

"He should be expelled," she said.

"Unbelievable," Kulee added.

Pell came running back, much quicker than any of us had expected.

"Okay, we're going to take a 10 minute break. Robyn, come with me. Everyone else, stay here."

I started to follow him but he stopped and turned around.

"After the 10 minute break, we will restart the sixth game. Are we clear?"

He looked at Crim, who nodded back.

"Yes, sir."

Pell led me to the middle of the zone, where the other cadet-captains were deep in conversation. One of them—the one that had jumped between us—stepped forward.

"Robyn, I want to apologize on behalf of 20th squadron. Teer's behavior was unacceptable, and he will be punished accordingly."

I nodded.

"Thank you, sir."

Pell turned to me.

"We spoke with Porr and she spoke with Cife. We are ejecting Teer from the exercise, and Porr is on her way to pick him up. Cife asked to give you a choice: you can continue or you can opt to take the rest of the day off. What do you prefer?"

Cife—this had gone all the way up to the cadet-general of 7th Wing.

"To continue, sir."

"Okay then, you'll continue. Return to your division and await the start of the sixth game."

I nodded and did as I was told. 20 minutes later, we won the sixth round and the exercise.

72

Teer was back at his squad table that evening for dinner. I didn't notice and, to some degree, I didn't care. But many of my divisionmates were furious, especially Drel.

"What the hell is he doing back at the table? Crim, can you talk to Pell about this?"

Crim hesitated.

"I can try, but I don't know what he can do."

"He should be expelled, don't you think?" she asked.

Crim shrugged.

"I don't make those decisions, and neither does Pell. Hell, neither does Cife. We're all pretending to be officers. Real officers make those decisions."

His eyes turned to me.

"Not that I don't think he should be. What he did was unacceptable."

Drel was winding up for a response but I cut her off.

"Can we not have a fight over this?"

Drel looked at me and then nodded.

"Can I ask what's going on?" Rolin interrupted, quietly.

I looked around the table at the others.

"Someone else, please. I'm tired of it."

Once again, I was the topic of discussion—or was it Teer? In either case, I was over it. While everyone else was obsessing over what had happened with the cadet from 20th squadron, I was obsessing over my seeming lack of pain.

All day, I had used the gloves and felt the rifle shock, and not once did a headache overpower me—as far as I could tell, the only pain I felt was from the hits themselves. Had one week of training with Commander Kelt, combined with a horrible, traumatic experience, cured me of my ills?

No, I told myself, this was different. In my special elective, I had trouble shooting because of where I was and who I was with—each attack was a reminder of that wretched experience. But outside, with my division and group? There, I didn't have to relive the terrible nightmare from a week ago. There, I was just a cadet like any other.

No, I realized, that wasn't true either. I was still an outlier among outliers, I just didn't want to admit it.

73

The next day we played similar games, but 20th squadron was down one man. While I focused on the task at hand, I had to admit I was glad to see Drel relax. I assumed the issue was handled and would soon fade into the background, but I was mistaken.

Going into the second week of the second month, some of our military work was at the group level or higher, which included Teer. I had no trouble ignoring him—after all, he was nothing compared to Commander Kelt—but when I caught him staring me down during two or three meals, I thought it best to send Pell a message. He agreed to meet me in the squad room after dinner on 6day.

"Robyn, how can I help you?"

I took a seat next to him like I had at our previous meeting. This time, a few other squad-mates were in the room, including Crim and Drel, and I felt silly for not specifying a private meeting.

"It's about Teer."

I kept my voice low, and Pell replied in kind.

"Has he done something?"

"No, but I'm worried he might."

He gave me curious look.

"Do you know why he attacked you?"

I told him about the first climate excursion and he frowned.

"That seems excessive," he said.

I nodded.

"I agree, and I don't understand."

He sighed.

"Robyn, this is exactly what I warned you about. He finds you threatening for whatever reason, and he's acting out. Unfortunately, there's probably a whole squadron that will argue Teer is a good guy, cadet material. He made a mistake, but doesn't everyone?"

He raised his eyebrows to emphasize his sarcasm.

"I'm biased so I disagree—I want him expelled—but it can't work that way. After all, they could be right. Maybe he was having a bad day? Plus, he didn't actually hurt you."

Pell paused, shaking his head.

"I shouldn't try to excuse him, but you get the point. Right now, there's nothing we can do. But if anything happens, you let me know immediately, okay?"

I nodded, frustrated by the conversation. It wasn't so much I was worried about Teer attacking me, but more so that I didn't understand why. Was this really just a reaction to the climate excursion? As Pell had said, it seemed excessive.

And while I hesitated to match Drel's level of anger, I had to admit I was curious about his seemingly light punishment. What did it take to get expelled from the Academy? Relaxants, attacking a fellow cadet... or just willfully withholding information about a pair of blurry memories?

74

The second weekend of the second month, we had our first snow at the dorms: a light layer of white powder that hinted at what was to come. I had worried the squadron-based exercise might include 20th, but we stayed within the confines of 17th, the upperclassmen teaching us how to use special watersuits.

During my third week, my academic courses expanded into new areas. As Wilor had told me, biology went beyond the boundaries of the Terian empire, describing and explaining all sorts of creatures throughout the galaxy. Communication Analysis stayed at the bottom of my list, although the occasional glimpse into Terian dialects and translation caught my attention. My morning OT course was starting to cover more and more obscure topics, but it was Interplanetary and Terrestrial Tactics that had really taken off. These two courses presented a major challenge, and it was one I was enjoying every step of the way.

It was also during the third week that I really started to get along with Grie. We had already bonded over his fitness upgrade, but during the first two weeks I had made a point of spending meals next to Drel, or meeting her in the squad room—no doubt spurred by subconscious guilt over a partially repressed memory.

Yet it wasn't just guilt that drove me to Drel: where my best friend complimented me on my aptitude, Grie seemed more in awe. Was it because of Advanced Fitness? I couldn't remember this admiration before we roomed together, but I also didn't pay him as much attention then.

In the end, I learned to embrace his respect for me and became something of a big sister to him. It was certainly preferable to what Drel had to deal with.

"Robyn, is Grie hitting on you?"

"Hitting on me?"

I gave her an amused look.

"Yea, you know, the thing you do with Pell?" she fired back.

I shot a glance around the squad table but most of the seats were still empty.

"Drel!"

I hissed at her, and she put her hand up in apology.

"I'm sorry, it's just Epore is getting on my nerves. For real this time. I think he and Kulee had a thing going as roommates but I'm not interested."

I glanced across the room at Kulee, in line for her food.

"Well, did you tell him that?" I asked.

She shrugged.

"I did and he goes to see her and it stops for a few days until one day it starts over again."

Relationships at the Academy were strictly prohibited. If Drel was right and Epore and Kulee were breaking the rules, they had to be discreet—especially since Kulee was now rooming with Crim.

"Next time he does something maybe you should casually mention Crim?" I suggested.

"As in, I might tell on him?"

Drel frowned, clearly turned off by the idea, but I pushed on.

"Yes. First off, it's only an implication, you don't have to go through with it. And an implication should be enough. Secondly, it's better than saying you'll go to Pell or Porr—or an actual officer."

I could see the wheels turning in her head before she nodded slowly.

"Besides," I added, "you saw what happened when I talked to Pell about Rolin. It all worked out."

She peered at me, some of her frown returning.

"Yea, but there were other reasons that worked out."

I gave her a look.

"What do you mean?"

She looked around at the ever-filling table, where our whispers were becoming less effective, then shook her head.

"I'll tell you another time."

75

For our third weekend, the wing cafeteria was repurposed as a presentation hall. Officers from around the empire came to explain some of the careers available in the Fleet and which academic tracks would lead where. On the second day, we were given the freedom to chat with them, but I knew better than to assume I had any say in that decision.

"You don't have anyone you want to talk to?" Grie asked during a break.

I shrugged.

"Not really."

He peered at me.

"You know, your skillset would make you valuable to many of these sections…"

I smiled, contemplating the future my mysterious superiors had plotted. All this intensive training, surely Commander Kelt and Commander Hurren had something lined up for me? Maybe an appointment with SOD? Where was their table, I wondered.

"Thanks Grie, but it's too early for me to know."

He shrugged.

"Fair enough."

"And you?" I asked. "Any of them catch your eye?"

He nodded.

"I've actually been thinking about Infantry."

I raised my eyebrows.

"Terra, huh?"

He nodded again.

"Yea, but maybe that's because I haven't piloted a ship yet. Hard to say."

There were certainly advantages to the Infantry. For one, their members typically saw much less action—it was a statistically safer career path. The only problem was when they did see action, it was almost always deadly. And with the uptick in terrestrial terrorist attacks, those statistics were changing.

"You're not in terra tactics, are you?" I asked.

He shook his head with a frown.

"Yea, that's the other problem. I don't think I can handle double-dosing, but I also wouldn't want to start terra too late. Oh well, I have some time to think about it."

I looked at all the stations set up around the cafeteria and wondered how many of these officers were actually involved in the areas they presented. Most had warm smiles and engaging voices—they were chosen for a reason, and it wasn't for their knowledge.

I had seen the Fleet as an outsider—there were no warm smiles there. In fact, I thought, I had seen the Fleet from the inside too—deeper than most. And that was even worse.

This brief bout of introspection brought my existential crisis front and center, and I realized just how deeply I was falling into this routine, into this life. Yes, I was desperate to fit in, to feel like a cadet, but at what cost?

Three weeks had passed since the incident at the outpost—three weeks during which my offensive tactics saw marked improvement. At first, I had channeled my anger into the lessons, telling myself I was exacting some kind of revenge, but deep down, I knew this was a lie.

Each improvement I made with the gloves marked another victory for Commander Kelt. Every time I hit her, every time she hit the ground in convulsions, was another justification for her vicious and terrible act.

I had been worried my life after the Academy might turn me into a broken woman, but now I realized it could happen well before I graduated. War wasn't the only thing that could turn a cadet into a monster.

76

"Ready for the weekend?" Drel asked.

It was 6day evening of the fourth week, and I was back in the squad room with Drel, Grie, and Tyla. There was something particularly inquisitive about my former roommate's tone.

"Fine, why?"

"It's the group exercise," Grie interjected, not looking up from his desk. "She's talking about dealing with Teer."

Drel kept her eyes on me, waiting for a response.

"Still fine," I replied.

She frowned.

"I don't know, Robyn, I've seen him glance over at you one too many times during our drills."

"I know you think she's overreacting but I've noticed too," Grie added, still working on the active surface.

"Are you actually working or pretending to work?" Tyla asked.

Grie looked up.

"Pretending."

We laughed.

"So you're not worried?" Drel persisted.

Grie answered for me.

"Drel, I know you care about Robyn, but think about it: if Teer does anything, he's out. Last time he got away with it, but there's no way he can get away with it twice. Plus, it's Robyn. He didn't even faze her last time, that's the whole reason he freaked out. If I were him, I'd be keeping a low profile."

Drel considered his words, not quite convinced.

"True, but you're not him."

Grie shrugged.

"I guess we'll find out in three days then. Until then, I have work I need to pretend to be doing."

Three days later, we were in the shuttle with cadet-colonel Porr, and I hoped for Grie's sake he had gotten his actual work done—the climate excursions didn't really give us any free time.

"This weekend we will simulate the conditions of Devra," Porr announced. "There's a special training facility in the northwest quadrant built specifically for this purpose. I hope you got a good night's sleep."

Devra was one of the least habitable planets in the empire. Its revolution and rotation lined up almost perfectly, so each day—and each night—was over three years long. They were such an anomaly, they didn't bother using their own time system—everything ran on Terian time.

As an added bonus, the never-ending day saw extremely high temperatures, and the equally prolonged night dipped just as low. Because of these conditions, all permanent settlements were closed-off, climate-controlled environments with artificial circadian cycles. The only time inhabitants would venture outside—barring an emergency—was during a transition period: dawn or dusk, each of which lasted about 30 Terian days. Based on what Porr was saying, we wouldn't be simulating one of these climate-controlled settlements, and I doubted we would simulate a three week dawn.

No, as soon as we stepped into the facility, we entered a faithful recreation of the Devran day. The building itself was massive, about two kilometers long and three deep, and the entire interior mimicked a hot, dry desert. The fake sun was unforgivingly hot, and we were each given just one liter of water to use sparingly. Several other groups of third-class cadets were visible, but Porr told us communication with anyone outside our group was strictly forbidden. Our first job was to make some kind of shelter from the sun, and we set about using the fake terrain to do so.

Most of the ground was sand, dotted with large rock formations. The trick was finding the right rock formation. After some searching, I spotted a large overhang and pointed it out to Crim.

"Over there, that overhang should work, sir."

He nodded.

"You heard her, that overhang looks perfect—it's almost a shallow cave. We should get over there before some other group does."

The 18th and 19th cadet-commanders nodded but the 20th cadet-commander hesitated.

"You sure that's a good idea? It's too shallow. If the sun moves—"

"It's Devra, the sun won't move," I interrupted, knowing time was of the essence.

The cadet-commander gave me a look.

"It's not Devra, it's Alder. This is a simulation. And that's sir to you."

Crim eyed him wearily and interjected.

"Okay, it's a simulation. A simulation where the sun doesn't move. Now we should get moving before—"

"Why is she in charge of what we do?" he asked, a hint of anger in his voice.

"Cadets you better get your act together, now!"

Porr interrupted the building chaos, no doubt frustrated by the same blaring heat that seemed to be fouling some moods. Crim didn't wait to start another argument—he just started walking. When the cadet-commanders of 18th and 19th followed, the dissident had no choice but to join.

Drel gave me a knowing look but I ignored her—after all, it wasn't Teer, just his leader.

We reached the overhang and found enough shade to cover our entire group. While everyone filed into place, the cadet-commanders plotted the next course of action.

"Our shelter is set, now we need to start searching for water."

"What about stills?"

"We should split the group into quarters: half rest, one quarter searches, and the last quarter builds stills."

"20 minute shifts?"

"Let's try 20 minutes and adjust as needed."

Having agreed on their plan, each cadet-commander chose half of their division to help with the water situation. Crim nominated himself and Kulee to search, and Tyla and Deena to build a still. The rest of us would stay at the shelter, conserving our energy in the shade.

"Thank goodness he's gone."

Drel came and sat next to me, both of us leaning against the rock.

"What?"

She pointed at the people leaving—specifically at Teer—but I didn't react. At this point Drel was overdoing it; as Pell would say, this isn't unity. But I kept my thoughts to myself—now was not the time.

"Can you believe there's a world like this, and it's inhabited?" Grie asked.

"Only because of the mining," Epore answered.

Devra provided a staggering 40% of the empire's metals and alloys for ship-building. This came not just from rich and plentiful ore deposits, but also from the most extensive and efficient recycling system in the empire. For being one of the most desolate planets, it was also one of the richest.

"That mining created this empire, don't forget," another cadet added.

She was referring to the Terian War, where Terius overthrew the Moffans. Arguably the most significant turning point in the struggle was when the Terians took Devra.

"Terius created this empire, and he did it on Raviir," a different cadet replied.

I jumped in before the first could respond.

"And Terius was born here on Alder, and we can start arguing about which system is the best or we can remember the Fleet's motto and perform our duty."

My divisionmates smiled, but the two who had been arguing didn't look so happy.

"Are you ordering around my division, cadet?"

It was the 20th cadet-commander, standing as he spoke.

"She isn't, but I will."

Porr glared at him, and he sat back down.

"She just reminded your cadet of our motto, and what do you do? Try to divide us even more. Right now, she is showing much better leadership qualities than you are. If this is about the incident three weeks ago, it's your job to make your cadets drop it. If not, we will drop you."

And just like that, cadet-colonel Porr made me another enemy.

77

The rest of the weekend passed by without any major conflict, though the tension between certain members of 17th and 20th escalated considerably. I knew Porr meant well, but she'd done exactly what she was trying to avoid: foster conflict. Of course, if she hadn't spoken up, it would likely be worse… there really was no good solution.

This tension manifested itself when we had military work together on the following 2day, and it was noticeable enough for Pell to call a special meeting with our division.

"Cadets, I'm disappointed in what I'm seeing. I've heard what happened during the climate excursion, but I was under the impression Porr's message was loud and clear. Apparently that's not the case."

His eyes scanned our faces.

"If you feel another cadet has acted wrongly, that does not give you permission to act wrongly in turn. This needs to stop, now. Is that understood?"

"Yes, sir," we answered.

As much as I hated to admit it, Drel was only making things worse. I had angered Teer and their cadet-commander, but I kept my mouth shut and did my job. Drel, on the other hand, would complain every time they gave me a dirty look. Not quietly, not privately, but publicly, loudly. Crim had even talked to her about it, but instead of listening to him, she came to me to complain.

After the meeting with Pell, I pulled her aside.

"Drel, promise me you'll drop it. First Crim, now Pell. You're my best friend but this isn't helping me, it's only making things worse."

She nodded with a frown.

"I know it's just… it's not fair."

I shook my head.

"Drel, please."

She sighed.

"Okay, I'll stop. For you."

At lunch the next day, I got my usual glares from Teer, but I was focused on Drel: it was clear she was fighting the urge to comment.

"She's awfully protective of you, isn't she?" Rolin whispered to me.

"She means well," I replied.

He gave me a smile.

"Relax, it's not a big deal. Your first session there's always going to be a some drama. And your second session, and your third, and after you graduate. Our motto is impossible. You just have to do the best you can."

In a way, Rolin was right: unity was impossible. Especially for me.

78

The second month wrapped up much quicker than the first. Part of it was me adjusting to the routine, learning what to expect from my classes, but I knew the absence of traumatizing events also contributed to a smoother experience. Of course, the memories of what had already occurred still haunted me, especially during my time with Commander Kelt.

In my special elective, despite major improvements on the offensive side, Commander Kelt continued to outclass me. Each time I took a step forward, she stayed one step ahead, a smug smile etched on her face. Yes, I was hitting her fairly often, but never more than the day before.

It was only in the final week of the second month that I realized what this meant: she was actually teaching me. She had lowered to my level and was adjusting as I caught up. This discovery threatened to paint the commander in a more human light, but the threat was short-lived: every time I looked at her face, I remembered the night she kidnapped my best friend and almost killed her.

Still, I had to wonder how much of my training was planned and how much was improvised. Had they really expected me to get this far? Commander Hurren seemed to think I would barely last a day, and at the time, I was inclined to agree. Yet despite a rocky start, here I was, ending the second month with a new appointment.

"Congratulations, Robyn. You're the next cadet-commander."

Pell shook my hand, as did Crim, and I shared an excited glance with Drel. We were in the squad room on 9day of the fifth weekend, enjoying some well-earned rest.

"Your new averages are coming now," Pell announced.

I got the notification and opened the message. APA: 98, MPA: 93, PPA: 95, CPA: 95.

"The switch from OT to MC is automatic," he continued, "but you need to log in and verify you know your new course location and instructor. That's more or less all you have to do this weekend."

His eyes locked on mine.

"Robyn, we'll meet after dinner."

"Yes, sir."

He turned to Crim.

"Crim, I'd like you there as well."

"Yes, sir."

He turned back to the division.

"At ease everyone. Enjoy the weekend."

With that, he took his leave.

Crim took cap off his and turned to me.

"I voted for you this time."

I smiled in reply.

"Thanks, Crim," then, turning to the group, "Thanks, everyone. I'll do my best."

I looked at the seven faces in front of me and thought about how close I had gotten to these people over the past two months. To be sure, I still knew some better than others, but it was in that moment—when all of them placed their trust in me—that I decided to place my trust in them.

"I have something I need to share with you all."

Drel nodded approvingly as the others gave me curious looks.

"I'm on the integrated commission program," I announced, surprised by how easy it was to say.

I expected a moment of reflective silence, perhaps shifting expressions as they digested what I had said, but Crim broke the tension before it had a chance to build.

"Ha! That explains a lot!"

"Well," Grie added, "I think that goes to show we made the right choice."

"If only 20th could learn to do the same," Drel quipped.

A few others laughed, but I knew I needed to nip this in the bud.

"Please everyone, can we stop?"

The laughter died down and all eyes were on me.

"I'm glad we're capless right now: I don't want to speak as your cadet-commander, but as your friend. And I'm asking you to stop. I know these comments seem harmless, sometimes even justified. I agree, mistakes were made, but they were handled by the proper channels."

I paused, my eyes going from Deena to Grie, from Epore to Tyla.

"If you don't agree, I understand, but either keep it to yourself or talk to Pell. This negativity isn't healthy, and you're all starting to feed off each other. If anyone has a right to be upset, it's me, wouldn't you agree?"

A few of them nodded.

"Trust me, I was upset. And I'm thankful so many of you would go out of your way to defend me. But this isn't the way to do it. I mean, Pell talked to us about it, and here we are again. So let's stop. Let's focus on us, and making our division the best division possible. Okay?"

For a while, a tense silence held the room, but it wasn't long before Crim broke it again.

"Well, at least with me you guys didn't get any lectures."

They let the sentence hang for a moment, then burst into laughter.

"You got it, Robyn," Tyla added, stepping forward to put her arm on my shoulder.

I smiled in response, but my eyes were on Drel: she hadn't laughed at Crim's remark, and as the rest of the division crowded around me, she turned and walked away.

79

My third month started with a new roommate and a new course. I had gotten quite close to Grie, but now I was with Deena—our division's enigma. Perhaps in these five weeks I would be able to figure out what went on in that head of hers?

As for the new course, Grie managed to summarize it in one question.

"So Manual Combat is without our gloves?"

We were on our way there with Tyla and Drel; Manual Combat replaced Officer Training, and the entire class transitioned together.

"I think so," Drel replied.

"So what we did in basic?" he continued.

Drel shrugged.

"I'm sure it's more complicated."

I hoped she was wrong. Manual Combat marked a new opportunity for me to expose myself—something I hadn't had to deal with since my first week. Still, I wasn't nearly as worried now as I was then; if I had managed to adapt to military training, I was sure I could handle this hand-to-hand combat course. What worried me was the opposite: what if I was surprisingly good? The last thing I needed was more questions about my mysterious past…

"Welcome, cadets, to Manual Combat."

The room was similar to the one we had used for weapons training, but instead of target spheres, we had sets of small pads propped against the walls.

"I know some of you are wondering how this course relates to Weapons Training, and others have already gotten the scoop from their senior squadmates. Basically, this course prepares you for situations where your gloves are useless."

He paused, scanning our faces.

"There are three main reasons this could happen. Can someone tell me one of them?"

Several arms shot up.

"Yes, you."

A cadet near the front responded.

"Sir, glove removal, sir."

The commander nodded.

"Glove removal, correct. This is rare, but is sometimes necessary or forced. While the gloves have an anti-removal mechanism, it's not foolproof. Can someone tell me a second reason?"

Less hands were up.

"Yes, you."

"Sir, lens malfunction, sir."

She nodded again.

"Correct. This one is far more rare, but it does happen. We tend to depend on these lenses, but we must be ready to operate without them, if the situation arises."

She paused again, eyeing the 100 or so cadets lined up in front of her.

"There is one more reason your gloves may be rendered useless, and it is the most common. Does anyone know it?"

I shot my hand up, and only two others mimicked me. The commander looked straight at me.

"Yes, you."

"Sir, wet gloves, sir."

She smiled.

"Very good, someone was paying attention during the watersuit training."

The commander had us remove our gloves and pick up a pad. While I was no stranger to taking off my gloves—I had to do it twice a day, switching from my sleepsuit to my uniform and back—they usually came right back on. Keeping them off was odd—my hands felt naked.

My lenses indicated a specific pad, and I went to pick it up, surprised by how unsettling it felt to hold something in my bare hands. The pad itself was large and thick—enough cushion to strike without pain.

"Now everyone pair up according to the directions."

The system put me in a standing position facing Drel. It was strange to see everyone with their caps on but their gloves off—like half-transies.

"We're going to start with a review of the exercises you did in basic. First up, arm strikes. One of you, take both pads and put them on, palms and pads forward."

I looked at the back of my pad and saw two straps. Drel handed me hers and I slipped my forearms through both.

"The pads can be set to variable cushion. For now, we will keep them on high, but remember your enemies might not be so soft."

For the next few minutes, I held the pads while Drel struck them with fists or palms at varying heights, angles, and speeds. It was clear that she had practiced these movements before.

"Okay, switch pads with your partner."

We did as we were told, and I prepared for the first round.

"Punches, both arms, chest and head level. Go."

Having watched Drel's attacks closely, I felt confident in my stance and movement. But as I geared up for the first punch, I felt a familiar discomfort—a subtle but unmistakable pain in my head—and my follow-through was weaker than expected. It wasn't enough for Drel to notice, but it was enough to catch me off guard.

I rotated and punched with the other arm, trying to ignore what I had felt. This time the discomfort was more pronounced—as my fist approached the pad, the air felt thicker, almost like water—but I pressed through it, managing a more respectable strike.

I tried not to hesitate, in case the commander's eyes were on me. With some effort, I managed to mimic Drel's movements, and by the time she lifted the pads to head height, the feeling had started to fade.

After several rounds, we switched places, and I held the pads while Drel attacked with her knees and feet. I knew I needed to watch closely, to study her stance and movement, but I couldn't stop thinking about what had just happened. The similarities between this strange handicap and my former issues with the gloves were obvious, and even though the pain was never unbearable, now that I had noticed, I found it hard to explain away.

"Switch pads, this will be our last set for the day."

The instructor snapped me out of my train of thought and I gave Drel the pads, preparing to copy her movements as best I could.

"Defenders, hold the pads almost horizontal at waist height. Attackers, upward knee strikes. Ready? Go."

I looked at the pad and brought my right knee up into it, trying to micmic Drel. For a split second, I hoped the discomfort was gone, but it happened again. Nothing unmanageable, only a shadow of what the gloves had caused, but present nonetheless. Thankfully, by the end of the exercise, I could barely notice.

Unfortunately, I wasn't the only one exhibiting odd behavior during the exercise. There were subtle differences in Drel's body language and tone, a change in the way we interacted. Was this because of what I had said, or was this because I was a cadet-officer now?

Deep down, I knew the answer, I just didn't want to admit it. To think I had made her upset, after everything I had put her through, after the nightmare she wasn't even aware of... I didn't want to consider the possibility.

80

I found the more the days filled up, the faster they went by. My duties as cadet-commander added to an already-full plate, but the promotion included at least one perk: frequent cadet-officer meetings, often with Pell. Unfortunately, these meetings were rarely one-on-one; most were with the other two cadet-commanders in our squadron, while some included other cadet-captains or even Porr. I didn't have much input at these meetings, but it was a way to see what the cadet-officers did, and I gained an appreciation for the work they put in to keep the Academy running.

Thankfully, 20th had elected a new cadet-commander, one who didn't seem to have any problems with me, making even our most inclusive meetings tension-free. The change of command also smoothed out any joint military work, and in general, it seemed like everyone was finally putting the situation behind them. Everyone except Teer and Drel.

The cadet from 20th continued to give me dirty looks, but as usual, I hardly noticed—I had so much on my plate, I didn't have time to deal with him. But Drel? That was something everyone was beginning to notice, starting with my new roommate.

"You need to talk to her."

I looked up from the simulation above my desk, surprised by Deena's sudden announcement.

"Drel?" I asked, as if I didn't already know the answer.

She nodded.

"She doesn't want to lose her friend."

With that, she turned back to her work, leaving me speechless. Fourteen days into the third month, and this was the first time she had really talked to me. To be sure, we had relatively frequent conversations—what pair of roommates didn't?—but that was the polite side of her, the one forced to adapt to social norms. This? This was honest, and this was real.

I turned off my own simulation and stood. Deena was right, of course. Not only was this no way for a cadet-commander to behave, it was no way for a best friend to behave. I needed to talk to Drel, the sooner the better. So why not now?

"Thanks, Deena."

She turned to me and smiled.

"Don't mention it."

I left our room, made my way a few doors down, and knocked.

"Hey Robyn!"

Crim's welcoming grin made me smile, but my eyes scanned the empty room behind him.

"Drel?"

He gestured toward the squad room.

"With the others."

"Thanks."

I made to leave but he put his hand on my shoulder.

"Be careful," he said, looking down the hall then back at me. "She's pretty upset."

I frowned. If it was this clear to her roommate, I had already failed— not just as a leader, but as a friend.

"Thanks, Crim."

He let go of my shoulder with a nod, and I made my way to the squad room, my feet a little heavier than before.

81

There was only a handful of cadets in the squad room, some alone and others in pairs. I found my former roommate off to the side, working on a simulation with Tyla.

"Drel, do you have a minute?"

She looked up at me, glancing at my bare head.

"Officially or unofficially?"

There was no malice in her tone, but Tyla looked away, uneasy.

"Both."

She peered at me for a moment, then turned to Tyla.

"I'll be right back."

She followed me into the hall, where dozens of cadets walked to and fro. Even though there were more people around us, everyone was minding their own business—it was easier to have a private conversation here than in the squad room.

"What is it?"

This time, I heard it—a subtle anger in her voice, something I had never heard her direct at me.

"Drel, I wanted to apologize."

Frustration came over her expression.

"You're coming to me now?"

Her voice was louder than expected, and I fought the urge to see if anyone was watching.

"Drel—"

She put her hand up to stop me.

"Tell me, why do you think I'm upset?"

I hesitated.

"Because you were trying to defend me, and I punished you for it."

She frowned, then shook her head.

"Wrong. It's not what you did, Robyn, it's how you did it."

I thought back to the conversation with the division, trying to understand where I went wrong… and Drel scoffed.

"Even now, you don't understand, do you?"

At that point, confusion became frustration.

"No, but you're not helping me understand. Tell me what I did, Drel. Tell me so I can try to fix it."

To her credit, she didn't hesitate to reply.

"You didn't come to me as a friend. You knew I was the source of the problem, and before you were commander, you came and talked to me about it. And yes, I should have stopped there, you're right. I made mistakes, no doubt about it. But when it happened again, instead of asking me to stop, instead of coming to me as a friend, you sidestepped our friendship by talking to everyone."

I could feel the disappointment in her words, and each statement brought another dose of shame.

"And now this. It's been almost two weeks and you haven't come talk to me. Why did it take you so long?"

She paused, and I tried desperately to come up with a reply.

"I—I didn't know how to handle it."

Her frown deepened, and I felt a stab of guilt much stronger than any I had ever felt before.

"Not like this."

She turned back to the squad room, leaving me standing in the hall, alone.

82

My conversation with Drel overshadowed everything: decisive victories for our division during the second weekend, a barrage of information from my academics courses, even my daily training with Commander Kelt.

It wasn't like I hadn't noticed her suffering, and not just during an awkward session of Manual Combat; ever since I had given my little speech, our interactions were strained, almost forced. So why had it taken me so long to act?

Yes, my workload was heavy, and yes, my duties as cadet-commander took most of my free time, but it was this new role which represented the root of the problem: Drel was right, I had sidestepped our friendship by addressing the division, but that was the point—I was a cadet-officer now. Where did I draw the line between friendship and leadership?

The problem was exacerbated by our history—a history Drel knew nothing about—leaving me frozen, unsure of what to do. In hindsight, this was the wrong course of action—I had ignored the issue instead of addressing it head on, and now it was far worse than before.

I knew I couldn't make the same mistake twice, but I found it impossible to talk to her in private. Any attempt at a meeting was met with an excuse—some reason or another she was unavailable. And while I saw her every day—at the squad table, during military work, and in Manual Combat—I couldn't get more than the bare minimum out of her—a polite response, not an honest one. In fact, when I finally managed to have a real interaction with her, it wasn't verbal.

Twelve days after our talk outside the squad room, we were paired us up as partners in Manual Combat. Since our first lesson, I had sparred with several other cadets, each time facing the same strange inhibitions. I was adapting to the impediments, but so was the class: each time I pushed through a barrier, our technique would advance, and the discomfort reappeared.

It was a bizarre and troubling parallel to my special elective, and while it lacked the blinding pain I once felt with the gloves, I was convinced it was connected to my neurological issues—this had something to do with my past, something to do with my memory loss, or both. At first I considered my trauma a contributing factor, but I hadn't ever grappled with Commander Kelt. Not yet, at least.

So why did I struggle with the course? Frankly, I had no idea, and again, I had other things on my mind. Namely, the person who was now paired up with me.

It didn't take long for me to feel the anger in Drel's attacks. I was glad Grie and Tyla were paired off in other parts of the room, but Drel needed to be careful—she was already catching the attention of the cadets closest to us, and it was only a matter of time before the instructor noticed her aggression.

Unfortunately, my lackluster counterattacks only seemed to anger her further. I could almost see the gears turning in her head, asking me why I wasn't matching her effort, why I wasn't responding in kind. But the truth wasn't some ethical high ground, that I refused to stoop to her level—I was just that bad at the technique.

"Cadet, is there an issue?"

I was so focused on trying to defend myself I hadn't noticed the commander approach us. Drel stopped at once, and we both stood at attention.

"No problem, sir," she replied.

The commander's eyes went from Drel to me.

"I disagree. Do I need to separate you two?"

She directed the question at me.

"No, sir," I replied.

"Very well," she said, then gestured to Drel. "But you need to tone it down."

"Yes, sir."

When we left the class, I wanted to stop Drel, to apologize again, but she walked away quickly, avoiding any chance of conversation.

"You okay, sir?"

Grie's voice caught me off guard, as did the salutation—even three weeks in, it was odd being called sir.

"I'm fine, Grie."

Tyla stood beside him, watching Drel walk away.

"Nothing happened, Tyla. Drel is just frustrated, and I don't blame her."

She frowned.

"This isn't good."

I nodded, ignoring the fact she had forgotten to call me sir.

"You're right. It's not."

83

Over the next week and a half, things only got worse. Drel avoided any one-on-one time with me, and on top of my unrelenting workload, I had to deal with an increasingly potent guilt.

Again, this wasn't just about me upsetting my best friend—this was about what she had already gone through, about her unwitting participation in my perverted training. Every day I went into my special elective and sparred with Commander Kelt, I was reminded of the direct relation between my progress and Drel's involvement. And while I had used my life as a cadet to distract me from my secret ties with the commander, it was hard to separate my Academy functions from one of my divisionmates. Least of all when I had to lead her.

"As some of you may have noticed, we are heading the exact same direction as last month."

It was the fourth weekend of the third month, and Porr was leading us to our next climate excursion. This was an exercise I had dreaded, but not because of its difficulty—with the rest of our group on board the shuttle, including Teer, I had a nice reminder of the origin of my conflict with Drel.

"That's because Devra is a generous world. She has given us not one, but two extreme climates to work in."

The cadet-colonel gave us a knowing smile, but my eyes were on my best friend. Would there be any issues this weekend? Military training between 17th and 20th had improved over the course of the month, but there was still some tension among certain individuals—one of those individuals being Drel. Would I have to lecture her again, sidestepping our friendship to fulfill my duty?

We landed in front of another massive complex about a kilometer south of the original. From the outside, it looked almost the same as last month's building, but thanks to Porr, we knew the inside was quite the opposite.

"Let's go 5th Group!"

As soon as we entered the facility, the brutal cold hit us, and I asked myself what would be worse: 40 hours of a scorching hot day or 40 hours of a dark, frigid night? Neither, I realized, so long as I didn't have to reprimand my best friend.

"We need warmth," the 18th cadet-commander announced.

I nodded in reply.

"I have an idea on how to warm up. Let's hustle to a rock formation."

The other cadet-commanders followed me without objection, and as we explored the terrain, we realized it was exactly the same—this complex matched her daytime sister, so we knew where there was shelter and water. Still, Devra had no moon, and the false stars didn't give much light.

"Let's head to the same spot," I suggested.

Again, the other commanders acquiesced, and I was thankful for our operative cohesion. As we approached our destination, I explained my plan.

"The rock formations are riddled with conductive ore deposits. Using our gloves, we should be able to heat up the face of the rock enough to keep us warm."

There was a murmur of approval from the ranks, and when we reached the formation—unclaimed, thankfully—we pressed our hands against the rock and fired. The ore was not as conductive as I had hoped, and keeping a low, continuous arc was more difficult than I had expected; we had been trained to fire our gloves in strong bursts, this was the exact opposite. Still, with 32 pairs of hands working together, the slab began to warm. Between that, our uniforms, and ignoring the notion of personal space, it wasn't long before we were comfortable.

"We need to keep the slab warm throughout our stay," I announced. "We can set up a rotation, one division at a time, 10 minutes at a time. Sound good?"

Three affirmative responses later, 17th took the first shift.

"What about water?" the 20th cadet-commander asked.

"You can take your division to refill now, and we can rotate that as well, whenever necessary."

He nodded.

"Yes, we'll go now. 20th, let's get some water."

"Why do you keep asking her what to do?"

We were huddled too close for me to see who had spoken, but I knew the voice. It wasn't Teer, it was the former cadet-commander of 20th. I shot a glance at Drel, worried she might react, but it was the cadet-colonel who spoke up first.

"Cadet, are you serious? Last month you were cadet-commander, and I spoke to you about unity. This month you aren't cadet-commander, and you still haven't learned your lesson. If you don't want unity, then we won't have it. 20th, you will remain here at the rock formation. And you, you are in charge of refilling our entire water supply for the remainder of the excursion. Do I make myself clear?"

The former cadet-commander hesitated, and our close quarters only heightened the tension. For a moment, I thought he may lash out at Porr.

"Yes, sir."

The rest of the exercise Teer stared me down, and this time I noticed.

84

On 4day of the following week—the final week of our third month—it all came to a head. I was in the room with Deena after dinner when someone knocked at the door.

"Are you expecting anyone?" I asked.

She shook her head, eyeing the door curiously. I got up and opened it.

A body came at my center full force, bringing me down to the floor. I saw a flash and heard Deena cry out, then the door closing. I knew what was coming next.

When two uniforms or gloves touched, any attack was felt by both parties. The former 20th cadet-commander, who had me pinned to the ground, could not activate his gloves against me or we would both get shocked. But Teer, who was standing over us, could hit my exposed head without hurting his friend. I needed to protect my weak spot and get out of this compromising position.

I thrashed about violently, and even though I could tell my strength was beyond his, prying him away was surprisingly difficult. Every time I got a good hold, it was wasted, thrown away. Besides the heightened adrenaline and immediate danger, this was just like grappling in Manual Combat.

"Quit letting her move, Jule!"

I felt the grip on me tighten but continued to fight, knocking my chair over while Teer jumped around, trying to get a clear shot. I managed to get my feet on the side of my bed and pushed, knocking him down on top of us.

"Fuck!"

Enough of this. Trying to wriggle my way out was taking too long, and now that we were in a pile, I knew my advantage. I fired my gloves and the shot travelled through three bodies, sending us all into convulsions. But where Jule and Teer struggled to regain composure, I was already out and up, Commander Kelt's hundreds of hits behind me. I fired on them again, this time with more force, then sent an SOS to Pell.

"Robyn…"

I jumped to Deena, who was starting to get back up. Teer had hit her hard.

"Are you okay?" I asked.

She nodded, but it was clear she was in pain.

"I just—"

The door opened and we turned to see Pell, his eyes jumping from the two of us to the two of them.

"Robyn—what happened?" he asked.

"They attacked us," I replied.

Teer and Jule started to move, but Pell kept his eyes on me.

"Are you okay?" he asked.

I nodded.

"Yes, but Deena is hurt."

He turned around. There were three cadets from first division behind him.

"You three, detain these two and keep an eye on Robyn. I'm sending a message to Cife. Robyn, I'll take Deena."

Two of the upperclassmen pulled Teer and Jule into the hall. Pell came in and took Deena, putting his arm around her to help her walk. They hobbled out of the room, then the third upperclassman blocked the doorway. I was not allowed to leave.

"What's going on here?"

I recognized Cife's voice before I saw her: the cadet-general of 7th Wing had given many talks in the cafeteria but this would be the first time I met her.

"These two attacked two of our cadets. One is still in the room and Pell took the other to the infirmary."

The cadet in the door stepped away and Cife came inside.

"You're Robyn, yes?" she asked.

"Yes, sir."

"These two attacked you?"

"Yes, sir. Myself and my roommate, Deena."

She nodded.

"Tell me exactly what happened."

I gave her the entire story and she nodded, then went outside the door and stood over Teer and Jule.

"Cadets, what are your names?"

"Teer, sir."

"Jule, sir."

"Is what Robyn said true?"

Jule looked at Teer, who didn't say anything.

"Answer me, cadets. Now."

"I'd like to speak to a real officer, sir."

I couldn't believe my ears. The senior cadets were appalled—even Jule seemed shocked. A few tense moments passed, then Cife's face formed a malicious smile.

"Okay, Teer. That's exactly what we're going to do."

85

20 minutes later, Pell and I stood outside the office of the Puric commander, the officer in charge of our dormitory. On the other side of the door were Teer, Jule, the 20th cadet-captain, and Cife. They had been meeting for approximately 10 minutes.

"Sir, what do you think is going to happen?" I asked Pell.

He didn't hesitate to reply.

"Expelled. Without a doubt. He crossed a line, and that's twice now."

I nodded.

Another 10 minutes passed before the door opened. All but Cife walked out. Something about Teer's face didn't sit well with me...

"Could you two come in, please?" the commander's voice beckoned us.

Pell and I entered the office and the door closed behind us. I glanced at Cife—she looked upset.

"Robyn, is it?"

The Puric commander sat behind his desk, giving me a once over. I didn't like his tone.

"Yes, sir."

He nodded.

"Robyn, I want to apologize for what happened. I spoke with Teer and Jule and gave them a final warning. If either of them behave aggressively toward you or any other individual in the future, they'll be expelled."

"Sir?" Pell's voice sounded from beside me.

I'd never heard him sound so unsure of himself. It made me uneasy.

"Yes, cadet-captain?"

"You're aware of the previous incident between Teer and Robyn, sir?"

The commander raised his eyebrows.

"Yes, cadet, why?"

I wanted to tell Pell not to answer—something was wrong here and he needed to be careful—but I didn't dare speak.

"Just making sure, sir."

He nodded slowly, but I saw the contempt in his eyes.

"Listen, I understand the punishment may seem light, but take a look from the other side, will you? These two cadets were frustrated, and they made a mistake. One fired on Deena, but Robyn, you fired on them twice, isn't that right? Once while grappling and then again when you got free?"

I couldn't believe my ears.

"Yes, sir."

"Right. For that, I should be punishing you as well, but I don't think that would be totally fair."

He gave us another once over.

"You're dismissed."

"Sir, may I speak with you in private?" Cife asked as we started to leave.

"No, Cife. It's late. Another time."

Before we could get too far, Cife beckoned for us to follow her. We went all the way to the 7th floor, and she had us enter her room, closing the door behind her.

"Robyn, I don't know what just happened, but I'm sorry."

Pell nodded in agreement.

"Yea, something doesn't add up here."

"I never liked him, but tonight was over the top," she continued. "And to think I thought he would rip Teer a new one."

"Sir, do you think that's why he asked to speak with a real officer?" I asked.

She looked at me, then nodded slowly.

"Probably."

"Can we ask what happened in your meeting?" Pell prodded.

She shrugged.

"Nothing that would tell me why he didn't expel him. He gave them a spiel about behaving better, and he told them it was their final warning, but there was something about Teer... like he knew he would get away with it. Even Wol was in shock."

Wol was the 20th cadet-captain.

"Sir, how is Deena?" I asked.

"Completely fine," Cife replied. "She's back in your room. Teer hit her pretty hard but no lasting damage."

"May I be dismissed, sir?"

Cife nodded.

"Of course, Robyn. And sorry again. This should not have played out like this."

I nodded, and Pell put his hand on my shoulder.

"Robyn, I want you and Deena to keep this to yourselves for now. I'll organize a meeting tomorrow for the squadron."

"Thank you, sir."

I turned around and rushed back to my room, trying once more to understand the root of this conflict. Why had Teer attacked me during the rifle exercise? Had the first climate excursion soured his opinion of me to the point where assault seemed like a rational reaction?

"Deena, are you okay?"

She sat up in her bed and I gave her a once over.

"Yes. Are you?"

I sat next to her and told her everything—how the meeting with the commander went and what Cife and Pell had said afterwards. As she listened to my explanation, I saw her expression change in a way I had never seen before—she was angry.

"That's not okay."

I nodded.

"Even Cife is confused. I don't know what happened."

She lay back down.

"There's something wrong about this."

I nodded.

"Yes. Yes there is."

I got up from her bed and went to my locker, a part of me beginning to see the cruel irony of the situation. Twice now, I had caused my roommates suffering. Twice now, my friends had been fired upon because of me.

Despite the inconsistencies surrounding the situation, I didn't think it had anything to do with Commander Kelt. Yes, Teer had gotten away with it, but the commander was looking for secrecy, and this situation was now front and center on everyone's minds.

I wondered how Drel would react to this escalation. Time and again I had told her to drop it, and in the end she was right—more than right. Unfortunately, I knew this would only make things worse. At the meeting tomorrow, Pell would do what a cadet-captain had to do—emphasize unity —and I, as cadet-commander, would have to echo his call. As much as I knew it was the right thing to do—especially as a leader—I couldn't help worrying how it would affect my friendship with Drel.

Of course, there was a silver lining to this mess. For three months I had fought to fit in, to feel like a normal cadet in order to escape the reality of my special circumstances. Well, I had succeeded. For the moment, Commander Kelt wasn't even on my radar.

Welcome to the Academy, I told myself.

86

The next day was an awkward one. Only a few other first-class cadets knew what had happened, but their behavior and our own was enough to prompt questions, questions we shot down by referencing the scheduled meeting.

Of course, keeping quiet meant all sorts of rumors started, even over the span of a few hours. Crim was bold enough to bring something up with me, but respected my desire to change the subject. And while Drel could tell something was up, she made no effort to ask me directly.

Unfortunately, the meeting went more or less how I had expected. As Pell, Deena, and I addressed the squadron, I noticed the growing fury in Drel's eyes. But I was done letting this situation own me, letting it own our relationship. As soon as Pell dismissed us, I ran after her, catching her before she could get away.

"You were right, Drel. One hundred percent."

My words caught her by surprise. A few of our divisionmates were within earshot, but I didn't hold back.

"You were right about Teer, right about his friend. But that's not what's important. I'm sorry for the way I acted, and I'm sorry for not coming to you sooner. That's not the way I should treat my division, and it's not the way I should treat my friend. Most of all, I'm sorry for whatever is still going on between us, because it's driving me crazy not being able to talk to you about this."

As I spoke, her anger faded, replaced by a wary curiosity.

"You think I was right? You're not worried I'm going to lash out?"

I shook my head.

"You're not like them. I know you're angry—so am I—but I also know you won't do anything stupid."

She shrugged.

"I've done stupid things before. Acting passive-aggressive with you, for one."

She smiled a sad smile, and I felt an enormous weight come off my shoulders.

"Will you two make up already!"

Crim hit both of us on the back, and Drel shot him an angry glare before shaking her head with a smile.

"I hate you, Crim."

He laughed.

"As long as you don't hate Robyn."

She looked up at me, and I saw a hint of the old Drel behind those eyes—my best friend, the one who helped me survive everything my secret life threw at me, even if she didn't know it.

"How could I hate Robyn?"

She opened her arms and gave me a hug—the first hug of my life—and I felt stronger than I ever had before.

87

Four days later I was reelected cadet-commander, and the day after that, I moved in with Kulee. I felt bad leaving Deena so soon after the accident, but in an odd way, I was glad to have shared it with her. I suddenly felt a lot closer to my quietest divisionmate.

Kulee, on the other hand, was quieter than I expected—too quiet. During our first week as roommates, I noticed a change in her behavior around me. Normally this would be a mystery, but thanks to my renewed relationship with Drel, I was reminded of an issue we had already discussed, an issue that would make Kulee very quiet around me. The problem was I had no idea how to approach this particular issue, and I wasn't sure if Pell was the right person to ask.

"I didn't do anything this time, did I?"

I smiled. I was in Rolin's room again, having asked to meet privately.

"I need your advice."

He nodded.

"Sure, take a seat."

"Were you ever cadet-commander?" I asked, sitting down.

He shook his head.

"Never wanted to. Why?"

"I'm not sure you'll be able to help but I still want to ask. Before I do, this is strictly between you and me, okay?"

He sat up straighter.

"Okay."

"I think Kulee and Epore are… seeing each other."

Rolin nodded, waiting for me to continue.

"I don't know what to do. If I see evidence they are fraternizing, as cadet-commander, I have a duty to report it. I mean, I know that's the reason she's acting funny, but I also want her to be honest with me. What do you think?"

Rolin nodded his head slowly then sat back in his chair.

"Well, I think you're not going to like my advice."

I shrugged.

"That's fine, I can always disagree."

He nodded again.

"Right. Well the problem is right there in how you said it. You want her to be honest with you, yet you say you'll turn her in for being honest with you. What else do you expect?"

I nodded, and he continued.

"In my opinion, I think you should leave them be. Whatever they're doing is their business, and frankly, relationships like that happen all the time."

"How often do they happen?"

He thought for a bit before responding.

"More often than not. At least ninety percent of cadets I know have had some kind of relationship with another cadet, one time or ongoing."

His words surprised me, but I tried to hide my reaction lest I come off as naive.

"And the cadet-officers turn a blind eye?"

He shrugged.

"Sometimes yes, sometimes no. Look, part of being a cadet-officer is learning to lead, right? And the hardest part of leadership isn't the black and white stuff, it's the grey stuff. If you have evidence, it's your job to turn them in. But do you have evidence?"

I shook my head.

"I thought so, otherwise we wouldn't be sitting here. In that case, I say don't go looking for it. If it happens, it happens."

He was right, I didn't like this advice.

"But what about Kulee? What if something happens and she feels uncomfortable coming to me about it? I'm supposed to be their liaison to the chain of command. I know she won't go to Pell, and certainly not a real officer."

"Ah!" he exclaimed, smiling. "Now you see the absurdity of it all. I don't know what you want me to tell you, Robyn. At some point, you may have to do what you think is right instead of what you've been told is right."

I took a moment to digest his words, then nodded.

"Thanks, Rolin."

He smiled.

"Anytime."

I got up to leave.

"By the way, Robyn…"

I turned back around.

"How are you doing?"

I shrugged.

"Trying to move past it."

"Right. Understandable…"

He hesitated, and I saw he was struggling to speak his mind.

"What is it?"

He stared at me for a moment, then frowned.

"Listen, I feel like I should tell you… one of the cadets in 20th is a friend of mine."

I could see he was searching for the right words, clearly uncomfortable.

"The senior divisions were embarrassed by the whole thing, so they did a little digging…"

He hesitated again, giving me a concerned look.

"What?" I asked. "What did they find?"

His frown deepened.

"His family name. You know who shares that family name? A class 3 general. His mother."

I stared at Rolin in the silence that followed, trying to process what he had just told me. So Teer had escaped punishment by his family name?

"I'm sorry, Robyn. I know you're trying to move past it, I know you want everyone to move past it, I just figured you should know."

I shook my head.

"No, Rolin, thank you. Thank you for telling me."

For me, this revelation proved two things: unity was a lie, and the dark side of the Academy extended beyond the confines of my special elective. Only why did it need to focus so much on me?

88

Over the next few weeks, the situation with Teer and Jule worsened. The angry stares were gone, replaced with something worse: arrogance, a smug disposition that grated every member of my division and spread into the rest of the squadron.

I had asked Rolin not to share what he had learned, but with a handful of upperclassmen already aware, it was only a matter of time before word got around. I never heard anyone mention anything explicitly, but soon even Pell was starting to show his disapproval.

Several divisionmates tried to have conversations with me about it, but I could tell they were careful with their words: after weeks of emphasizing unity, even talking about Teer and Jule was a linguistic minefield. Frankly, this worried me most of all. I had created a paradox: I wanted my division to communicate openly with me, and yet I had told them over and over not to discuss the situation.

It would be easier to ignore if their table wasn't so close to ours, or if they didn't have military work with us two to three times a week. But it was and they did, and we had chosen the high road, the road most difficult. Thankfully, they hadn't actually done anything—at this point I was afraid one of our own might snap. Worst of all, I had a feeling if that were to happen, their meeting with the Puric commander would go very differently.

While we were lucky enough to be free of them the first three weekends, there was no way to avoid them at the climate excursion, so it came as no surprise when Cife called a special meeting the day before the exercise.

We met in the wing conference room—both third divisions of 17th and 20th, along with the two cadet-captains, Porr, and Cife. Our cadet-general started us off.

"Good evening, cadets. You all know why you're here. There is a wound in 7th Wing, and it's an ugly one. I know your cadet-commanders, cadet-captains, and cadet-colonel have all spoken to you at length about the importance of unity. 17th and 20th, you've been going through the same classes, the same training, and now the same speeches. I'm not here to rephrase something you've heard many times. I'm only here to say your actions in the coming weeks, and of course this weekend, will speak volumes about your character. Robyn and Olen, would you please come forward."

I joined the cadet-commander of our sister division—the same one that had replaced Jule and held his position since then—and saw a hint of shame in his eyes. I thought back to what Rolin had told me and realized maybe it wasn't just the senior divisions that were embarrassed by their peers.

"As an exercise in unity and hopefully in healing, I'm enacting a special policy for your climate excursion this weekend."

Cife's words snapped me out of my train of thought. A special policy?

"During the entirety of the exercise, you two will switch commands. Robyn, you will be the cadet-commander of the third division of 20th Squadron, and Olen, you will be the cadet-commander of the third division of 17th Squadron. Is that understood?"

"Yes, sir," we answered in unison.

She turned to the others.

"And cadets, you will obey your cadet-commanders, is that understood?"

"Yes, sir!" came the response, with varying degrees of enthusiasm.

Cife dismissed everyone except the cadet-officers.

"Okay, Olen and Robyn, you understand what we're doing, yes?"

"Yes, sir," we replied.

"Porr will give you the specifics this weekend, and determine when the switch begins and ends. Is that understood?"

"Yes, sir."

"Do you have any questions?"

We looked at each other.

"No, sir."

"You're dismissed."

We made our way out, and Olen stopped me as soon as we were in the hall.

"Robyn, I'm sorry."

There was a sincerity in his eyes that made me frown.

"Olen, you don't have to apologize."

He shook his head.

"Yes I do. You're being asked to lead Teer and Jule. I'm being asked to lead a division that doesn't hold any grudges against me. This is unfair."

I nodded slowly.

"And the rest of your division—everyone besides Teer and Jule—do they hold grudges against me?"

He hesitated, then shook his head.

"No."

"Then don't worry about it. Cife is doing her job. She's trying to fix this situation. Let's do ours."

He smiled, and gave me a quick nod.

"Fair enough. See you soon."

I watched him walk away and frowned again. I was glad I could make him feel better, because I was still trying to process it. Command Teer and Jule? I understood what Cife was trying to do, but I wasn't sure it was going to work.

89

The atmosphere during our flight was clearly different—everyone, even those in the other squadrons, was curious to see how this would play out. How many of them knew what had happened between Teer and I? How many had heard?

"This weekend we'll be in another special facility, not too far from the first two, with a wholly different environment. A mix of Dathleran and Yontaren—a different kind of heat."

Right as the shuttle hit the ground, Porr gave us the signal, and Olen and I officially switched positions. I looked at the seven faces in front of me. This was my new division. I was their leader.

"Okay cadets, up and out, 17th!"

I turned my head to answer Porr's call but caught myself just in time, glancing over at Olen.

"17th Squadron, let's go!" he announced.

I watched my old division follow their new cadet-commander out of the shuttle.

"18th!" Porr called out.

I turned back to the faces in front of me, to my new division.

"18th Squadron, let's go!"

Most were alert—very alert.

"19th!"

Were they trying to make up for the others?

"19th Squadron, let's go!"

Maybe this would go better than I thought.

"20th!"

I smiled, encouraged by most of what I saw.

"20th Squadron, let's go!"

I made my announcement and jumped out of the shuttle, following the last cadet of 19th. Our group ran to the entrance of the facility and stopped, waiting for Porr to let us in. She hustled to the front of the line and led us inside.

A wave of humidity hit me: damp, heavy air so thick I could feel it. A sea of greens, yellows, and browns lay before us, denser than anything I had ever seen—at least in person. I had seen simulations of these environments in my biology course, and I recognized the larger plants ahead.

With each climate excursion, Porr's involvement diminished, and it was clear we were meant to operate as independently as possible. Once we were all inside, she expected the cadet-commanders to lead the way.

"Shelter and water, let's start with the first," the 18th cadet-commander announced.

I thought back to what I had learned about Dathleran and Yontaren.

"The ground is too wet to sleep on, and rains are frequent," I explained. "We'll need lifted beds under roofs."

"A-frames?" the 18th cadet-commander asked.

I nodded.

"We could do one per element pair."

"How are we going to build them?" the 19th cadet-commander interjected. "I'm familiar with funnel trees—we had them on Nommir. Those branches are hard to break."

"You're right," I said, "but we have a saw right here."

I lifted my hands about half a meter apart and shot from one palm into the other, creating a temporary band of electrical discharge. My colleague smiled.

"Brilliant."

We split into our divisions to do a quick search of the area. Our goal was to determine density patterns and elevation changes in order to locate an area with less trees and higher ground. For efficiency, we decided to spread out in a large circle, one division per cardinal direction, staying in our elements. I noted a brief hesitation from two of my elements, but no other issues.

An hour later we had a decent plot of land and were starting to make A-frames. My clever idea was not as clever as I had imagined: the gloves needed to be at very high power to cut wood, and sustaining that level for more than a few seconds was difficult. But for now, time was on our side. As long as it didn't rain while we were building our frames, we would be fine. I had no idea if it could rain in this simulation, but I wasn't putting anything past the Academy.

While constructing our shelters, I noticed some minor disagreements within the same two elements, and I kept my eye on them. I knew I would have to address it eventually, but so far Teer's partner and Jule's partner had it handled. It wasn't until Teer's roommate dropped a funnel branch in exasperation—catching the attention of the rest of the division—that I knew I had to act.

"Cadet, what's the problem?" I asked, approaching them.

"Sorry, sir. Won't happen again, sir," he answered.

I felt a certain degree of pity: I knew he wasn't the culprit, but he was the one who had dropped the branch.

"Cadet, you and your roommate have been at odds for the entire exercise. So I'll ask you again, what is the problem?"

He looked at Teer then back at me.

"Sir, my roommate wants to swap elements for the weekend."

"What do you mean, swap elements?"

"Sir, Teer wants to be partnered with Jule and have me partner with Finnen."

I turned to Teer.

"Is this true, Teer?"

He smiled a smug smile, and for a moment, the image of a young, male Commander Kelt popped into my mind. Was this what she was like as a cadet?

"Yes, it is," he answered.

"The rest of you, get back to work!"

Porr's exclamation took me by surprise, but I was thankful. More and more people were paying attention to our conversation.

"Do you feel like you can't work with your current roommate?" I asked. Teer shook his head.

"No, but if you and Olen can switch, why can't we?"

I frowned.

"Cadet, despite any personal misgivings you may have, you are required to refer to cadet-officers of higher rank as 'sir' unless off-cap or in specific situations dictated by higher ranking members of the Fleet. Is that understood?"

He smiled again but my question went unanswered. Several people had stopped working, and I knew if Porr wasn't yelling at them she must be watching.

"Cadet, I will ask you again, is that understood?"

Our eyes were locked, and I kept my composure as calm as possible.

"Yes, sir."

He had said the words, but I knew it wasn't enough. Not after what had just happened. As he started to turn back to work, I made my choice.

"You're dismissed from this exercise, Teer."

He whipped around, the smile gone.

"What?"

"Cadet, did you forget the entire conversation we just had? You have now failed to refer to a superior cadet-officer as 'sir' three times. You're dismissed from this exercise."

He stared at me, no doubt calculating his reply, but I didn't give him time to think of one.

"Cadet, if you don't leave this exercise immediately, you'll be expelled."

His eyes widened, and I could feel the stares of everyone around us.

"Get back to work, NOW!"

Porr snapped the others to action and hustled to us.

"Cadet, you heard your cadet-commander, you're dismissed. Come with me."

He hesitated, shooting another glance at me, then followed Porr toward the exit. Just before she left the area, she turned to address us.

"5th Group, I'm temporarily delegating leadership to Robyn. When I get back here all these frames better be done. Move it!"

Two reactions caught my eye: Drel, smiling with glee, and Jule, fuming with rage.

90

An hour after Porr left with Teer, I received a message to pass leadership to the 18th cadet-commander and leave the building. I made the announcement reluctantly—each of these distractions was destroying any sense of immersion—then privately urged him to whip them into shape.

Porr was outside, waiting by a shuttle. Her frown told me exactly where this was headed.

"Yes, sir?"

She gestured to the shuttle.

"Hop in, we have a meeting with the Puric commander."

I nodded and got on board. She didn't say a word to me the entire flight, her hands busy making gestures on the lenses. As we approached the dorms, I felt a familiar pit in my stomach, reminding me of my first few visits with Commander Kelt. It was hard to believe, but at this point I would rather see her than him.

Pell and Cife were inside the office, their expressions only adding to my concern.

"Good afternoon, cadet."

I still didn't know the commander's name, but it didn't matter. Where was Teer?

"Good afternoon, sir."

He looked me up and down.

"Cadet, could you explain to me what happened today, specifically between you and Teer?"

"Yes, sir. I was acting cadet-commander of 20th Squadron 3rd Division from the start of the exercise. We entered the facility and proceeded to find and build shelter. I noticed some minor hesitation from Teer's element and Jule's element, but it was quickly self-corrected."

"Hesitation?"

"Yes, sir. I don't know the details."

He nodded.

"Carry on."

"Yes, sir. During the construction of our shelters, Teer's element and Jule's element exhibited further inter-element disagreements. At one point, Teer's roommate threw down a piece of a funnel tree, distracting the rest of the division. I talked to the element and was informed that Teer had been asking to swap roommates with Jule."

"Wait, Teer's roommate threw down the branch in frustration?"

"Yes, sir."

"Because Teer wanted to swap roommates with Jule?"

"Yes, sir."

He nodded.

"Anything else?"

"Yes, sir. I asked Teer if this was true, and he confirmed it. I asked why he wanted to swap roommates and he cited my switch with Olen. Both of these answers came without a 'sir' so I reminded him he was required to use that title with me. I asked if he understood and he did not reply. I asked again and he replied affirmatively. Because of these transgressions I dismissed him from the exercise. He resisted until cadet-colonel Porr came and removed him."

"Is that all, cadet?"

"Yes, sir."

He nodded again, but by the way he was looking at me, I knew what came next—I prepared to go on the defensive.

"So let me get this straight: an element was having disagreements, at some point it became a disruption, and when you asked for the reason behind the disruption, it was due to their desire to copy the change in command. Correct?"

"Yes, sir."

He looked at Cife.

"The switch was your idea, was it not?"

"Yes, sir."

He turned to me.

"Cadet, what your cadet-general did is not unheard of, but it's certainly abnormal. I can understand the confusion. If your superiors demonstrate that a switch of cadet-commanders between squadrons is admissible, then perhaps a minor switch between elements is admissible as well? Now you say you had an issue with him calling you 'sir,' correct?"

I ignored the spark of frustration, holding my composure like I had with Teer.

"Yes, sir."

He pointed to his cap.

"Tell me, cadet, if I didn't have this insignia would you know I was a commander?"

"No, sir."

His hand came down.

"Now all of you, as cadets, have the same insignia. Your cadet-general just made a switch of cadet-commanders. It should come as no surprise they may be slow to call you 'sir,' particularly in the hours following the change."

Frustration turned into anger, and I pushed back even harder. This was no place to let emotion get the best of me.

"Furthermore, after he failed to call you 'sir,' you repeated the request, and he acquiesced, correct?"

"Yes, sir. But—"

He raised his hand to stop me.

"Is that correct, yes or no?"

"Yes, sir."

He nodded.

"Sir, if I may," Porr began.

"You may not," he shot back, with surprising severity.

He glared at her, then turned back to me.

"Cadet, did you threaten to expel Teer?"

"No, sir."

He raised his eyebrows.

"Are you saying Teer lied to me? I was told you explicitly told him if he didn't leave the exercise, he would be expelled."

I almost sighed, but caught myself.

"Yes, sir."

"A cadet-commander does not have the authority to threaten another cadet with expulsion except in the case of egregious infraction. Do you think him not calling you 'sir' would qualify as an egregious infraction?"

"No, sir. But—"

He raised his hand again and I shut my mouth. As much as I hated this moment, as much as I wanted to show him everything I had learned from Commander Kelt, I knew if I didn't heed that raised hand, I would be in a world of trouble—not just from him, but from her as well.

"Cadet, it is my opinion you have not acted in a manner appropriate of a cadet-commander. As such, effective immediately, you are demoted. 7th Wing 17th Squadron 3rd Division will have no cadet-commander for the remainder of the month. You are also out of the climate excursion for the rest of the weekend."

He paused, giving me a once over.

"This is your final warning. Another incident like this and you'll be expelled."

"Sir—," Cife began.

"Silence! All of you are at risk of being demoted over this incident. How could you let a cadet-commander threaten expulsion for something as simple as improper address? After an unusual switch of command, no less? This discussion is over. You're all dismissed."

As I turned to leave, I caught a glimpse of Pell's face; never had I seen such fury in his eyes.

91

After the meeting, Porr had to go back to the fake jungle, Cife had other tasks to attend to, and Pell had an exercise with our first division. I went back to my room and sat at my desk, trying not to let my rage consume me.

I wondered if Teer had been allowed to return? My poor divisionmates —and poor Olen. What a mess. All because someone's mother was high up in the Fleet. Disgusting.

A knock on the door interrupted my solitude. Was Pell back already? Or—I thought as my hand hovered over the button—was Teer here to greet me once more?

"It's me, Rolin!" came the familiar voice.

I opened the door. Something about the familiar face, the half smile, and the clear worry in his eyes pushed me over the edge. I jumped at him, arms wide, and gave him a hug.

"Well, uh, nice to see you too?" he quipped.

I let go and stepped back, laughing at his surprised reaction.

"Did you hear what happened?" I asked.

He nodded.

"Pell told us—that's why I'm here. Is everything okay?"

I shrugged, hesitated, then shook my head.

"No, not really."

"You know Robyn, I've never heard Pell talk that way before. He didn't give us the details, but he insinuated the commander was unfit for duty, something I would never expect him to say."

He smiled.

"It's funny now, looking back at every call for unity, every little meeting and lecture. But Pell's the best. I would've done the same. This situation is just crazy."

I nodded, trying not to think too much about my cadet-captain's reaction. I wanted to ask Rolin where he was, but I knew that was pushing it.

"This is what I was talking about though, unity is bullshit. I mean yes, we should try to be united, but look at where that's gotten you. You've done everything right, more than right, and just because mommy is a general, somebody is automatically better than you. And now you're not cadet-commander? That's bullshit."

I didn't stop him. For once, I let the words flow unhindered—they were addictive.

"Teer deserves to be expelled. I mean, Pell said it himself! It's crazy."

Deep down, I knew I was being hypocritical, that I shouldn't encourage such talk. But at that particular moment, I didn't care.

"Well, I don't know how you feel about this, but we're going to have a small get together in the squad room tonight at 900—no drugs, of course! If you'd like to come, you're welcome to."

Rolin's words ignited something inside of me. Another party? Last time I had laughed with Drel at their insanity. This time, I really wanted to go. I had so much pent up frustration, so much anger at being punished for doing what I thought was right...

Just as I was about to say yes, a notification appeared on my lenses. And from the way Rolin was staring into space, his too. A simple request from our cadet-captain to be extra careful due to the circumstances of the weekend. Both of us knew exactly what that meant.

"Well, never mind," he said.

That night, cooler heads prevailed, but I had to ask myself: where did this high road end? Was it even worth it?

92

The next day, I had breakfast with the senior divisions, painfully aware of the seven empty seats at the table. My squadron made up for it—even the first division made an effort to interact with me, and I finally got to know some of the faces I saw every day. It was surprising how little I knew about them almost halfway through the session, and even more surprising how much they knew about me. I wondered if Pell had filled them in, or if they were more observant than I gave them credit for. In any case, they opened up in a way I never would have expected, and I almost forgot my little predicament.

Unfortunately, once breakfast was over, I was on my own. I passed most of the time in my room, running extra simulations for my tactics courses. As lunch approached, my mood improved, excited to see the upperclassmen, but I found the cafeteria almost deserted: the third divisions were still on their climate excursions, and apparently the first and second divisions had their own exercises.

There were only two other cadets in a room made to fit 500, and the empty tables around me compounded my loneliness. As I sat there, playing with my goop, I realized neither of the other cadets was Teer, but it barely fazed me. With this much time to myself, my thoughts had gone well beyond our little conflict.

The warning from the Puric commander had ripped the facade off my life as a cadet, reminding me of the stipulations of my situation. Suddenly, it didn't matter if I mastered all the drills or learned how to grapple—now, despite overcoming all of these obstacles, I was just as close to my undisclosed punishment as I had been the day I woke up on Kurotar.

The longer I spent with my squadron, the more I considered myself one of them—like Drel or Crim, like Rolin or Pell. But I wasn't. They were free to leave, to quit, to drop out at any time and go back to their homes or their lives outside of the Fleet. Certainly, some had a tough past and several had no home to go back to, but they were still free. I was not. I had decided against going to the detainment center, but what was my situation at the Academy, if not a form of confinement?

Occasionally, my divisionmates would talk of family and friends, but I had neither. Some even talked about alternate career paths if they didn't finish out the three sessions. My alternate career was incarceration, if not execution. And so I spent the hours leading up to dinner in a growing pit of darkness, reality threatening to shatter every illusion I had worked so hard to craft. By the time Kulee walked through the door, I wasn't sure if I'd ever feel the same again.

"How are you?" she asked.

"I've been better."

She looked me up and down, frowning.

"We missed you out there, Robyn. Your division missed you."

I looked up and saw her wringing her cap. Clearly, I was worrying her.

"How did it go?" I asked, trying and failing to sound normal.

"We did surprisingly well, given the circumstances," she replied.

I nodded absentmindedly, and she put her hand on my shoulder.

"Come on, Robyn. Let's go to dinner."

I saw the concern in her expression, but what could I say? She probably thought this was about Teer—if only it were that simple.

"Okay," I replied, standing.

We put our caps on and she straightened.

"Ready, sir?"

The word was like a hit from Commander Kelt—no one had told them.

"Kulee... I've been demoted from cadet-commander."

She nodded and opened the door.

"Pell told us, sir."

Behind her, standing in the hallway, were six cadets—seven, once Kulee filed into the line. The rest of my division, standing at attention in front of our room.

"Good evening, sir," they announced in unison, then gave the customary nod.

93

My division's defiant support was enough to clear some of the darkness hanging over me, and their protest helped me get through the final week of the fourth month. What they were doing was technically prohibited, but Pell let it slide so long as they kept it out of anything official—and since it was the last week, that really only meant military work. In all other circumstances, it was as if I was still cadet-commander.

While my divisionmates thought they had cheered me up by rejecting my demotion, in reality, it was their friendship that had shined a light into the darkness. Their actions showed me I wasn't just imagining things—I wasn't a stranger or an outsider, I was a cadet of the Academy, despite all that had happened. Sure, this didn't erase my special circumstances nor did it clear up my existential doubts, but it was enough to let me focus on what a cadet would focus on during their last week of the fourth month: the coming weekend, the halfway point of the session.

Not only were five of my courses coming to an end, we also had the cadet-captain election on the agenda. Pell told us to make it clear to the whole squadron if we didn't want to run, but no one bothered. We all knew Pell would win again, and that was exactly what we wanted.

9day afternoon, we gathered in the squad room to perform the vote. Since the other divisions did their monthly cadet-commander votes on their own, this was the first time we had the entire squadron together for an election.

The format was the same: the lowest scoring candidate or candidates were eliminated by round until there were only two options left. At that point, a majority was needed to win.

There was only one preliminary round, and the two names that came out were Pell and Robyn.

Robyn? I did a double take of the name projected on my lens. Why was I even in the running?

Then the final round began and Pell was elected immediately.

"Okay divisions, now for your cadet-commanders."

The familiar interface popped up and I chose my name.

"Congratulations, Robyn, you're the new cadet-commander."

I was still waiting for the final two names to pop up, and Pell could see the confusion in my eyes.

"A unanimous vote, no second round."

He reached out his hand and smiled.

"You've earned it."

I shook his hand, and looked at my divisionmates with a gratitude I wasn't sure I could properly express.

"Third division," Pell continued, "you have a little more work this weekend than usual. Robyn?"

I composed myself.

"Yes, sir. Cadets, back to your rooms for course selections."

Our desired course list was due at 750, which gave us over three hours. For most first-session cadets, the four month mark was where these decisions would start impacting their career tracks, so there was some pressure to make the right choices. The situation with Teer had distracted us from these decisions, but hopefully three hours would be enough to figure out our classes.

Our classes? No, I realized, my choices didn't matter. While my friends had a future to consider, a future of their own choosing, I had the whim of some mysterious superiors plotting my course.

Again, I wondered about the path laid before me, about the people pulling the strings. The same questions from last weekend plagued my mind, and in the hours leading up to dinner, the darkness threatened to return, to highlight the differences between myself and my peers.

How long would I be fighting this battle? How long would I struggle to figure out who I was?

94

This cloud hung over me through dinner, a subtle separation between myself and the others. I watched as my divisionmates shared excited words about their course assignments, envious of their carefree laughter. It wasn't until we left the cafeteria and headed to the squad room I realized someone had noticed.

"What's wrong, sir?"

Deena was kind enough to speak softly, away from the others, and I gave her a thankful smile.

"I've got a lot on my mind, Deena."

She nodded, responding without looking at me.

"I can imagine."

A few minutes after we reached the squad room, the schedules came through, and there was a scramble to activate desks and check lenses. I welcomed the stimulus as a brief respite from my depressing thoughts, and took a moment to look over the next month's course list.

Most of the changes I saw were not what I had chosen, though that didn't surprise me. What did surprise me was one of my choices making it through: I was moving from Galactic Biology to Advanced Biology, its upper-level counterpart. It was still an odd day only class, now paired with Terian Politics on even days. And in place of my alternating Galactic Militaries and Galactic Politics courses was Computer Science I, a daily class. While it hadn't been one of my selections, I did remember positive feedback from members of the second division. Hopefully they were right.

Wrapping up the replacements was the next step after OT and MC, Fleet Unity. This course discussed the ways different parts of the Fleet worked together, but I almost laughed at the name. For one, I no longer believed in the motto—I had seen too much that proved otherwise—and to make matters worse, the title was a cruel reminder of my past, present, and future: could I ever truly be united with my peers?

"So, what's the consensus?"

Drel snapped me out of my daze.

"The consensus?" I asked.

She gave me a concerned look.

"You okay?"

I sighed.

"I've got a lot on my mind."

She nodded, not entirely convinced.

"Ok, what'd you get?"

I listed out my new schedule to her.

"Excited about bio I'm sure?"

I nodded, managing a smile.

"And you?"

She started telling me about some of her new engineering courses, then stopped abruptly.

"Robyn, you sure you're okay?"

"I…"

The genuine concern in her eyes was a thin ray of light cutting through the dark cloud above me. But what could I tell her? The truth was forbidden, and Drel deserved nothing less than the truth.

"You don't want to talk about it, do you?"

I gave her a sad smile.

"Sorry."

She scoffed.

"No need to apologize. Just tell me later."

She winked at me, and it took all my willpower not to frown. Would I ever be able to tell her? Would I ever be able to tell anyone that mattered?

95

The next day I said goodbye to Kulee and hello to Tyla. Having done several of these room changes, I began to understand the reasoning behind them. While I was still closest to Drel, each month helped strengthen the bonds among us, bringing us closer as a division. I wondered how universal that was—surely there had to be friction among certain pairs. Teer and Jule came to mind, but what could I say about the inner workings of 20th? In any case, I was lucky to have the division I did.

Unfortunately, even my division wasn't enough to improve my mood—not this time. My mind drifted to dark places, and I struggled to pull it back. This was a dance I knew far too well, which only it made it worse: how many times would I get complacent, get comfortable, and then something would remind me of my unique situation, of how I was different?

Even if I finished out my time at the Academy, even if I became an officer of the Fleet, my origin would follow me. In a way, Commander Hurren had lied: when I finished, I wouldn't get my freedom—I'd be constrained to do what they wanted. And what about after that? Would I ever be allowed to retire? To live a normal life? Was that even possible?

I knew these thoughts were premature. I was only four months into my first session, with plenty left to go. Barring any more kidnappings, and excepting my special elective, I had several months of normal cadet life ahead of me. Was I going to deny the only joy I knew in my life based on some dire prediction?

I turned to my new roommate, eager to distract myself.

"Tyla, are you ready to start the fifth month?"

She turned to me and shook her head, wide-eyed.

"I can't believe we're halfway through the session," she answered.

"Time flies when you're shooting lightning out of your hands," I quipped.

She laughed.

"It sure does. But I have to say, I miss home. I love it here, of course, but knowing that we have two more sessions and specs in between doesn't make it any easier."

I nodded, almost wincing. There it was again, the one subject I wasn't sure I'd ever understand: home. Not in the sense of belonging—I had that at the Academy. In the sense of origin, family, history…

"Where is home for you, Tyla?"

It was a polite question, with just a hint of curiosity. But the answer changed everything.

"Raviir."

96

Having a roommate from Raviir proved immediately difficult. My curiosity, dormant for so long, reawakened stronger than ever. But it was a vague and frustrating curiosity, like a word on the tip of my tongue. I didn't know what questions I wanted to ask, and I certainly didn't know why. All I knew was I had to be discreet. Something about this desire related to my life before Kurotar, those hazy red recollections I had kept entirely to myself.

In the past four months I had had plenty of time to learn about the planet of red. From biology to OT, Raviir figured heavily in many Academy courses because it figured so heavily in the Fleet. So why had none of those lessons sparked this fire? What made Tyla's revelation different?

Still, there was a silver lining here: it gave me something to focus on, a place to channel my thoughts. To be sure, it was essentially the same problem—my origin—but instead of worrying how it affected my future, I was wondering how it shaped my past. Perhaps a new perspective would fill in the blanks?

For most of the first day of the fifth month, I fought the urge to talk about it, not least because I didn't even know what it was I wanted to talk about. As far as I could tell, Tyla was unaware of the storm inside of me, though I wasn't sure how long that would last—I found myself staring at her during our first Fleet Unity class, barely listening to our instructor's introductory remarks.

"Good morning, cadets. This course is about inter-group Fleet relations and operations. We will discuss the various ways the Guard, the Infantry, and Intelligence interact and perform their duties among themselves and with the rest of the Fleet. We will also look at inter-command operations and the basic mechanics of command transfers."

Tyla seemed to sense someone was watching her, and I shot my eyes to the instructor. Was this going to be the theme all day? We only shared two classes, but even at lunch I found myself drifting toward my new roommate.

"Tyla, where on Raviir are you from?"

She looked up at me curiously.

"U14, why?"

I shrugged, trying to play it off.

"I've always wanted to visit and never had the chance."

She nodded.

"There's not much to it. Lots of red. Red, red, red. It's beautiful to an outsider but when you grow up there you get used of it."

She pushed her spoon deeper into the goop.

"Though I do miss home-cooked meals."

I nodded, annoyed she hadn't asked a follow-up question. I had to accept this was going to be a slow process. Besides, what was the rush? I still didn't know what I was looking for. Did I expect one of her statements to unlock my past, to bring back another memory?

If so, I needed to curb my enthusiasm. So far, only one other person had been able to do that.

"Good afternoon."

"Good afternoon, sir."

While I would never say I was growing comfortable around Commander Kelt, there was a certain familiarity between us—after all, she was the instructor I saw most often.

"Now that you're done with MC, we're going to add that curriculum to your training."

I had a moment to ponder what she meant before a hidden sprinkler system activated, drenching me in cold water. The surprise was enough to catch me off guard, and by the time I realized the commander was coming at me, it was too late.

Her shoulder dug into my stomach, while her arms and legs threw me off-balance, sending me to the ground. I managed to grab her arm and tried to fire, but my glove was soaked and unresponsive—I needed a different way out.

After two months of Manual Combat, I had managed to overcome my handicap, to subdue the looming discomfort. But this wasn't Manual Combat, and within seconds of trying to escape the commander's grasp, the headache was back, surging to levels I hadn't felt in months.

I tried to tap out but she ignored it, and as I struggled to break free, to find some leverage, a familiar fear crept into my system. How far would she take this? Was I moments away from another blackout?

She twisted me into another position, locking my neck in her arm and pulling hard. The pressure on my arteries would knock me out in a matter of seconds, and again I tried to tap out, slapping the wet floor with as much urgency as I could muster. But the commander only tightened her hold, squeezing the life out of me. I stopped resisting, knowing the darkness was on its way...

Then reality flooded my senses and the commander let me go, standing as I struggled to breath. Had I fallen unconscious? I swore I had felt her come off of me...

I got to my feet slowly, almost slipping on the wet floor, and eyed her warily. But where I had expected more smug satisfaction, more psychopathic pleasure, I saw something I hadn't seen in months: fear.

"Expect the unexpected," she said.

There was no conviction in her tone, none of the usual self-assuredness. I wanted to revel in her discomfort, but something about the situation only worried me further.

"Yes, sir," I replied.

Three times now, I had seen that fear, and each time when she was on the verge of crossing a line. Was this her inner struggle? Her attempt to control the evil inside of her?

It didn't matter, I thought to myself. This was the woman who had kidnapped and almost killed my best friend—that evil was well beyond control.

97

The entire first week, my hunger for knowledge of Raviir plagued me like an itch I couldn't scratch. Every time I was alone with Tyla, I realized that despite my appetite for information, I still had no idea what I was looking for, what I was trying to find. This lack of clarity only added to my frustration, feeding a cycle of disappointment.

At times, I would try to revisit the instances where the red memory presented itself, but if I had had trouble recalling them in the immediate aftermath, I could scarcely remember anything now. Still, it was an exercise for my mind, a way to try to piece together the puzzle.

The first incident happened more or less on its own: my first night at the Academy, trying to remember my past. Why that had only worked once—and so weakly—I couldn't say. Of course the second incident was hard to forget... that was the true flashback, the one that proved it was more than just a figment of my imagination... and the one that put me squarely in danger, as I hadn't reported it like Commander Hurren had asked.

That last bit, I tried not to think about.

"I don't understand how there can be anything harder."

At dinner on 8day, Drel could barely walk.

"Fitness II?" Epore asked.

"Robyn and Grie are crazy, that's all I have to say," she added.

"Grie, what're you doing this month?" I asked.

I knew he was ahead of the curve, having moved up to Fitness II a month in advance, but I wasn't sure if that had continued.

"I've got another month of Fitness III," he replied.

"You going to try for Advanced after?" Epore asked.

He smiled.

"Of course."

"You're crazy," Drel added, shaking her head.

We laughed.

"Robyn, you want to visit Raviir?" Crim asked.

I tensed unconsciously then tried to relax. I had to be better about controlling my outward appearance.

"Yea, why?"

"Tyla was telling me."

Again, I winced.

"Maybe you will soon," Rolin interjected.

"What do you mean?" I asked, monitoring my tone.

"Specs," he answered.

"We get to choose?"

This time, a little of my eagerness slipped through.

"Not really, but Raviir is a popular spot. We're going to talk about specs later this month to start getting you ready."

I nodded.

"Where did you do your specs, Rolin?" Tyla asked.

"Borrin. Also known as boring."

We laughed.

"Hey, I'm from Borrin!" one of the first-class cadets interjected.

Rolin smiled.

"Sorry, Syrto. But my specs was boring."

"How involved do you get?" Tyla continued. "Are you part of the ops or do they treat you like basic?"

He raised his hands up in mock fatigue.

"We'll tell you all about it in two weeks, don't fret."

Tyla rolled her eyes.

"Fine."

98

Two weeks later and I had made no progress on Raviir. Thankfully, the third weekend was our weekend to discuss specs, a welcome distraction I secretly hoped might bring me closer to the red planet. Pell led us off with a brief overview.

"Special assignments are a first-hand glimpse into life after the Academy. As you all know, you will have three specs as a cadet, one after each session, each lasting 100 Alder days. Remember that last detail: you'll likely be stationed on a planet with a different time system, or if you're on a ship, you'll use the Terian clock. In both cases, 100 will translate to a different number."

He paused for emphasis. A hundred days seemed like a lot, but I was already over 200 into this session. Still, how long it felt really depended on what I would be doing.

"Each cadet will receive their specs at the start of the final month. You won't choose your specs, it will be chosen for you. However, the classes you're taking and the track you declare will help determine where you're placed. Some specs have a lot of cadets, others have just one. In all cases, overlap will be minimal: seeing someone from your mock command is rare, seeing someone from your squadron simply won't happen."

I remembered Rolin talking about how much he missed Bett and Wilor.

"Now we'll go off-cap and your second-division partners will give you more details about their own experience. Feel free to ask around for someone that may have taken the same courses as you, to find a better match for where you might end up. Cadets, caps off and at ease."

I took off my cap and turned to Rolin.

"Well, I'm all ears," I said.

He smiled.

"It's really not that exciting. I got placed on a carrier hangar deck. I learned a lot about how they deploy and take in ships but not much else. It's rare to get a great first specs, they usually get better each year."

I gave him a curious look.

"100 days on a carrier hangar and nothing exciting happened?"

He smiled.

"Not much. I was lucky to have pretty relaxed oversight. My superiors were helpful and gave me plenty of flexibility. Wilor had a horrible experience."

I raised my eyebrows, inviting him to continue.

"Well, he was stationed on a destroyer, which at first glance is the jackpot. I mean, they can't really put you on a scout frigate, so a destroyer is probably the best ship you'll end up on. Anyways, he goes in excited to see what they'll have him do and… well, in his words it was like being a transie all over again. He was cleaning bathrooms and running laps. That's part of the deal with specs though, you don't know what you're going to get."

"What command was he in?"

"Veller."

"And you were Borrin, right?"

"Yep."

I wanted to ask if anyone in his division had gotten Raviir, but I held myself back.

"Did anyone in your division take similar courses to me?"

He paused in thought.

"Have you declared your track yet?" he asked.

I shook my head.

"Ah, well, no one in my division. Actually you should talk to Pell. I'm pretty sure he double-dosed for a while."

I looked over at our cadet-captain, explaining something to Crim.

"Okay, thanks Rolin."

"No problem. Sorry I don't have any more information. Let's just hope your superiors are more like mine and less like Wilor's."

I smiled and nodded, then walked over to Pell and Crim. Both of them turned toward me, and Pell stopped his explanation to greet me.

"Hello, Robyn."

His smile hit me harder than I expected, and I turned to Crim.

"Sorry to interrupt."

He shook his head.

"I'm just listening to what Pell did for his second specs. Go ahead."

I turned back to the cadet-captain.

"How can I help you, Robyn?"

"Did you take space and terra your first session?"

He smiled.

"Not quite. I took it my first four months, so you're three weeks past me now. But yes, I double-dosed. Although I didn't do Advanced Fitness until the last two months of my first session. Have you declared a track yet?"

"No, sir."

He smiled again.

"Robyn, if you keep calling me sir when we're off-cap, you're going to make me think I've graduated, so could you please stop?"

I nodded, slightly embarrassed. Most of my time spent with him was official—it was hard to break the habit.

"I'm guessing you're curious what I did for my first specs," he continued, then glanced at Crim. "Sorry for the detour here."

Crim shrugged.

"Not a problem."

Pell turned back to me.

"I was stationed on Gonn with Intelligence. I spent most of my specs on terra, learning about communication analysis in a two-world system."

Gonn and Soortah were each two-world systems, as opposed to the other nineteen one-world systems in the empire. Since commands were based on systems, each of those two worlds shared a command. This made for a lot of unique policies and procedures.

"Are you on the Intelligence track, Pell?" I asked.

He nodded.

"Indeed I am."

Five months in and I was just now learning this.

"And what about your second specs, if you don't mind me asking?"

He laughed and gestured at Crim.

"I think both of us would be more than happy to answer. My second specs was at Raviir Three, where I got a good look at some of the work Intelligence was doing to keep tabs on the MR."

Crim gave me a knowing look, breaking my attention from the mention of Raviir.

"Our cadet-captain was spying on the Resurgence."

Pell laughed.

"Not quite. I was watching other people gather intelligence about their activities and members. I was really lucky with that placement. I hope I get something similar for my final specs."

The final specs were often a job interview; about 40% of cadets left their final specs, graduated, and went right back to the same position.

"Do you get any more say in your final specs?" I asked.

Pell nodded.

"You do, thankfully. You can be as specific as you want, and the Academy will look at your performance averages and previous specs, then determine from there."

Interesting. I wondered how much that would apply to me.

"So what happened after they made that positive ID?"

Crim took the opportunity to jump back to their previous conversation. Pell looked at me to see if he could continue and I nodded—I knew what I needed to know.

"We tracked their whereabouts to another region on Raviir, and caught a signal in the Raviir 18 spaceport. Now here's the interesting part: even though we had a position and were in contact with our peers at 18, he was never found."

"He boarded a civilian ship?"

Pell shook his head.

"Unless he yanked out his ID chip, we would have caught him. We scan everyone going through any port. But I have my own theory. I think he was a robot."

Crim had been totally absorbed in the story, and now I was too. Robots were absolutely forbidden in the Terian empire—any that were found were promptly destroyed. But there was a problem with this policy: robots were not a well-defined concept. Put simply, there existed an entire spectrum from human to machine, and many beings fell into both categories. Frankly—and while it would be unwise to say so publicly—the ID chips, ear wigs, lenses... all that equipment was pushing Fleet cadets away from the fully human.

Still, the most basic robots would never make it inside the empire—what the Fleet had to look out for were hyper-realistic androids. Here too there were different layers of complexity: fake skin on a body of metal was the most basic type, but what if the skin tissue was grown in the lab? Was that not natural? Was that not human?

"A robot? An android then?" Crim asked.

Pell nodded.

"I saw video of the target myself. It looked human to me."

"But how could it be a robot? Wouldn't you be able to pick up the signal?"

Since the empire had to draw the line somewhere, it drew it at the brain. Even with a fully human body, an artificial brain—or a non-human

one, to be more precise—made its owner a robot. These types of brains—
or at least most of them—had inbound and outbound signals which could
be picked up by Intelligence, and that was the most common way of
weeding them out.

"Normally, yes."

"So why would this one be any different?"

Pell shrugged.

"I don't know, I could be wrong. But a robot might be able to fake an
ID chip."

Crim nodded, lost in thought.

"Anyways, there you go, that was the most exciting thing that happened
during my second specs."

Watching ships dock, cleaning bathrooms, or chasing robots. Out of
the three, I hoped for the latter.

99

As the next weekend approached, I noted a bit of tension among my
division. If I had to guess, it was less about the fifth climate excursion's
location and more about its personnel. At first I was surprised—how had I
had managed to go four weeks without so much as acknowledging Teer's
existence? Even the few times he was involved in our military training, I
ignored him and Jule completely.

Yes, Tyla and Raviir consumed my idle thoughts, but I knew there had
to be more to it. Sure enough, as soon as I started paying attention, I
realized neither of my classmates were behaving in their usual manner. I
didn't know when the change occurred, but now that I was looking for
their smug attitudes and stares, I couldn't find them. It was almost off-
putting.

When the weekend came and went without a hitch, I wasn't the only
one surprised.

"What's going on with Teer and Jule?" Tyla asked me.

It was 10day evening, a few hours after we had wrapped up the exercise. She looked at me as if I knew the answer, but I just shrugged.

"I have no idea."

The next day, Pell asked to meet me privately during lunch. I grabbed my food and met him in the squad room.

"Hey, Robyn."

"Hello, Pell."

He smiled and gestured to the chair next to him.

"Have a seat, please."

I took my seat, surprised by how much more comfortable I felt around him. While I still hadn't let my guard down, I wasn't as hyper-aware of my movement, my expression, my speech.

"Do you know why I wanted to see you?" he asked.

"The climate excursion?"

He nodded.

"Do you know why things have changed?"

I shook my head.

"I thought as much. First, 20th had a special meeting where the upperclassmen strongly encouraged certain members of third division to get their act together."

Pell gave me a knowing look.

"And second, the Puric commander was replaced."

I hesitated, surprised by his words.

"Is this normal?"

"I'm not sure. Cife told me about it but didn't give me too many details —she just wanted me to know."

"Do I need to do anything?" I asked.

He shook his head.

"No. Nothing's changed. The previous commander put both of you on your final warnings. This was likely noted on your records. Normally these warnings are reviewed at some point, and may be lowered or even rescinded. That is entirely up to the new commander."

I nodded.

"Pell, do you know which of those two things was the reason he stopped?"

He smiled.

"No, and I'd rather not guess."

I smiled back.

"Thank you, Pell."

"Of course. Anyways, you don't need to do anything but keep an eye out for a message from the new commander—you may be called into a meeting. And most of all, assume you're still on that final warning."

I nodded, then grabbed my food and made to stand.

"What are you doing?" he asked.

I looked at him and sat back down.

"I thought we were done," I replied.

He laughed.

"Just eat with me."

Of course. At least I didn't say yes, sir.

100

After my lunch with Pell, we had military work with our entire group, including 20th. Between my duties as cadet-commander, I snuck a few glances at Teer and Jule, contemplating what Pell had told me.

A lecture from the upperclassmen and a new Puric commander? I had a feeling I knew which change had caused this shift in behavior, but how? Were Teer's family ties not important anymore?

I could wonder about this for the next few days, but my curiosity was occupied with a different problem—one that had an ever-approaching deadline.

"Tyla, have you ever seen a trone?"

We were in our room on 6day evening and I couldn't hold it anymore—I would be moving out in four days. At this point, I was grasping at straws, but it was better than nothing—or so I hoped.

"A trone?" she said, giving me a curious look. "Not in person, no. There's a lot of them on Raviir, but they're deep in the wilderness—nowhere near the cities. How do you know about trones?"

I hesitated.

"We had a lesson about them in biology."

She nodded.

"Ah, okay. They're super dangerous. The only thing on Raviir that's a threat to humans."

"Do people avoid the wilderness then?" I asked.

She shook her head.

"Not really. You'd have to go pretty far out to find one, and they're nocturnal. I never heard of an encounter myself but I know they happen."

Yes they do, I thought to myself. The real question was why: why would an animal native to Raviir find itself on Alder—a planet with only one patch of wilderness?

Deep down I knew the truth—I always had—yet I still couldn't believe it. Was I thrown into a life-threatening situation just to see how I would handle it? Were my rescuers watching me, ready to step in when necessary, or would I have been left for dead if I hadn't killed the trone?

I remembered Commander Kelt's face when she let me out of the chokehold—the same face I had seen in the infirmary, and the first time she had asked me to attack her. Had the same thing happened up there? Had she been watching me suffer, pinned under the boulder, then suddenly had a change of heart?

Ultimately, the commander's damaged psyche wasn't high on my priority list. What worried me more was the connection between the trone and my hazy recollections. Did she somehow know about my memories? Did she know about my past?

If she did, she wasn't telling me about it, and so far Tyla was my best chance at learning more. But as I wracked my brain for a follow-up question, some thread to sow a conversation with, I realized it was futile. How was I supposed to figure anything out without knowing what I was looking for?

Four days later, I moved in with Epore, my curiosity unsatisfied.

101

By the sixth month, I was used to being a cadet. I was used to Advanced Fitness, even when I was sore. I was used to my tactics double, even if it was still difficult. I was used to military work, the most variable course of all. I was even used to my special elective, Commander Kelt's occasional episodes notwithstanding.

What I wasn't used to was being flirted with, and that's exactly what Epore was doing.

"Drel, how did you deal with this?"

She laughed.

"I told you! Ask Deena—it happened to her too."

"Seriously, Drel. I put my cap on and he's a great cadet. Respectful, calls me sir, no funny business at all—ever. But as soon as we're alone in the room, it gets weird. And it's not like he's going way over the line—that would almost be easier to deal with. No, he's standing on the line stretching his foot over it and touching the other side with his toe."

She burst out laughing.

"That's great, Robyn. Perfect. Listen, just be firm with him and he'll tone it down. I'll be honest, it never really went away, but after a while you get used to it."

She shrugged and smiled, but I wasn't amused. I knew I had to say something, but I didn't want to blow this out of proportion: he was being a minor annoyance, not degrading me.

The last time I had an issue with a roommate, I resolved it with the help of one person in particular. So I sent Rolin a message and met him a few days later.

"Hey, Robyn."

"Hey, Rolin. Thanks for meeting me again. Is Olla here?"

He shook his head and gestured for me to sit at her desk.

"She's in the squad room."

I nodded and sat down.

"So what's the latest drama?" he asked.

I smiled.

"Another roommate conundrum. This time it's Epore."

"Ah, Epore. Kulee's other half, right? Can't you say the same things you said to her?"

I shook my head.

"It's not that. He's been flirting with me. Normally he's a great cadet, and it's never affected our working relationship, but when we're alone and off-cap, he'll do things that are borderline unprofessional."

Rolin raised his eyebrows.

"Oh boy."

"What?"

He smiled.

"You're not going to like my answer—again."

I shrugged.

"That's why I'm here."

"Right, in that case you probably know what I'm going to say. To me, this doesn't seem like a big deal. You say so yourself: on-cap, he's professional, correct?"

"Correct."

"And off-cap, it's only when you're alone, not around others, right?"

"Yes."

"And even when he does it, you're saying it's borderline unprofessional. So which is it, professional or unprofessional?"

I hesitated.

"Well, technically it's unprofessional."

"And technically he's not a professional. He's still got more than two sessions to go. Besides, why are you hesitating to tell me he's unprofessional? It's almost as if you're trying to defend him."

I sighed.

"I… I don't know. It's not disruptive, not even when we're alone. Just annoying. I'm mostly worried it might grow into something unacceptable."

Rolin smiled.

"Well there you go. You've found the crux of the issue. Tell him that."

I nodded.

"Also, Robyn, tell me this: was it professional of you to hug me the other day?"

I didn't answer. He had me there.

"Technically, no. But did I care? No. Quite the opposite. Did you ask for permission to hug me beforehand? No, and that would've been absurd. Not everything is black and white here, Robyn. Sometimes, you're going to have to decide what's acceptable and unacceptable. You're right, if it crosses the line you have to do something, and it's a good idea to let him know you don't want that to happen. But that's all there is to it—at least, in my opinion."

He was right. After all, every time I was with Pell, I wanted to break the rules, to act 'borderline' unprofessional. What made that any different?

The door opened and Olla walked in.

"Oh, hello Robyn."

I stood from her chair.

"Hi Olla. Sorry to steal your desk, I'm on my way out."

She looked from me to Rolin and back, then nodded.

"No worries."

I turned back to my second-division partner.

"Thanks again, Rolin."

"Of course."

I headed back to my room, trying not to read too much into Olla's expression. Right now I needed to focus on Epore.

As soon as I took my cap off, it started.

"Hey Robyn. Glad to see you back, it's much better when you're here."

He smiled. I took a seat in my chair and turned to face him.

"Epore, listen, I want to talk to you about this."

He gave me a confused look.

"About what?"

"You flirting with me."

I could see the defenses coming up, the wheels turning to formulate his response, but I put my hand up.

"Please don't, Epore. I'm not trying to lecture you, and my cap is off. I just wanted to ask you to tone it down a bit. And most of all, please don't let it evolve into something that crosses the line."

There was frustration in his expression, This was not going to be the same as Kulee.

"What are you talking about Robyn? Flirting?"

I sighed.

"Epore, there's a clear difference between your actions when we're alone and off-cap versus any other time. Do you disagree?"

"No, of course not, there is a difference. When we're here, I let my guard down. I can be myself. Just because I compliment you, maybe I admire you. Am I not supposed to be honest with you? Kulee told me you wanted us to be open?"

He was right about that.

"Yes, but... just don't go any further. Don't make it unprofessional."

He nodded, but his expression didn't match the gesture. I had offended him, less than a week in. Only four to go.

102

For better or worse, I started to see less of Epore after our chat. He was rarely in the room after dinner, and any conversation we had was concise, almost curt. Technically, I had succeeded: he wasn't flirting anymore. Part of me wanted to find a way to fix this—I remembered how the tension between Drel and I had affected our entire squadron—but another part of me just wanted to let it be. After all, was there even anything to fix? Hadn't I already fixed it?

I had plenty to keep me busy, of course. Our second month of Fleet Unity covered several interesting topics, including an in-depth analysis of the interplay between different groups in major Fleet operations. Put simply, Intelligence determined as much as it could about the situation, the Fleet flew in to establish interplanetary control, then the Infantry established terrestrial dominance.

While these sorts of massive operations were mostly a thing of the past, recent attacks by the Resurgence were mobilizing more and more Fleet resources, especially in contested regions. Despite these terroristic threats, however, the majority of Fleet operations were dedicated to maintaining peace and order.

Peace and order—I had heard these words over and over, used to describe the Fleet's domestic mission, but it didn't take much to read between the lines. An industrial region on Lefforan calling for better working conditions? Send in the Fleet to maintain peace and order. A protest on Veller against leisure development on sensitive land? Send in the Fleet to maintain peace and order.

Was this another reason seasoned officers seemed so contemptuous? The Academy painted the Fleet as the good guys, but I had to believe most cadets were smart enough to understand this was an indoctrination process. We were being fed information in a carefully selected manner, with enough opposing views to seem objective but not enough to promote critical thinking.

I was reminded of military work, of the drills we practiced to hone our obedience. What would happen after graduation, if I was tasked with something I didn't feel comfortable doing? No, I realized, I was already well past that—everything I was doing in my special elective had cause supreme discomfort.

Still, that had more to do with my neurological issues than ethical ones. What happened when the rifle in my hands was a real one, or the person I was sparring with actually wanted me dead?

No, I realized again, I was already well past that too. Thanks to Commander Kelt, I had the most realistic training available.

103

"I think this weekend is going to be it," Crim announced.

As we approached our sixth climate excursion, my division was taking bets on what environment we had in store. All third-class cadets went through the same eight climate excursions on a rotating basis. Having talked to other members of our class in different wings or commands, we knew which three were left. The question was, which one was it going to be?

"You're probably right," Epore replied. "That's the pattern some Oser guys in my fitness course went through."

Most of us agreed this weekend would be the basic Alder forest, and we certainly hoped we were right: it was by far the simplest.

"Did they say anything specific?" Crim asked. "Was it just the usual shelter and water?"

"I think so," Epore answered.

"That almost seems too easy," Crim said, turning to me. "I mean, that's got to be easier than a day in Advanced Fitness, right?"

Some of them laughed and I smiled.

"Maybe we should do it with weighted uniforms and oxygen-deprivation masks," I suggested.

Crim shook his head.

"Yea, on second thought, let's not."

A few days later, our shuttle landed in a well-forested area of the grounds. We had guessed correctly, but this wasn't going to be as easy as we had hoped: sleet came down from the overcast sky, icy rain dancing in the cold wind. While the rest of us groaned in dismay, Porr seemed pleased by the conditions.

The cadet-commanders agreed to search for high ground and start building A-frames, but there was a problem: our gloves were soaked—we couldn't cut the trees. We had to find branches, which weren't necessarily plentiful, so we gathered as many as we could while we searched for a good spot.

Over the next hour, the sleet worsened to the point where we decided to cut our losses and start our shelters at the nearest clearing. Since we were still short on wood, 19th went to look for more while the rest of us put together what we could.

Overall, it was an unpleasant process. Our branches were oddly sized and all of our materials were already wet. Even when we put together our first few A-frames, they were just as wet inside as out. All told it took three hours to get the shelters in place, and not once did the sleet clear. At least water wasn't an issue.

Once each frame was up, we huddled inside our wet shelters with our roommates. I lay next to Epore on an uncomfortable bed of twigs and leaves under a leaking roof, trying not to think about the awkwardness between us. The setting sun was only exacerbating the cold, and via lens communication, the cadet-commanders agreed that our current setup would not be enough for the night temperatures. But as long as the sleet was coming down, we couldn't have an open fire.

Our solution was to have each element dig a hole under their frame and use the driest plant matter they could find to start a small fire. One person dug the hole and found the kindling while the other kept their gloves as dry as possible and started the flame. It took another hour, but soon each A-frame turned into a sort of stove.

Admittedly, this plan was dangerous. The holes and fires had to be the right size: too small and it would be too cold, too large and the frame might catch fire. Smoke was also a hazard, so we dug the holes deeper and opened up the roofs. We agreed if the sleet subsided during the night, we would start new fires just outside our shelters.

Until then, one roommate was on fire duty while the other rested or slept. It was still unpleasant, but it was working. Even in the middle of a nasty winter night, I was warm. I thought about my first and only night alone in the Alder wilderness—the night I met the trone. My current conditions might be unpleasant, but I preferred this night to that one.

A loud crack interrupted my thoughts, followed by several more. A shelter had collapsed. Then a scream, a scream I recognized, and I jumped to my feet, breaking our A-frame in the process. There, twenty meters away, Drel and Deena's shelter was up in flames.

I sprinted towards them, watching two bodies emerge from the burning pile, the sleet already fighting against the flames. Their uniforms protected their bodies, but not their heads.

"Drop and roll!" I shouted.

They listened immediately, falling to the ground and extinguishing their hair. It was over in seconds, but as soon as I got to them I knew it was serious.

"We need a medic, now!"

I knew everyone in the area was on their lenses and making it happen. I knelt down next to Drel while Porr went to Deena.

"Drel, listen to me, you're going to be fine, just relax."

Her face was marred by red and white splotches, and I could see the blisters forming. I leaned over her to block the rain and made sure Porr was doing the same for Deena.

"Second and third-degree burns on the face and head," the cadet-colonel said. "This is serious but you'll be fine."

I almost wished she hadn't said anything. The entire group was around us now, out of their shelters, helping shield my two divisionmates from the never-ending sleet. Yet despite the clear camaraderie, I felt sick to my stomach. The fires were a terrible idea, why had I agreed to that?

I heard Drel whimper and looked down. Her wounds had started to swell, and I watched the water drip off me, joining the tears falling from her eyes.

104

The next few hours were difficult. Within minutes, a medevac shuttle arrived for Drel and Deena, and Porr had me accompany them while she stayed with the rest of the group. We reached the infirmary a few minutes later, and I watched helplessly as they were ferried away for surgery. The staff put me in a waiting room, water still dripping from my uniform, and I did exactly that—waited.

A few minutes later, Pell walked in and I stood.

"How are they?" he asked.

"Second and third-degree burns to the head and face, sir. They went into surgery about ten minutes ago."

"What happened?"

I explained the sequence of events in detail.

"So the shelter caught fire from the flames underneath?"

"Most likely, sir."

He nodded again.

"But one of them was supposed to be monitoring the fire at that time?"

"Yes, sir."

"Thank you, Robyn. Do you want to stay here?"

"Yes, sir."

"Then we'll wait together."

We took a seat next to one another and he went into his lenses. I wanted to talk to him, to get his guidance, to hear him explain to me why this wasn't my fault…

"Robyn, this is a terrible time, but I need to ask you something."

He broke the silence, startling me.

"Of course, sir."

"Is there anything going on between you and Rolin that I should be aware of?"

Olla. It wasn't just a passing thought.

"No, sir."

He nodded, but that wasn't enough for me.

"Permission to elaborate, sir?"

He looked at me.

"Go ahead."

"I've been meeting with him for advice on certain things, and usually in private."

Pell smiled, taking some of my stress away.

"You know why I'm asking you, I take it?"

I nodded.

"Yes, sir."

"I thought so. In any case, I also want to elaborate. Your squadmate who came to me about this did the right thing, and not just because of the rules. A relationship between divisionmates is against regulations, but a relationship between someone and their second-division partner is worse. When these things happen, they never end well."

I nodded. What about relationships between a third-division cadet and their first-class cadet-captain?

"Of course, if anything ever does happen, you shouldn't hesitate to talk to me. Relationships are forbidden, but sometimes I can get forgetful when it comes to my reports."

He smiled again, and I felt relieved. Relieved to hear he accepted my explanation, relieved to see he was able to talk to me now—a good sign for Drel and Deena—and relieved to find out I was leading in the same style as he was, a style I wanted to emulate.

"Yes, sir."

Then the relief was over, and we waited in silence. It wasn't until 932, well into the night, that an ensign came to address us.

"Cadets Pell and Robyn?"

We nodded.

"Cadets Drel and Deena are in post-op care, stable and in good condition. They had several second and third degree burns on the head and face, but we were able to cover them with rapid-form grafting. There will be some superficial differences, including permanent scarring and temporary lack of hair, but they should be fully recovered and off-hold by 4day. If you wish to see them you'll be able to do so 1day afternoon."

"Thank you," Pell replied.

The ensign took his leave and Pell turned to me.

"I was going to ask if you wanted to go back to Puric or back to the exercise, but I think I can guess."

"The exercise, sir."

He nodded.

"Like I said. Come with me, I'm in a hovcar and Porr can send me the coordinates."

105

On 1day, Pell got special permission to spend our military training visiting Drel and Deena as a squadron. As soon as we walked in, our division rushed to their sides, and I made the conscious decision to see Deena first because I knew less people would head in her direction.

I braced myself for the worst, but the face I saw was almost the same as the face I knew.

"Good afternoon, sir," she said.

I smiled.

"Your cap is off, cadet, don't call me sir."

Deena had a scar along the back of her right cheek and a discoloration across her forehead. There was also something slightly different about her nose, but I couldn't pinpoint it.

"How are you, Deena?" Kulee asked.

"Good, thanks. And you?"

Kulee rolled her eyes and Deena smiled.

"I'm good, Kulee. Just waiting to get off-hold."

"What happened?" I asked.

She frowned.

"I—I don't know. I was watching the fire but… it all happened so fast."

There was something in her tone and expression that worried me. Her earlier smile had seemed forced, although that could be the surgery. Some of the others started crowding around the bed, so I walked over to Drel.

I was happy and a little surprised to find her in more or less the same shape as Deena. Why I would be surprised by the medical prowess of the Fleet, I didn't know. After all, hadn't I fully recovered from the encounter with the trone in just a few days?

"Hey, Robyn."

"Hey, Drel. How's it going?"

There was discoloration over most of her face, almost like a weird tan, but I didn't see any major scarring.

"I've been better. Did you hear the good news, though?"

"What good news?"

"I get to take four days off from Fitness II."

I laughed.

We spent another ten minutes with them before we had to leave. For the most part, I was relieved. Their wounds were all but healed, and they seemed in good spirits. Or at least Drel did. There was something off about Deena—I would have to keep an eye on her.

106

Drel and Deena returned to regular duties a few days before the fifth weekend, and the mood in our division improved dramatically. With the added excitement of the rapidly approaching first specs, there was an electricity in the air that helped me forget my troubles. Even Epore's cold shoulder softened, though by the time I had noticed, I was sharing a room with Crim.

Crim was the last member of my division to room with me, even though we had another month after this one. On the first day I had noticed this discrepancy, and a few weeks ago I had learned the reason: on the eighth and final month of the session, every third-division cadet would room with their second-division partner. Next month, I was rooming with Rolin, which made Pell's inquiry all the more important.

For the time being, I was with the only other former cadet-commander in our division and, in my opinion, the funniest of my peers. After a quiet month with Epore, I was excited.

"Robyn, I just want to set a few ground rules here. First off, sorry, but I'm not interested."

He smiled, giving me a knowing look from across the room.

"So please, no flirting."

I couldn't stop myself from smiling. Thank goodness we were off-cap.

"Thank you for clearing that up," I replied.

His smile disappeared and he straightened at attention.

"Of course, sir. Always ready to be of service, sir. But not to be taken advantage of, sir."

I shook my head and turned to my work. Maybe I wasn't ready for this after all.

The seventh month also brought with it a new course. In place of Fleet Unity, I had Current Affairs: this was the final of the 'first session four': Officer Training, Manual Combat, Fleet Unity, and Current Affairs. I worried it might be a bit redundant with Terian Politics, but only time would tell.

With the fire incident behind us, Epore out of my room, and Teer effectively subdued, the seventh month promised great things. But there was something in the back of my mind that bothered me, something more concrete than Raviir: I had only two more months with Pell.

The session, which started out so new and so fresh, was almost finished. But where I had two more, our cadet-captain was on his last. And while this issue was more clearcut than my obsession with Raviir, it was equally irresolvable.

The reality kept replaying in my head: romantic relationships were forbidden, especially between the classes, and even more so with superior cadet-officers. For better or worse, I was one to follow the rules. As much as my crush intrigued me, it was not worth any major problems down the road, and besides, I didn't want to risk our friendship.

"Robyn, now that we're getting towards the end of the session I wanted to talk to you about next year."

He had asked for a private meeting during lunch. At this point I was used to such things.

"You will very likely be elected cadet-captain, you know that, right?"

The thought had crossed my mind after my surprise appearance during the midterm election.

"Really?"

He nodded.

"I wanted to make sure you understood something: in most cases, if you're on track to be a cadet-captain as a second-class cadet, you'll move up to cadet-colonel or higher your third session."

I thought about Porr and Cife, the tasks they carried out and the schedules they kept. Did I want a position like that?

"As you can guess, being a high-ranking cadet-officer has its disadvantages. You're no longer part of a squadron, you're in a more administrative position."

I nodded. I had learned about this as a cadet-commander. The cadet-officers were often in charge of the transie's assignments, helped schedule certain exercises, and even planned some of the activities.

"How are the higher cadet-officers selected?" I asked.

"Everyone is elected at the end of the session, before specs. Cadet-colonels are chosen by the acting cadet-colonel, the acting cadet-captains of the group, and the outgoing first divisions of that group. Cadet-generals are chosen by the acting cadet-general, the acting cadet-colonels, and the acting cadet-captains of the wing."

"And cadet-admirals?"

He smiled.

"Aiming high, are we?"

I smiled back.

"Just curious."

"Cadet-admirals are elected at the end of the session as well, by the acting cadet-admiral, the acting cadet-generals, and the acting cadet-colonels of the command."

I pondered his words for a moment.

"If someone is trying to become cadet-admiral but only cadet-colonels and up get to choose, how does that work? Aren't most cadet-colonels and up in their last session?"

He nodded.

"Yes, but the candidate pool is not limited to the electors. The entire command is eligible."

I nodded.

"That's a very isolated position, I take it?"

"Yes, very. At that point, you're directly underneath the actual commander. I've rarely met with the cadet-admiral myself."

I nodded, then he continued.

"But... don't let that hold you back. Honestly Robyn, if you wanted to, I think you could do it."

I caught his look and wished I hadn't. Was there more than pride there? More than friendship? It didn't matter. I already knew I couldn't pursue it. The best I could do was enjoy the last two months and try to move on. Pell wasn't the only star in the galaxy.

107

The first morning of the seventh month, Grie joined me in the hall. It was the first time I had seen one of my divisionmates up as early as me on a weekday.

"First day in Advanced?" I asked.

He gave me an apprehensive nod.

"They warned me against it."

He shivered as we walked, and I thought about what awaited him: all of the pain I was already used to, but where I had the luxury of starting in the fall, Grie was starting in the dead of winter. It was much colder in these halls now than it had been our first month.

I gave him a pat on the back and tried to sound encouraging.

"Don't worry, I'm still here, aren't I?"

As it turns out, that was not the right response: at breakfast, struggling to get the spoon to his mouth, Grie echoed Drel's sentiments about Fitness III.

"I think I've made a huge mistake."

Despite his struggle, he was in the hallway again the next morning, and the one after that. By the second week, he was still limping to and from his classes, but he didn't have any trouble eating.

Deena, on the other hand, sometimes did. Not only was she eating less than usual, she was speaking only when spoken to. In the first few months, this would have been normal, but even Deena had warmed to the group over time. Something was wrong, and while it was reasonable to assume the fire was the culprit, I had to wonder if these symptoms were physical or psychological.

I tried my best to keep an eye on her, but the seventh month proved harder than the sixth, thanks in part to the new required course. Where Fleet Unity had been simple enough, Current Affairs assigned daily reviews, each related to some recent operation or attack. As annoying as the workload was, it was a sobering reminder of the MR's relentless and ever-escalating conflict with the empire.

Here too, the information taught was one-sided, but I would never vocalize such a thought. As much as I was a fan of objective learning, the MR's actions were often deplorable, with hundreds if not thousands of civilian casualties resulting from their attacks.

On top of being stretched thin with coursework, I had an interesting issue in my special elective: I was getting better. After months and months of training, my offensive and defensive movements were quicker, more precise. My Manual Combat weakness was fading, almost a memory. And most important of all, the scales were tipping—infinitesimally, almost imperceptibly—in my favor.

Normally, this would be good news, were it not for the commander herself. Having noted the shift in the scales, her attacks had grown in intensity, though this only served to widen the gap. The harder she came at me, the better I adapted.

It was a strange situation, but deep down, I felt an emerging triumph. I knew before the end of the session, I would be able to put her in her place. The thought gave me an alarming amount of pleasure, and I did my best to contain it. After all, this was Commander Kelt—she had a penchant for the unexpected.

108

Midway through the third week, Pell called me for another private meeting.

"Robyn, I want you to talk to Deena."

I frowned.

"What happened?"

"Her CPA is falling below acceptance. If she doesn't correct her averages, she'll be expelled."

I felt a pang of guilt, wishing I had done a better job of watching her.

"What do you want me to do?"

Pell shrugged.

"Just try to talk to her. See if she'll open up to you. Maybe you can lead her out of this mess."

I nodded, contemplating the best way to approach the situation. At dinner, I made sure to sit next to her.

"How are you Deena?" I asked.

She looked up from her meal and faked a smiled. I wasn't fooled.

"Fine, sir."

I ignored the capless sir.

"How are your classes going?" I asked.

"Okay."

She wasn't interested in talking.

"Deena, we need to talk," I whispered.

She looked at me, a hint of confusion in her eyes.

"Your CPA is falling below the acceptable threshold," I added.

She frowned.

"You were told?"

I frowned back, concerned by her reaction.

"I was told."

She sighed, looking away. I waited for her to speak, but she just started eating again.

"Robyn! I told you not to sit next to me anymore!"

I turned at Crim's comment, watching him crack a smile as he sat. By the time I turned back around, Deena had already made her escape. I watched her walk away, a knot forming in my stomach.

"Is she alright?" Crim asked.

I shook my head.

"I'm not sure."

"I'm sorry if I…"

I turned and shook my head.

"It's okay. You didn't mean to."

Pell was absent from dinner so I sent him a message. He had me meet him in the squad room.

"It didn't work?" he asked.

I shook my head.

"I didn't really get to talk to her. Should I ask to meet her in private?"

He shook his head.

"No Robyn, I will. Thank you for trying though. I thought maybe she would be more open with you but it sounds like that's not the case. If I need your help, I'll let you know."

The next day, Deena wasn't at breakfast.

"Cadets, in case any of you are wondering about Deena, she had some follow-up treatment from the fire that she had to attend to. Please don't be alarmed."

I knew Pell was hiding something in that announcement, but it was up to him if he wanted to fill me in. After all, Drel was sitting there listening with us, confused by what was happening. Confused enough to pull me aside right after the meal.

"What do you think that's all about?" she asked.

I frowned. Even if I didn't know the details, I wondered what kind of precedent she expected. There had to be a line between friendship and leadership.

"Drel, you know I have access to certain privileged information I can't share."

She gave me an angry look.

"I can't be worried about the person that was in the fire with me?"

She had me there.

"You're right, I'm sorry. But I don't know any more than you do."

I looked her up and down then continued.

"How are you? You seem to be pretty much back to normal."

Her expression changed. Something about it was different, different than I had ever seen.

"Yep, pretty much."

Her speech was different too. What was going on here?

"Drel, is something wrong?"

She shook her head.

"No."

In that moment, I knew she was lying. I felt a pang of betrayal but tried to stay professional.

"Well, if you ever need to talk, I'm here."

I walked away before it got worse. I trusted Drel completely. Did she not trust me? Her and Pell lying on the same day... what was happening in our squadron?

109

The weekend came and went and there was still no sign of Deena. In the six days she'd been absent, I'd met with Pell many times. Each time I expected an explanation, and each time I left empty-handed. Or almost empty-handed. The way he talked, the way he looked at me—he knew I wanted to know, but he wasn't telling me. That only worried me more.

On 1day of the fourth week, I'd had enough.

"Pell, can you tell me what's going on with Deena?"

He frowned.

"No."

We were alone in the squad room, but I brought my voice down all the same.

"Can you at least tell me if she's okay?"

His frown deepened.

"Robyn, as cadet-captain, I am entitled to—"

"What about as my friend?"

Just as the question finished coming out of my mouth, I realized how brazen I was being. Brazen and hypocritical: didn't I just have a conversation like this with Drel?

A look of surprise and concern crossed Pell's expression, and for a moment I thought I had crossed a line. But when he looked away and sighed, I knew I had him.

"What I'm about to tell you is strictly between you and me."

He turned and put his hand on my arm.

"Okay?"

His glove hadn't fired but the touch was electric. I could feel the hairs on the back of my neck standing up, and it took everything in my power to keep my eyes on him.

"Okay," I replied.

He let go, and I fought the urge to look down at my arm, where his hand had been.

"Deena blames herself for what happened. She believes the fire is her fault. She's been purposefully neglecting her cadet duties in the hopes of being expelled for an unacceptable CPA."

I wasn't surprised, but the confirmation was important. There was a difference between believing something and knowing it.

"Where is she now? Is she still a cadet?"

"She's in reconditioning therapy but they won't tell me anything. The fact that it's been six days is enough to make me worry."

Reconditioning therapy? I had a much better idea.

"Pell, why don't you get Drel to talk to her?"

"I thought about that, but what can she say? If Deena is convinced it's her fault, even Drel won't be able to change her mind."

I shook my head.

"No, something else."

I laid out my plan to him, the details of what I had in mind, then let him mull it over for a moment.

"It's a good idea, but we'd have to get permission," he said.

"From who?"

He gave me a knowing look.

"The new Puric commander. I'll set up a meeting as soon as possible."

110

As the afternoon wore on, I contemplated the upcoming meeting with the new commander. I was finally going to learn who had saved me from Teer and Jule—or, at least, from their arrogance—but I wouldn't say I was excited. If this commander was anything like the previous one, it would be difficult to get them to agree to anything a lowly, third-class cadet was propositioning. Even with Pell on my side, it was an uphill battle.

Still, when it came to difficult commanders, I had plenty of experience.

"Good afternoon."

"Good afternoon, sir."

While I continued to advance in the hopes of surpassing her, I had made a point to restrain myself, holding back my full potential. The rage in her eyes began to worry me, and while I enjoyed her frustration, I had to be careful—if I pushed her too hard, she might snap, and I might not be the only victim.

At dinner, I found myself staring at the best friend I had almost lost so many months ago. Drel caught my eye, giving me a confused look, but it wasn't because I was staring at her. Pell had told her to join us for the meeting with the Puric commander, but didn't tell her why. She also wasn't allowed to discuss it with anyone else.

"The suspense is killing me," she said.

The table was packed, so I gave her a confused look.

"For what?" I asked.

She rolled her eyes at me.

"For the food of course."

She was still upset with me for not telling her everything before, and now that she wasn't in on the secret with Pell, she was lashing out.

Thankfully, she waited until we were on our way to Pell's room to pester me again.

"You're not going to tell me what this is about?"

"Drel, you know what this is about," I replied.

Pell met us in the hall.

"Ready?" he asked.

"Yes, sir."

We headed downstairs and I went over the plan in my head. It was simple: instead of having Drel try to convince Deena it wasn't her fault, Drel would tell Deena we needed her. Our squadron, our division, and most of all Drel herself. If she could frame it in a way that surviving the fire would be a waste if Deena were to quit, it might bring Deena back. But only if it came from Drel.

The walk to the office brought bitter memories, but this time would be different. There was a new face behind the desk, a new beginning. We stood in front of the door and paused for the ID scan. A light turned green and it opened.

A wave of confusion and surprise hit me, and I did everything I could to contain my reaction. What? Why? These thoughts needed to be repressed immediately, as they threatened the very lives of Pell and Drel. If I hesitated, if I made the wrong gesture, they would be in grave danger, and so would I. But it was going to be a difficult show. Sitting at the desk in front of us was the new Puric commander, someone I knew as Commander Kelt.

111

"Good evening, cadets."

She, of course, was unfazed. It was as if she had never met me.

"Good evening, sir."

For now, I let Pell do the talking, and her eyes stayed on him.

"You had something you wanted to run by me?" she asked.

"Yes, sir. The cadet-commander of our third division has an idea to reinstate our cadet in therapy."

Commander Kelt nodded and turned to me.

"Is that you?"

I nodded.

"Yes, sir."

She looked at Drel.

"And you are the other victim of the fire?"

I could feel the anger bubbling beneath the surface. Here she was, pretending she didn't recognize the person she had almost killed. I needed to keep my emotions in check.

"Yes, sir."

Her eyes came back to me. There was no recognition, no acknowledgement of the fact that we had been together less than an hour ago.

"Go ahead, cadet. Explain your proposal."

"Yes, sir."

I told her my idea and tried to dissociate from the situation. The less I thought about where I was and with who, the better.

"Is that it?" she asked.

"Yes, sir."

Commander Kelt turned to Pell.

"And you agree with this proposal?"

"I do, sir."

She turned to Drel.

"And you? It looks like you are just finding out about this, yes?"

I turned to my divisionmate and saw the surprise in her eyes.

"Yes, sir. I am."

"I apologize about that."

Again, a pang of fury. Why don't you apologize about knocking her unconscious, then firing on her defenseless body?

"Your cadet-officers were under strict orders to keep the status of your divisionmate under wraps as long as possible. It was not their decision, but mine. In any case, do you agree with this proposal? After all, you are the key component. Feel free to take a moment."

Drel shook her head slowly.

"No sir, I don't need a moment. They're correct. I agree with this proposal, and I agree to do what is needed."

Commander Kelt nodded.

"Excellent. The faster this is done, the higher the chance of success. Cadet, would you feel comfortable talking to her now?"

Drel's eyes widened, clearly overwhelmed. She had just found out she was the main piece of the puzzle and was now being asked to act. Still, to her credit, I knew what the answer was going to be before she said it.

"Yes, sir. As soon as possible, sir."

Commander Kelt nodded again.

"Very well, you all have my permission. I will notify the therapist of your coming and give you a hovcar. You are dismissed. Good luck."

"Thank you, sir."

112

The ride across the grounds was an uncomfortable one. I could tell Drel was angry with me for not telling her, despite Commander Kelt's explanation. I just hoped she could focus on the task at hand. In fact, given who we had just met with, I hoped I could focus on the task at hand.

Why was she the new Puric commander? Did she intervene because of Teer? What could she have told him without breaching the secrecy of our relationship? And what about the general?

I pushed these questions to the back of my mind, focusing on the current situation. Deena was being held in a special section of the infirmary and it took three security checks for us to reach her room. On the final leg, a lieutenant therapist had to escort us.

"Who is entering the room?" he asked when we reached the door.

Pell gestured to Drel.

"She is."

The therapist nodded.

"Okay, the three of us will wait outside."

He raised his arm to press the button.

"Sir?" Drel asked.

He paused, and Drel looked from him to Pell and from Pell to me.

"Could you two come in with me?"

Pell looked at me then at the therapist.

"Is that alright, sir?"

He hesitated, then nodded.

"I will wait just outside. Are you ready?"

We looked at Drel.

"Yes, sir," she replied. "Sorry, sir."

He pressed the button, the door opened, and we went inside.

The room was similar to any other in the infirmary, but there were far fewer objects: just a bed, a desk, and a chair, all built into the floor and walls, all with soft edges. Deena was at the desk when we entered, and the sight of her made me pause. There were dark bags under her eyes and her hair was in a fray. She had lost weight, how much I couldn't say, but her frame seemed much more fragile. When she turned to look at us, there was an emptiness in her gaze that made me shudder. Once her eyes locked on Drel, however, they came to life, and it was as if Pell and I were invisible. I felt a ray of hope—maybe this would work after all.

"Drel?"

Deena's voice was soft, almost a whisper. Drel moved toward her while Pell and I stayed by the door.

"Hey, Deena. How are you?"

There was no reply, but her eyes stayed fixed on Drel.

"Deena, we need you to come back."

Drel stood over her, struggling to contain her anguish. I realized how unfair it was to thrust her into this situation, given Deena's state. How could this have happened in six days?

"Deena, you've been gone for too long. Your squadron needs you. Your division needs you."

Silence. It was almost too much to bear. The tears that had been welling up in Drel's eyes started to break free, one by one.

"Deena, you and I had an accident, and you and I survived. I need you back with us, Deena. I need you back with us because if you're not there, it was all a waste. If you quit now, the fire will bring us both down. If it defeats you, it will defeat me. You can't let that happen, Deena. You can't let that happen."

Deena shot up from her chair fast enough to make us jump, and Drel let out a yelp. Her eyes darted to and fro, no longer fixated on Drel.

"It was all my fault..." she began.

"No! Stop. Enough. Do you want to hear the same things you've been hearing from all these doctors? You were on watch, I was resting. We both built that shelter. And who built the fire pit? I did. You just lit the fire. Stop with this, Dee—"

Before she finished the last word, she had to dip and catch Deena, who fell into her arms and burst into tears.

"Drel, you don't understand, I'm so sorry."

As I watched, my own eyes started to water.

"Deena, I don't want to hear any more about any of this. Will you just come back?"

Deena looked up at Drel, still limp in her arms. They stared at each other for a long time, then Deena turned to us, suddenly aware of our presence.

"Will they take me back like this?"

She was asking me but I looked to Pell.

"Deena, if you are ready to be a cadet again, just say the word. But you have to drop this, all of this," he answered.

I looked back to Deena, still in Drel's grip, and watched her straighten and stand on her own.

"Okay. I'm ready."

She turned to Drel.

"I'm doing this for you."

Drel hugged her.

"Thank you."

I struggled to keep my composure, hoping this solution would hold. We had won the battle, but the war was far from over.

113

A few minutes after Deena agreed to return, we asked the lieutenant to come in and help us figure out the details. It was decided she couldn't return right away, as her appearance would bring too much unwanted attention. Instead, she would remain in the infirmary for three more days to rest and gain her strength, accessing her coursework via the desk. Drel and I volunteered to come in to help her as much as possible, but Pell declined my offer, citing the importance of having me around my division as cadet-commander. Drel, however, was given permission to skip military training for the next few days and would have her meals in the infirmary with Deena.

An hour later, we were back on our floor, and Pell bid us goodnight.

"I need to speak with you in private, sir."

The tone in Drel's voice worried me. It was an odd time for formality, given the events that had just transpired.

"Of course, Crim might be in the room but I can ask him to step out."

She shook her head.

"No, sir. I suggest we use my room, sir."

I gave her an exasperated look. This was ridiculous.

"Okay."

I followed her to the door and walked in after her.

"Grie, could you leave us for a moment?"

Grie looked up from his desk. I thought she had chosen her room because she knew Grie wouldn't be there. Why was this different than mine?

"Of course."

He put his cap on and gave me a quick nod.

"Sir."

Then he walked out the door, closing it behind him.

"Permission to go capless, sir?"

I stared at her. She was angry. This wasn't going to be easy.

"Of course."

We took our caps off and each took a seat.

"What is it Drel?"

She glared at me.

"What is it?! What is it?! Why didn't you tell me what I was getting myself into? Do you know how difficult that was for me? To see Deena like that? How did that even happen?"

I had a flashback to the third month, when Drel was silently angry at me. There was no silence this time.

"I had no idea it was that bad. I haven't seen her since she left. Pell didn't tell me anything until today during lunch when I forced it out of him."

She raised her eyebrows.

"You finally went for it? Congratulations."

I shook my head, frustrated.

"No, Drel, not like that. Listen, I'm sorry, okay? I really am. Pell told me what was happening at lunch and I came up with the idea on the spot. We set up the meeting with the commander, and she told us very specifically not to let anyone else know."

I hadn't thought about it earlier but how had Pell explained my own knowledge of Deena's situation? Would he get in trouble for telling me?

"This was your idea and you didn't think it best to run it by me first?"

Her eyes were bloodshot, her tears dried up from the meeting with Deena. It was the only reason she wasn't crying now.

"I came up with it on the spot, I didn't realize I wouldn't be able to warn you. I'm telling you that was all the commander."

"So the commander told you not to say anything. Okay. But couldn't you have at least told me on the way to the meeting? So I wasn't finding it out as you explained it to her? Even that would have been better."

She was grasping for an argument now, her anger taking control.

"I'm sorry Drel, what was I supposed to do? If we were alone maybe I would have told you, but we were with Pell. And Pell knew the rules. I couldn't disobey an order right in front of him."

"Pell," she scoffed. "It's all about Pell."

She shook her head, and I felt the frustration rising up within me. Why was she going on about Pell? This had nothing to do with him.

"Drel, what are you talking about?"

She stood up and started pacing the room.

"I don't know, I…"

She stopped and looked at me, the anger suddenly gone from her expression. In its place, I was surprised to see something else, something unexpected: shame.

"Robyn, I'm sorry."

The tears were coming back—how did she have any more?

"Sorry? For what?"

"I'm mad at you for keeping something from me but I'm doing the exact same thing."

The lie—the lie she had told me the day Deena left.

"Drel, you don't have to tell me everything…"

She sat back in her chair.

"I don't but I should. You're my best friend, Robyn. But you're also my cadet-commander. That's why I haven't told you."

Her going on about Pell—it clicked in my head.

"Drel, are you seeing someone?"

A slow nod answered my question.

"Grie," she said.

Grie? That took my by surprise. My surrogate little brother?

"Ever since he started Advanced Fitness he's been helping me with Fitness II, giving me tips… it was all an excuse to spend time together, we knew we shouldn't, but then there was the fire and I moved in with him…"

She shook her head.

"He's the reason I was able to pull out of this mess. He's been the crutch I've needed, the one Deena never had. I should've told you earlier but—"

"No, Drel. You do whatever feels right to you. Of course you'd hesitate to tell me. After all, it's my job to report you for it."

A hint of worry came over her expression, but I shook my head.

"That doesn't mean I will."

I thought back to what Pell had told me, about being forgetful in his reports.

"Thanks," Drel replied.

"Is this why you've been acting like this?" I asked.

She shrugged.

"Things have been crazy since the accident, and after seeing Deena… I feel guilty I had Grie and she had no one. She's always been kind of an outcast."

I shook my head.

"Drel, now you're turning it around on yourself. Deena fell down a hole of guilt, don't follow her. Maybe she didn't have anyone before, but she does now. She needs your help to get out of it, just like you needed Grie's."

She nodded and I stood.

"Okay, today's been a long day, and we've got a lot of work ahead with Deena. If you need anything, let me know."

Drel stood, then grabbed me in a tight hug. When she let go, she was smiling.

"I can't believe it Robyn. That first month I felt like your big sister, making sure you stayed involved. Now I feel like the little sister."

I smiled back.

"As long as we're still sisters. Of course, Grie is like my little brother, so that makes your thing a little unconventional."

She laughed and gave me a playful hit on the shoulder.

"Get out of here."

"Good luck with Deena. I'll see you tomorrow morning."

114

The next day was a bucket of ice water—of cold, poignant clarity—poured over everything that had transpired.

First, Commander Kelt was the new Puric dorm commander. Expect the unexpected. But the same questions I had had after our meeting lingered in my mind. Did her appointment relate to my problems with Teer? If so, how had she solved the issue?

Then there was Deena. Why had she seemed so frail? There was something else to her condition, something beyond the guilt she had, but I didn't know what it was and I wasn't sure I wanted to find out. Now that she was on the mend, opening these wounds would cause more harm than good.

And finally Drel. I had voluntarily swept aside my cadet-commander duties for my best friend and I didn't realize until the morning after. Could I always look the other way about these things? I tried to defend my actions—maybe she needed Grie because of the fire—but if she started her relationship emotionally vulnerable, that made it even worse.

These thoughts swirled in my mind at breakfast, and I tried to clear my head. Worrying about these situations did nothing—I had to analyze each one and act according to what felt right.

What felt right. I had used that as my excuse to look past Drel and Grie's relationship. After all, wasn't that Rolin's advice? Do what feels right, not what you've been told is right? Yesterday, I thought I knew what felt right, but today?

Pell interrupted my mental struggle to announce Deena's scheduled return, something that clearly cheered the rest of my division. I wondered what the others were thinking now, her having disappeared for so many days. Would they respect her privacy? There was only one person I worried about when it came to gossip, and she was the main one involved.

I realized right then I needed to talk to her.

"Drel, you didn't tell Grie about Deena, did you?"

The change in her expression told me everything I needed to know.

"Drel..."

"He asked about where we were and I told him. We all care about Deena."

"Yes but it should be Deena's decision who knows and who doesn't, don't you agree?"

She shrugged and I felt the frustration inside me growing, not just at her but at myself. This was definitely not right.

"Everyone knows she's gone, everyone cares about her..."

"And everyone is going to treat her differently if they know the truth. The best thing for her is to be treated like a normal recruit. If she feels the need to share what happened, she will. Promise me neither of you will tell anyone else."

She sighed.

"I promise."

"Thank you."

That afternoon, I met with the new Puric commander in our usual spot for my special elective. I had told myself she wouldn't so much as mention what had happened the night before, and I was right. I toyed with the idea of asking if I was still on a final warning, but I knew it would get me nowhere. For now, I had passed the test of not revealing our association. The question was, how long could I keep it up?

115

At 4day dinner, Deena returned. If I had been shocked by the change she underwent before we saw her in therapy, I was almost as shocked by how much better she looked now. It wasn't the same Deena I roomed with, but it was close.

To our squadron's credit, we welcomed her back as if she hadn't missed a beat, and there were no awkward questions or comments. The best thing about that evening was seeing her smile—it was the most I had seen her smile since I met her.

But my own questions about Deena lingered, and I decided to talk to Pell about it.

"Pell, don't you think Deena was in terrible shape when we went to see her?"

He frowned.

"Yes, you're wondering how that could have happened? I am too. I tried to get some more information from the infirmary, but they aren't giving me anything else."

"Would they hide things from us?"

He hesitated.

"If they need to… I know you're trying to be a good cadet-commander —I'm trying to be a good cadet-captain. But in the end, the Academy is above all of us, and we have to trust the professionals at the infirmary."

I nodded, then noticed his eyes linger on mine.

"You're a good person, Robyn. You're going to make an admirable officer."

I felt the blood flooding my cheeks. For the first time in months, Pell had made me uncomfortable.

"Thank you, sir."

He laughed and continued eating.

"I thought you were done with calling me sir while we were capless."

In that moment, I realized how much of a hypocrite I had become. When it came to the ongoing question of Drel and Grie, I was starting to make up my mind. The longer I thought about it, the more I disliked it. At first I was happy that she had told me, now I wish she hadn't. At some point, I had to transition from friend to leader. I had to do my job.

I had thought about talking to Pell about this friend versus leader issue, as he was no doubt most qualified, but I had decided against it. After all, now that the two of us were growing comfortable, I didn't want him to think twice about our own relationship.

Therein lay the hypocrisy: do as I say but not as I do. And what happened to him not being the only star in the galaxy?

116

The last week of the seventh month passed fairly quickly. Deena was coming back into her own and all of us were excited for the coming weekend, the weekend we would finally receive our specs assignments. It was enough of a distraction for me to ignore Drel and Grie.

But if I was being completely honest, it was my time with Pell that kept my attention, more so than the upcoming chance to be stationed on Raviir. The fact that my interest in the cadet-captain consumed me beyond my obsession with the red planet was troubling, but like any true hypocrite, I buried these worries in the back of my mind.

"One month left and you'll be done with your first session, can you believe it?"

He smiled at me over another private lunch. He was smiling more often now, and I was pretty sure there was no official reason for being in the squad room instead of the cafeteria.

"Can I believe it?" I replied. "You're the one about to graduate."

"Yea don't remind me. Not to take away from you getting your first specs but me? The assignment I get this weekend might well dictate the next few years of my life."

"And if you get something similar to last time, on Raviir Three?"

"Oh, then I'd be fine. Counterintelligence work is exactly what I want to do."

"Even against robots?"

He smiled again.

"Especially against robots."

Spending time with Pell put me in such a good mood, I became a master at coming up with excuses for my behavior. I understood now, at least obliquely, why Grie had been so important to Drel's recovery. Deep down, I knew what both of us were doing was wrong, but I did it anyway.

9day came and I was elected cadet-commander unanimously for the fourth month in a row. A few minutes later, the entire squadron filled the room, and a tense silence took hold.

"Okay everyone, 2 minutes until you receive your specs."

I glanced at my cuff. 598. Most everyone was seated at a desk, a few glaring intently at lens projections only they could see. It was interesting to see the first class as nervous as the third. As Pell had said, the final specs assignment was a good indication of your first deployment after graduation.

I wondered what Commander Kelt—or whoever was controlling my destiny—had cooked up for me this time. I tried not to hope for Raviir lest I be let down. Better to be pleasantly surprised than disappointed.

25 soft beeps went off in unison and each of us opened our messages.

I was assigned to the Destroyer *Tyran* of Nommir Command. Captain Reyn was the ship's superior officer. And that was all the information I got. I thought about Wilor's experience on a destroyer. Was I in for 100 days of cleaning floors and running laps?

People started talking around me, asking each other what they had been assigned. The ones doing the asking were clearly happier than the ones answering. A few people, such as the first-class cadet sitting next to me, got up and left without a word.

I looked at Pell from across the room, and he gave me a hint of a smile —did he get Raviir Three?

"What did you get?"

Rolin came over to me, no doubt interested in what the double-dosing third-class cadet had been chosen for.

"A destroyer. Nommir."

He nodded and took the open seat next to me.

"Could be great," he suggested.

I shrugged.

"Could be great. Could be Wilor."

He smiled.

"I was about to say."

"And you?"

"Another carrier. This time Dathleran, and not on the hangar deck. They're having me in the engine room."

Rolin was on an engineering track, specializing in propulsive systems.

"Congratulations! That's exactly what you wanted, isn't it?"

"Pretty much. Carriers aren't very mobile, so there won't be too much to do, but I'm not complaining. As long as they're there to teach me not use me. That remains to be seen."

"Looks like we're in the same situation then."

He nodded, then gave me a once over.

"You know tomorrow's the big day, right?" he asked.

I laughed.

"We're moving in together, yes I know."

He smiled.

"It's a big step. I'll try not to be as bad as Epore."

I laughed again.

"I hope not. If you did that, where would I go for advice?"

He gave me a curious look.

"Good question. I'm flattered you've chosen me as your confidant."

"Of course. You've helped me get through some tough patches this year, Rolin."

He smiled and stood.

"That's what a second-division partner's for. No more surprise hugs though, this time I want a warning."

117

Something changed between Rolin and I when we moved in together, something that well into the first week, I couldn't quite define. He wasn't noticeably quiet like Deena or borderline obnoxious like Crim, and he certainly wasn't flirting like Epore. And yet, things were different.

Of course, as I couldn't immediately see the explanation behind it all, I continued to do what I had become so good at over the past few weeks: I buried it in the back of my mind. After all, it was Rolin— someone who had helped me from day one. Why worry about him when I only had a few more weeks to worry about somebody else?

"So?"

Another private lunch, 2day of the first week. I'd made it a point not to ask Pell what his specs were before then, as if it were a secret. But it wasn't. A cadet talking to their cadet-captain was entirely normal. So why was I acting like this?

Actually, I knew why, I just didn't want to admit it.

"Raviir Three again. They actually asked for me specifically, can you imagine?"

I smiled, genuinely excited for him.

"That's great! So you'll be in the same division?"

He nodded.

"Yep. Same commander, same division, same place. I really enjoyed my time there and it's Raviir Three: one of the top bases in the empire. Now instead of worrying whether I might get stuck there, I have to worry about whether I'll be moved out after specs."

"Oh please, they asked for you specifically, I think that gives you an idea of what's coming."

He smiled.

"I hope you're right."

His eyes lingered on me for a bit longer than usual and I tried to focus on my food. There was no doubt in my mind what was happening now. We were having private meals almost twice as often as necessary. He always had a pretext for them, but he also had a pretext for more and more lingering touches. It was intoxicating. The rational part of me screamed to stop, if not for me then for him, but it was useless. Epore and Kulee never caused any issues. Same with Drel and Grie. And all four of those people had two more sessions together.

Unfortunately, I was not the only one to notice all the extra one-on-one time.

"Tell me Robyn, what does a cadet-commander do alone with her cadet-captain?"

Drel was smart enough to whisper her comment when we were well away from the others, but I still shot a look around. She caught my glance and gave me a sly smile.

"Guilty as charged," she said.

"Nothing happened, Drel. We can't."

"Ah, can't. But want to?"

I shook my head.

"I don't want to talk about it."

A flash of anger preceded her words, no longer a whisper.

"Oh, so I tell you everything about Grie but your life is secret?"

"Drel, please. I'm your cadet-commander. I didn't ask you to share that with me, you did it voluntarily."

She gave me a frustrated look then walked away.

"Uh-oh, trouble in paradise?"

Rolin gave me a look as he approached down the hall.

"Same old trouble. Friendship versus leadership. I think I'm going to go to the squad room today, you?"

We walked side by side toward our room.

"Robyn, I'm beginning to think you're avoiding me. Seven months I barely see you in the squad room now all of the sudden you're there every evening?"

He was right, I was spending a lot more time in the squad room. But he of all people should understand.

"There are less than four weeks left, Rolin. I want to see everyone as much as possible."

We reached our door and it opened.

"Understandable. I might come by later."

"Okay, see you then."

He walked into the room and I continued down the hall. Why was that so awkward? I couldn't put my finger on it, but something was definitely off. Hadn't he said the party during the first month was because of how much he missed Wilor and Bett? So why was he in our room now?

"Don't think so hard or you'll break your brain."

Crim gave me a smile as I sat at one of the desks.

"She's been doing Advanced Fitness all this time, her brain is already broken," Tyla quipped.

"Wait, does that mean my brain is breaking?" Grie asked.

"Will you kids keep it down? The real cadets are trying to have a conversation," Bett added.

The squad room wasn't the best spot to get work done, but it didn't matter. Most of our performance averages were safe, all except Deena's.

She and Drel were locked away in one of their rooms right now, getting her caught up.

"Robyn, I heard you got put on a destroyer," Wilor said, coming up to me.

"Yes, I just hope I have better luck than you did," I answered.

He shrugged.

"You never know with specs. But I have a feeling they wouldn't squander a talent like yours."

I never did take compliments very well, and not knowing what to say, just nodded politely.

"By the way, where's Rolin?" he asked.

"In the room."

He gave me a confused look.

"In your room? It's the last month, what's he doing in your room?"

I shrugged.

"I'm asking myself the same question."

He gave me a quick nod then headed toward the exit.

"I'm bringing him in here."

Even Wilor thought his behavior was odd. A few minutes later, he came back into the squad room, alone. We locked eyes and he shrugged. What was going on?

118

As the second week came to a close, the Rolin situation started to creep forward from the back of my mind, refusing to be ignored. By 10day, I was curious enough to confront him about it.

"Why are you spending so much time in the room, Rolin? Don't you want to see everyone?"

He shrugged.

"I still see everyone at meals, in class… and specs is only 100 days."

I frowned. He was evading the truth—another close friend lying to my face. I wracked my brain for an answer, for some kind of explanation, but I couldn't find one. The change came when we moved in together, but besides the room swap, nothing had happened—no confrontation, no situation, nothing to warrant what he was doing.

At this point if I ignored it, it was more for Rolin than for me. I was saddened by his dismissive answers, but I told myself there was a reason for his actions. If he felt like he was ready to tell me, he would.

The next day, Pell managed to take my mind off things.

"By the way, you have another special exercise this weekend."

I stared at him, confused.

"What do you mean?"

"Another special exercise for all Puric cadets in Advanced Fitness."

I felt the familiar pit in my stomach, the premonition of what was coming.

"Is it individual?"

He nodded.

"Yep. And once again they haven't given me any specifics. Try not to get injured this time, okay?"

He shot me a smile but I hardly noticed. So close to the finish line… what did Commander Kelt have in store for me this time?

119

As soon as I woke up on 9day, the message was waiting for me.

"Reach the target location by 500."

Next to the words was a map with a familiar location marked—the same location I had been told to deliver the package.

I stared at the readout before me, frowning. I had spent the last few days dreading this weekend, contemplating the various possibilities, yet this particular outcome hadn't occurred to me. To have nearly the same assignment, with such a clear reference to the previous one?

Expect the unexpected.

I got out of bed with far less haste than the first time, wondering if another trone was waiting in the mountains. Even though I had some 80 kilometers to cover, I had made sure to secure permission to use a hovcar beforehand. No more fun encounters with the guardians, unfortunately.

My vehicle was parked outside Puric, and I hopped inside, turning it on. I had my lenses plot a course through the grounds and estimated my arrival time: while the hovcar couldn't take me all the way to the target location, it would get me to the base of the mountains. According to my readout, I didn't have much leeway, so I started off, heading toward the gap in the tree ring.

The sun was still hiding behind the horizon, though I knew it wouldn't be long before it came out— we were still seeing snow multiple times a week, but the days were starting to get longer. Grie would be happy, I thought.

Grie! He was in Advanced Fitness now, I realized—was he doing this too? No, I thought to myself, he was doing a special exercise, but not mine —mine was extra special. I contemplated taking a quick detour to see the person responsible, to ask her if there were any trones waiting for me. Maybe she could tell me why she continued to do these things to me?

Up ahead, I saw a wall of forest and a few openings—hovcar paths, one of which was mine. I turned slightly and headed in, holding right in case another hovcar decided to come the opposite way.

As I made my way through the forest, I managed to forget Commander Kelt, focusing instead on the surroundings. While I had had plenty of time to explore the grounds in the past six months, it was always with a larger group—I hadn't been alone in the wilderness since the last special exercise. Something about being on my own was soothing, and while I knew I couldn't get too complacent—I was almost guaranteed to find an ugly surprise at the end of this journey—I let myself enjoy the moment.

The sun started to peek between the thinning trees, and I noticed a few more hovcars pass me by. I wondered what it was like to be an officer at the Academy—there were so many parts to this base I didn't know about, and to think there was a fully operational sector completely separate from the academic side... even having seen it in person, it was hard to believe.

I went back to my lenses and looked at the second section of my journey, the part after I left the hovcar. Most of the vertical distance I needed to cover was in that section, but at least I could do it without an annoying package... and hopefully without any unwanted visitors.

The terrain was getting rockier, and I could see the foot of the mountains ahead. This wouldn't be the same path I had taken before, as I was approaching from a different vector, but it would be similar. Most important of all, I was starting in the morning rather than the afternoon, so the weather would get better—not worse.

Once I was within a kilometer, my lenses projected my destination, guiding me to the spot I would stop. I had thought this would be a remote area, but I saw another hovcar up ahead, next to where I was headed. Another Advanced Fitness student?

As I approached, I saw a figure standing a few meters from the hovcar, and I realized it wasn't a student—this was an officer, a lieutenant to be precise. The lieutenant who ferried me to and from Commander Kelt.

I felt the pit in my stomach and tensed involuntarily. What was he doing here? What was going on?

As I brought my vehicle next to his, I saw he was shifting his weight, staring at me with a sort of nervous agitation. The pit in my stomach grew, and I brought the hovcar to a stop.

"Robyn."

He took two steps toward me and I recoiled, confused and suspicious. He seemed to notice my uneasiness and took a step back.

"Sorry, I... I need to talk to you. There's not much time."

I stared at him, keeping one hand on the controls. Maybe I shouldn't have turned it off?

"What are you doing, sir?"

He looked back the way I had come, as if making sure I wasn't followed.

"Don't go to the target location. You're in danger."

The anxiety in his words was contagious, and I felt the dread growing inside me.

"What are you talking about, sir?"

He shot another nervous glance behind me.

"Kelt. She—she wants you dead."

My heart was pounding in my chest. I tried to read his expression, to understand what he was trying to tell me.

"Sir?"

"This assignment—it's a trap. If you go up there," he gestured into the mountains, "you won't come back."

I stared at him, confused. A trap? I knew it was a trap from the moment I got the message, but a trap I wouldn't come back from?

"The general," he continued. "You've brought too much attention to yourself. We needed to keep you a secret, but now they're asking about you."

Teer, I realized. Was his mother investigating the Academy?

"You can't go up there, Robyn. If you go up there, you'll die."

There was no headache now, no blinding pain in my mind, but the fear burned just as deep. I shot a glance back the way I had come, overwhelmed by what the lieutenant was telling me. Commander Kelt wanted me dead, and she finally had her excuse.

"I can help you," he added.

I turned back to him, struggling to process what he was saying.

"What?"

He took a step forward, looking around and lowering his voice.

"I can smuggle you out of here. If you come with me, I know some people that can get you out."

I stared at him again, suspicion outweighing fear.

"Who?"

He leaned forward, giving me a knowing look.

"The Resurgence. They can get you out, they can save you."

I was speechless. The lieutenant, part of the Resurgence? I tried to respond, to form a coherent statement, but I could barely form a coherent thought.

"You need to make a choice, and you need to do it now. If she bugged me, there's already a patroller on its way."

I felt rooted in place, unable to move or speak. The lieutenant looked around, the terror in his expression exacerbating my overwhelming despair. Commander Kelt wanted me dead, and the Resurgence was offering a way out. The Resurgence, here at the Academy, here in this lieutenant...

Commander Hurren had given me the illusion of choice, and the Academy had given me the illusion of freedom, but now I had a real choice—and one of the options was real freedom. Or was it? Was this not just like his proposal? Two choices: one suspicious and likely dangerous, the other straightforward but certainly dangerous.

"Robyn, we don't have time!"

He jumped into his hovcar and gestured behind him.

"Get in!"

I stared at him, still frozen in place. Why did I hesitate? If I stayed here, the commander would kill me. She had held herself back so many times, but now she had the perfect excuse to fulfill her desire. Yet despite the looming danger, I couldn't move.

Then suddenly, I made my choice.

"What are you doing?"

The lieutenant saw my hands up, interacting with the lens interface, drafting a message.

"Stop!"

He jumped out of his hovcar toward me, lifting his arm and firing. I dropped my hands to catch his arc then jumped down to meet him on the ground, pulling him into a hold and firing decisively into his bare face. He screamed in pain then went limp, and before I could think twice, I threw his body into my hovcar, shooting another glance at my surroundings.

That's when I heard it—the patroller. The lieutenant was right, Kelt had bugged him.

I jumped into the hovcar and started it up, making a sharp turn to head back the way I had come. Where now? Did I try to hide? The grounds were open fields here, and the forest was still a ways away. I knew the patroller could shut me down but maybe if I could reach the trees…

A familiar horn broke my train of thought, and I had just enough time to brace myself before the hovcar came to a halt. The lieutenant's body crashed into my back, sending me into the front panel and knocking the wind out of me.

I pulled myself back to my feet, pain shooting through my body. I could hear the patrol vehicle coming to a hover behind us, and I glanced up into the cockpit, half-expecting to see Commander Kelt in the pilot's seat.

Instead, I saw two guardians—not the ones I knew, but another vice sergeant and corporal pair. They brought their vehicle to a hover and hopped out, visors lowered and rifles armed.

"Get out of the—"

I leapt out of the hovcar, ignoring the incredible pain, and ran toward the nearest guardian. He fired his rifle and I caught the shot in my glove, then fired at his chest. My arc made contact, but the distance diminished its power, and he stumbled backward without falling. I caught a shot from the other guardian with my right arm then leapt onto the first one, firing another arc into his chest, this time from less than a meter away. He collapsed to the ground, dropping his rifle, and I felt a familiar pain surge through my head, temporarily disorienting me. In that moment's hesitation, the other guardian fired, and the pain compounded to an unbelievable degree, shooting through every fiber of my body.

Everything went black, and then it went red. I was on Raviir, in the familiar field of grass. I could see the person clearly now—a woman, her build similar to mine—but they had their back turned. I felt a strange kind of sadness, then the image disappeared, as did my consciousness.

120

I woke in a familiar bed in the infirmary, with a familiar face standing above me. But this wasn't my doctor, this was my primary liaison.

"Good afternoon, Robyn."

A visceral fear took hold of me, and pain shot through my body as I tensed in shock.

"I wanted to congratulate you."

I felt the nakedness of my hands and wondered how I could defend myself, how I could escape. Commander Kelt had me cornered, it was the end of the line. Why hadn't she killed me? Did she mean to make me suffer?

"You've passed your latest test."

I stared at her, noting something odd about her expression—for the first time ever, there was no disdain in her eyes.

"It was a mistake to draft the message to your cadet-captain, as that might reveal your association with me, but we'll let that slide since you didn't actually send it."

She studied me for a moment, and I tried to understand what I was hearing. The whole thing was just a test?

"As always, the details of this exercise related to our relationship are to remain strictly confidential. The doctor will see you shortly, then you will be taken to your target location to ensure you complete your cover assignment."

Her lips formed a small smile—a genuine one.

"Good luck," she announced, then turned around, walking out the door.

I found myself staring at the place she had been, a swarm of emotions battling to take hold: anger, confusion, relief…

The doctor walked in and stood next to the bed.

"Your vitals are good and all scans are normal. The rifle hit knocked you out, but there's no permanent damage we can see."

She gestured to the wall.

"Your uniform is in the regular spot. You're free to go."

I gave her a nod.

"Thank you, sir."

She nodded back, then walked out of the room.

For a moment I stayed in bed, my mind still racing. All of that was just a test? The lieutenant's confession? The presence of the Resurgence? The Guard's intervention?

I knew I shouldn't be surprised at this point—the commander's motto played through my memory—but this was absurd. What if I had hurt the lieutenant more? Or one of the guardians?

And what about the way she looked at me, the way she talked to me? It was almost as if she was treating me like a human being.

Still, all of these questions paled in comparison to the return of my red memory, now clearer than ever—and not just visually. I had felt a strange sadness at the sight of the turned figure, as if I was experiencing a kind of loss. Who was that woman? What was that feeling?

It had been so long since these questions had plagued me… why were they coming back now?

121

After I put on my uniform, I walked out of the room and found one of the guardians waiting outside—the one who had shot me down.

"This way, cadet."

He led me out of the outpost, and I saw the patroller parked outside on the same landing pad I had arrived on from Kurotar.

I was still reeling from everything that had happened, trying to comprehend the depths of deception these people were willing to go to.

What was the purpose of that exercise? To prove my loyalty to the Fleet? Why? It wasn't like my divisionmates had to endure such a test...

As I got into the back of the patroller and the corporal started our ascent, I realized the answer wasn't all that hard to find. I hadn't undergone basic, and even I had considered the possibility of a past life in the MR. If they didn't know my history, the Fleet had to test my allegiance.

I knew there was a connection between the outcome of this exercise and Commander Kelt's change in behavior, though that was harder to pinpoint. Did she not trust me fully before? Did she think I was part of the Resurgence?

Then I contemplated another possibility: maybe they weren't testing me because of an unknown past, but because of a known one. What if I had been a member of the MR and they were aware? It would explain some of her earlier hatred, and the importance of this assessment. But why would the Fleet ever risk a former agent of the Resurgence joining the Academy?

As clear as my memory had been, it lacked the context to answer these questions. I wished I had gleaned more from the vision, but what could I do, ask the corporal to shoot me again and hope I learned more?

The guardian dropped me off at the target location, and I spent the rest of the weekend juggling a difficult assignment from Advanced Fitness with the burning questions in the back of my mind. By the time I made it back to Puric for 10day lunch, I was physically and mentally exhausted.

"How was the Advanced Fitness special?" Wilor asked, joining me in the line.

"Tough," I replied

He laughed.

"As usual."

I glanced around the cafeteria, frowning. I had hoped to see my friends and distract myself from my troubles, but there was less than half the usual crowd inside.

"Is everyone still on their exercises?" I asked.

Wilor nodded.

"I only just finished. Some of them might not be back until dinner."

I grabbed my portion and headed to the table, trying to stay positive. I might not see them now, but dinner wasn't so far away.

After lunch, I went to my room and worked on simulations until Rolin returned.

"Well, that was rough," he announced, throwing himself into his chair.

I paused my work and turned to him, glad to have someone to talk to.

"That bad, huh?"

He shook his head.

"I barely got any sleep last night, I got back so late."

I gave him a look.

"I had to sleep in the forest."

He stared at me, then shrugged.

"I should've done that."

I smiled, surprised by the flow of conversation. I didn't know if it was the trial I had just endured, but it seemed as if the awkwardness between Rolin and I had faded away.

A message interrupted my thoughts; Pell asked me to meet him before dinner.

"What is it?" Rolin asked.

I left the interface and looked at him.

"Pell wants me to meet him," I said, standing.

He frowned, and I gave him a curious look.

"What's wrong?" I asked.

He shook his head.

"Just never see you in here, that's all."

I realized I might have made a premature assessment—something was still off.

"I'll see you at dinner, Rolin."

I made my way into the hall, trying not to read too much into his behavior. Besides, someone else was on my mind. The one person who had the power to distract me from my ordeal.

"I'm going to talk to the first division about electing you cadet-captain for the next session."

I smiled at Pell, grateful for his support.

"I think you're the most qualified out of everyone," he added, "including the second division."

"Thank you. I don't really know what to say."

He smiled back.

"No need to say anything."

I didn't care whether I became cadet-captain or not. In that moment, I didn't care about anything—not even the commander's elaborate test. All I cared about was his hand, coming down to give my forearm a quick squeeze. I didn't want it to end.

122

The next day, I met the same lieutenant in front of Puric, noting the dark mark along the side of his face—a byproduct of my attack. I had wondered if he would pick me up, yet seeing him was still a surprise. As I got into the hovcar, I couldn't stop replaying our encounter, the way he had convinced me of my imminent doom.

While seeing him proved awkward, my session with Commander Kelt was stranger still. Our movements were the same and our technique hadn't changed, yet everything about the class felt different. Gone was the crippling anxiety accompanying my every move, as was the fear of imminent danger. Despite no outward changes, it was clear the commander no longer wanted me dead.

This was actually more problematic than I would have thought, as it once again threatened to paint her in a more human light. Worst of all, it was working. The woman who had brought me to the brink of death and kidnapped my friend seemed far more human to me now than ever before.

I tried to shake this feeling or at least ignore it, but the rest of the week was more of the same. With only one week to go, I hoped I wouldn't have to endure her much longer, though I wasn't sure specs would be an escape. After all, wouldn't my mysterious superiors want to keep tabs on me there too? Maybe they would bring the commander aboard the *Tyran* to continue my training? How would they explain that without revealing too much?

In truth, my desire to be rid of her was outweighed by my desire to hold on to Pell. With only ten days remaining, I started finding any excuse I could to spend time with him, to the point where Drel warned me about it.

"Robyn, you need to cool it, everyone's going to notice."

"We haven't done anything, Drel."

She sighed, shaking her head.

"That's the point, you two are more suspicious than Grie and I and we're actually together."

I frowned, worried by how brazen she had gotten. Should I encourage her to be this open with me so I could stay informed, or was I crossing the line as cadet-commander? Was I her friend or was I her leader?

Neither, I realized, I was a hypocrite—her advice did little to change my behavior. I figured Pell would let me know if I crossed a line, and so far, he seemed happy to spend more time together. Besides, I thought to myself, everyone was busy getting ready for the end of the session. Who had the time to notice what we were doing?

"Leaving again?"

I stopped at the door and turned to my roommate.

"Another meeting," I replied.

Rolin nodded.

"See you later."

"Bye!"

I stepped out of the room and walked down the hall, ignoring all the red flags in my mind.

123

Red flags or not, the last week went by in a flash. Suddenly it was 9day, the last day of the session and our last day on Alder. Tomorrow we would transfer to our specs, to our 100 day special assignments all over the empire. I struggled to understand how the time had flown by, but first I had to get through the day's business.

We started with our transfer instructions. They were sent to us after breakfast so we could see our departure time, shuttle, etc. I had a shuttle from the main dormitory landing area at 384 which would take me to the milport. From there I had another shuttle at 412, directly to the *Tyran*.

The Nommir system. Now that I had a session's worth of courses under my belt, I knew a bit more about where I was headed. But I didn't know if I'd ever see Nommir's surface—the shuttle would take me right to the ship. Did it really matter?

At lunch, the cadet-admiral came by and gave a speech about the outgoing first class. It was full of congratulations, several individual mentions, and an overall message of good luck on their final specs. I had my eyes on Pell most of the time.

This was it—the last day I'd see him, unless we had a similar departure tomorrow. Again I asked myself how the time had gone by so quickly…

After lunch we gathered in the squad room for the elections. First was cadet-captain. There were two preliminary rounds, and it came down to myself and Olla. On the final round, I won the first vote.

"Congratulations, Robyn, you will be the new cadet-captain at the start of the next session."

Pell reached out his hand and I shook it. It was so different to feel it like this, so official.

"Okay divisions, now for your cadet-commanders."

I waited for the vote to pop up but it never came. After a moment's confusion, I realized as an upcoming cadet-captain, I was technically no longer in my division. I looked around at my friends going through the voting process. This was the last day I would be on the same level.

After a few rounds, Crim was elected the new cadet-commander. Like me, his ascension wouldn't take effect until after we returned due to the timing of the election. For the last few hours I would remain cadet-commander, although it didn't matter that much.

I smiled and shook his hand.

"Congratulations, Crim—again."

Now the real work began. Before 750, we needed to compile a desired course list for when we returned. I had planned ahead, as had most everyone, but it was still nerve-wracking. Pell took us off-cap and urged us to stay in the squad room. I entered my choices on one of the desks, aware as always of the futility of my decisions.

While everyone else continued working on their course lists, I reminisced on the past eight months. To think I hadn't expected to make it one day, and here I was, nearly done with my first session. I had excelled in many areas—often surprisingly so—and I had formed true bonds with my peers. So much so, that for the first time in my life, I thought I might have a way out.

Every little situation and relationship had added a layer of protection, a way for me to ignore Raviir or my weird proficiency with the gloves. But now that I was leaving? Now that I was entering the unknown?

I looked around at my squadron and realized just how much I was going to miss them. This was my family now. This was my home. What would happen when I left?

124

At 750, we headed to our last dinner as a squadron. I was surprised to see food set out in each spot—servings of meats, breads… and Alder berries: a local delicacy, saved for special occasions.

"Wait, where was this every other day?" Crim asked.

"We ate it before you come," Tyla shot back.

The conversation around the table was cheerful, if not bittersweet. The first and second division kept mostly to themselves, making promises of future plans and reminiscing on their time together. Our division skipped the former but did plenty of the latter.

"Remember the first day, when she hit the target sphere?"

I rolled my eyes at Drel, but Crim beat me to the reply.

"That was love at first sight for me."

After dinner there was a quick meeting between the outgoing cadet-captains and cadet-colonel of our group with the incoming individuals for each position. Porr smiled when I walked in with Pell, then went on to explain several logistical issues such as cadet-captains having their own private rooms.

"And the empty spot in the division?" I asked.

She smiled.

"Filled by the integrated commission program."

Of course—someone who didn't need the first session could slide in as a second-session cadet, taking my spot on the roster of eight. I thought back to when I had first heard about my cover story, and how crazy it had all sounded. So much had changed in these eight months, it was hard to keep up.

After the meeting, there were only a few hours left in the day. I—and pretty much the entire squadron—went to the squad room to spend it together. While the first class discussed their future, the other classes received their course assignments.

I opened the message and skimmed through it. Advanced Fitness continued, then immediately into two hours of my special elective. After that military work, followed by lunch. Then I had another tactics double, this time with interstellar on even days and interplanetary on odd days. My day wrapped up with two hours of Interstellar Flight.

I did a double take, surprised by what I was seeing. Other than the special elective, I had gotten everything I had asked for. Or had I asked for everything I was going to get?

Before I could get lost in thought, the voices of second and third division joined those of the first, and everyone discussed their upcoming session. Unsurprisingly, most of my division had different classes than their peers—in the second session, things were more specialized.

"Robyn, are you taking IS?" Tyla asked.

"Flight or tactics?" I replied.

"Flight."

I nodded, and she smiled.

"Me too, actually."

"For the full flight program?" I asked.

She nodded.

Interstellar Flight was a required course for all cadets, the bare minimum being two months. More advanced pilots would take four months and then move into Planetary Flight. This one could also take up to four months, but if you did well on both of those, you were allowed to take Interplanetary Flight, the most advanced of them all. IP flight, if done to completion, took an entire session: eight months. Therefore, if a cadet wanted to go through all of IS, PL, and IP flight, they had to start right at the beginning of the second session. That was what I was doing, and so was Tyla.

"So, you ready to take my place?"

Pell joined our conversation.

"Have you seen her lead us? Yea, I'd say she's ready," Crim replied.

Pell laughed.

"Are you all ready for specs?"

Some nods, a few shrugs.

"I heard about what happened to Wilor… I just hope my superiors are somewhat invested in my success," Grie said.

Pell laughed again.

"That's a common hope, yes. But Wilor's case is the exception, not the rule. After all, did anyone else have a story like that?"

It was true, his was the only one. Some had been bored, like Rolin, or gotten assignments that didn't teach them much, but only Wilor had been put through the wringer.

"Well third division, it's been a pleasure watching you grow into true cadets. I will see most of you tomorrow at breakfast, but for those I don't, good luck with everything. Perhaps, in the future, our paths will cross once more."

He gave us a nod then caught my eye. There was a sadness there I didn't expect, and a knot formed in my stomach as he turned around and walked out of the room. Was that it? He was leaving already?

I glanced at my cuff. 892.

"Well I for one think Pell has the right idea," Grie announced as he stood. "I'm going to get some sleep. I will see you all in the morning."

I knew at that moment my best friend was trying to determine how best to escape without attracting attention. I decided to save her at least a bit of embarrassment.

"Me too. Goodnight everyone."

"See you tomorrow, Robyn," Tyla said.

I left the squad room and walked through the hall.

This was it, I thought. My first session. I had managed to be an outlier while having a tight circle. My first month with Drel was rough, but I had found my footing pretty quick. Then came Grie, who was like a brother to me now. Then Deena, who frankly had a more transformative year than any of us. Then Kulee, Tyla, Epore, Crim…

And now Rolin. I stopped and stared at the door in front of me. What had changed between us? At that moment, it didn't matter. Rolin was not behind the door because the door in front of me was not my own.

I knocked.

125

"Robyn? What are you doing here?"

Pell eyed me curiously, but his body language betrayed his nerves.

"Can I come in?"

He moved aside and I walked into the private quarters, closing the door behind me.

"I… wanted to see what my room will look like next year."

He glanced around the room then back at me, but said nothing. I had never seen him like this before. He was always in control, always in charge. This was different.

Without thinking, I came up next to him, close to him. I could hear his breath quicken, the tension increase. His face was so close to mine, his eyes so clear.

I knew what I saw in there, I knew why he hadn't said anything yet. Our faces were moving, covering the remaining distance. My eyes closed, our lips touched. This was it. It was happening.

"No."

He pulled away.

"Robyn, no, what're you doing? We can't."

Reality was like a knife in my chest, and suddenly the walls were spinning, a nausea coming over me…

"I'm sorry, Pell, I…"

I felt the tears coming, a rush of emotion I had never felt before. Happy, sad, ashamed… it all came together.

"I shouldn't have come here."

Before I let anything else slip, I ran past him, out the door, and into the hall. I ran all the way to my room and closed the door behind me. For once, Rolin wasn't there, and thank goodness. As soon as I hit the bed, I cried.

I cried for the first time in my life. I felt the waves of emotion deep inside of me, and I let the feeling consume me. I had never felt so alive, never felt so real. I was sad, I was upset, but something about it was liberating. Something about it was intoxicating. I let the feeling course through me, consume me.

I didn't know how long I cried before I heard the door open. Twenty minutes? Forty? The tears had run out long ago, but the pain remained.

"Robyn."

Rolin came to the side of my bed and put his hand on my shoulder. I looked up with tired eyes and shuddered.

"I saw you running," he said.

Even though his eyes were on me, it was as if he was looking through me, beyond me. The half smile on his face seemed out of place, bizarre. There was something wrong here.

"What?" I asked.

"I saw you running from his room," he replied.

From Pell's room. I had been so overwhelmed I hadn't thought about other people in the hall.

"He hurt you, didn't he?" he continued.

"What?"

"It's okay, I can make you feel better."

He leaned in to kiss me but I pushed back.

"What are you doing!?"

He let go and stood over the bed, the half smile still on his lips, now scarier than ever.

"I know he rejected you. But I won't."

He grabbed me harder this time, with both hands, and pressed his face into mine. I struggled to get free and he put more of his weight on me.

"Stop, Rolin! Stop!"

His hands wandered toward the seam in my uniform. I pushed them away but he tried again, with more force.

"Rolin, stop now! Stop!"

He started to undo the seam. I threw one hand onto his face and fired my glove. His body went tense and collapsed to the floor.

My heart beat in my chest harder than ever before. I was hyper-aware of my surroundings, pumped full of adrenaline. A wave of nausea rose within me and threatened to take me under. The walls were moving again, dancing, swirling...

The body on the floor made a grunt and I snapped out of it. Rolin rolled to his side and vomited. I needed to deal with this, now. I made a voice call, the first person that came to mind.

"*Robyn, I—*"

"*Come to my room, now!*"

I heard his footsteps in the hall, running, then the door opened. Pell's expression jumped from confusion to concern as he looked from me to Rolin.

"Robyn, what..."

"Close the door!"

He stepped inside and closed the door.

"Pell, Rolin is on drugs and he tried to take advantage of me."

The vomit-covered mass on the floor turned over and grunted in protest.

"No, I, I, I..."

I looked at Pell. Concern became disgust, disgust became anger.

"I'm calling the commander."

I jumped off the bed.

"No, wait!"

He looked at me, bewildered.

"Don't, please."

He stared at me.

"Robyn, you just said—"

"I know what I just said. Pell, he was on strong drugs, look at him."

As if on cue, Rolin let forth another portion of his dinner all over the side of my bed. Pell shook his head.

"Robyn, I have to report this."

I nodded.

"I know, Pell. Report him for the drugs but I'm begging you, leave the rest out."

He gave me a sad look.

"Robyn, I know you two were close but if he assaulted you, he needs to be punished."

"Pell I just assaulted you and I'm completely sober. Am I going to be punished for that?"

A flash of anger crossed his expression.

"Robyn, that's not the same."

"Why, Pell? I made a mistake, it's only human. Rolin made a mistake. A big one. He is way too far gone to be making conscious decisions. Please, you've known him longer than I have, is this the Rolin you know?"

He hesitated, then shook his head.

"No, but that doesn't matter."

I felt the frustration burst within me.

"Then what does matter, Pell? What matters? Does it matter he assaulted me? Does it matter I, the victim, am asking you to keep that information private? Does that matter?"

Pell sighed.

"Listen, Robyn…"

"Don't patronize me, not now! Won't the drugs lead to his expulsion anyway?"

He hesitated. I knew the answer was yes.

"Why are you protecting him?" he asked.

It was a good question. In my mind it all made sense, it was clear. But was my mind really clear? First I kissed Pell, then Rolin tried to kiss me…

"Robyn you're going to be the cadet-captain now. You need to be a leader, not a friend."

And there it was. The truth I was trying to avoid. The truth exposing my own hypocrisy, the truth threatening my relationship with Drel and Grie, but the truth nonetheless. It hit me so hard I had to take a seat, my mind reeling from the implications of his words. Pell called the commander but I didn't hear it. All I could hear was his statement, repeating itself in my mind like an echo that wouldn't go away.

You need to be a leader, not a friend.

126

A few minutes later, Commander Kelt joined us, accompanied by two members of the Guard. Rolin was taken away, still incoherent. The commander asked us both questions. I kept my answers brief. It went by quicker than I expected, and I found myself alone with Pell in the hall.

"Goodnight, Robyn."

There was a sadness in his eyes, but I felt nothing. I had used up all of my emotions already.

"Goodnight."

I went back to my room alone, the vomit already cleaned up, a hint of air freshener masking the events of the past hour. I thought about the transies that had come through—so thorough, so quick.

For the first time, I spent the night alone in a dorm room meant for two. I didn't sleep.

The next morning I got a notification from Pell. He would handle questions about Rolin. I could eat my breakfast in peace. But I decided not to go. A few of my divisionmates sent concerned messages. I gave noncommittal answers. No one came by the room, they were all busy with their own departures. For a moment I wondered if Drel had chosen to be with Grie rather than come check on me, but it didn't matter.

I walked the familiar path to the outcropping near the dorms. I had come here so many times with my division or my squadron, the beginning of a weekend adventure. This was about to be the beginning of a two month adventure, but I felt empty, cold.

I reached my shuttle and opened the door.

"Good morning, Robyn."

Commander Kelt sat inside, waiting for me. I hadn't expected her to be in the shuttle, but at this point I was past her surprising me. Besides, after last night, she was the last thing on my mind.

The shuttle lifted and I strapped in across from her. I felt the familiar vibration and saw a green landscape out the window, emerging from the white. Spring was coming to Alder.

"You know Robyn, I've spent eight months wondering why a fugitive was allowed to join the ranks of the best recruits the Fleet had to offer."

I glanced at her, confused. She was being frank, open. What was going on?

"Finally, this very morning, I got my answer."

Something about her tone begged my attention, but I was having trouble escaping my apathy.

When I was born, I was a small flame fighting to stay lit. My time at the Academy had built me up as a person, with twigs at first and then logs, until right at the end I was a true fire, my emotions overwhelming me with their potency.

But that was gone now. Last night, the fire was put out. Only a few warm embers remained.

"Robyn, you may not know your past, but I do. You're not going to the *Tyran*. You're going to Raviir."

She poked the embers and out came a spark.

www.ingramcontent.com/pod-product-compliance
Lightning Source LLC
Chambersburg PA
CBHW072119250626
47159CB00007B/2500